W9-AMT-033

The Lady Who Would Be Queen

A wary light entered Anne Boleyn's eyes. "Your village women jeer at me when I pass?"

"Yes," I said.

She gave me a look that held the strength of emperors. "I will be queen, Frances. It is in my stars, and things are falling into place. The court is a dangerous land, but if you are quiet and obedient, you can hold your own. You have not much to recommend you," she said, her gaze critical, "but I need good and loyal friends, and I will reward them well. Can you be loyal?"

"Oh, yes," I cried.

I had been asked to attend the beautiful lady Anne, who would soon be queen. And hers would not be a court of constant prayer and rosaries, like Queen Catherine's—in effect, an extension of my mother's house—but a court of dancing and laughter.

To my seventeen-year-old eyes, this was much to be desired.

Alas, I ought to have remembered that I had such troubles with a single word Lady Anne had mentioned.

Obedience.

A Lady Raised High

A NOVEL OF ANNE BOLEYN

LAURIEN GARDNER

JOVE BOOKS, NEW YORK

THE BERKLEY PUBLISHING GROUP
Published by the Penguin Group
Penguin Group (USA) Inc.
375 Hudson Street, New York, New York 10014, USA
Penguin Group (Canada), 90 Eglinton Avenue East, Suite 700, Toronto, Ontario M4P 2Y3, Canada
(a division of Pearson Penguin Canada Inc.)
Penguin Books Ltd., 80 Strand, London WC2R 0RL, England
Penguin Group Ireland, 25 St. Stephen's Green, Dublin 2, Ireland (a division of Penguin Books Ltd.)
Penguin Group (Australia), 250 Camberwell Road, Camberwell, Victoria 3124, Australia
(a division of Pearson Australia Group Pty. Ltd.)
Penguin Books India Pvt. Ltd., 11 Community Centre, Panchsheel Park, New Delhi—110 017, India
Penguin Group (NZ), Cnr. Airborne and Rosedale Roads, Albany, Auckland 1310, New Zealand
(a division of Pearson New Zealand Ltd.)
Penguin Books (South Africa) (Pty.) Ltd., 24 Sturdee Avenue, Rosebank, Johannesburg 2196,
South Africa

Penguin Books Ltd., Registered Offices: 80 Strand, London WC2R 0RL, England

This is a work of fiction. Names, characters, places, and incidents either are the product of the author's imagination or are used fictitiously, and any resemblance to actual persons, living or dead, business establishments, events, or locales is entirely coincidental. The publisher does not have any control over and does not assume any responsibility for author or third-party websites or their content.

A LADY RAISED HIGH

A Jove Book / published by arrangement with the author.

PRINTING HISTORY
Jove mass-market edition / March 2006

Copyright © 2006 by The Berkley Publishing Group.
Excerpt from *Plain Jane* by Laurien Gardner copyright © 2006 by The Berkley Publishing Group.
Cover design by Erika Fusari.

All rights reserved.
No part of this book may be reproduced, scanned, or distributed in any printed or electronic form without permission. Please do not participate in or encourage piracy of copyrighted materials in violation of the author's rights. Purchase only authorized editions.
For information, address: The Berkley Publishing Group,
a division of Penguin Group (USA) Inc.,
375 Hudson Street, New York, New York 10014.

ISBN: 0-515-14089-9

JOVE®
Jove Books are published by The Berkley Publishing Group,
a division of Penguin Group (USA) Inc.,
375 Hudson Street, New York, New York 10014.
JOVE is a registered trademark of Penguin Group (USA) Inc.
The "J" design is a trademark belonging to Penguin Group) USA Inc.

PRINTED IN THE UNITED STATES OF AMERICA

10   9   8   7   6   5   4   3   2   1

If you purchased this book without a cover, you should be aware that this book is stolen property. It was reported as "unsold and destroyed" to the publisher, and neither the author nor the publisher has received any payment for this "stripped book."

One

I Gallantly Save a Lady

JULY 1532

ACCOUNTS of the execution of my queen said she'd been attended at her death by four women, three named, and one left unnamed.

The unnamed one was me. Why my presence should not be recorded, I never understood, because everyone knew Frances Pierce, Anne's favorite lady, a foolish nobody Anne had brought to court and who fancied herself a poet.

On the humid, misty day in 1532 that I first saw my lady Anne, going to court and dressing like a lady was the farthest thing from my mind. I had planned only to ride out and watch her and the king's hunting party from Hunsdon, because I wanted to see what a whore of Babylon looked like.

My aunt, who had married an English baron and lived five miles from us, was all a-flutter. "The king, Frances, just think."

We were having a grand clear-out at my uncle's estate, Aunt Mary having nothing for it but that the tapestries must be taken down and rehung, the bedding removed and replaced, the silver plate polished again and again, the linens washed and ready.

She'd convinced herself that Henry could at any time bring his entourage to her manor tucked far off the road in our remote corner of Hertfordshire.

I shook out linens and folded them and with difficulty held my tongue. I suppose there was a remote possibility that His Grace would bring his gentlemen and ladies here for a rest and a glass of wine, but I thought it farfetched. But he would, I knew, bring his hunting party through the village on his way to and from the woods, because he'd done such a thing before. I was determined, if I could escape the eagle eye of my mother, to watch.

My mother was, at the moment, busily glaring at a maid who polished plate. "The king and his strumpet. What does he mean, bringing her on progress?"

"She will be queen soon," Aunt Mary said. "Have a care with your tongue."

My mother, who was French, gave her a superior look. "He will never marry a mistress. Did he marry Bessie Blount when she gave him a son? Nay. Catherine is a good and pious woman, and she will always be queen, and let that be an end to the conversation."

"He has put aside the queen," Aunt Mary pointed out.

"Temporary madness," my mother said in a hard voice.

My aunt Mary obviously wanted to say more, but like the rest of my father's family, she stood rather in awe of my mother.

My father was a baronet and therefore called Sir Lionel Pierce, but he was not much more than a farmer. He lived on land in Hertfordshire that his father and his father's father and so on had lived on since time immemorial. Through wars and famines and plagues, the Pierces had held onto their estate. My father rode his bounds every day and sometimes worked with his tenants during harvest, when every hand was needed to bring in the crops.

My mother, a French baron's daughter, had married a bit beneath herself and never ceased reminding us of the fact.

Mary, my father's sister, had managed to snare herself a baron and pop out five children, four sons and a daughter.

My mother had only managed to bear me, and this was the one area in which Aunt Mary felt the slightest bit superior.

My mother flicked her sharp gaze to me as I folded linens. I tried to look innocent, as though I was not waiting for a chance to steal to the stables. She'd take a strap to me if she thought I wanted to have a look at the king's mistress. But she had for so long decried Lady Anne—the nobody daughter of a courtier of Kent—that I was very curious to see her.

Every time I saw an ease in the work, however, my aunt Mary would put panicked hands to her head and discover some other meaningless task that simply *must* be done. Until, at long last, my mother sent me on an errand to the buttery. Deceitful daughter that I am, I passed the errand along to one of my aunt's maids and hied myself to the stables.

It is not the thing for a seventeen-year-old young lady to throw herself across the back of one of her uncle's hacks and kick it into a gallop across the countryside, but that, God forgive me, is what I did. My confining wimple I left behind on a pile of clean hay, and I'd slid leather breeches under my skirts in preparation this morning.

I felt wild and free and childlike, sailing over the hills with my hair streaming and the horse moving with sinewy grace beneath me. My mother *would* take a strap to me when she found out, but this heavenly freedom, however brief, was worth it.

I planned to watch the hunting party and pen verses about it. I'd taken to writing poetry after my uncle had come by a copy of Sir Thomas Wyatt's verses that were currently circulating at court. I'd read them and been smitten. I thought it a wonderful thing to make music with words, even though mine did not sing as Sir Thomas' did.

So many visions danced in my head, and I struggled to put them onto paper. Late into the night, I wrote crooked lines of badly metered verse, the parchment dotted with my tears because I could not twist the syllables the right way.

My mother, of course, did not approve. Whenever she caught me, she'd rip up my costly bits of parchment and slap my fingers. "When you marry," she'd say, "you must be quiet and obedient, ready on an instant to serve your husband. He will not want to see you with ink on your fingers, staring into space like you've lost your wits."

"I do not wish to marry," I'd answer, my fingers smarting. "I will stay home and keep house with you and be an obedient daughter."

My mother never argued. She simply bent others' wills to her own. "No."

"I have heard that ladies of the court write verses," I would point out.

"Certainly," said my mother. "*After* they have husbands."

My mother had ambition to marry me well. She had at first wished my father to procure me a place in the household of Queen Catherine. There, I would learn manners, and in time, get myself a husband. I thought her optimistic. Gentlemen of the court set their sights on ladies more high born than a baronet's daughter, and then they had their pick of beauties.

None would ever call me a beauty, by any means. I had a long nose, small, dark eyes, a pale complexion, and a thin mouth. My hair, which I kept tucked modestly under a wimple, was the color of dark wheat—not light blonde as was the fashion nor black like that of the fascinating Lady Anne. No court gentleman would trip over his feet looking at me.

I had been secretly pleased when, last summer, we heard word that King Henry had banished Catherine from court, and so all my mother's plans to send me to the queen had collapsed.

I knew I should feel sorry for the queen, or outraged, like my mother, but I'd felt only childish glee at my escape.

I let my horse scramble down hills and through streams, as I made for the road to Hunsdon where the crowd had already gathered. Children happy to leave off work ran about shouting, and when they saw my horse, they ran to me, to the horse's alarm. I reined him in before he could do any damage, and guided him down to the road at a walk.

I was recognized right away by what I termed "the

crows," four middle-aged women in dun and black who saw everything, heard everything, and knew everything about everyone in the village and for miles around.

"'Tis young Frances," Mistress Longacre said. She turned steely eyes to me and took in my tangled hair and hiked-up skirts. "How is your lady mother? Did my blackberry wine cure the pains in her stomach?"

Mistress Longacre considered herself more learned than any physician and constantly dosed everyone within ten miles, young and old, lowborn and high. The truth of it was, she generally always cured us.

"Aye, she is well," I said.

Mistress Longacre looked satisfied. "I knew it. She came by the pains eating too many winter roots. Ah, well, she is French."

I had not realized that eating root vegetables was a French trait, but I said nothing. The other three ladies looked me up and down, and I knew that before the hour was out, a report of my wild behavior would reach my mother.

I diverted them by pointing down the road at a cloud of dust. "Is it the riders? Is it the king?"

Mistress Longacre and her crows scuttled out into the middle of the road. "Aye, there are a good many horses coming."

Anticipation heightened in the milling villagers. Children ran about, shouting at each other. The men pulled off caps, ready to wave them. And then, to my alarm, I saw Mistress Longacre and her friends begin gathering up handfuls of mud.

I nudged my horse to them. "What are you doing?"

"Preparing a welcome," Mistress Partridge said. She was younger than the others, but she'd already developed a steady gaze that made me squirm.

"You cannot throw mud at the king," I said. "You will be arrested."

Mistress Partridge smiled, which was a chilling thing. "This is not for the king, but his whore."

"The lady Anne?" I asked faintly.

"It ain't natural, is it?" Mistress Longacre snapped, "for the king to set aside the good queen his wife? It upsets the order of things."

"My auguries have shown it," Mistress Partridge said. "The wrong stars are in the sky, and the signs are clear. If he does not put away this mistress, chaos will visit us."

Mistress Partridge always made dire predictions, so I did not tremble. Sometimes, though, some of what she predicted did come true, so I could not completely dismiss her.

"Chaos is certain to visit us if you throw mud at the king's lady," I remarked.

A few of the other village women looked worried, but Mistress Longacre stood firm. "'Tain't natural," she repeated.

I circled my horse to the edge of the crowd, my stomach knotting in foreboding. They would be mad to throw the mud, but Mistress Longacre feared no man. She obeyed my mother, but no one else.

The children began cheering, and I craned to view the horses coming into sight. The hunting party was returning. It had been successful, I saw; a huntsman drove a cart at the forefront with the carcass of a deer piled carelessly onto it.

Next came the banner bearers, far enough behind the cart to keep from the stink and the flies. Behind these, the king rode with his gentlemen. I rose in the stirrups to look long and hard at him. Henry wore a brown doublet and cloak and long boots suitable for riding. I had often heard of our king's prowess on a horse, and I well believed it now. He sat straight and guided his horse with the merest touch.

I had heard rumor that his girth had thickened, and perhaps it had, but he still looked muscular and strong. I could not see his face clearly from where I watched, but the sun flashed on his red gold hair as he turned his head to laugh at something the man beside him had said. The gentlemen with him were handsome, their clothes fine, and their laughter and easy nature inspired us to cheer.

To my disappointment, I saw no lady perched on a horse beside Henry, no Jezebel gazing upon him with lovelorn eyes. The king rode alone surrounded by his gentlemen.

They passed, talking and waving to us gawking on the side of the road. I cheered at the top of my lungs, and so did the men and children around me. Some of the women cheered as well, although Mistress Longacre tried to glare them to silence.

So focused were the villagers on the king and his glittering gentlemen that the ladies riding somewhat behind them, surrounded by grooms, had nearly passed before we noticed them.

My hungry gaze took in every detail. About five ladies rode on horseback in a cluster, astride like me, their skirts trailing like banners. In the midst of them rode my lady Anne.

She wore brown to match the king, a gown of modest cut that shielded her neck and shoulders, and a fine brown cloak embroidered with gold. Her headdress was different from the usual. While my mother wore the stiff, gabled wimple that sat heavily on the head—and unfortunately required me to do the same—Anne wore a simpler headdress. A curved band pulled back her long hair, and a wisp of silk flowed to her waist over her loose, dark tresses.

Despite the rumor that she was the king's mistress in truth, she still dressed like a maiden. I thought her beautiful.

As soon as I set eyes on her, she threw back her head and laughed. The sound entranced me. It was like dark chimes, deep and golden, ringing for pure joy. That laughter struck something within me, and I suddenly longed to laugh with her, to feel the same joy she did.

At that same moment I saw Mistress Longacre and her women move.

They ran at the ladies, bobbing up and down like a flock of geese, waving skirts like they were shooing away something distasteful. The horses shied and danced, and the groom cursed.

"Whore," the women screamed at Anne. "Restore the queen! Return to Babylon!"

In the confusion, the grooms dispersed. Two or three of the ladies rode into the ditch, to be confronted by the women of the village. The village women hissed and spat like cats. Mistress Longacre drew back her hand.

Without waiting for thought, I kicked my horse forward, plunging between Mistress Longacre and the lady Anne, just as the handful of mud flew.

The wad caught me on the shoulder and half splattered my face, stinging my eyes. Mistress Longacre had packed the mud with pebbles. They cut my cheek, and I tasted blood on my lips.

Lady Anne's horse swerved away. I rode my horse in a circle around hers, trying to hold the village women off, like a dog protecting a sheep from predators.

The lady Anne flashed a look of dangerous anger. A groom moved his horse beside mine, blocking me from following her, but keeping her from the village women and their missiles.

Lady Anne called to another groom. "Guide the young woman's horse," she commanded. "I want her to follow."

She said nothing directly to me, but turned her attention to her mount, calming it with an expert touch. She and her groom rode on.

Another groom commanded me to follow him, and I let him herd me into the group of Anne's ladies. They looked at me with startled eyes beneath colorful veils, highborn women surprised to find a hoyden in their midst.

I heard Mistress Longacre shriek. "Frances Pierce, come away from there at once!"

My heart beat wildly. My face stung where the mud and rocks had hit me, and my entire body quivered.

"I will go to your lady mother," Mistress Longacre cried. "You ought to be ashamed. No good will come of this."

I ignored her. Lady Anne, at that moment, had far more weight with me than Mistress Longacre.

The procession continued up the road, this time with me in it.

I rode directly behind the groom along the road to Hunsdon, my gaze fixed on the up-and-down motion of his horse's mahogany hocks. The right hind had a white patch just above the fetlock. It rose and fell under my fixed gaze, and for some reason, I could not look away from it.

After a long time, we rode through a set of high gates and up the long avenue and into a courtyard of a long, brick house. All manner of people swarmed about us, and the neat line of riders dissolved into disorder.

The king habitually made a summer progress about his realm, staying in his manor houses to hunt and hawk and entertain those he wished to impress. Sometimes he went east, sometimes west, occasionally, north. He went accompanied by his favorite gentlemen, the queen by her favorite ladies, and servants of the bedchambers, cooks, footmen, maids, and the same number of people to care for his horses and other animals as cared for the people. Now they were all at Hunsdon, and the house teemed with activity.

I quickly lost sight of the king and his entourage and the lady Anne and hers. The groom who pulled me into the train dismounted his horse and disappeared toward the stables, having better things to do than to answer questions of a mud-splattered girl.

I slid from my horse, legs shaking. A lad immediately grabbed its reins, then looked at the nag in surprise and distaste. I started to ask him what I should do, but he turned and led the horse off toward the stables without a word.

I was left alone in the midst a whirl of activity. At first glance it looked like confusion, but as I watched I realized that everyone knew exactly what to do. Lads unsaddled horses, the grooms headed for the mews and the stables, porters carried things into dark doorways, foodstuffs appeared and were trundled out of sight. I heard the clucking of fowl and the squeal of pigs. A woman hurried by with a basket on her arm, overflowing with bright, ripe fruit.

The only person with nothing to do in this flurry was me. I debated whether to latch on to one of the lackeys and follow him inside, or whether to slip out of the gate and make my way home. I would return to a certain beating. Even my father would be angry with me for taking my uncle's horse without leave, not to mention leaving it behind at Hunsdon.

While I debated, I noted a gentleman, one I'd seen riding with the king, watching me. He was older than me, in his midtwenties, I guessed, and he wore a dark green doublet, lighter green coat, and a fine velvet cap. He had deep brown hair, tightly curled, and very sharp, dark eyes. He was tall, and, I supposed, handsome, with a beard trimmed close to his face and muscular calves in well-fitting boots.

I turned away from him after my first assessment, deciding such a highborn gentleman could have no interest in a creature like me. Then I became aware that he was standing at my shoulder, glaring as well as Mistress Longacre ever could.

He said in a hard voice, "Why do you tarry here, girl?"

Now, usually, when I see an important gentleman, such as my uncle and his cronies, I at least take it upon myself to curtsy or show some sign of deference. I really have no excuse for what I did. But I was nervous and uncertain, and my face hurt dreadfully, and I was all alone and ignored.

I managed a sneer that would do my mother proud. "I take orders only from my lady Anne."

"Lady Anne has ordered you to stand about like a lost dog?"

"She requested I be here," I said loftily. "When she has need, she will send for me."

The trouble with my bluff was that he knew it was a bluff. His disdainful eyes took in my old gown, my mud-splattered face, and the tangle of my wheat-colored hair. He was not impressed.

"I will advise one of the ladies to find you something to do," he said.

He turned on his heel and stalked away. To relieve my childish frustration, I put out my tongue at him.

A bony hand clenched my shoulder and turned me around. I found myself looking into the face of a lady only a bit older than Anne herself. She wore a French hood and had a long nose and hard eyes.

"What is your name?"

I gulped, wondering if everyone at court was this startling and abrupt. "Frances Pierce," I managed.

"My mistress believes you very brave." Her expression told me she doubted her mistress's wits. "She called you a lady knight, gallantly throwing yourself between her and a dreadful missile."

"I did not want to see her struck with the mud," I said faintly.

The lady looked me up and down much as the gentleman had, but she seemed to see a little beyond the mud and tangles; at least, that is what my pride told me. She removed her hand from my shoulder. "Come with me."

"Have you found work for me?" I was slightly unhappy that I'd escaped the tyranny of my aunt and mother only to be bullied by Lady Anne's hard-eyed servant.

"My lady wants to meet you," she said. "She has few friends, and she needs many."

With that, she turned in a swirl of skirts and marched away. She expected me to follow without question. I did.

Two

MY MOTHER CONTEMPLATES
MY FUTURE

The great hall of Hunsdon manor, a lofty room with dark wooden beams, held a chill, as though winter never fled it. Effort had been made to usher in summer, such as sweet herbs strewn through the rushes, the shutters from high windows flung back, and garlands of summer flowers woven through the lattices of the gallery.

I followed the long-nosed woman up a steep staircase at the end of the hall and along the gallery to a fine chamber. Here, sunshine reached into the room, dancing on the gold threads in the bright arras on the walls and picking out jewels sewn into the ladies' garments as they swarmed busily about.

I did not see Lady Anne right away. The woman who'd led me here, who turned out to be a Mistress Lombard, hauled me round by the hair and thrust a cloth against my face. "Clean yourself, girl."

I took the cloth and tried to wipe off the worst of the mud. Another lady thrust a veil over my unruly hair and viciously pinned it in place. I was still patting my face with the cloth when I was dragged behind a wooden screen that divided the room, and there beheld my lady Anne.

She was commanding that her writing things be set up, a small table, parchment, a horn of ink, and pens. I found myself standing in the center of the floor, knees trembling, the tight veil rubbing my ears.

She did not look at me. She'd put off her wimple, and her hair tumbled down, sleek and dark and unadorned. Her skin was pale, almost milk-white, her face an oval. She did not possess brilliant beauty, but there was something about her that arrested the attention. Once one looked at her, one did not lightly look away.

Her body was slender, and she was tall, but not awkwardly so. Her gown was cut to emphasize the best of her figure, slim waist, trim hips, long arms. Around her neck she wore a medallion with a large *B* positioned to rest on the hollow of her throat.

Vicious people liked to say that she wore the necklace to hide a large mole or some other sort of defect on her neck. This is simply not true. People who'd never seen her before said this, when whispers began that she used witchcraft to enchant the king. They wanted to assure themselves that she indeed bore the mark of the devil. Likewise, lies and gossip gave her a sixth finger on one hand, but this, too, was utter nonsense, although I admit it makes a good story.

The truth was, she was simply an ordinary woman of extraordinary character, related through her mother to the great Howard family, and wise enough to use what she had to gain as much as she could.

All this did not occur to me, of course, as I waited, trembling, for her to notice me. My only thought at that moment was hope that I would not hiccup as I sometimes did when nervous, or do anything else as undignified.

At last, Lady Anne raised her eyes and looked directly at me.

I gaped and stared.

Her eyes were black. But instead of being pools of darkness, they glowed with strange, silver fire, as though something glorious burned behind them. They were eyes that seared you and bewitched you, and made you forget why you stood there in your old gown with your hair a mess and your mouth hanging open.

I understood that instant why King Henry had fallen in love with her. When she fixed you with that gaze, she willed you to love her. She had speared the mightiest in the land with her eyes, and he'd fallen.

"I am trying to decide who you are," she said, as I stood a-tremble. Her voice was clear and low. "You ride well on a horse that can only belong to a nobleman's stable, yet you dress like a peasant and gape like one, too. Perhaps, my dear, you should close your mouth."

I popped it shut. I heard titters behind me.

Lady Anne smiled faintly, the corners of her lips just lifting. "Excellent. Now, cease teasing me, and tell me who you are."

"F-Frances Pierce," I said, dry-throated.

"Do you always stutter? Is it a defect?"

"N-no, my lady," I answered in French. "But I am all amazed."

That flattered her. "Frances Pierce. A good name. But you have not told me who you are, nor why you so gallantly interposed yourself between me and a nasty bit of mud."

"My father is Sir Lionel Pierce, a baronet. And I did not think it right that your beautiful cloak should be marred."

She took this explanation with a lift of brows. "So you are a lady, Frances Pierce of Hertfordshire."

"I try to be," I said. "At least, my mother tries to make me one."

"You speak French well."

"My mother is French," I answered.

"I see. Can you also write?"

"I was able to this morning. I am by no means certain at the moment."

She laughed, while the other ladies watched us from the corners of their eyes. "You are droll. Come, sit, and copy out this song for me into my book."

I tottered forward to the stool that she indicated. The other ladies looked on as they brushed Lady Anne's cloak and gloves or folded away her things. I'd seen some of them riding with her, and they looked me over much as they had then, some curious, some indulgent, some jealous.

The ladies wore gowns of every color, deep blue, greens, yellow, and violet, and either French hoods as Lady Anne had in the hunting party, or gabled wimples with gaily colored veils. Each was young and quite pretty, with jewels as bright as their eyes gleaming on throats and fingers.

I noticed when I sat down and took up the pen that my hands were very grubby, which was my own fault for not snatching up a pair of gloves. I tried to fold my fingers under so Lady Anne would not see, but she either did not notice or did not care.

Mistress Lombard spread out a manuscript from which I was to copy a little song, all about a sparrow singing in a meadow and a man hearing it and giving glory to God. I trembled, but I managed not to blotch ink on the clean page of the book she opened for me. My fingers knew what to do, despite my agitation, and I wrote quickly and precisely.

When I finished, Lady Anne leaned over my shoulder, the spice of her perfume tickling me. "Very good. Your hand is neat and quick." She held the book to her other ladies, who each took it in turn and pronounced my writing fine.

They were smiling and not serious, and I knew they were making fun of me, but I did not care.

"Your governess should be pleased," said one, handing the book back to me.

"I have been writing for many years," I said, stung. "I write verses."

That invoked laughter from all except Lady Anne herself. "A lyricist, are you? What do you write verses about?"

"Anything, my lady. From nature and love to the milkmaid stumbling out of the buttery. My mother does not like it."

"But many ladies compose verse." She pointed to a blank page in her book. "Here, write some for me."

I suppose she meant for me to compose lines out of my head as I sat before her, but my mind had sunk into a kind of numb haze. Everything seemed a bit unreal, as though I did not truly sit in this sunny chamber with these butterflies of ladies and the king's mistress hovering at my elbow.

But I'd had lines running through my head since this morning, when I imagined the procession of the king and his train, and I wrote them now.

> A maiden fair, and round her all beguiled.
> A gentleman too, a heart too long tossed
> On seas of love, a ship teetering and lost.
> But tempests calm when on them the maiden smiles.

She watched every word. I swallowed, looking at the pathetic rhymes, the meter of the last line not true. I waited for her to, like my mother, snatch the paper from me, tear it to shreds, and tell me I'd never amount to anything.

"Is that about me, Frances Pierce?" Anne asked.

"Yes, my lady."

A wary light entered her eyes. "Your village women jeer at me when I pass, and you write of me smiling upon tempests and beguiling them?"

"Yes," I said.

"You are an unusual young woman." She gave me a look that held the strength of emperors. "I will be queen, Frances. It is in my stars, and things are falling into place. The court is a dangerous land, but if you are quiet and obedient, you can hold your own. You have not much to recommend you," she said, her gaze critical, "but I need good and loyal friends, and I will reward them well. Can you be loyal?"

"Oh, yes," I cried.

While she spoke I had a vision of myself in splendid velvet skirts and a brocade stomacher, following the lady Anne, carrying writing implements and composing verses for her pleasure. The court would admire me, and the gentleman I'd met downstairs, whoever he was, would see that

I was somebody. And my mother would at last concede I'd made something of myself.

"Splendid." Lady Anne's expression softened, and she looked upon me with something near to affection. "You will, of course, need better clothes."

"Yes, indeed," I breathed.

She began to turn away. "Mistress Lombard will look after you."

Mistress Lombard, from across the room, bent an eye on me that boded more scrubbings, but I did not mind. I had been asked to attend the beautiful Lady Anne, who would soon be queen. And hers would not be a court of constant prayer and rosaries, like Queen Catherine's—in effect, an extension of my mother's house—but a court of dancing and pleasure and laughter.

To my seventeen-year-old eyes, this was much to be desired.

Alas, I ought to have remembered that I had such troubles with a single word Lady Anne had mentioned.

Obedience.

MY mother shrieked. The sound echoed from the rafters of the great hall in my uncle's house. My aunt simply fell to the floor.

"You wished me to go to court," I said stiffly. "It would be the making of me, you said."

Despite the presence of Mistress Lombard behind me, my mother strode forward and boxed my ears. "How *dare* you?"

I reeled back, my face stinging. "I thought you would be glad for me."

"Impertinent, wretched girl," my mother cried. "I wished you to learn manners from a queen, not write lewd verses for a trumped-up, dog-mannered—"

She broke off as Mistress Lombard stirred in indignation. "She will be queen, and rightful queen," she said. Mistress Lombard had not looked *very* angry when my mother slapped me, because no doubt she thought I deserved it.

"You ought to be ashamed," my mother snapped at Mistress Lombard. "The Boleyn is nobody, a plain gentlewoman of no royal blood. My daughter has as much connection as she."

"Mistress Anne's uncle is a duke," Mistress Lombard pointed out.

My mother's eyes narrowed. "Queen Catherine is a good and pious queen, a lady to look up to. Is she not a learned woman, has she not been a good queen these twenty years? What can my daughter learn from a demimondaine but lewd manners and lecherous ways?"

I listened, tears spilling down my face. My aunt likewise sobbed, prostrate on the floor.

It was Mistress Lombard who changed my fate. She listened calmly to my mother's tirade, and then made a single statement.

"Frances will be introduced to gentlemen of the king's privy chamber, many of whom are in need of a wife."

My mother's diatribe cut off in midsentence. My aunt raised her head.

My mother slowly closed her mouth, her expression becoming thoughtful. Lady Anne came attached to a king, the same king whose gentlemen my mother had wished to send me to Queen Catherine to meet. I saw her weighing her choices: keep me from the woman she despised and have me on her hands the rest of her life, or send me off with a lecherous woman who might just help me marry a highborn man.

She thought, while my aunt and I held our breaths. Then my mother, so righteously angry a moment ago, succumbed to ambition.

"With luck, she will be married within a six-month," she said, half to herself. "And setting up her nursery."

"I do not wish to marry," I broke in.

My mother gave me a long-suffering look. "Yes, you do, Frances. There is nothing for a woman if she does not marry."

"I can always take the veil."

I had absolutely no intention of doing so, but the threat nearly always drove my mother mad. She was fond of piety, yes, but not of giving my dowry to a convent.

She turned a bleak gaze on Mistress Lombard. "I will want to hear of any connection she makes, great or small, right away."

"Of course," Mistress Lombard said. "I would wish nothing different for my own daughter."

My aunt picked herself up and hung onto the stair banister for support. "Just think, Frances," she breathed. "You might marry an earl."

My mother sniffed. "At this point I'd settle for a gentleman knight. One of steady years and firm hand."

I would never dream of encouraging such a man, so I said nothing.

"She will need new clothes," Mistress Lombard said.

"She will have them," my mother answered, and then I knew that the argument was won.

I rejoined Lady Anne at Hunsdon, quivering with excitement for my new life to begin. My golden-haired cousin Mathilde often put on airs because she was married and had three babes, though she was but a year older than I. But what was a husband and a household when compared to waiting on a queen?

Or at least, Lady Anne would soon be queen. My mother was wrong. Our king was changing the world so that he could discard the beloved Catherine and have his Anne. And at the moment, I wanted him to do so with all my heart.

Lady Anne smiled at me when I appeared before her again three days later, hands washed and hair combed, in a new and hastily made gown. She nodded approval at the change in me but ordered one of her seamstresses to take me in hand. I would need much more, she said—riding clothes, gowns for dining and for balls, for feasts and entertainments. I would need gloves and veils and hoods and wimples and shoes and stockings and chemises. When the seamstress finished, I'd be dressed from the skin out in finery I never dreamed would touch my body.

She introduced me to the other ladies and admonished them to treat me kindly. They did, for the most part, though they were the daughters of dukes and earls, and I was really nobody. They wondered why Anne had brought me into their circle, and I wondered, as well. I thought perhaps she saw in me something of herself, a plain gentlewoman with no one to recommend her. Pity, I was certain, had much to do with it, but I did not mind.

I never was formally introduced to the king. The night of my arrival, I accompanied Lady Anne to Henry's chamber, where they entertained the French ambassador. Our king looked at me, his red gold hair burnished by candlelight, the rings on his fingers bloodred. His glance turned puzzled, then Lady Anne leaned and whispered to him.

Henry's dark eyes became fixed, pinning me like a marsh bird he particularly wanted to shoot. Then he laughed. His great mouth opened, as red as his rubies and filled with pearl-white teeth.

He lifted his cup. "God bless my lady's rescuer. Give us a curtsy, girl, we'll not bite you."

I dropped my gaze and bent my legs. At the same moment, a hiccup came out of my mouth and landed in the silence.

Henry stared at me a moment, brows raised, then he burst into louder laughter. The rest of the company followed suit, including the ambassador. They thought me fine entertainment. I blushed, mortified, but Lady Anne smiled and winked at me, and I knew I'd not been disgraced.

Henry called for a song, then, and completely ignored me.

After that, oddly, I seemed to be accepted. My new life was strange at first, but I soon fell into a routine.

I was housed with the unmarried ladies, looked after by Mistress Lombard. I shared a bed in a cold chamber with three other misses of different ranks, and there was much whispering and giggling as we huddled under the quilts each night.

We woke at dawn, dressed hurriedly, ate a bite of bread, and then went to Lady Anne. While the ladies of her wardrobe dressed her, we younger girls ran errands or sorted her gloves, or conversed with her when she asked us to. We would go with her to Mass on Sunday, and on weekdays, listen to her read out scriptures in French, which we would then discuss.

Lady Anne breakfasted at a table alone, and we would stand ready to hand her a kerchief or send for more wine or meat. Sometimes the king breakfasted with her, and we would retreat to the side of the room and be decorative while they talked.

During the day, Lady Anne wrote letters or received visitors and read books and dispatches—usually about the king's divorce, which she knew much about, and could discourse on like a lawyer. She would then join the hunting or hawking in the king's private park. Because I could ride well, she took me with her.

In the evening, she dined, usually with the king and whatever person he'd brought to be entertained, often an ambassador he wanted to impress.

Each night after supper we had merrymaking with musicians and dancing. Sometimes Henry would play the hurdy-gurdy and sing. He had a fine baritone, although I preferred the music of his minstrels and the jokes of his fool. The gentlemen also would sing, even the cross gentleman who had accosted me in the courtyard, whose name was Sir John Carlisle. The king's closest friend, Henry Norris, also sang, and flirted quite blatantly with any lady near him.

The king's gentlemen never flirted with me, because as I said, I was plain and small, but I did not much care. I was giddy with excitement simply to watch the king and Lady Anne and their court in miniature, and write of it when I could snatch a moment to myself.

My duties were to keep near Lady Anne to bring her

what she needed, run errands, sing or dance for her, and entertain her when she wanted diversion. She seemed to like me, although Mistress Lombard chivied me a great deal and found fault with everything I did.

Lady Anne also had me write verses for her and read them out. I quickly realized that what the court ladies prized was wit, and I tried to master puns and double entendre— often without understanding what the double entendre meant. I was an innocent creature.

Lady Anne rewarded me with cloth for new clothes, a maid of my own to dress me, and gifts such as little books or pieces of jewelry. In all my life, I'd never felt so rich.

I had hoped that when I joined Lady Anne, we'd travel northward to places I rarely ventured, but as it turned out, we went no farther than Hunsdon.

Incidents like Mistress Longacre throwing mud and rocks had happened all too often, the other ladies told me. Therefore, Henry no longer wanted Anne to ride out publicly with him. Instead, they would hunt in the park and entertain the French ambassador, who'd come to talk about the king's upcoming trip to Calais.

I was disappointed, but I began to be caught up in the happenings of court. The Calais trip, it seemed, would be quite important. Henry wished to meet with the French king to put the final seal on an arms treaty they'd worked out together. He also wanted to take Lady Anne with him. If Francis, the French king, agreed to the meeting, it would indicate a tacit acceptance of Anne as the new queen of England. Henry and Anne seemed to want this more even than they wanted the treaty.

I came to realize that always at the back of Henry's mind was the fear that when he divorced Queen Catherine, Catherine's nephew, who happened to be the Holy Roman Emperor, would invade England. This new treaty with France meant that France would help England if such a thing happened.

Lady Anne showed us a portrait of King Francis. He was quite handsome with his dark hair and beard and flash of light in his eye. Francis' relationship with Henry was a rivalry of sorts, a game of one-upmanship, each king trying to best the other in pageantry, wit, and prowess. He and Henry were both robust men, strong militarily and politically. Francis, however, had one thing that Henry lacked: a horde of children, including several sons.

Henry spent much of his time proving to himself and the world that he was better than Francis. I do not know what Francis made of this game, but the dry humor in his painted eye told me he let Henry play it because it amused him.

This time, Henry wanted to show that he had—or soon would have—a new queen who would give him a bushel of sons.

Lady Anne was certain she could.

"I am young and strong and healthy," she would say. "God has seen fit to send me to the king to give him strong sons."

That, I think, was the secret of her ambition. Not to be queen and surrounded by pomp and glory—although she craved this as well. Not even for great love of the king. But if she married Henry, then *her* sons would be kings of England, the children of *her* body would climb to greatness.

The king of France apparently took some convincing, to judge from the way Anne and Henry lavishly entertained the French ambassador. The ambassador was inclined to be pleased with everything, but of course, when you are an ambassador, you cannot very well say that your meals are horrible and your room is cold and your host is most unpleasant. If you say such things, the king will dispatch you back to your country, and you lose your post.

One day, a few weeks after I'd joined her, Lady Anne returned to the manor looking pleased.

"An excellent ride," she said, stripping off her gloves. "Most invigorating for the humors."

A lady took the gloves and a damp cloth and began cleaning them. I could only watch a task that I was supposed to have done, but earlier I'd torn my new brocade skirt, and Mistress Lombard had not only made me sew it up but bade the rest of the maids and ladies hand me their mending as well.

"Was the French ambassador in good spirits?" a lady called Anne Savage asked.

"He was indeed." Lady Anne settled herself on a chair and allowed a maid to remove her boots. "I believe all will be well for me to go to Calais. I cannot go until invited, but I predict that the king will receive a request from the French king before long." She let out a sigh. "It will be a fine thing to see old friends again. Frances, would you like to accompany me to Calais?"

I dropped the mending all over the floor. I blinked a few times, then managed, "Yes, please, my lady."

She gave me an indulgent smile. "Then I shall take you. I would be pleased for you to attend me."

She stood up, clad in slippers while her maids removed her riding clothes and dressed her again in the lavish brocade in which she'd take supper with the ambassador. "We will return to Greenwich soon. You will be finished with the mending before then, I trust?"

I blushed at my clumsiness, and the ladies laughed. Lady Anne's splendid eyes twinkled. She liked to tease me, but she was not cruel. She enjoyed banter and laughter and clever talk, and she liked it when I quipped back.

"Indeed," I said, trying levity. "My needle will go in and out like lightning, as the stableboy said to the milkmaid."

The ladies giggled. The sparkle in Lady Anne's eyes heightened, but she shook her head, pretending to admonish my lewdness. Mistress Lombard tightened her lips. My mother should be receiving a report shortly.

A few weeks later, when Anne and Henry had finished softening the French ambassador, we rode back to London.

My life by now had been completely transformed. It was odd to be one moment nobody Frances Pierce, scolded by the crows in the village, riding pell-mell across country on her uncle's horse, the next a young lady in charge of writing witty verses and keeping Lady Anne's everyday jewels close by in case she wanted them.

Lady Anne's seamstress had made me clothes that would be the envy of my mother, aunt, and cousin. The latest dress, cut from cloths that Anne had given me, had a pointed stomacher of fine green velvet embroidered on its edges with stitches of gold. The bodice had long, straight sleeves that belled from the elbows. The kirtle, narrow because the farthingales that were to become the rage years later had not been thought of yet, was flowing yellow satin, with a green velvet robe over it.

My hair, no longer tangled and snarled, hung in a long, sleek wave, covered with the veil of a French hood. Lady Anne liked her attendants to dress modestly, so the bodice hid most of my bosom, leaving room only for a little chain to rest against the hollow of my throat. But for the first time in my life, I felt pretty.

Lady Anne had given me a ring, too, which I wore on my right hand. It had an emerald in it, large as my little fingernail. This band was nothing compared to the beautiful rings that Henry gave Anne, but I felt pleased and proud to wear such a thing.

My new clothes and new status meant that I traveled like a young lady. I rode on a lively mare Lady Anne lent me, on a finely tooled saddle. My new riding clothes consisted of soft leather breeches and a skirt that trailed gracefully across the horse's back.

The sun shone on us as we rode from Hertfordshire to Middlesex to London, I in the midst of laughing, clever ladies. Gentlemen, grooms, and outriders circled us, the king's banners flapping. My heart soared with pride. I was young, Anne was young, and we rode through the English countryside under the sun and sang songs. Life was perfectly splendid.

The only blight on this life was a man.

His name was John Carlisle. Sir John, for he was already

a knight, was also the son of the Earl of Pennington. He was handsome and arrogant and a bully. It had been he who'd accosted me at Hunsdon manor house and demanded to know what I was doing standing about like a lost dog.

The king and his friends addressed him as Jack, and he was a member of the king's privy chamber. This means he was one of a body of young gentlemen who waited on the king and amused him and held his shirts when he got dressed in the morning. They were among the most privileged in the land, and they were happy and confident in their power.

Jack Carlisle was as arrogant as the others. He and young Henry Norris played tennis or hunted with the king, and they made sure that the rest of us knew it. Mr. Norris was a scandalous flirt. Mr. Carlisle was a bit more haughty, and I believe that he was sent by God to drive me mad.

The morning we were to ride into London, he caught me outside the stables stroking the neck of one of the king's horses. Now, I was fond of horses, and to see such fine examples of horseflesh delighted me. I absorbed every detail of them for my letters to my father, also a lover of horses.

"What are you doing there?" Jack Carlisle asked in his displeased tones.

I thought it perfectly obvious what I was doing, so I did not deign to answer.

"The king does not like his animals to be touched," he said.

"I am not hurting it."

"Nevertheless."

Really, he was as bad as Mistress Lombard. But while I was apt to allow Mistress Lombard to bully me, I was not afraid of Jack Carlisle. Not because he had no power over me, because he did. All he had to do was suggest to Henry that young Frances Pierce was not good for Anne, or even worse, that my family supported Queen Catherine. And Henry could say, *Ah, well, Frances, back to your father with you, and by the way, I will confiscate his lands for my friends.*

But for some reason, while I always scrambled to obey Mistress Lombard, Jack Carlisle only put my back up.

"You will accompany Lady Anne to Calais?" he asked. He put his hand on the horse's bridle as though afraid the beast would bolt under my bad influence.

I gave him a lofty look, having to tilt my head back to do so, he was so tall. "I go where my lady asks me to go."

"A simple 'yes' would suffice."

I eyed him narrowly. "Aye, then. If Lady Anne goes to France, I will go with her."

"She will," he said. "The court of France is a different place from the English court. It has an elegance, but it is very treacherous. I do not think it will be good for you."

"Piffle on what you think," I said. "I will be attending my lady. I doubt the king of France and his courtiers will be asking my opinion on the threat of the Holy Roman Empire."

He ignored my attempt at wit. "That is at least sensible of you. Give the French courtiers a wide berth. You will not know how to handle them."

"Thank you very much for your advice," I said. "I am sure you have superior wisdom over all of us."

He looked annoyed but did not rise to my banter. "And do not compose verses while you are there, pray. I read a few of your lines that Anne showed His Grace the king. Do not make yourself a laughingstock."

I stopped, my face heating. "You read my verses?"

"Yes. You should either practice much before you show them to people, or cease writing them altogether."

I balled my fists, wanting nothing more than to stoop to the ground, snatch up a piece of dirty hay, and fling it at him. He made me as bad as Mistress Longacre. "How *dare* you?"

"I say it for your own good, Mistress Pierce."

"You insult me for my own good?"

His eyes went hard. "You are too young to be here."

"That is utter nonsense. Mary Howard is years younger than I, and she is here."

"She grew up in the house of a duke and understands

the intrigues of the court. You know nothing of it. These waters are deep, and you do not belong in them."

I wanted to scream like a fishwife but remembered my dignity in time. "I realize that I am countrified, but I came to court to learn, and to marry well. Not, I must add, to you."

I did not want to marry in particular. That part of my education could be put off a long while, as far as I was concerned. But I hoped that when a handsome and highborn and wealthy and *polite* courtier begged me to be his wife, Jack Carlisle would be there so that I could rub his nose in it.

He gave me a disdainful look. "I am not prepared to marry."

"Excellent, then I will not have to suffer a proposal from you."

"You are a child."

"You are a prig," I retorted.

The horse did not like our raised voices. He snorted and danced aside. A groom hurried forward and caught his reins, shooting us an irritated look.

Jack managed to be handsome even when he was angry, and that annoyed me still further.

"Run and play games with your king," I said. "And leave me be."

I swirled around to stomp away. I expected him to try to get in the last word, and I was pleased when he said nothing. But when I turned before I left the stable yard, hoping he watched me with his mouth open, I saw that he'd disappeared.

The man could not even be bothered to wait while I stormed away from him. I thought of colorful names to call him all the way back to the house, nasty ones I'd learned from the lowest of my uncle's servants.

Three

❦

THE MARQUESS OF PEMBROKE

SEPTEMBER 1532

WINDSOR Castle tingled with anticipation. Two months had passed since I'd joined Anne's company. In my thoughts now, she was simply Anne, and the king, Henry. How quickly I had gotten used to my new station! Today, I would stand with her while she was elevated to the peerage. In the king's presence chamber, she would become the Marquess of Pembroke, receiving all the lands and moneys conferred with the title.

This step was necessary, she explained, if she was to journey to France with the king and meet with the great ladies there. She could not go as plain Anne Boleyn, daughter to a newly made earl. She must meet the ladies of the French court as an equal, or near equal, and likewise have charge of a household of highborn ladies.

It was also, I knew as well as Anne did, a sure step in her becoming queen.

I loved pomp. Parade and ceremony could lift my spirits on even my lowest days. I looked about me carefully, knowing that I would write an account of this day for my aunt, who also loved ceremony, the more lavish the better. My mother would pretend to care nothing for what the king did for his strumpet, but I imagined her straining to listen as my aunt read out my words.

I helped dress Anne in deep red velvets and ermine. Her hair, which I combed out, hung straight and long down her back in a shining fall. We hung many jewels upon her until she glittered whichever way she turned.

I would not walk in the procession, so when Anne was ready, I ran out to watch the nobles of the court make their solemn way through the halls to the presence chamber.

Standard-bearers led the way, carrying a flag with Anne's symbol, a falcon. Next came the Duke of Norfolk, her uncle, smiling a little, his dark eyes triumphant in his narrow face. He'd gained much influence, I'd heard, since his niece had caught the king's eye. Her elevation was his, too.

I wondered fleetingly how he felt about his wife's refusal to have anything to do with the ceremony today. The duchess, her daughter Mary Howard told me, should have carried Anne's robes of state and her coronet, but had refused point-blank. She would not toady to a Boleyn nobody, she said. She was friend to Queen Catherine, and nothing would move her.

I had not met the duchess, but suddenly I longed to see the woman who could make our powerful king and the haughty Duke of Norfolk back down.

But watching the way the duke held his shoulders straight while his eyes narrowed, razor-sharp, I decided that he did not bother about his wife's opinion at all.

My new friend Mary Howard had been ordered to take her mother's role. Mary had whispered to me under the bedclothes the night before that she was terrified she'd drop the robes or trip or do something equally dreadful. Mary was thirteen, much younger than I, but I found her sweet and kind, and we'd become friends. I'd patted her hand and told her she would do fine.

True to my prediction, Mary acquitted herself well. She was pretty with her light brown hair and her young face lit with excitement. She held Anne's robe and coronet in hands that trembled, but she held them securely.

The Duke of Suffolk, husband of King Henry's sister Mary, was there as well, looking disapproving, but not making a fuss. His wife, too, though not present because she was ill, was not happy with Anne Boleyn as the king's choice. After all, a queen should be royal, a foreign princess, not a lesser nobleman's daughter. Mary Suffolk had once been the queen of France, albeit for only a few months, so she knew all about what it took to be queen. To put aside the daughter of Isabella of Spain for a Boleyn, even if she was a duke's niece—well, it was simply not the thing.

Anne cared nothing for this. It was her day. She held her head high, letting all know her triumph.

I followed the procession to the presence chamber, slipping inside just before the doors closed. The huge, high-ceilinged chamber glittered with candles and the deeper fire of braziers. A canopy of cloth of gold hung over the platform on which Anne was to stand. The king waited for her there, as well as Bishop Gardiner, who would say prayers and read the patents.

The blight, and by that I mean Jack Carlisle, stood a little behind the king, dressed in velvet and brocade finery, a feathered hat, and glittering rings. The king, his red gold hair shining, his red beard combed, radiated satisfaction. This was not his ceremony—it was Anne's—but by some token it was his as well. By this move, he was showing the world his intentions. He would move forward to make Anne queen, whether they liked it or not.

Plus, he was giving his lady a gift, elevation to the peerage, the sort of gift that most men could not give to the ladies of their hearts. This was the equivalent of a merchant boasting that he'd provided his wife with the best linens on the street.

Mary walked behind Anne to the platform. Two countesses, one of Sussex, the other of Rutland, accompanied Anne up the shallow steps and helped her kneel.

There followed many readings and speeches in Latin, which I ill understood, but the spectacle was splendid. Bishop Gardiner, who was also the king's secretary, performed the ceremony. Bishop Gardiner, gossip told me, had recently had to forfeit his house, Hanworth, to Anne, because he had not been happy about the recent act that made Henry head of the Church in England. Bishop Gardiner had voiced his disapproval quite loudly. Henry then informed the bishop that he might be spared if he would give up his house and beg for mercy.

I remembered my father telling me that the king had done much the same to Cardinal Wolsey. Wolsey, who'd been lord chancellor, had failed to obtain a swift divorce for Henry, and plummeted from favor. He'd died before the king could bring him to trial for treason, but not before Henry had seized his sumptuous houses, Hampton Court and York Place. I suppose the moral is that if you are a clerical man with a fine house, you had better guard your tongue.

Bishop Gardiner seemed neither worried nor resentful as he performed the ceremony, or perhaps he'd simply learned to hide his feelings.

The happiest part of the hour was when Henry took the robe from the white-faced Mary Howard and settled it about Anne's shoulders. When he placed the coronet on her head, they shared a look that sparked for all to see.

We are all, that look said. *And none may oppose us.*

I could make lovely verses from this, I thought. I let words flow through my head, my fingers moving against my skirt as I counted out the meter.

I caught Jack's eye on me. He looked fine today, and I knew that more than one of Anne's ladies liked to admire his strong legs.

It was not his legs I noted now, but the disapproving glance he tossed at me.

Whenever my father looked disapproving, I felt humbled and wished to do better to please him. When Master Jack looked at me, I had only the urge to kick him. Or, more ladylike, stick my nose in the air and walk away.

I could do neither of those things while my lady Anne became her ladyship the marquess, so I frowned at him until he looked away.

I did not let him stop me, however. I thought out my verses as I watched Anne be embraced and kissed on both cheeks by the king. The nobles bowed to her, and she stood before them, smiling her triumph.

I read the poem out to Anne the next morning as we drifted in barges to Hampton Court. From there we would ride the short distance to Hanworth and set up her new household.

I enjoyed traveling in the comfortable barge, sitting against cushions while the land floated by and the bargemen whistled. I read to her:

> Sparkling from raven hair to dainty foot,
> My lady received her homage due
> Which upon her the great king did imbue.
> A lady from a noble family's shoot,
> A king who from great love has long wooed.
> At last their love is able to take root . . .

I did not believe the lines very good, but they pleased her. "Lovely verses, Frances," Anne said, dark eyes dancing. I knew she teased me, but she teased everyone. "You captured the moment splendidly."

I heard a snort in the accompanying barge, which was filled with the king's gentlemen. Sure enough, Jack Carlisle leaned against the gunwale, his look scornful.

"Some gentlemen seem not to appreciate poetry, my lady," I remarked.

Jack glanced away, but I saw the irritation in his eyes. Anne's smile turned sly. "Perhaps he can recite verses better? Come, Sir John, entertain us with poesy."

Jack did not squirm or show embarrassment as I'd hoped. Instead, he bowed politely. "I have not the skill, my lady. Perhaps our minstrel will perform for us."

The man who lounged in the stern of the gentlemen's boat plucked a few strings of his hurdy-gurdy.

Anne winked at me. I sat back, disappointed that she did not make a fool of Jack. I hoped she'd demand that he sing or make verses to please her and threaten him with the king's displeasure if he did not. But she merely nodded at the musician and bade him to begin.

That night, when I put away her jewels at Hanworth, she said to me, "You too much wished me to punish Sir John Carlisle. Why, I wonder?"

She spoke in low tones while I sat at her feet, tucking her rings safely into their silk bags for the night. "He was rude, my lady," I said.

"Many people will be rude to you, Frances. The court is filled with people who will cut you to ribbons if you let them. You must return rudeness with a smile, with grace, to show it does not touch you." She leaned to me and put her lips to my ear. "Never let them win."

I was a bit confused, but I nodded. "Yes, my lady."

"His Grace the king is fond of Sir John."

"Is he, my lady?"

"Indeed, Sir John is rather a favorite." She looked thoughtful. "I will speak to His Grace."

I looked at her, astonished. "You would have the king scold him?"

She looked wise, her eyes difficult to read. "Perhaps. That and other things. But never mind. You are finished here. Off to bed with you."

I closed the box, got to my feet, and curtsied. "Yes, my lady."

I did not quite understand her preoccupation with Jack Carlisle then, but I would come to.

The next day, still at Hanworth, I waited on Anne as she and the king dined with another French ambassador called Monsieur du Bellay. Thomas Cromwell sat nearby, watching the king and queen dine. These days, Cromwell, a rather long-nosed man with animated eyes, was rarely far from Henry's elbow.

Cromwell, I was given to understand, though lowborn, had risen sharply in the king's favor, because he'd become quite adept at preparing things for the divorce. He was a member of the king's council and had taken over quite a lot of duties. Now, he'd become Henry's most trusted advisor. Indeed, much of Henry's conversation with Anne of evenings was a catalog of what Cromwell had said or done.

What I learned about politics since I'd come to serve Anne was that each person scratched the back of another who could help him. Woe betide you if you scratched too hard or forgot to scratch at all. Thomas Cromwell had proved himself very adept at scratching.

"Is there word?" Anne asked the ambassador.

Monsieur du Bellay twitched. "Alas, my lady, I hear that the queen of France will not come to Calais, or Boulogne."

Anne stilled, trying to hide her disappointment. If the French queen and her ladies did not accompany Francis to the meeting in Boulogne, Anne could not attend. Court etiquette forbade it, and Anne and Henry, so blatantly dismissing convention over the divorce, wanted to strictly adhere to all other rules. Anne must be seen as a proper consort.

Henry went red in the face. "Blasted man, how dare he—?"

The ambassador broke in quickly. "Do not worry, Your Grace. He has told me to inform you that the queen of Navarre will attend instead. I believe she was her ladyship's friend of long ago? Here is the letter."

He handed a document bearing many seals over to Henry. Thomas Cromwell smoothly intercepted it. He opened it, read it through, then said, "Your Grace, it is an invitation from the king of France himself to her ladyship to attend him in Boulogne. The queen of Navarre will await her."

His voice was dry, matter-of-fact, but Anne and Henry shared a satisfied glance. "Dear Marguerite," Anne said. "How happy I will be to see her again."

Henry's expression said he could care less about dear

Marguerite, but he had what he wanted: the French king's invitation to Anne. He was quite merry the remainder of the night.

AFTER the ambassador's good news, we did nothing but prepare for the trip to Calais. For Anne to meet the king of France smoothed the way for him to accept her as Henry's wife and queen. This trip, if all went well, would put France in Henry's pocket.

Anne was determined to enter the French court fully equal to the queen of France and the queen of Navarre, who was King Francis' favorite sister. Anne had left the French court as the mere daughter of an English gentleman; she intended to make them fully aware of how far she'd come.

I learned this with a vengeance when Anne took me with her the next day to Hampton Court, where she'd been summoned by Henry. I put on my best clothes, the aforementioned green frock, and traveled with her the short distance from her house to Henry's.

A flurry of renovations were in progress at the redbrick manor, to make it over for Henry, erasing the influence of Cardinal Wolsey. These renovations had begun a few years ago and were to carry on for quite some time.

We rode through a pointed-arched gateway to a long sweep of drive through a greensward, which ended at the house itself. A herd of gardeners worked with backs bent in the beds, setting out glorious autumn blooms and pruning back summer greenery.

Anne swept into the dim interior, me in her wake. In the hall, workmen stood on scaffolding, plastering over a coat of arms that I took to have been Wolsey's, erasing the poor man forever.

I wanted to wander about the great house exploring and looking at things, but I followed the attendant who came to meet us. He took us up a grand staircase and through smaller rooms to a chamber in which the king was meeting with Thomas Cromwell.

Henry was seated at a table that was heaped with papers. Cromwell sat next to him. A younger man I had not met hovered nearby, his expression worried.

Cromwell looked up when we entered the room, and rose and bowed. His chill dark eyes roved over me once, then dismissed me.

The king was in fine looks that afternoon, his muscular frame set off by gold-slashed sleeves and a red velvet doublet, his face nearly as red from his morning hunting. He was forty, but no gray marred his hair, no lines creased his skin.

All the ladies admired Henry, and he was not beyond flirting with them. Even now, he caught my eye and let his gaze lock a little too long with mine. I paid no attention, because I did not truly think he had interest in me. How could he want plain Frances when he had glittering Anne?

Besides, while it might be flattering to have a king notice me, Henry unnerved me a little. His eyes held a hard light, and when he looked at people, I sensed him sizing them up, trying to decide whether they threatened him or not.

I'd seen him lose his temper at Bishop Gardiner a few days before. Henry's face had gone bright red, cords had stood out on his neck, and he'd balled his fists and shouted, spittle flecking his lips. I'd watched in stunned amazement the transformation from good-humored Great Hal to a furious animal with rage in his eyes. I had been happy to duck behind a pillar and wait for the tantrum to be over.

> King Henry, an English bull, with voice
> That rises over all who tremble . . .

Oh, dear, what rhymed with "tremble"? Dissemble? Amble—perhaps, if one stretched the point.

It annoyed me that each time I tried to devise a rhyme, I saw in my head the disapproving eyes of Jack Carlisle, heard the snort of derision he'd made at my verses to

Anne. That gentleman had ruined some of my pleasure at poesy, and I decided to not forgive him.

Henry came forward, holding his hands out to Anne. "My dear, come and see."

She walked to the table, leaving me behind. When we ladies accompanied her, we were to stay unobtrusively out of the way until called for, but I had an overwhelming curiosity to see what was on the table. I sidled along the stone wall and craned my head to look.

The tabletop was strewn with drawings for jewels. A long chain with huge medallions of gold and rubies was for the king. Another cluster of diamonds held together in a gold brooch like a flower was apparently for Anne. I wanted to see more, but if I stretched farther, Anne might notice and send me from the room.

"They are excellent," Anne said.

I thought Cromwell's shoulders relaxed the slightest bit. Henry lounged back in his chair, at ease.

"Yes, well done," he said. He nodded to the younger man. "Make it so."

"Master Vaughan," Anne said, addressing him. "What about the queen's jewels?"

The room went utterly silent. I heard a man far below in the gardens, whistling. Cromwell moved his hand on a paper with a sound like dry leaves.

At last, Henry sat up, giving Cromwell a sharp look. "Indeed, we should send for them. My lady should not face the court of France in anything less than their ladies would wear." He fixed a beady gaze on young Master Vaughan. "Tell the Duke of Norfolk that he is to go to the queen and fetch away her jewels."

Vaughan dropped lids over his eyes, but I saw the spark of agitation in them before he bowed. "Yes, Your Grace."

Vaughan left the room, presumably to run this errand. Anne and Henry continued to turn over the jewelry designs, making comments on each, but overall, quite pleased.

Anne's pleasure soured in a few days, however, when

her uncle Norfolk returned to tell the king that Queen Catherine refused to relinquish the jewels.

Anne told me nothing of this, but the ladies, of course, gossiped and whispered.

"I heard that the queen had a great fit of rage and told my father the duke to leave her house at once," Mary Howard told me.

Another lady gave a smile of glee. "Did you not hear what she said about our lady? 'I will not give them up to a person who is the scandal of Christendom.' The king is furious."

Mary Carey, Anne's pretty, blonde sister who would go with us to Calais, smiled. "Anne will have them, in the end."

Mary, I had been told at length by the other ladies, had once been the mistress of the king. I often wondered how she'd felt watching her sister not only take her place in the king's affection, but also rise toward becoming his queen. Mary had been already married herself when the king drew her to his side, so she could not have hoped to be wife to the king. Her husband had died a few years ago of the sweating sickness. Now she lived at home with her father in Kent, on a tiny allowance. Anne frequently sent for her.

If Mary was resentful, she hid it. Mary was a lovely woman, all golden hair and blue eyes, with a body not overly thickened by her pregnancies. The king still spoke with her and laughed with her, I'd seen, but he treated her as a friend. His eyes now were only for Anne.

Mary's prediction was correct. Queen Catherine said that she would only relinquish the jewels to a direct order from the king. She might have been hoping that Henry would feel kindness to her, his wife of so many years, but Henry had already finished with Catherine. He gave the order, and the queen's jewels were sent to Anne.

I helped unpack them the evening they arrived. Anne held up a flashing diamond and sapphire diadem, and smiled.

The sparkle of the jewels could not match that of her eyes.

Four

⁂

FRANCE AND A DELAY

OCTOBER 1532

MISTRESS Lombard did not go with us to France, to my delight. She asked permission to return home and care for her ailing father, and Anne let her go with good grace. I never saw the woman again.

I was happy, because Mistress Lombard not only reminded me of my mother, she often wrote to my mother. The result of this correspondence was many letters to me admonishing me to pray harder, mind my manners, never forget who I was, and forbidding me to speak to gentlemen.

This last was rendered difficult, because I could hardly avoid gentlemen on the ship across the Channel.

I feared I would be seasick, having never ventured upon water except the barges on the Thames. As the misty cliffs of England dropped behind us, and the first real wave rolled under the hull, I nearly screamed in fright. The ship came down, crash, in the trough of the wave. Freezing water dashed against my hands, which were clenched hard on the rail.

The ship flew upwards again, and I held on, eyes wide, as we rode the crest.

Anne and her ladies, many of them already ill, had gone to

her cabins. I had come out because the closeness and the odor threatened to sicken me as well. On deck, I could breathe.

The sky was blue, with only a few clouds racing before us. The wind filled the square sail, snapping it taut. Brown sailors climbed over the rigging, a contrast to the white sail, and the sun shone with all its might.

"You should not be up here."

He shouted over the boom of the waves, and came to rest on my right at the rail. The wind blew his dark brown curls every which way; no hat could stay upon a head in this weather. I'd tied my own unruly hair into a tail, but my hood I'd left below. As usual, Jack Carlisle wore a disapproving frown.

"Master Carlisle," I said. I never called him "Sir John" because I liked to annoy him. "I am out of the way. I asked the captain where I might stand, and he said here."

"You should be below with your lady," was his answer.

"I could not bear it, below. I will be sick if I do not stand in the wind."

His frown deepened, but he left the argument there.

He held onto the rail, his hand next to mine. His leather gloves, dark with water, stretched over his fingers and ended in wide cuffs that covered his sleeves. In spite of the ship tossing every which way, he managed to look immaculately washed and brushed, his beard neatly trimmed against his chin.

He was a study in contrasts to Henry. Where Henry was golden fair, Jack was dark; where Henry was muscular bulk, Jack was tall and tightly lean; where Henry laughed loudly or shouted in rage, Jack remained quiet and controlled. I'd never seen the man laugh, although he smiled at his king's quips as required.

"You do not know my mother, do you?" I asked him.

He looked slightly perplexed. "No."

"Because she, too, enjoys telling me what to do at every turn. I thought perhaps you were in league with her to plague me."

He did not look amused. "I do not know your mother, or

your father. That is what I came to discuss with you. Who are you? Do you belong to a family of great ambition, like the Boleyns?"

"Or the Howards?" I countered.

"The Howards have ambition, but you are not in their league. Who is your father? A baronet, I gather."

"If you already know, why ask me?"

"That is all I know," he scowled. "Tell me of him."

"He is a good man," I flashed. He always put my back up, and I did not know why. Other gentlemen teased me, and I simply shrugged them away. Jack's barbs seemed to dig under my skin and stay there. "He is a farmer. He loves the earth."

Jack's brows rose. "A farmer? That is all?"

"He inherited the baronetcy from his father, who received it from old king Henry for valor against the Yorkists. His estate is near Hunsdon."

"Hunsdon," he said thoughtfully. "So that is the connection."

"What connection?"

"Do you not find it odd that Lady Anne plucked you from nowhere and now has you carry her jewels? A duchess or an earl's wife should do that. Why you?"

Of course I had marveled at my good fortune. But my aunt had had my horoscope cast earlier that summer, and it had said that in this year, great things would be bestowed upon me. I accepted this because it was in the stars, and the stars do not lie. Unscrupulous astrologers do, I grant, but I'd met this particular astrologer. He wore a high hat and a robe embroidered with stars and moons. He had great affinity with the four elements, and I trusted him.

"I serve my lady," I said.

"Yes." He looked out to sea, where, when we crested the top of a wave, we could clearly see the low-lying shore of France. The wind teemed with salt and water and a freshness I'd never smelled before.

He turned back to me with another rapid question. "What think you of the queen?"

"Catherine of Spain, you mean?"

"Catherine of Spain. Who is still queen, by the way."

"Why do you ask what I think of her?"

He leaned down to me, blocking my view of the sailors behind him. He spoke in a low voice, his lips quite close to my ear so I could hear him.

"There are many near the king who think one thing and say the other. A great change is coming upon the kingdom, Mistress Pierce. Who you favor will determine your place and possibly even whether you live or die. Now, what think you of the queen?"

"Live or die?" I echoed. I thought of Cardinal Wolsey, disgraced and displaced, of Thomas More, the king's great friend and advisor, resigning his chancelorship, to the king's fury. Even poor Bishop Gardiner, forced to beg forgiveness for his outspokenness. All of these men had been quite close to the king, dearest friends, in fact. And now they were disgraced or dead or scrambling to regain favor.

"This must be difficult for the queen," I said, choosing my words. "But she must know that the king needs an heir. If he died, God keep him, without one, we could go back to war, could we not? Henry must have an heir."

He was watching me, an odd look on his face. "You think well, Frances. Hold fast to that opinion."

"Why?"

"Because these days, it is the right one."

"It is what I believe. I do not understand you."

"You do not need to. When there is another subject upon which you need to form an opinion, seek me out and discuss it with me."

I gave him a haughty look. "You presume much."

"It is important. Are your mother and father for queen Catherine?"

I sighed. "My mother is, God help me. She very much loves and admires the queen. My father . . ." I hesitated. "He has expressed no opinion on the matter."

"Is he a reformist?"

I laughed. "Dear heavens, no." I recalled one day at home when I'd expressed impatience with priests and their archaic Latin and asked my father why we could not read the Bible ourselves in decent English.

Both my mother and father had gaped in horror. They'd remonstrated with me and told me that on no account was I to *ever* voice such a radical idea in public. "My father is afraid of the Lutherans, I believe."

"Anne is a reformist, and so is Thomas Cromwell. Anne is guiding Henry to reformed religion."

"Are you saying I should be a reformist as well?" I asked, truly curious.

"I am saying that you ought to support your lady Anne, but look to the king for which way he leans. He is not entirely comfortable with reform, and while he admires the German princes for their stand against Rome, he does not want Lutheranism to take root here."

I lifted my chin. "You wish me to change my opinion to meet the whim of the king, and to consult you to discover what that whim is?"

He nodded. "For your protection. You are nobody. You have no friends."

"I have Anne."

"Who has only the king as her friend. For now."

I gave him an indignant look. "Her uncle is the Duke of Norfolk, a very powerful man."

"A man ruled by ambition. When Anne's sister fell from the king's affections, and her husband died, Norfolk did nothing to help her. Mary had no money, no husband, nothing. She was reduced to begging her own family to take her back. If Anne should fall from favor before she is queen— there could be nothing for you. That is why you should look to the king's whims."

"My family would take me back," I said stoutly. Inwardly, my heart gave an uncertain beat. My mother had been quite angry that I'd serve Anne rather than Catherine, and had only let me go because of the possibility that I'd get a husband. But so far, none of the gentlemen had shown any interest in aligning themselves with a baronet's daughter from Hert-fordshire. If Anne were to lose, what would happen to me?

He eyed me narrowly. "Are you this argumentative at home?"

"I am afraid so. Not for lack of my mother trying to bring me up well. I have trouble with obedience, you see. I believe it is a flaw in my character. Or perhaps an imbal-ance of humors."

One brow twitched upward. "You do not seem unduly troubled by this flaw."

"If I was as obedient and quiet and good as my mother liked, I would not be here, sailing to France on this fine day." I smiled. "To think, I shall meet the king of France and his courtiers."

He watched me for a time, leaning one arm on the rail and wrapping his gloved fingers around a rope. "Ambition is a dangerous companion."

"I have no ambition. I simply go where my lady bids. So far, where I have gone has been quite splendid. I bless my luck."

"You wish to be a poet," he reminded me.

My face heated. "That is different."

"Writing verses for your friends is one thing. Seeking more, that is dangerous."

I scoffed. "What is dangerous about wishing my poetry read? And if you came here to laugh at my verses again, I shall—I shall walk away from you."

He opened his mouth to say more, but suddenly he closed it. "I will not laugh at you today, Frances."

That is all he would say. He turned his attention again to the waves, a little frown on his face.

We landed in Calais later that morning. The autumn day was crisp and clear, but to me, we could have had the most dismal weather in the world, and I would not notice.

I was abroad. I, who thought she'd never see much be-yond Hertfordshire with the occasional lucky journey to London, had crossed the Channel. I know that Calais was English in truth, taken more than a century ago and still fortified against France and Burgundy, but to me, it was foreign and faraway.

The town was small, and we landed on a muddy wharf that ended in more mud. In all this mud were litters intended to bear us to our lodgings, and even the litters looked damp and small.

But the sun caught on the stone and whitewashed buildings and on the clothing of the townspeople. The women wore red scarves that shone like fireflies above their drab black and brown shawls and gowns.

Other than that, the women were a bit somber, watching us with dark eyes. They reminded me very much of Mistress Longacre and her crows, showing me that nosy women who could not mind their own business were common across the world.

The children, on the other hand, were more frank in their interest. They swarmed around us crying, *"Le roi! Le roi!"* although in truth, Henry had disembarked first and was already on his way with Anne, her sister, her cousin, and his own immediate attendants. I was left with the rest of the ladies and the baggage.

I talked with the children in French. They laughed at me and called me a pretty demoiselle, and I ended up scattering coins to them, which, I believe, was their intention in the first place.

Men loaded the baggage into waiting carts that had come. It did not all fit, so they unloaded the carts again, and then everyone stood about and scratched their heads, and fell into talking about everything but loading the baggage.

At last, Jack Carlisle, who I was sorry to see hadn't gone immediately with the king, entered the fray and directed the loading. Nothing went exactly right, of course. A horse slipped and the cart fell, scattering boxes and trunks through the mud. Jack was frustrated and red-faced, which pleased me.

Second, there were not enough litters for the ladies. The gentlemen were riding or walking, but there were only two small litters and five ladies. One younger lady started to cry, fearing she'd have to ride, and she would never last all the way to the castle, she declared.

I immediately said I'd ride because I was a country girl and used to rough ways. This did not elevate my standing with the ladies, but the other four did scramble eagerly for the litters, leaving me behind.

I bade one of the grooms bring me a horse and help me into the saddle. My dress was wrong for riding, but it was not my best, because of course I could not have worn costly velvets on the wet boat. The groom assisted me into a saddle, and I hooked my skirts around my legs the best I could. I dropped the little whip he handed me at once, and the horse shied and turned in a circle several times while I struggled to settle myself. The groom moved off and left me quite alone, and did not answer my cries for help.

A hand caught the bridle and the horse quieted. I looked round, expecting the interfering Jack, but I found myself staring into a pair of dancing black eyes as glowing and sparkling as my lady's. A smile like Anne's, but handsome and masculine, beamed up at me.

My entire world stopped. The horse ceased to matter. The lovely waves against the sky, the mud, the wind, the bags tumbling about, the children and the curious crows, all faded to nothing. This man, with his square face and brown hair and laughing eyes became the only thing I could see.

He settled my foot in the stirrup and gave it a pat. "There, my lady. All ready?" He picked up the whip and handed it to me.

Simple words, simple gestures, but they touched me deeply. I think I said, "Yes, thank you," but I could never be certain.

I knew who he was. He was George Boleyn, Viscount Rochford, and he was Anne's brother. He had not ridden in my ship, but already waited in Calais to meet us. While I had heard much about him that summer, I had not yet seen him. The king sent him as envoy to France often, and George had done much to organize this Calais meeting.

The ladies spoke of him with smiles and sly glances.

Even Mistress Lombard approved of him, because he had
as much reforming zeal as his sister. Anne spoke of him often, referring to him as "sweetest George," or "my dearest
brother."

The way he looked at me now, the words he spoke to
me, were in no wise improper. But, as I had when I'd first
met Anne, I stared like a simpleton.

"The litters have gone," he pointed out. "You cannot
ride to the castle alone. Come, you will ride with me."

A dry little voice deep inside me told me that he was
only being polite, watchful over a young lady of whom his
sister was fond. But my heart zoomed to my throat, and I
gave him an idiotic smile.

He laughed with Anne's dark laugh, one that said he
saw much but would never tell.

He shouted to a groom to bring his horse, and then he
mounted. I watched him, tall and lean and young and well-
formed. In that moment, on that muddy beach in Calais, I
lost my heart, and I lost my reason.

George did not ride next to me; he bade his groom stay
near me while he rode with the other courtiers. As I left the
wharves for the lane, it never occurred to me to look back
and see what Jack Carlisle thought of me riding away with
Viscount Rochford. I had forgotten all about Jack Carlisle
and his handsome face and cryptic warnings as easily as
one forgets a dream in the morning light.

WE reached the castle all too soon. George bowed to me
as the groom helped me from my mount. With a smile and
a careless wave of his hand, he went off after the other gentlemen, and I watched him go, dazed.

A servant kindly took me into the castle proper and directed me to the queen's rooms. I found the other ladies
there before me. None had missed me, but I no longer
cared. I'd ridden from the wharves with George, watching
his legs and back sway as his horse moved. What was the

snubbing of a few ladies compared to that? I smiled to myself and let the ladies wonder at my spirits.

We settled ourselves and Anne, putting away her tumble of gowns and gloves and shoes and cloaks and linens.

Later that evening, Anne received bad news. A gentleman brought a message for her to read. We paid no attention, because such a thing happened all the time, but suddenly, she startled us with a cry of rage.

"He promised," she said. "Oh, he promised."

She stood in the middle of the room, fury on her face, the paper crumpled in her hands. We ladies exchanged looks, but none ventured to ask what was wrong.

Anne glared at us. "We will not be journeying to Boulogne," she snapped. "We will not be going to the French court, despite all assurances to the contrary."

I remembered the supper at Hanworth, when the ambassador had brought King Francis' invitation for Anne and Henry. I wondered, with sinking heart, whether Francis had changed his mind and would snub Anne altogether.

Only Anne's sister, Mary Carey, dared ask the question. "Why not?"

"Because the queen of Navarre will not accompany the French king," Anne said in clipped tones. "She is ill, it seems. And so we must stay here and let Henry and the gentleman go without me. Hell's teeth."

"Oh," I said, acutely disappointed. I was in Calais, but not properly in France, and I wanted very much to see the French court. I had heard that it was much more sophisticated than the English court, and I wanted to learn what sophistication meant.

Anne continued to glare. I waited for her to express concern that dear Marguerite was ill, but she did not. Perhaps she worried that dear Marguerite was feigning her illness in order to prevent a meeting.

We waited in silence until Anne tore up the paper and flung the pieces into the fire. She sat down, staring moodily about, as though daring one of us to say a word.

* * *

HAPPILY for me, Jack Carlisle accompanied the king, along with most of his men, when Henry went to Boulogne. Unhappily, so did George Boleyn.

I, at seventeen years of age, had never before fallen in love. It changed me. My entire body felt different. I could not keep my mind on any task given me. I would think upon George Boleyn's smile, and laugh out loud. My limbs tingled. Warmth coursed through me whenever I imagined him touching my face, or pressing a kiss to my lips, or simply smiling at me.

I was giddy with it. I'd lie awake in the chill Calais castle next to Mary Howard and think through ridiculous girlish fantasies of George Boleyn. He had certainly charmed his way into my heart in a few short moments.

I knew he was married. He had married Jane Parker as directed by his uncle Norfolk, for her money and connections. I knew, from gossip that never ceased, that he disliked his wife, and she, him. Even Anne made no bones about discussing her brother's marriage "to plain, dull Jane."

At court, I'd learned, one's relations with one's wife or husband did not seem to matter. One married for the good of one's career and family and enjoyed love and merrymaking with a mistress or a lover. My mother would be shocked, and frankly I had been, too, but after meeting George on the cold wharf, I had decided this arrangement made some sense.

I did not quite understand intrigue and the dangers of it, but at the moment, wildly in love, I did not care.

I encouraged Anne to talk about her brother. The other ladies were as anxious to hear of him as I, and Anne was all too willing to speak of him. So while the October winds moaned in the castle eaves, Anne told us about George, and what a dear brother he'd always been to her.

Anne also liked to reminisce about her girlhood in France and the Netherlands. While we passed the time sewing and embroidering or weaving, we listened to her speak of days gone by.

"I went first to attend Margaret of Austria, who ruled as regent in the Netherlands when I was just a girl. I must have seemed very rustic to her, never having traveled far from Kent. She seemed the greatest lady I had ever known. But she taught me to write well and to speak well and how to carry myself. I owe much to her."

From there, Anne had moved to the French court. She had been summoned there when Mary, Henry's sister, had traveled to France to marry Louis XII in 1514.

"He was an old man, and ugly, and he smelled," Anne said, dismissing the king of a powerful nation with a shrug. "The princess Mary cried very much. But she was lucky; old Louis died within a few months of the wedding. I believe God felt sorry for her. And then she married Charles Brandon."

Anne dismissed him with a shrug as well. I had seen Brandon, now the Duke of Suffolk, at Anne's elevation: a square, hearty man with a red face. He was not handsome but had a vibrancy about him that was attractive.

I had already learned the story. After Louis had died and Francis had assumed the throne, Mary was kept in France. Charles Brandon traveled to Paris to negotiate with Francis to bring her home. There Francis helped Mary snare Brandon, who was already in love with her, into a secret marriage, before they journeyed back to England.

Henry did not forgive them for years, and I was not certain he had done so, even now. Henry had promised Mary that after Louis of France died, she could marry whomever she wished, and Mary had been determined to hold him to that promise. Henry seemed to have swallowed his promise with poor grace.

But Mary was disgraced all the same for marrying beneath her. That is the trouble with being a royal princess. One can marry only royalty, and there are only so many royal princes lying about.

Henry was flagrantly flaunting that convention with Anne, but I suppose it is different for men.

As for Francis, he'd married Queen Claude and had

plenty of children by her, including robust sons. She'd died still young, and he'd married Eleanor, a Spanish lady whom he did not like.

"I told the ambassador," Anne said, her eyes dancing, "that the French ladies of court should not wear Spanish dress, because Henry looked at Spanish dress and saw the devil in them."

We all collapsed into laughter, including myself. How awful, I thought, to be old and Spanish and ridiculed. How fine to be young and English and happy.

As a girl, Anne had stayed in France and attended Queen Claude while they were both quite young. Anne had liked the queen and had learned much from her and the other French ladies.

"We had a lightness in dress and conversation that is now much admired. Wit was prized, not ponderous piety, although do not think that we were not pious. But it is one thing to obey God and to pray and to follow the teachings of Christ, and quite another to cling to a rosary and mutter constantly like a madwoman. Love of God is in your heart and in your faith, not in reciting the incantations of priests."

I was a bit shocked by her blatant ideas, but pleased by them, too. Why should we listen to priests who were old and stuffy and never followed the piety and clean living that they taught? Plenty of monks and priests owned vast estates, possessed decadent fortunes, and had plenty of lovers, of both sexes, I had heard. Cardinal Wolsey himself had had several sons, and he'd certainly amassed a fortune.

Anne's ideas that priests should live simply and that we should read scripture and strive to be good ourselves seemed refreshingly simple, and I eagerly embraced them. Better to follow the teachings of the beautiful Anne, I thought, than listen to foul old cardinals. I decided then, in the living quarters in Calais, that I was a reformist.

I would keep this to myself and not write my father of it. I could imagine my mother falling into a swoon and staying in such a state for days. Worse, they might find some way to snatch me home, and I'd never see Anne again.

Anne continued with her tales. She had stayed in France until after the Field of Cloth of Gold, that glittering pageant in which Henry had made negotiations of peace with France.

The spectacle had been magnificent, with tents of cloth of gold glittering in the sunlight on the plain east of Calais. There had been a grand jousting in which Henry and Francis had much enjoyed themselves. They, being kings, had won most of the matches.

But the peace had not lasted, and the English had quickly become bitter enemies of the French. When you are a king, you see, it is all very well to become great friends with another king, but when it comes down to it, you have to do what will hurt your country least. Francis was always courting the Holy Roman Empire because they were stronger, and both France and the Empire went back and forth in their allegiances with England.

After the Field of Cloth of Gold, Anne had been called home to become a lady to Queen Catherine.

"I had so learned the manners of the French court that those who did not know me assumed me French." She smiled, her dark eyes lighting with amusement. "And then one day, we had an entertainment. We ladies took on the guises as womanly vices, haughtiness and disdain and so forth, and hid in a fortress built in the great hall at York Place, to entertain the ambassadors. The king and his gentlemen set siege to us."

She winked at her sister, who pretended not to notice. "And the king danced with me," she finished.

"He danced with me first," Mary said, her eyes on her sewing.

"But he danced with me last," Anne said, smug.

"He is still dancing," Mary returned.

Anne's eyes filled with anger, but only briefly. "Soon the dance will end, and we will be seated," Anne said. "Side by side. As man and wife."

Mary said nothing. She knew the truth of it, as we all did.

That night, Mary bade me brush out her hair. "You seem surprised, Frances," she said, "that I do not hate my sister."

"Yes." I pulled the brush through her hair, admiring the way the gold danced through the bristles.

"I loved the king," she said. She held my gaze in the mirror. "Once. But no longer."

"You should not say you do not love the king," I said hastily. "The wrong ears might hear."

She smiled at my fear. She was a very beautiful woman, with her blonde hair and dark blue eyes. She was more beautiful than Anne, but she did not have the presence that Anne had.

"I no longer love him as a man," she said. "Nor as a lover. We had what we had, and then, we were finished."

"He dismissed you."

"He did." She bowed her head, and I stilled the brush. "He ruined me. My sister believes herself clever, but she is a fool. I saw." Now, true venom entered her voice, but I was not certain at whom she directed it. "My husband had no use for me. Now I have no husband, no friends, and I never see my children."

"I am sorry," I whispered.

She looked up again, the fleeting anger vanishing. "It no longer matters. Anne looks after me. She has no need to, but she looks after me and looks after my son. She can give my son what I cannot." She turned in the chair and put her hand on my arm. "When you find someone who cherishes you and takes care of you, do not discard that. Hang on to that person, and cherish him in return."

I nodded, not entirely certain what she meant. She smiled, knowing she confused me, and patted my hand. "I will cease. Brush my hair a little longer, it feels fine."

IN spite of Anne's irritation at being left behind, she was not forgotten. The king of France sent Anne a huge diamond, which we all pored over with wide eyes, then pretended that we were used to such things. Then Henry returned, to our cheers from the battlements of Calais's walls, and after that, Francis himself came.

Five

❖

A STORM AND A PROPOSAL OF MARRIAGE

ANNE prepared a lavish entertainment for the king of France. At least, it was as lavish as we could prepare in the rather cramped quarters in Calais. Anne was set on a masking, with us ladies dressed in white and gold with masks to hide our faces.

I dressed with shaking fingers, trembling with excitement and delight. I could barely contain myself as I fastened the queen's jewels about Anne's neck, but she supposed I was simply thrilled to meet the king of France and his courtiers.

I did not tell her, because I did not want to embarrass myself, that my secret delight was to see her brother. George had ridden in with Francis, conversing with him in French as fluent as his sister's. Anne had greeted George with a fond embrace, then their lips had met in a brief kiss. She had taken George's arm and walked away with him. He scarcely noticed me, but I did not mind. Simply to gaze upon him enraptured me.

Tonight he would be there with the courtiers, and he would dance. I was humble enough not to believe he'd dance with me, as I'd not perfected my dancing yet, and besides, I was a nobody. But at this point in my infatuation, simply to look upon him filled me with joy.

Anne and Henry dined with Francis. I did not join that ceremony, not being highborn enough, but I saw Francis walk to the dining hall. We ladies who would not attend had gathered in the gallery to watch the French gentlemen pass. It does not take much to induce young ladies to spy upon gentlemen.

Francis looked as rakish and handsome as his portraits. He had rather a long face, but his eyes sparkled with wit and mischief, and his lips were turned up in a smile. One of his courtiers spotted us. He pointed upward.

Francis doffed his feathered hat and bowed to us. We giggled. Mistress Lombard would have sentenced all of us to winding wool for days, but Mistress Lombard was not there. We were young, and pretty, and away from home, and handsome gentlemen waited below.

Francis bent to speak to his courtier, and they both laughed. They waved hats to us and continued the procession for their dinner with Henry and Anne.

What I did not know until later was that King Francis had the courtier he whispered to choose one of our ladies to stay with him that night. The courtier had chosen me. However, a certain gentleman of the English court had explained that I was still a maiden, so another girl was selected.

That certain gentleman was the interfering Jack Carlisle, as you may have guessed. But when I heard, I was quite grateful to him for interfering in this case.

Oblivious now, I hurried back to our quarters to dress in costume with the other ladies, and processed down to the hall for the masking.

I had not yet been to any ceremony besides that of Anne's elevation, and that had been solemn and filled with priests and lords and Latin phrases. Here was dancing and joy and splendor. We spoke English and French and flirted, even me.

Anne was beautiful. She was dressed and masked like the rest of us, but who could not distinguish her graceful form and vibrant wit?

The king of France certainly knew who she was. He led her out to a dance, and Henry watched, smiling indulgently. They chatted, Francis and Anne, while they went through the steps.

"Will you dance, my lady?"

I turned at the sound of the male voice, then my spirits plummeted. It was Jack standing by me, not George Boleyn.

"I do not dance well," I said, turning away.

"His Grace wishes all the English ladies to dance. He sent me to you."

"You are very flattering, Master Carlisle."

"Do not be haughty. It ill becomes you."

He took my elbow and steered me to join the circle.

The tune was stately but quick. Jack held my hand high while I tried to remember the steps. Right foot, left foot, hop back to right, turn left—no, right. No. Jack was pulling me back into line before I could tread on the skirts of the lady in front of me.

I was mortified, but his expression remained neutral. So skilled was he in dancing and pulling me this way and that, that none of the others noticed.

I wondered what had become of George Boleyn, but I did not see him in the hall. Indeed, I looked quite hard for him. He was not among Henry's courtiers, nor among the gentlemen who'd come with Francis. I craned my head to see if he stood in the shadows near the doors.

"Do not twitch about so," Jack said as he passed me before him.

I reddened. "I am agog at the festivities."

"The king is pleased," he said in a low voice. "The signing of this treaty means a stand against the Empire."

I looked to where Henry danced with one of the masked ladies. "Does it?"

"He hopes this alliance with France will be a deterrent to those who oppose the divorce."

Henry was wise, I thought, to turn Europe to his side in the Great Matter. A few years ago, my father had told me, the question of a ruler's supremacy over the Church in his own country was posed to the universities of France and England. They had ruled, my father said, in favor of the king having supreme authority in his own country. The pope could still give his clerics and cardinals orders, but if the ruler overrode them, then they should bow to the authority of the king. Henry took these words to heart, and this is why Bishop Gardiner fell from grace and Thomas More resigned.

"He believes the way is clear then?" I said.

"He does."

"I am glad."

He tugged my hand, pulling me back into the proper steps of the dance. "Are you?"

"Of course." I'd tied myself to Anne, and her rise was mine.

"The king's actions are not popular." He lowered his voice and leaned to me. "But it is not wise to say so."

I nodded. I was learning that in Henry's court, one watched one's tongue.

"Why do you constantly give me warnings?" I asked, somewhat crossly. "Do you think me a fool?"

"You do not belong here," he answered. "You belong in a provincial town marrying a provincial gentleman and raising a provincial family. The last place you should be is in a court of slippery intrigue. You were not raised to play the game."

The trouble with Jack's insults is that most of them bordered on truth. I had not been raised to this life, but his intimation that I was not sophisticated enough to learn was infuriating.

"I would walk away from you," I said. "But that would not be the thing. I will smile and finish the dance so that the French king will know English ladies have manners."

He gave me an unreadable look, but at least he ceased talking. I tried to concentrate on the dance, but I continually got the steps wrong. Jack pushed and pulled me surreptitiously, and at least I ended in the right place. The courtiers applauded.

In the middle of the floor, Anne curtsied to the king of France, and he bowed to her. They walked from the floor, her hand resting on his arm, all smiles.

Francis complimented Henry on Anne, on his courtiers and ladies, accompanying his flattery with a humorous glint in his eye.

Henry sat back, satisfied. His mission to France, in his opinion, was a success.

AFTER the French king departed, a deluge of rain swept the coast of France.

The foul weather kept us penned in Calais for a good long time. The sailors said that the Channel was too dangerous to cross in heavy rain this late in the year. I observed the driving wind and white, tossing waves and decided they were wise.

I, who had been so eager to come abroad, now chafed at the delay. Calais was a garrison town, which meant soldiers and towers and not much else. I had not been able to go to France proper, which disappointed me greatly. I wanted to see Boulogne, and perhaps Paris, but I was not destined to this time. Now, I longed to return to the comforts of Greenwich palace or Anne's house at Hanworth. Besides, George Boleyn had left with Francis and his entourage, and did not return.

Anne kept us ladies busy weaving tapestry or sewing or reading to her—and me making verses about the king of France and the masking ball, the ocean and Calais. But my fingers ached from tying knots in wool and became too cold to hold the quill.

Occasionally, I escaped to ride through the rain down the beaches of Calais. Gray, chalky cliffs rose beside me, mirrors of the white cliffs of Dover, where I longed to be.

I, Frances, world traveler, was terribly homesick for the green fields of England.

Jack sometimes rode out with me, saying it was not safe for me to ride alone. I let him—because he was right; there were too many soldiers and sailors roaming about for my comfort—but I rode fast and hard so we had no opportunity to speak.

I thought of George Boleyn often, reliving the way he'd spoken to me on the wharf, every look, every word. My fixation on George was silly, I knew that deep inside, but I was in love with being in love. Love made me happy and impatient, restless and at peace. My humors went one way and then the other, and if any asked me what ailed me, I flushed and stammered.

One of the ladies at last said, "Frances is in love."

I panicked and told her to keep quiet. I feared that Anne would think me horribly presumptuous to fall in love with her brother, and she might banish me from her side. The only thing worse than being stuck in muddy Calais was being sent home and never seeing Anne—or George—again.

Two people were quite happy with the situation: Anne and Henry. Henry met with his gentlemen every day to write letters or documents or whatever kings and their gentlemen found cause to write down. Then Anne and Henry would dine together and be entertained by their ladies and gentlemen. This entertainment included reading poetry or improving books, me making verses and reading them aloud, a few of the ladies playing the virginal, and gentlemen or ladies singing.

It was a court in miniature, with the benevolent king and his lady watching us in pleasure. They were relaxed and happy, stealing glances like young lovers.

I found that I could make the ladies laugh with my verses, and became quite the jester, creating funny rhymes that bordered on the bawdy, and daring to poke fun at others. I was careful not to direct my barbs at anyone Anne or Henry loved or respected. I confined myself to, God help me, Queen Catherine and her supporters, namely the Holy Roman Emperor's ambassador, a stuffy gentleman called

Chapuys. The king and Anne laughed uproariously and pronounced me quite a wit.

The only person who did not laugh was Jack, as one might have guessed. He shot me looks of disapproval and once told me that I had become quite the performing dog. I was tired of him comparing me to a dog, and so we quarreled, and did not speak for a week.

My resolution to have nothing to do with Jack Carlisle came to an end on a particularly vicious night. Rain beat against the walls with unceasing monotony. Inside, we had braziers and roaring fires, but all the firelight could not banish the numbing cold that crept under my skirts and stiffened my fingers.

The hour was late. I sat with Anne in a tower room, smaller and squarer than the hall below, which, thankfully, meant easier to heat. Almost everyone had gone to bed, except Henry himself, who paced the floor like an expectant father. He'd dismissed his gentlemen, and I suppose he'd expected Anne to do likewise with her ladies.

But while her sister and cousin and other ladies had gone away to bed, Anne had bidden me to remain.

"Foolishness," Henry snapped. His good-natured calm had vanished, to be replaced by red-faced impatience.

Anne continued to sew. "My reputation, Your Grace. I am a virtuous woman."

He growled. "We are practically married, Nan. We have waited six years. Why will you not yield, blast you? I am your king."

"But we are *not* married," Anne pointed out. A smile hovered about her mouth, but she kept her head bent so Henry would not see. I, sitting at her feet, saw her expression clearly. She was pleased.

"Bloody women," Henry said under his breath. He stopped his pacing abruptly and fixed a chill glare on me. "Frances, go to bed."

My limbs immediately moved to obey, but Anne pressed me back down. "Frances, stay."

Henry reddened. "Frances, go."

I looked up at Anne, miserable. She laughed. "Do not tease her, poor thing. Sit still, Frances."

Henry made a rumbling noise in his throat, like a bull ready to charge. The sound terrified me, but Anne remained serenely sewing.

Silence fell while Henry looked at her. I watched him out of the corners of my eyes. Here was a powerful monarch, one of the most powerful in Europe, made silent by my lady Anne. He had faced down his parliament and the entire clergy of England, he was defying the pope and popular convention, and he vied with France and the Holy Roman Empire to have the most lavish court in the world.

Here he stood in a small room in rainy Calais, a medium-height, muscular man just beginning to fatten, his red hair glinting in the firelight, silently observing the woman for whom he was changing the world.

His breathing was noisy, hoarse and raw. Anne kept her head bent.

Along with Henry, I studied the strands of dark hair that fell to her lap, the sleek sweep of her veil, the demure curve of her hair against her forehead. Her hands had long, tapered fingers, crooked gracefully around the needle. Her movements as she pushed the needle through the fabric and drew the sinuous thread through, were elegant yet understated. She did not draw attention to herself. Attention naturally drew to her.

Her skirts hung over long legs, and the linen shirt that was draped over her lap only emphasized the curve of her limbs. Even performing the mundane task of sewing, she was all that was grace and womanliness.

Henry's thick-fingered hands curled into fists. I saw the impatience in his eyes change to desire. But the desire was edged with tenderness. Here was a man not simply looking upon a fair morsel, but a man looking at a woman he cherished.

"Nan," he said.

She glanced up. Her dark eyes were subdued, but I saw a spark buried deep inside them. "Your Grace."

"I crave you."

Her cheeks pinkened modestly. "It will not be long. All the pieces are in place. You have made yourself supreme authority. You have befriended France. Your new ministers are loyal to you. When Canterbury has Cranmer for archbishop, then it will be finished."

"It is too long to wait." He moved closer to her, forgetting all about me perched on a stool at her feet.

I bowed my head but could see his strong thighs in trunk hose, smell damp wool and sweat and masculinity.

"Not long," Anne said softly. "Not long, my heart, I promise."

I saw the moment when Henry's patience, stretched for six years, thwarted by first one hurdle, then another, snapped. Queen Catherine, the papal legate, Henry's own cardinals, his friends, public opinion, and shifting alliances in Europe had all swarmed to keep him from his desire.

By stubborn perseverance, he'd swept all those obstacles away. He could now see a clear path, and he wanted to charge down it.

I saw the moment. His muscles tightened, his hand, inches from my face, curled into a fist. Gold and ruby rings sank into his flesh. He drew a long breath, and turned the game to his advantage.

I think it was that moment, more than any other, that marked the turning point. In that room, Henry moved from devoted and desperate lover to commanding king, all in the space of one breath.

"We will fetch a priest. If you will not comply as mistress, you will comply as wife."

Anne started. I peeked through my lashes at her. She looked surprised and then hopeful. "Is a priest to be had? One that can keep silent?"

"He will be silent."

"It must be witnessed," she argued. "Else it will not be valid."

"It will be witnessed." I felt the weight of Henry's stare. "Frances."

I raised my head. "Your Grace?"

"Fetch—damnation, who do I want?"

"Master Norris is loyal," Anne said.

"Master Norris is too frivolous."

"Master Weston, then. He might strum a tune as well."

Henry's brows furrowed. "No, I need someone who will not be tempted to tell a soul, not until Cranmer is in place. I have it. Sir John Carlisle."

Anne wore a small smile of satisfaction. I understood then that she'd deliberately put forth unsuitable candidates until Henry came around to who she'd wanted all along, the gossip-hating Jack Carlisle.

"Fetch him, Frances," Henry said to me.

I looked to Anne. She gave me an almost imperceptible nod. I gathered my skirts and rose to my feet, my heart beating swiftly.

Henry's hand clamped on my shoulder. I looked up into small eyes that pinned me with the weight of power. "Have him bring a priest," he said. "And tell not a soul."

"Yes, Your Grace," I said, voice shaking.

"Frances is a good girl," Anne said. "She understands."

I did not think I did, but her faith buoyed me. I managed a scrambled curtsy, then ducked out of the room.

I now blessed the rain that had confined us here, because I'd used the time to learn the ways of the castle. I gathered my skirts in both hands and sped down the stairs and through the maze of little corridors on the upper level until I came to the quarters the gentlemen used.

A servant lay asleep on a pallet outside a great door. Behind it, I knew, the gentlemen slept. I hurried to the lad and nudged him with my toe. He barely moved. I nudged harder.

He moaned. I resisted the temptation to kick him in the ribs and continued nudging, rolling my leather-shod foot across his back.

He came awake with a snort, blinking sleep out of too-young eyes. "My lady?" he mumbled.

"I need Jack Carlisle. At once."

The youth took his time getting to his feet. "Ladies not allowed. Her ladyship ordered it."

"Then go in and fetch him out. Hurry!"

"*Sir John* is asleep."

"Then wake him. Oh, you stupid boy. Go in and fetch him, or I will myself."

The lad looked me up and down. He was strong-limbed, but about the same size as I was. I drew myself up, ready to shove him aside and charge into the gentlemen's quarters if he did not hurry.

He must have seen the desperation in my face, because he gulped, spun, and hurriedly tugged open the great door.

I paced in agony until I heard the servant coming back, murmuring answers to the deep tones of Jack Carlisle.

At last Jack appeared at the door. He wore only a shirt and trunk hose that he held together where they should be fastened. His black hair was a mess, and his close-trimmed beard was shadowed with new growth.

He stared down at me with astonishment that quickly turned to annoyance. "Frances? What do you here?"

Mindful of the listening boy, I grabbed a handful of Jack's hair and pulled his head down so that I could whisper into his ear.

What I told him amazed him. He stared at me, his eyes red with sleep, his dark eyelashes clumped. "If this is a trick, or a game . . ."

"It is not. Please, hurry."

He at last believed my agitation real. "Wait here," he said tersely and disappeared back into his quarters.

Again I paced, waiting in trepidation. I worried in case some wakeful lady or lord should spy me here and demand to know why I was wringing my hands outside the gentlemen's rooms. Their first guess would be that I had a tryst, and to protect Anne and the king, I would have to pretend that their guess was true. My mother would hear of it and either drag me home in disgrace or else send me long, heavily worded letters about honor and virtue. Either way, I'd be ruined.

Before I had to make any such sacrifice, the door opened again, and Jack, fully dressed this time in doublet, hose, shirt, and shoes, emerged. Without saying a word, he took my arm and propelled me into the dark bowels of the castle.

Six

I ATTEND TWO WEDDINGS

THE garrison priest spoke the service in the tower room with a tremor in his voice. The man had gone green with fear when Jack fetched him from his rooms and explained what he was to do. Anne promised that he'd be rewarded well for performing the ceremony and keeping quiet about it, but the old priest looked in fear of his life. I thought it well he did. If news of this secret ceremony leaked before Henry was ready, the priest might pay with his life. Or Jack might. Or me.

I stood beside Anne, and Jack stood beside Henry. Other than the priest's wavering voice, there was no other sound. Anne smiled, her breathing quick. One gold thread running through her veil held my eye. It glinted brightly at the crown of her head and trailed off into nothing.

Henry rocked back and forth in impatience. The priest noticed and stumbled over his words even more. Jack murmured something to the king. Henry shot him a baleful look but calmed a bit.

At last, the priest made his final sign of the cross and

breathed his final amen. Henry drew Anne into his arms and kissed her.

I'd seen him kiss her before, but this time it was different. His look was possessive, triumphant, and her returning look was no less so.

I had wondered how Henry imagined he'd take Anne to bed without all his attendants and servants knowing. He managed it by more or less dragging her to an unused bed-chamber just below the tower room. Jack and the priest and I followed.

The room was freezing. Jack carried a brazier from the room above and set about lighting a fire. I made the bed with linens I had brought at Anne's command. Jack heated a brick in the brazier, then wrapped it in a bed hanging, and I passed it through the sheets.

The priest stood over the bed, blessing it and possibly praying for his immortal soul at the same time.

Henry, who had been helping Jack at the fireplace, climbed to his feet. "Go, you miserable old man," he growled, but ended with a laugh. "You have done good work this evening."

He pulled coins from his pocket and pressed them into the man's hand. Anne walked him to the door. She gave him something surreptitiously—I thought I saw the glint of a ring—and breathed, "Thank you."

Henry would wait no longer. He would not even leave the room so that Anne could ready herself. She had to make do shielding herself behind the bed and its hangings while I undressed her. On the other side of the bed, Jack helped the king from his doublet. On mine, I loosened my lady's stomacher and pulled off her bodice.

Henry make ribald jokes to Jack, and Jack actually chuckled.

Anne winked at me. "They say cold weather does make a man's blood hot."

I swallowed. "It would need to, my lady. This room is sore cold."

Henry laughed, and Anne joined in, a sound like dark chimes.

Men are not so exacting in dress as ladies. I was still carefully folding Anne's satin skirts so they would not be ruined, when Henry, clad only in his shirt, bellowed. "Get out, the pair of you."

He started to remove his shirt, I averted my eyes, face burning, not wanting to see my monarch in his skin. Anne, in her shift, hugged me hard and kissed the top of my head. "Do not go far," she whispered.

She turned to the bed. She put her hand to her throat, as though to touch the necklace that I had removed, then she moved into the arms of her king.

Jack hauled me around by the shoulders and out of the door. He closed it on a peal of triumphant laughter, both Henry's and Anne's, then their voices drifted down into something more tender.

The stairwell was just as cold as the room had been. "She wants me to remain nearby," I said, my teeth chattering.

"Aye," he answered. "She wants witnesses that this marriage will be consummated and valid."

"But he is still married," I said in the barest whisper. "Is he not?"

"That is a matter for the priests and the lawyers, not you and me." Jack took my hand and led me up the stairs to the tower room, in which Anne and Henry had just been married. "We will stay here. It is warm, at least."

"You will stay with me?" I asked.

"I'll not leave you alone." He drew me to a bench before the fire, and we sat.

Side by side, we waited, while the fire consumed the logs on the hearth. Below the stones beneath our feet, Anne and Henry were at last satisfying their longing. Tonight, they were simply lovers who had waited a long time to be with one another. Tomorrow they would again be the king and a lady marquess.

I drooped with tiredness, and thought I'd fall, but Jack caught me with his strong arm and held me in place.

"Go to sleep if you wish."

"I am exhausted," I admitted. "All the same, I will never sleep."

He pulled me against him, my back to his chest, his arm still around me. I had to admit that he was a comfortable fellow, as irritating as he could be. "Lean against me," he said. "I will not let you fall."

My eyes ached, and I let them close. I knew that if anyone found us here, my reputation would be in shreds, but I did not care. And if anyone was mad enough to think that Jack and I . . .

I gave a tiny laugh. Jack leaned down. "What is it?"

"Nothing," I whispered, then I tumbled into sleep.

WHEN I woke again, the fire had burned down to the heart of the log. Jack was not asleep. He stared into the fire, the red glow making sharp shadows of his nose and cheekbones.

I stirred, and he switched his gaze to me. Very slowly, he drew his thumb under my chin, then he leaned down and kissed me.

It was a brief brush of lips, nothing intimate, little more than a kiss I would give my father or uncle. But Jack was not my father or uncle. He was a man, and as I lay in his arms and stared at him in stunned surprise, I realized that fact for the first time.

The feelings that moved through my body confused me. Hot and cold sensations chased one another, my heart pounded, and my fingers tingled.

The sensations were not unlike what I'd felt when George Boleyn had smiled at me, but at the same time, completely different.

I had no idea what to say or do. I could only stare at Jack, eyes fixed, while he watched me.

Then he laughed softly, a self-deprecating sound, and unwound his arms from my body.

He stood up. I must have looked like a fool staring at him, my eyes round and my lips parted.

"Stay here and keep warm," he said. "I will see if your lady needs you."

He departed while I still gazed at him, my mind spinning. I wondered what had just happened, and why I was not entirely displeased.

Jack returned in a few moments to say that Anne did need me, and gratefully I hurried down the stairs to the bedchamber.

Henry shot more ribald humor at Jack while he helped Henry dress and I laced Anne back into her clothes. Her skin was hot and flushed, her eyes heavy-lidded. I glanced at the folds of the sheets, but I saw no scarlet slash of blood staining them.

That worried me. Rumor had it that a long time ago Anne had been in love with a gentleman called Henry Percy, who was now Earl of Northumberland. They had promised themselves to each other in marriage, perhaps even been lovers. That would not bode well, even if it were far in the past. Henry Percy had been married off hastily once his master, Wolsey, had gotten wind of their love. Gossip hinted that Percy, up in his drafty house in Northumberland, still loved Anne.

"Did it hurt, my lady?" I whispered as we descended the stairs.

"A bit." Her voice sounded strained. "But not for long."

We proceded to the women's rooms. Inside her chamber, I undressed her for the second time and lifted the heavy covers so she could climb into her bed. Before she settled against the pillows, she clutched my hands.

"I did not mind the pain," she whispered. "Because it meant I am his. It meant I am *queen*."

Tears beaded in my eyes for no reason I understood. I leaned down and kissed her cheek. "God bless you."

She smiled with a glimmer of her usual humor. "Away with you, Frances."

I left her then. When I turned back at the door I saw that she was not asleep, but sitting against the pillows and staring straight ahead of her, smiling.

I made my slow way back to my own bed, my lips still feeling the soft imprint of Jack's kiss.

NOT many days later, the rains ceased. The clouds departed from the Channel, and blue sky reigned. We lost no time boarding the ships and making haste for England.

Henry and Anne never strayed far from one another the entire journey. They walked the deck of the ship together, and when we landed in Dover, Henry kept her by his side as he lingered to inspect fortifications.

The mood of the party was different from what it had been on the way to Calais. Then we had been wound tight with anticipation of the upcoming meeting with the French king. Now, we dawdled through Kent on the way to London, staying at country houses, lingering in the fine weather. We amused ourselves walking, riding, hunting, playing cards, playing music, and of course, gossiping like mad. Henry's favorite page, Francis Weston, gave us tunes and bawdy songs that made us laugh.

Jack and I became go-betweens for the newly married Henry and Anne. When she retired for the night Anne would dismiss all ladies but me. Then I'd finish undressing her and prepare her to receive the king. Jack, for his part, would clear the way for the king to creep through the passages in secret to Anne's chamber.

Not a few ladies expressed jealousy that I seemed to be quite close to Anne these days. In truth, the secrecy set my nerves on edge, and I would gladly have given the position to any of the others. Anne, however, wanted me.

Another thing that set my nerves on edge was Jack. After our kiss in the tower room, he refused to speak to me. Not about the kiss, not about Anne and Henry, not about anything at all. Whenever I stood in a chamber with him, he would pretend I was not there. If I happened to move toward him, he would turn and walk the other way. If it came about that he might have to partner me in a game or dance, he would deliberately cross a room to choose someone else. It was most vexing. He confused me greatly, and I wanted to speak to him about it.

No, in truth, I wanted to scold him and relieve my feelings. I was confused because my fiery infatuation for George Boleyn had not lessened. But George was a fantasy, an ephemeral dream. Jack had kissed me, and I did not understand why.

Try as I might, I could not make Jack stand still, and so I was left to stew. Men do it on purpose, I think, to madden women.

"Are gentlemen always such vexatious creatures?" I asked one night as I brushed out Anne's hair.

We looked into the mirror, our faces side by side, her glowing black eyes outshining my rather lackluster ones. "I am afraid so," she said. "But we do have a power over them, Frances. They cannot resist the mystery of us."

I slowed the brush. "Well, so far, they have resisted the mystery of me."

She gave a throaty laugh. "You poor dear. It will not last long. The wind will change for you, as it did for me."

I gazed at her in the mirror. She was so lovely, even more lovely in her chemise with her hair down. I could understand why Henry was so eager to tumble with her.

"Do you love him?" I asked suddenly.

She did not look startled, but then, nothing seemed to startle her. "Of course. He is our king."

"I mean do you love him entirely? With your whole body, so that when he comes near, you feel as though every limb is on fire?"

"That sounds quite fervent."

"Perhaps." The question welled inside me, for some reason so very important. "But do you love him?"

Anne turned in her chair. She tugged the brush from me,

laid it on the table, and took my hands in hers. "Frances," she said, her smiles gone. "Being courted by a king is the most heady thing in the world. Here is a man, one of the most powerful in Christendom, a man loved and feared by so many, and he bends his knee to *me*. He stops his country to give me what I want. Me, Thomas Boleyn's daughter. He is willing to make me his queen to have me." Her fingers dug into mine. "Aye, that sends a fire through me every time I see him. I am not a simpering miss to accept his gifts and prostrate myself at his feet. In return for what he has done for me, I will make his kingdom great. And you will be there with me."

My heart swelled. She might find it heady to be made love to by a king, but I found it heady to be singled out by her. She'd plucked me, quite literally, from the mud, and raised me up to be her handmaiden and her confidant.

I threw my arms about her neck and held her tightly. "I will try to be worthy of you," I cried.

Anne laughed and returned the hug. "Frances, you are too impetuous."

"I know." I sat back, wiping tears from my eyes. "I am quite useless, my mother says."

"Your mother is wrong. And we shall prove it."

She kissed me on the cheek and ordered me to return to brushing her hair.

After I had tucked her into bed, Henry arrived, Jack behind him. Jack barely had time to remove the man's dressing gown before he shoved both of us aside in his eagerness to be with his lady.

I found myself outside the door, alone in a cold chamber with Jack. I started to put my hand on his arm.

He looked right through me, turned around, and walked away through the next chamber, his footsteps loud in the silence. I ground my teeth in rage and marched off in the other direction.

It was not until I'd reached my own chamber and my warm bed with Mary Howard that I realized that Anne had never answered my question.

* * *

ANNE was now so buoyant that her happiness spilled over
onto the ladies and courtiers. We danced and played, the
ladies and gentlemen performed little plays to the delight
of Anne and Henry. I composed funny verses and set them
all to laughing. Jack would never dance or sing in the plays,
and the others took to dubbing him Master Long-face. I
laughed hard with the rest of them.

We hunted as well, chasing deer through the chill autumn countryside. Anne liked me to ride with her because I
was daring and would ride fast over rough terrain, clinging
to my horse with my skirts flying.

Henry always got his buck, and we'd feast on venison. I
was not highborn enough to carry a hawk—and, in truth,
the things frightened me with their long beaks and claws
and cruel eyes—but I rode out with Anne and the others
when they flew their birds.

I grew rather bored sitting in the clearings while the
hawks chased pigeons, so I listened to the ladies talk,
mostly about the gentlemen.

"I see Sir John Carlisle looking after you aplenty,
Frances," Margery Shelton, Anne's cousin, said to me
one day.

"Oh, yes, Sir John is smitten, depend upon it," said another lady.

I cringed inside. "Humph. I do not care a straw for Jack
Carlisle."

The ladies tittered, including Anne, and they proceeded
to tease me. I grew red but insisted that if Jack watched me,
it was to catch me doing something wrong so that he could
twit me about it. They remained unconvinced.

At last our leisurely journey came to an end, and we
reached Greenwich again at the end of November.

Anne began to spend much time planning her coronation. She and Henry reasoned that soon Thomas Cranmer,
their friend, would return to England and become archbishop of Canterbury. He would have the power to reopen

the divorce case and finish it. And then Anne would be truly married to Henry and truly queen. High time, therefore, to plan the festivities.

Anne wanted a full procession and ceremony and discussed the details one afternoon in December with Thomas Cromwell. Cromwell, normally her staunch supporter, looked at her askance. "The state apartments at the Tower have not been used in years, my lady."

"Then they must be made ready." Anne made a note with her quill on a paper. "I will take the queen's barge from Greenwich to the Tower and then progress in full pageantry to Westminster."

Cromwell made a dry harumph. "Is that wise? Public opinion about you, if you have not noticed, my lady, is dubious. You might be heckled, or worse, physically accosted. Take the barge from Greenwich to the stairs at Westminster on the day and have done."

Anne's eyes flashed. "No." She raised her hand as Cromwell began to speak. "I understand the danger. But I cannot be queen secreted away from all eyes. If we follow the procedure for a queen, then the people will realize that I am queen. Do you see? We must not behave as though anything is wrong or that we are afraid."

Cromwell eyed her with his narrow lawyer's eyes. "You mean that if you are seen as queen, you will be become queen," he said.

"Precisely. They will enjoy the ceremony, and their fading Spanish woman will disappear altogether."

Cromwell gave her a skeptical look down his long nose but said nothing.

Anne continued to be optimistic. The apartments at the Tower were torn apart, repaired, replastered, and repainted for Anne.

Henry gave her gifts, cups and plates from the royal treasury, land, houses, more jewels. He was a man setting up a household, and Anne stood at his shoulder to oversee every detail.

I went often with Anne to the Tower to look at the renovations. We went from there to York Place, where renovation was also being done, before returning to Greenwich. Everywhere, Henry was transforming his life and homes for his new bride. The court was alive with the excitement of change, of a new order entering.

Outside our enclosed world of the court, however, was a different story. When I traveled with Anne, we rode in slow barges protected by men-at-arms. When we traveled through the city or across the countryside, we rode with outriders and banners.

What I heard the few times I went out on my own with only a servant alarmed me.

Catherine was loved and revered; Anne was hated. The women could not be more plain. Anne was the king's whore, and they wanted to see her hanged. The view was widespread and prevalent. I never heard a voice rise in defense of her.

"You look pensive," Anne stopped me in the hall after one of my excursions in Greenwich. "Has something happened?" She placed her hand upon my brow. "Are you ill, poor Frances?"

I loved my lady. She liked me, the lowest of her ladies, and cared about my comfort. How to tell her that women cursed her and men thought the king a fool?

I gazed at her, so strong and lovely, her wit gentled because she thought me ill. I caught her hand.

"You can not have your coronation procession through the streets. What if they rise up against you? They could tear you to pieces."

Anne only looked resolute. "They will not. Do you not understand, Frances? When I am crowned, I shall be queen. That is different from being the king's mistress. They will not accost the queen."

She patted me on the head and told me to go away if I were going to be long-faced.

I did not share her optimism. I hoped, in spite of myself,

that the king would change his mind and send Anne away.
Then she could become plain Lady Anne again and marry
sensibly and live to old age with her grandchildren.

I wanted it in that moment, when she walked away from
me, her skirts swishing, with all my heart.

In the next moment, I told myself I was a fool. Anne
was right. She would be queen, and the people would accept her. They had to.

ONE January morning, when I helped Anne from bed,
she hurried to a basin and vomited into it.

"Oh, Frances," she said.

I handed her a cloth to clean her mouth and helped her
to her feet.

Her lips trembled, but her white face took on a look of
hope. "Do you think I am?"

I knew from watching my cousin with her many babies
exactly what a woman went through when she was with
child. "Are your courses late?"

"Yes. You know that."

"Well, my lady," I said, pretending to be severe, but
feeling delighted, "I believe you ought to speak to your
husband."

She laughed, then sent for a midwife, who was sworn to
secrecy. I waited with Anne, holding her hand while the
midwife poked and prodded and pressed practiced hands
over her belly. At last the midwife straightened and gave
her a wise look. "I think, my lady, that you should order a
cradle made."

Anne hugged me, and we laughed.

Her new condition transformed Anne. Before, she had
been merry and triumphant; now she radiated joy. Motherhood, she told me, was a woman's happiest state.

My mother had never expressed this opinion. Indeed, she
had seemed grateful she'd only borne one child, and often
asked my cousin why she wanted so many brats. I suppose
motherhood means different things to different women.

Anne told Henry of it, in private, which meant that only four of us knew: me, the midwife, the king, and Anne. We kept it secret because, despite Henry's impetuous marriage ceremony in Calais, the divorce was far from over. Cranmer was still wandering about the Continent, taking his time returning to England. He did not particularly want to be archbishop, I understood from overhearing Henry's tirades, because he would have to take oaths to the pope in Rome. Being a reformist, he did not want to take such oaths. I can understand why the man had trouble sleeping.

But one evening toward the end of January, Anne came to me and bade me journey with her to York Place. Henry, she said, was there already, waiting.

She did not take only me. Anne Savage went with us, as did Mary Howard. Likewise, a few of the king's gentlemen attended, including Henry Norris and Jack Carlisle.

When we reached York Place, Anne told me that she would marry Henry this night. This puzzled me greatly, because of course Anne and Henry had already married in that cold tower room in Calais.

Henry greeted Anne with a kiss. The ladies and I and Jack and Henry Norris walked behind them to a chamber that had been decorated with flowers and ribbons.

We ladies retired with Anne to an antechamber, where we dressed her in the clothes we'd brought with us. There had not been time to prepare a gown of cloth of gold, so we dressed her in a simpler gown of white with diamonds on the bodice. I clasped the state jewels about Anne's neck, the ones she had caused to be purloined from Catherine.

We returned to the main chamber. Henry waited there with a priest. Jack stood next to him, looking stuffy, Henry Norris, smirking. Mary Howard carried Anne's train, and we walked with her to the priest.

The priest, a man called Dr. Lee, was red-faced and uncomfortable. "If you cannot produce the license, Your Grace, I cannot perform the ceremony," he was saying.

"I have it," Henry said. "Elsewhere. Proceed." He was

smiling to himself and not in a temper with the man, which I found curious.

The priest looked dismayed. "But I must see the proofs that you have papal approval."

"I have the papers," Henry answered. "That is good enough. Continue with the ceremony."

The poor man looked back and forth from the smiling Henry to the smug Anne, then sighed and did his bidding.

And so, for the second time, Anne married the king.

Her voice was serene and true as she spoke her vows. Henry took her hand and slid a ring onto it. The priest put his hand on theirs and blessed them in Latin, his voice droning.

I looked sideways at Jack. He was rather splendid in a blue satin doublet, wide gold sleeves, and feathered hat, with a diamond on his finger. He would not return the glance, which gave me a chance to study him.

His face was a bit pinched, as though he were unwell. I could not recall him being sick, and I wondered what was wrong. While everyone else in the room was riveted to Henry and Anne and the service, I watched Jack.

He turned his head slightly and caught my eye. I looked quickly away. I had decided to be exceedingly angry at Jack Carlisle, and snub him as much as he snubbed me. Unfortunately, I do not think he noticed.

Seven

❦

THE KING'S GREAT MATTER

NEWS of the secret marriage leaked. How could it not? We'd made a hasty journey to York, taking servants, and the witnesses, while they were close family friends, had not been bound to silence. Neither had Dr. Lee. Rumors began almost at once, and Henry looked pleased, as though he'd wanted such a thing to happen.

Anne, in transports of delight about her pregnancy, saw no more reason to keep it quiet. One day when speaking to her brother and other courtiers, she began laughing and said she had a great craving for fruit.

"Tell us why, dear Anne," George said, his dark eyes glinting. He looked over at me and winked, which sent my heart thumping.

Anne walked a little way away from him, then turned and placed her hands on her stomacher. "I hear that women crave fantastic things when they are with child. I want fruit. Is there any to be had? Do fetch it for me, there is a good and dear brother."

"Frances, bring my sister fruit," he said. "She will have only the best."

Amid the ladies and courtiers agog at this gossip, I curtsied and slid away to do his bidding.

My heart was still pounding, as it always did when
George so much as looked at me. He did much more often
since we'd returned from France. Granted, he would pinch
my cheek and treat me like a girl, but that was better than
him ignoring me altogether.

The story of Anne's fruit craving was retold many
times, becoming embellished. Some said she'd told Sir
Thomas Wyatt of a longing for apples. But Sir Thomas was
not in London at the time, and apples in February are quite
wrinkled and shriveled. I brought Anne pears and oranges,
and she shared them with me and the ladies and gentlemen
nearby.

She enjoyed bragging about her condition, and everyone who saw her believed she carried the heir to the throne
and the future of England. I believed it, too, and we were
all perfectly content.

The spring days continued sweet. Anne was constantly
laughing and jesting, dancing a little with her ladies in her
chamber. George went back and forth to France, but he
spent much of the time at his sister's side, to my delight.

For myself, I was giddy with happiness. Anne had
promised I would continue in her household when she became queen, even with a great lot of ladies who were far
more highborn than I. George Boleyn actually conversed
with me, danced with me, and flirted lightly with me.

And Jack Carlisle went away. He never said good-bye;
one afternoon, he was simply gone. That was just like him,
I thought. When I asked after him, Anne said that he'd
gone to Dunstable where the divorce proceedings would
resume now that Cranmer had returned at last to England.

"Shall you miss our Jack?" Anne asked, a teasing light
in her eyes.

"No, indeed," I sniffed. "He is constantly cross. Your
brother—and the other gentlemen—are much more sweet-
tempered."

"That is true." She patted me on the cheek. "The other gentlemen are quite pleasant."

"They are," I said fervently.

I had succumbed, alas, to the game of flirtation. I studied it, I learned it, and I quite rapidly became good at it.

Flirtation takes an art of words, gestures, and looks. A fan drawn across the lips makes a gentleman hope for a kiss, the swish of skirts and a look makes him long to chase you. A lady encourages her gentleman to do deeds for her, hinting—only hinting, mind you—that he might be rewarded.

When the gentleman slays the deer or wins the joust, the lady can be generous and reward him with a flower, or a smile, or if she is very bold, a kiss. Likewise, the lady can be cruel and pretend she is angry with him no matter what spoils the gentleman lays at her feet.

Strangely, the cruelty only makes the gentlemen hotter. They become that much more determined to win a smile, while kinder ladies often see their gentlemen hanker after another.

That was one form of flirting. Another form was with words. Ladies and gentlemen would use jesting to skirt the topic of love. Winning the queen of hearts at a card game meant a promise, capturing a knight or a pawn at chess meant another. One had to become a master at double entendre, both to use it and to understand it.

I had the best teachers in the ladies who surrounded Anne Boleyn in 1533. In addition to Mary Howard, me, Anne's sister Mary, her mother, and Anne Savage, she now had beautiful Margaret Douglas.

Margaret was the king's niece by his oldest sister, and she knew the art of flirting certainly enough. The other ladies whispered that her reputation was quite bad. Margaret's mother had been married to the king of Scotland; at his death, her mother had married a Scottish gentleman, and Margaret had come from that union.

Margaret was red-haired and white-skinned and young

and quite handsome. She liked to favor a Scottish brogue and pretended to be more Scottish than English. I discerned a ruthless glint in her eye and decided to be wary of her.

Other ladies joined us, Margery Shelton, Anne's cousin, with an eye for the gentlemen; and other maidens from great houses, supervised by a woman called Mistress Marshall. Since I was a maiden, albeit not from a great house, she began to keep an eagle eye on me, much to my dismay.

This did not stop my flirting, however. I grew bolder about George Boleyn. I spoke to him in whole sentences, and once playfully winked at him. He returned the wink with a promising smile, which sent my heart racing.

I became quite the fool about him. I wrote poetry, which I showed no one, about the highlights in his hair, about his glowing dark eyes, and the fine shape of his limbs.

I kept these hidden in a box that no one touched, although frankly, no one paid much attention to my things. Along the margins of these papers I'd write my initials with his—FG, intertwined with vines and flowers. I thought it significant that the letters of our first names were next to each other in the alphabet. I even remarked about the fact to him, which made him pinch my cheek again, but this time the pinch ended in a caress.

Ironically, I wished Jack Carlisle could be there to see that I was a success with someone as important as George Boleyn.

JACK remained at Dunstable, witnessing the final proceedings of the divorce. Anne read each dispatch from him and Henry and Thomas Cranmer eagerly every day, and shared the facts with her ladies.

It seemed that Cranmer had summoned Catherine to the proceedings, and she had refused to turn up. The witnesses from her household likewise refused. The entire proceeding, Catherine implied, was invalid.

"The woman is a fool," Anne said acidly. "She still believes that Charles her nephew will ride in at the head of an army and force Henry to acknowledge the marriage. The emperor and pope have abandoned her, and she does not concede it."

I thought of the old queen, stubbornly holding on in her little house in the country, surrounded by aging retainers who suffered with her. I felt sorry for her. Why, I wondered, did she not realize that Henry would never take her back? She had enraged him, and he could scarcely speak about her without disgust. She ought to quietly retire as he had bade her.

"They are proceeding without her," Jack Carlisle wrote to Anne. "The witnesses who did turn up are hostile to her and speak openly about her carnal knowledge of the king's brother when she was married to him. Her insistence that she went to the king a maiden is quite ridiculed."

I read this paper out to Anne while she wrote at her table. She'd put her hair up like a matron, but dressed it so that it showed sleek and black at her forehead. She might be a married woman with child, but she was still determined to be beautiful.

Anne took Jack's words with delight. "Good, then we were right. Her marriage to Henry was never valid. If she fears to come to court to dispute it, she acknowledges that she was in the wrong."

The lawyers and priests went back and forth with the examinations, Jack informed us. Neither Catherine nor Henry would waver in what they saw as the truth. They were both proud and stubborn people, but I knew in the end who would lose: Catherine, because she was a woman, and because Henry was the king, and she stood no chance against him.

The trial dragged out all through February and March, while we pretended to be penitent at Lent and fast and sit vigils. At the end of March, Thomas Cranmer at last swallowed his misgivings and went through the ceremony that made him archbishop of Canterbury.

Henry's tricky friends came up with a way that Cranmer could both take the oath to the pope and break it at the same time. Cranmer had a proxy go through the ceremony in Rome, so that he himself would not have to speak the oath. At the same time, Cranmer wrote a protest against having to take the oath and sent it off to the pope. In this way, he was sworn in as archbishop but promised to obey *Henry* overall, not the pope.

I did not understand this convoluted thinking at all, but Anne did. Now that Cranmer was archbishop, Anne knew that nothing could stop her.

In Anne's chambers, after we heard the news of Cranmer's investiture, she caught me around the waist and whirled me about. Then she caught Mary Howard's hands and whirled with her as well. Laughing, she ran from her chamber, amazing the gentlemen without. She danced with each of them in turn, while Mistress Marshall begged her to remember her child.

At last Anne came to rest in a fur-strewn chair, laughing. "I am queen," she said. She threw back her head and laughed. Her wimple came undone, her black hair spilled down, and her dark eyes flashed. "I am *queen*."

On the Saturday that was Easter Eve, Anne went to Mass and was prayed for publicly as Henry's queen and consort.

Mary Howard carried her train as she stepped from the litter and ascended to the chapel. I came behind Mary, dressed in finery for Easter, and we settled Anne in her chair in the loft. She glittered with jewels and finery. The choirs sang thanksgiving for their king and, incidentally, for the resurrection of Christ our Lord.

All of London saw Anne, all heard her acknowledged aloud as Anne the Queen.

Then, toward the end of May, Cranmer sent word that he had at last pronounced Henry's marriage to Catherine of Aragon null and void.

Henry was divorced. Four long years after the first trial began, the king's Great Matter was settled at last.

* * *

ONE would think that after years of lawyers nitpicking the question to death, everyone would simply accept the resolution and let it be.

Not so. The great Thomas More, the philosopher and statesman, whom my father admired, expressed his disgust for the entire affair. He had already resigned as chancellor of England the year before, and now he spoke out against this new development. Pope Clement in Rome excommunicated Henry, the worst punishment a pope can inflict. Excommunication meant that Henry was no longer in the body of the Church, and his soul was in mortal peril.

Henry paid this no mind. Indeed, he seemed terribly cheerful for a man doomed to eternal fire.

My mother wrote me a letter in which she condemned me and my loyalty to Anne and told me I was cut off from the family. I wept copiously until Anne asked me what was the matter.

"It is the end of me," I said.

Anne watched me calmly until I stopped crying. "It is not. I am queen. You do not need the paltry allowance your father sends you. I will give you money and clothes and anything you want. Even a husband if you so desire it."

I dashed tears from my eyes. "Husband?"

"Do not look so dismayed. You deserve a good marriage, and I can fix one for you."

I gulped. I wondered what she considered a "good" marriage. She could not mean her brother, because he was married to Jane Parker, and Jane was in robust health.

"No," I said quickly. "I would rather serve you."

She cupped my cheek. "You are sweet, Frances. In a few years, when you are ready, I will find you someone appropriate. Your position is secure, my dear. Your mother can cry to the wind." She brushed her hands together as though dusting off my mother, the pope, Queen Catherine, and all others who disparaged us.

* * *

Anne kept her word. For the coronation I received cloth of gold for a gown finer than I'd ever had in my life. Also my aunt secretly sent me money and a letter saying that, although I might be plunged into mortal sin, I was her niece, and she'd be embarrassed to see me not well turned out.

I blessed my aunt but kept her secret. I knew my mother would not be above boxing her sister-in-law's ears if she found out.

On the twenty-ninth of May, we ladies dressed Anne in her finery and began the pageant that would end with her crowned in Westminster Hall. Such merrymaking we had! I will never forget those days as long as I breathe.

In the morning, we waited at Greenwich for a procession of barges to drift down to us. The first barge held a dragon that spat fireworks. I do not know how they managed such a mechanism, but it was exciting to see the shafts of fire spurting into the summer air. Other barges held the lord mayor, a flock of musicians, the highest noblemen of the court, Henry's and Anne's gentlemen, and aldermen from London.

One barge held a depiction of a falcon landing on a stunted tree stump, from which roses burst into bloom. This was a representation of Anne's own banner. She was the falcon, and she'd make the barren Tudor house blossom again. Her obvious pregnancy seemed to confirm that she was the fount of new fertility.

Once the procession reached us, we ladies and Anne climbed into the queen's barge, which had been appropriated, like the queen's jewels, from Catherine. Sunlight glittered on our gowns of gold and white velvet as we returned upriver with the flotilla. Anne was radiant, and we felt strong and happy.

The gentlemen in their barge amused themselves tossing flower petals and blooms at the ladies. Even Jack Carlisle, splendid in gold and white doublet and coat, smiled as he listened to the songs and banter.

The bargemen rowed us upriver, muscles straining. The shore drifted by, the May air soft and warm. As we passed tall ships along the river, their guns fired in praise of Anne.

The sun was bright on the water, and flowers floated where the gentlemen had tossed them. We ladies encouraged the gentlemen to try to throw them into our boat, then held the blooms aloft in triumph when we caught them.

"Even long-face is merry today," I said.

Jack at that moment chuckled at something another gentleman said. His teeth flashed in his smile, and the breeze tugged his dark curls.

Margaret Douglas tittered, and I realized I'd fixed my gaze on him. Blushing, I turned away. The ladies took up teasing me, and I was happy when the barge turned and made for the Tower steps.

Anne alighted, assisted by her footmen. The rest of us tumbled out, giggling when we should have been solemn. I brushed flowers from my hair and smiled at Henry Norris, lifting my skirts to daringly bare an ankle as I walked by him. He gave me an appreciative glance, and the ladies gave me puzzled looks.

I glanced over my shoulder to see if Jack had noticed. At that moment, he leaned to say something to Margery Shelton. I did not much like Margery, who flirted with the king under Anne's nose, although Henry did not seem to reciprocate much.

Jack was smiling down at her. My heart burned curiously, and I looked away.

I followed Anne up the steps and across the King's Bridge. Anne stopped to prettily thank the lord mayor and the nobles for the honor they did her. They bowed to her, then we processed into the Tower.

Henry, waiting for Anne, took her hands and kissed her. "Welcome, love," he said. I had never seen him smile so wide.

We continued through the Tower to the queen's apartments that the workmen had scrambled to finish. Tapestries draped the carved walls. A great bed hung with gold and red stood in the middle of one chamber, which was warmed with a high fire. The windows stood open to draw in sweet spring air.

We would stay at the Tower for two days, then ride to Westminster. Despite Cromwell's and my misgivings, Anne would ride openly through the streets. Pageants and tableaux were being set up along the way, where the people of London would greet her.

The feasting in the hall soon began. I attended to Anne, but I also ate and drank much. Minstrels entertained us, and then we danced.

I danced that night with many gentlemen, and, to be charitable, with Jack.

"Is it not splendid?" I asked. I performed the steps with much better coordination than I had in Calais. I had learned since then.

I expected Jack to admonish me, but he only answered. "Indeed."

"You do not seem happy about it," I remarked.

"I am to be made a Knight of the Bath," he said. "Tomorrow."

"Is that not an honor?"

"I am grateful for it," he answered. "It is the ritual I can do without. I will be bathed and put to bed in a hall with seventeen other gentlemen. 'Twill be ridiculous."

I started to laugh. "Are you so modest?"

"It is an arcane ritual that has not been used in centuries. I believe His Grace has run mad."

"Nothing is too good for his queen."

He gave me a narrow look. "You are enjoying my discomfort."

"Yes, indeed."

"You are impertinent, Frances."

He had his hands on my waist so that he could turn me in the steps. I'd had so much wine that my body was pliant, and his hands warmed me. "I know. My mother often slapped me for it."

"A husband does not like impertinence in a wife."

I faltered and lost my steps. As he had done in Calais, Jack steadied me so that none noticed my mishap.

"Her Grace the queen is impertinent," I told him. "And she got herself a king."

I hoped that would close his mouth. It did not. "Her Grace is an exceptional woman."

Anger seeped through me, but I decided to give him a cool look. "Meaning I am not? She is exceptional, I agree with you. You are also exceptionally insulting."

"You wish me to flatter you? I am not Henry Norris."

So he *had* seen me flirting. I rather liked that. "Indeed, you are not. He smiles and says pleasing things."

"For his enjoyment."

"Whereas you have decided to plague me for *your* enjoyment. You can smile, I know, but you would smile at me only if I were Margery Shelton."

He looked puzzled. "You have lost me."

"Have I? I do beg your pardon."

The dance came to an end. Jack began to escort me back to Anne, but I ran a little ahead of him so he could not speak to me further.

The ladies shot me teasing looks as I rejoined them, but I pretended to watch the next dance begin and ignore them utterly.

Eight

❦

ANNE THE QUEEN

JACK went for his uncomfortable ritual the next evening. Among the eighteen gentlemen so distinguished were Francis Weston and Henry Parker, brother to George Boleyn's wife.

I, of course, did not witness the ceremony, but we ladies had no compunction about speculating on what these young men would look like stripped to their skins. We became more and more raucous, debating which of them would be the most well-formed, until Anne put an end to our bawdy talk and sent us to bed.

The ladies had been given somewhat cramped quarters off Anne's large bedchamber. All of us tired, we crowded into our rooms to undress, rest, and gossip.

"You know why she is so fond of you," Margery Shelton said to me as we climbed into our beds.

If there was a lady I less wanted to speak to that night, it was Margery, but I did not give her the pleasure of knowing this. "I amuse her," I replied. "She likes my poetry."

The ladies laughed. Even Mary Howard put the bedclothes over her mouth to stifle her giggles.

"Your poetry is ridiculous stuff that makes her laugh," Margery went on. "She keeps you next to her because you will not attract the attention of the king."

"Why would I want to?" I asked, puzzled.

She snorted. "Because anyone who is the king's mistress gains much. Look how Anne's father was made an earl, her brother a viscount. All because Anne caught the king's eye. And her father had already been a viscount because of her sister. If you won the king's affection, your father and uncle would benefit. But of course, you will not. You are small and plain, and Henry never notices you."

I wanted to strike her, but I kept my temper and said icily, "He does not notice you, either, no matter that you flaunt yourself before him."

Margery reddened. "I do not flaunt myself. If he notices me, it is not my fault."

"Henry notices only Anne," I retorted.

"He notices many people," Margery said. "Except you. That is why Anne likes you so."

I wanted to dismiss Margery's hurtful words, but I thought of the many times that Henry and Anne had spoken frankly in my presence, as though what Frances heard did not matter, and how Henry had kissed her or knelt before her without noticing I was nearby.

This had never bothered me, because Henry was in love with Anne, and he could see only the object of his adoration. But I knew that Margery was correct in that I did not have the charm or the prettiness to truly attract him.

Mary Howard whispered to me across the pillow. "She is jealous. Anne favors you, and she cannot stand that, being Anne's own cousin."

"You are Anne's cousin," I pointed out.

"Yes, but Margery Shelton is a nobody. My father is a duke. My future is assured."

She did not speak boastfully but matter-of-factly. She was right, of course. When one is born a duke's daughter, one is certain of a place in the world, a good dowry, and a good marriage. Before my mother had banished me from the family, my father had despaired raising a dowry large enough to attract a decent suitor.

Now, of course, I had Anne's patronage. She could marry me well, as she had promised—to a duke's second son, perhaps. I hoped so, so that I could be Lady somebody and rub Margery's nose in it. My mother, too, might come around if I had a duke for a father-in-law.

I settled down to sleep, comforting myself with the thought. Anne's future was my future. Perhaps she did like the fact that I did not outshine her, but I would reap many rewards for being lucky enough to be plain.

THE next morning the tired Jack and the gentlemen who'd sat vigil most of the night were dubbed Knights of the Bath. This ceremony I could watch. Jack went down on his knees and kissed the king's ring, then Henry touched his shoulder with a sword, and that was that.

Henry made more knights that day, including his friend and cohort, Thomas Cromwell, and Henry Norris, his groom of the stool.

Late that afternoon, Anne's procession through the streets of London began.

We spent much time preparing Anne in her gown of cloth of gold, cleverly made to make her swollen belly not so obvious. We placed a gold circlet on her flowing dark hair, which she wore loose and long.

I thought her the most beautiful woman in the world. I thought of verses that Thomas Wyatt had written, people believed about Anne herself, although he would never say one way or the other.

> And graven with Diamonds in letters plain
> There is written her fair neck round about
> *Noli me tangere,* for Caesar's I am,
> And wild for to hold, though I seem tame.

With this coronation, Henry was certainly making Anne his, but the sparkle in her eye told me she was still wild and beautiful, and her spirit would never break.

We gathered in the Tower yard in bright sunlight to form the parade. Light caught the blue and violet banners that snapped in the wind and glinted from the gold canopy that the barons of the Cinque Ports, those Channel towns that paid no tax in exchange for garrisons, held to shelter Anne.

The new Knights of the Bath led the procession with Anne, dressed in violet robes and hoods. Behind Anne came the ladies, in order of rank, duchesses and countesses and their daughters. The elderly Dowager Duchess of Norfolk and the creaking Marchioness of Dorset rode in chariots. We lesser ladies brought up the rear, laughing and waving and throwing flowers to those along the streets.

I wore my cloth of gold robe and white kirtle, and had brushed out my hair until it shone. Over that I put a veil of transparent white and a cloth of gold hood. Happily, one can cover plainness with finery; one only has to look at old dowagers to determine this.

Margaret Douglas was there, her red hair shining, her wicked eyes snapping in delight. Mary Howard looked quite beautiful with her golden hair and young, round face beaming with excitement.

The only absent royal was the Duchess of Suffolk, the king's sister Mary. She'd written a letter of apology that she could not attend because of illness. Anne had been annoyed, although Charles Brandon, the Duke of Suffolk, confirmed Mary's illness and seemed quite distracted to be away from her.

I knew, from Anne's virulent comments, that Mary Suffolk hated Anne. Indeed, I'd heard a story of a banquet, the summer before I'd known Anne, where Mary had made such disparaging remarks about Anne that swords had been drawn, and one of Suffolk's men had been slain.

Henry himself was not there either. It was Anne's day,

he said, and Anne should take the stage. I had no doubt
he'd find some way to watch the proceedings, and he had
already made secret plans to meet her when they were
over. I had been sworn in as part of the plot, and this made
me feel slightly better about Margery's barbs.

French merchants and servants of the French ambassadors joined the procession. Then came judges all dressed
up from the Inns of Court, and clergymen in scarlet robes,
and aldermen in finery.

I eased my excited horse behind Anne Savage's, as we
moved out of the gate and made our way to Fenchurch
Street. Rails had been put up along the way to keep the
people back. Those at the rails, who leaned far over them
to see us coming, had been there all night, defending their
places. The crowd filled in behind them, each person struggling to see over the shoulders of the others. Children were
lifted high, women complained that they could not see and
elbowed the men out of the way.

When we reached Fenchurch Street, the procession
stopped. Children dressed as merchants performed a little
tableau to praise Anne. I could not see much where I was,
but as we started up again, I passed the flock of children
who'd started to pull off their costumes and tear into the
sweetmeats she'd given them.

At the intersection of Gracechurch and Fenchurch
Streets we found another tableau, this one of people
dressed as Apollo and the nine muses. Again, I could not
see much but understood that they were somehow paying
homage to Anne. As I rode past after the tableau finished,
Apollo snatched up a muse and kissed her soundly on the
cheek.

The procession wound on through Lombard Street and
the length of Cheapside to St. Paul's Churchyard. A choir
of children at the churchyard sang, their small voices rippling in the summer air. These children, too, were awarded
with sweetmeats.

It was all very orchestrated, all very formal, and all very
beautiful. We went on along Fleet Street and through

Temple Bar, then followed the Strand to Charing Cross.
Turning south, we moved past York Place and down to
Westminster Hall.

Exhausted and happy, we entered Westminster Hall to
take refreshment.

I heard vicious tales already that the pageant was a failure, that it resembled a funeral, that it paled against Catherine's procession, that people on the streets refused to
remove their caps or cheer. I burned at these lies against
Anne. The coronation procession, to my eyes, had been
enormously splendid. The people of London, aldermen,
merchants, guildsmen, and citizens, paid much compliment to Anne, and I, for one, heard plenty of cheering. The
people of London always loved a pageant.

We had a merry feast, and I drank much wine. By the
time we retired, my head buzzed and the floor seemed to
undulate beneath my feet.

I managed to walk with Anne back to the chamber that
had been prepared for her. As I did so, my excitement
mounted for what would come next. Once we were in her
chamber, Anne dismissed all but a few of her ladies. I was
mean enough to be pleased that Margery Shelton was one
of the dismissed.

As soon as we were alone, a manservant appeared to
Anne's summons. This servant led us, muffled in cloaks,
out of the chamber and down stairs to a wooden door. Beyond this was a set of stairs that led to the river.

As planned, a barge waited, one plain and unadorned.
The servant helped us ladies and Anne into the barge. We
huddled under blankets as we went the short way down the
river to York Place.

The night air was cold, but fortunately, we'd brought a
flagon of wine that we drained between us. By the time we
stopped at the slippery stairs of the palace, all of us except
Anne were giggling madly.

Serving men helped us climb out of the barge under the
small light of lanterns. We hurried up the servant's stairs
and through halls to the royal bedchamber. As we poured

into the room, half a dozen ladies tittering and whispering, Henry, surrounded by his own gentlemen, rose.

He embraced Anne and kissed her. "My queen," he said. "My triumph."

He tugged off her cloak with an impatient jerk and took her into his arms. She kissed him, face flushed.

The gentlemen of the chamber began to drift away. The ladies did as well, except me, because Anne had ordered me to stay and undress her. My fingers were clumsy with wine as I unpinned and unfastened her sleeves and skirt. Henry held Anne tightly and would not stop kissing her even while I unlaced her.

As soon as her bodice fell, Henry waved me away. "Go on."

I scuttled out the door, pleased to escape.

The other ladies had already run off to our chambers, taking their lanterns with them. I made my way out through the royal suite, which had emptied itself of all but a few servants. The passage without was dark, and I had to grope my way along the wall.

There should be another passage soon, I thought, cutting to the right, which would take me to stairs leading to the ladies' rooms. I hoped. If only the floor would cease tilting. I was certain I could find my way if the palace would just keep still.

Another lantern came toward me, a pinpoint of light in the dark. The person carrying it did not see me. I tried to sidestep, but my feet would not obey. He plunged right into me, and I gasped.

"Frances?" Jack Carlisle looked over his lantern at me, the light outlining his square face.

I put my hand over my mouth and giggled.

He raised the lantern. "Good lord, are you tipsy?"

"Perhaps."

I knew I should still be angry at him for his insulting remarks, but at the moment, I no longer remembered exactly why.

"Why are you wandering about by yourself?" he demanded.

I shrugged. "No one waited for me."

"Let us get you someplace warm, at least."

"Not yet." My mind spun with happiness and wine. I held out my hands. "Is Anne not the most beautiful queen that ever lived? Put down that lantern, and let us dance to her beauty."

"You *are* tipsy."

"Yes. Do dance with me, Jack."

He watched me for a bemused moment, then, to my surprise, actually set his lantern on the stone floor. "There is no music."

"We will sing, then."

I started skipping around him, warbling a carol about love and springtime. He caught my hands. I expected him at any moment to admonish me, but he did not.

We danced around the lantern, the light glowing upward in a warm, yellow beam. I sang softly, my heart light, happy I had someone to dance with.

We went around and around the lantern, me singing tra-la-la. Jack stopped. I stared at him, breathing hard, wondering why he'd ceased. The song was not over.

Then he pulled me close and kissed me.

I relaxed into his embrace and let him kiss my lips over and over. I felt very comfortable in his arms. With any other gentleman, even the handsome Henry Norris, I might have become alarmed and fled, but it felt so natural to kiss Jack in the dark hall that I thought nothing of it. Perhaps it was the effect of too much wine.

He slipped his tongue inside my mouth. The sharp taste surprised me, and I gasped.

Jack pulled away and stared at me, breathing hard. I felt suddenly bereft and cold. "Do you want to kiss me again?" I asked.

He shook himself, like he was waking from a dream. He took my arm. "You should be in bed."

"A spinster's bed is narrow and cold," I murmured.

"What?"

"It is not, really. The featherbeds are soft. And Mary Howard is plump, so she is comfortable to sleep against."

He made a sound like a laugh, but not quite. "Frances, you are too foolish sometimes. Or perhaps I am. I ought to ask the king to find a mission for me somewhere in the north."

"Oh, no." I grasped his hand in alarm. "Do not leave London. Fine things will happen now that my lady is queen."

He lifted his lantern and began steering me through the passage. "I doubt Henry will let me go where I will, in any case. Even home." He sounded depressed.

"That is well, because you will be happier at court. By the bye, where *do* you come from, Jack?"

"Gloucestershire," he answered. "In the Cotswolds. It is very beautiful, with the green hills and wide fields. Lovely hunting country."

I had spent much of this winter and spring inside great houses or walking in enclosed gardens. His words raised visions of green downs and warm winds, and me on a horse, racing across open lands as I had done as a child. I suddenly longed for it.

"It sounds lovely," I breathed. I caught myself. "I mean, I expect I'd find it a bit countrified, now that I am a queen's lady, and used to London."

"No doubt you would," Jack said. "Here are the stairs. Do not trip."

I gathered my fine skirts and stepped deliberately onto each high stair. I did slip once or twice, but Jack caught me.

Once we reached the doors that led to the ladies' chambers, he made a slight bow to me. "Good night, Frances."

Impulsively, I stood on my tiptoes and kissed his lips. He did not move his lips to kiss me back.

I smiled at him, lifted my skirts once more, and hurried inside to find my soft featherbed and the comfortable Mary Howard.

* * *

I woke with a raging headache and a dry, aching mouth. I was not the only lady thus indisposed, but I imagined myself the only one who'd made a fool of herself with Jack Carlisle.

Fighting nausea from my small debauch, I helped dress Anne in her cloth of gold. We trudged down to a waiting barge that would take us back to Westminster for the coronation ceremony itself. I felt white about the mouth as we made the short journey upriver, and hoped I would not disgrace myself.

Anne, six months gone with child, having survived a lengthy ride through London and then a night with the king, looked fresh and bright. I, on the other hand, could not draw a breath without hurt and hoped I would not have to put my head over the side of the barge to be sick. I thought the world not fair.

When we entered the chapel at Westminster Hall, I saw Jack, dressed in his robes as Knight of the Bath. He saw me but mercifully looked away. I was mortified. Sadly, I remembered every detail of what had happened in the hall the previous night, and I knew he did, too.

I tried to focus on the coronation, Anne's triumphant day. Mary Howard carried her train, as usual, as Anne walked to the altar of the chapel. Archbishop Cranmer waited for her, holding the crown of St. Edward.

The crown was a huge, gaudy affair that no one was meant to wear, really. Anne knelt with her robes trailing behind her, and bowed her head. Cranmer held the crown high, its jewels catching the sunlight, then placed it on her. The choir sang.

Sunlight fell into the room through bright stained glass, touching the stone arches with variegated blue and red and green. Every noble in the kingdom had packed themselves into the chapel, their robes and doublets every color of the rainbow. The smell of warmed velvet and wax mixed with the acrid tang of incense.

I fancied I saw tears in the archbishop's eyes. He had tutored Anne, and she and he were both zealous in pursuing reform in the church. In her, he had a friend and a colleague, and now he'd made her a queen.

The archbishop kindly removed the heavy crown once the ceremony was done, and placed on her head a smaller circlet that had been made for her. Then he said Mass.

Under the spell of the archbishop's clear Latin words, my headache receded, though my mouth remained unmercifully dry.

At last, the archbishop raised Anne to her feet and turned her around to face her people as queen.

As one, the nobles and gentlemen and ambassadors and ladies went down on their knees. The Dukes of Norfolk and Suffolk, the imperial ambassador, and every man who had been her enemy, bent their knees and bowed their heads. Watching her, watching them, I felt the power of it.

Anne had gotten her triumph, and her vengeance, at last.

Nine

❦

A Brief Journey Home

THE banquet that followed was the most lavish I'd ever seen. Four enormous tables ran the length of the Great Hall with Anne's table at the head on a dais. A great canopy was erected over her, and here she sat with her ladies and the archbishop, who had a smaller canopy of his own.

Down on the floor, the lords occupied one long table, noble ladies occupied another. Bishops, the mayor of London, the barons of the Cinque Ports, and the gentlemen from the Inns of Court filled the remaining tables.

The Duke of Suffolk, despite his dislike of Anne, had agreed to be earl marshal for the festivities. That meant that he rode about the hall, on his horse, no less, to see that everything was served properly and no servant was out of place or too slow to fill a cup of wine.

At the head table, Anne had only highborn ladies to wait on her, to hold her napkins, hand her her wine cup, and do for her any little thing. I sat at her feet, ready to help at a moment's notice, but mostly to keep her fine skirt clean from any dropped food or wine.

She was served by the new Knights of the Bath and others of the king's gentlemen. The knights brought her platters of food and flagons of wine, and Sir Thomas Wyatt brought her an ewer in which to wash her fingers.

Jack, as one of the knights, kept her supplied with roast peacock whenever she wanted it. He stood before the table in his violet blue robe, a deferential look on his face. If he saw me huddled on a stool at Anne's feet, he made no indication. Through a gap in the tablecloth, I saw his strong calves and broad feet in brocade shoes, muscles moving as he came forward to serve my lady.

The king, I knew, watched from behind a latticed screen in a gallery, letting Anne have her day.

I managed to eat quite a lot: wild fowl and goose, roast venison and oxen, lovely fresh greens, soups of clear broth, and piles of strawberries, along with light breads and lovely, velvety cream. I drank enough wine to assuage my thirst, but was careful to drink slowly.

The banquet went on all day and well into the night. As the entertainments rolled on and fireworks streamed over the river, I rode with Anne back to York Place, this time officially in her queen's barge, and saw her again to Henry's bosom. This time, I stayed with the crowd of ladies until I reached my bed, and avoided gentlemen with lanterns.

The next morning there was jousting. A new tilt yard had been built just for the coronation, rather hastily I heard. Anne took us ladies to her box in the stands, so that we could watch the king best his opponents. He was excellent at the joust and loved to win.

I sat near Margaret Douglas at the end of the box, relegated to this seat because I was not as highborn as the duchesses and countesses who clustered near Anne. Margaret sat next to me so that she could see better.

I was not terribly interested in watching two thousand pounds of horse with three hundred pounds of man and armor on its back hurtling at another through the mud. It looked to me like a recipe for disaster, but the gentlemen loved it. Sunlight flashed on silver-colored armor made to fit by skilled armorers in London and France and the Italian states. Gentlemen took as much pains with their armor and its decorations as ladies did with gowns. More so, to hear them boast.

Jack was to joust today as well. I spied him strolling about the field, his helm under his arm, the wind catching his curling hair. He seemed confident in his surcoat of white and green, with a green feather in his helm. I heard the ladies say that he was one of the finest riders, and often won.

The ladies liked to talk over Jack because he was young, unmarried, and of good family. He was also handsome, and close to the king. An excellent catch, they said, and speculated on who he would one day choose as his wife.

I thought of how I'd shamelessly kissed him the night before the coronation and grew hot and uncomfortable. To distract myself, I poked Margaret with my elbow and asked her, "Who is that young lady on the other side of the queen? In the dark yellow."

Margaret knew who I meant without looking. Ladies did not move to and from court without everyone knowing everything about them. "She is Jane Seymour, Sir Edward Seymour's sister. She was Catherine's lady, and now that Anne is queen, she will join us." Her eyes sparkled with mischief. "She is even more of a nobody than you, Frances."

"Perhaps I should befriend her then," I said. "I know what it is to be nobody."

"She might not speak to you," Margaret said. "Not because she is haughty, but just the opposite. She is shy and has little to say for herself."

I could understand why Anne would find that refreshing. The court was filled with ladies who had plenty to say for themselves, including Margaret, and Anne's mother, who was a haughty Howard. The quiet deference of Jane Seymour must be a relief.

The jousting began, and I forgot all about Jane. She was self-effacing, and I had eyes only for Anne.

Jack was one of the first to joust. I watched him ride his charger at an easy pace to the end of the lists and accept a lance from his attendant. He saluted his opponent, then the two men leaned forward and clapped heels to their mounts. The horses jumped forward into a dead run. I held my breath as they thundered toward each other.

With a *boom*, Jack's lance landed square on the other knight's shield and splintered all the way to its hilt. The second knight swayed mightily, then lost his balance altogether and toppled off.

I found myself on my feet, waving my handkerchief and cheering with the others. Jack saluted us ladies, then he raised his visor as he trotted his horse past our box. Ladies threw flowers at him, some of which he caught. He did not look at me, however, which suited me.

The jousts went on. The king won many, Jack won many, and both were unhorsed a few times. The king did not like his gentlemen to let him win—he wanted to prove his own prowess. However, he did not like to lose, either.

By the end of the day, I was tired, my throat hoarse from cheering. I wandered through the halls of York Place, dismissed while Anne rested before tonight's feast. I was warm with the happy tiredness that comes of enjoying oneself all the day long.

I was happy, that is, until I saw Jack walking toward me across the huge white hall that was being renovated for the king. He limped slightly, the result of a heavy fall on the tilt field, but seemed none the worse for wear.

He had not noticed me. I turned to flee, but in my haste I swung into scaffolding, then twisted my ankle and nearly fell. A strong hand on my arm pulled me to my feet. "Frances."

I stood up, mortified. My face was hot, my mouth dry.

"I have been looking for you," he said.

"Have you?" I waited for his lecture, for him to remonstrate with me, but his look was worried, as though he did not remember our encounter in the upstairs halls.

"Aye. A messenger has been trying to find you. I am

sorry to bear bad news, but your father has sent word your mother is quite ill. You are to return home at once."

MY journey to Hertfordshire made me feel very odd. The road there was not long—I passed Hunsdon the morning after I'd left York Place—but I might have been making a journey to the other end of the world.

On my last day home, I'd been in a mud-spattered gown with my hair hanging in snarls. I'd been pouting and rebellious and very angry at my mother.

Today, I wore a gown of brocade and velvet and was perched upon a fine horse. My hair, brushed and untangled, was covered with a costly silk veil. I wore leather shoes for riding and fine leather gloves that covered my hands and wrists. Behind me rode a page and a maid, spared to wait on me while at home.

The village crows were out in force. They had lined up on the High Street to disparage me. That much at least, had not changed.

"Here she is home again, all fancied up, with her nose in the air," Mistress Longacre said. "Come to boast, has she?"

I gave her a cold nod. I could show her that I was civil. "Good morning. I have come home because my mother is ill."

"Aye," said Mistress Partridge. "She's taken to her bed these last three days and cannot move from it."

"She feels the illness of the kingdom," Mistress Longacre said, her voice gloomy. "Its despair has gone into her bones, and she aches with it."

"She is not long for this world, I am certain of it," Mistress Partridge continued, pinning me with her watery stare.

Mistress Longacre put her hands on her hips. "Ungrateful child. Are you the king's mistress, too?"

I looked at her, horrified. "Good heavens, no."

She nodded wisely. "Ha. We'll see."

I spurred the horse forward and sped through the village. I looked back before the road bent around a corner

and saw Mistress Longacre standing in the middle of the
High Street, watching me, her black gown billowing like
wings of a dark angel.

I rode hastily until I turned in the gates of my father's
house. The redbrick manor crouched at the end of the lane,
its windows small and dark, the dirt stable yard like a
wound in the green. What I had once thought fine now
seemed small and disappointing.

I gave the reins of my horse to our stableboy, who
looked over the mare in awe. The servants I'd brought from
court openly sneered at the house. The maid lifted her
skirts disdainfully as she stepped over the threshold.

Inside, I found everything much as usual. Two maids argued as they scraped the trestle boards of the table in the
hall. A boy crushed herbs for the rushes, and another maid
clumped across the gallery with her arms full of linen.
Dobbin, my mother's housekeeper, was lumbering down
the stairs, keys clanking at her waist.

When she saw me, her round face blossomed joy. "Mistress Frances," she cried. "Thank heavens you've come.
Everything is at sixes and sevens with the mistress abed."

Secretly, I was pleased to see the busyness. My mother
could not be too ill if she was ordering the servants about.

"Is she better?" I lifted my skirts to start up the stairs,
but Dobbin blocked my way.

"She will not want to see you." Her breath smelled of
garlic, as usual. "It is your father who wants you. He's dis-
traught, poor man."

My heart squeezed. "Where is he?"

"Not here. He went to visit your uncle, saying he
couldn't hear himself think in this house."

I grew puzzled. If my mother did not want to see me and
my father hadn't waited for me, why had they sent for me?

"Frances!" My aunt's thin voice floated from the top of
the staircase. She pattered down, but instead of embracing
me, she stood still and clasped her hands to her bosom.
"My goodness, how fine you are." She touched the embroidery on my bodice. "Silk thread and silver cord. How

lovely. And skirts are higher this year, I see." She smoothed her fingers over my velvet-covered waist, her eyes greedy.

"I have brought you cloth from the queen," I said. "And for mother."

"What a thoughtful girl you are." She looked delighted, then her face fell. "Your mother will not let me have it."

"We shall see. I want to see her. Dobbin, please."

My aunt looked surprised. "Well, of course. Come along."

She grasped my arm and pulled me around Dobbin and up the stairs. Dobbin watched with misgiving but did not try to stop us.

"She is a bit poorly," my aunt whispered as we neared my mother's chamber. "Try not to tire her. I'll not go in. She says I make her weary, but she is not herself."

She nudged me toward the door, gave my gown a last hungry look, then hurried away.

My mother's chamber was the best in the house. It lay in the front, over the hall, far from the smells of the kitchens. The room was large and airy, whitewashed and painted, with dark beams curving to support the roof.

My mother's bed was wide and high, brought over from Paris when she married my father. Four thick posts rose to the carved top, which supported brocade draperies of green and gold.

I'd always thought the bed a magnificent and awesome thing, and now, even to my court-jaded eyes, it still was.

My mother lay in the middle of this vast bed with the coverlet pulled all the way to her chin. Her eyes were closed, her cheeks sunken.

"Maman?" I hurried to the bed.

Her eyes opened a crack, dark pools on white. She looked at me for one silent moment.

"You look French," she said. Her voice was hoarse, but she still managed to insert acid into her tone.

"I am French," I answered. "Or, at least, half-French."

Her eyes closed. She began muttering prayers under her breath.

"Maman?"

Her lids fluttered. "God save me from an ungrateful child. Did *she* dress you like that? The king's strumpet?"

"She is queen of England, mother."

"There is but one queen," my mother said, strength rising in her voice, "and that is Catherine."

"Not any longer." I clenched my hands, leather stretching over my fingers. "Catherine is now to be addressed as Dowager Princess of Wales."

My mother turned bright red. She sat up straight, the covers sagging from her shoulders. "How dare you cast that in my face? The king's Frenchified whore will fall. When she falls, you will fall, and no one will be there to catch you."

I feared my mother would hurt herself in her rage, but I had to answer. "Anne was crowned queen of England yesterday. She is the most powerful lady in the land."

"For now," my mother spat. "I have seen it in the auguries. She will return to the dust from whence she came. Have a care, child, or you will go with her."

I lifted my chin. "She said she would make a marriage for me. A good marriage."

My mother ignored me and the fact that this was why she'd allowed me to go to Anne in the first place. "She corrupts everything she touches. She will destroy the Church and let the devil in. God will not forgive."

God might forgive, I thought, *but my mother never will.*

"I am going to see Father," I said.

"He is carousing," she answered, mouth tight. "Drinking with your aunt's feckless husband while I lie here, suffering. You and he will be the death of me, and you will laugh together when I am gone."

"No," I cried. I took a step forward but did not have enough courage to reach for her. "I wish you to get well. Truly I do."

She lay down and turned her head away. "Well, I cannot. I will be unwell until the king's whore is gone."

I drew myself up. "She will not be gone. She will never

be gone. She is queen, and her sons will be kings. Do not cling too much to the old ways, or you will be swept away with them."

Her gaze snapped to me again. "You threaten me? You dare? Get out. Get out at once. You are no daughter of mine."

Her words hurt me, but my anger burned bright. "You will see," I shouted. "You will see."

Then I turned and stormed from the room.

"SHE is afraid, Frances," my father said.

I had fled to my uncle's house and now sat with my father in my uncle's great hall. We warmed ourselves at the fire, and he'd bade a servant bring me warmed mead. The homey spice of it, for some reason, made me want to cry.

I covered my sentiment by speaking quickly. "Why should she be afraid? The new court is sophisticated and learned. It is nothing to fear."

My father's beard was black, speckled with gray. His eyes were blue and intelligent but softened with kindness. "When new ways come, many times the old ways are viewed with intolerance, and those who cling to the old ways are punished." He sipped his mead. "It happens, Frances."

I was not certain whether to believe him. I had lived my entire life surrounded by safety and people who took care of me. My first venture into the world had put me under the protection of a powerful woman, and so I still existed in a bubble of safety. So far in my life, the wolves had never howled at the door.

"Mother has no need to fear," I tried to explain. "Anne counts me as one of her favorites. She would never let harm come to my family." I leaned to him. "You do not see what I see every day, that she has great influence—with the king, with Master Cromwell, with the new archbishop of Canterbury."

He smiled at me, somewhat indulgently. "It is difficult for her, Frances. She fears for religion itself."

I burst out laughing, relieved. "Well, she is foolish. Queen Anne is quite pious. We pray in her chamber in the morning and at night, and we attend Mass with her. She speaks often of scriptures and teaches us, and we debate. She was once a pupil of the archbishop himself."

My father looked slightly dismayed. "It is not for young ladies to debate scripture."

"Anne says it is good for us to talk over the gospels and understand them. She has read the New Testament in English and will soon obtain a copy so that her ladies can read as well."

My father lost all his good humor. He caught my hand. "Frances, have a care. You speak of heresy."

"It is no longer heresy. The Church is reformed."

His worn hand clung more tightly. "Not yet. Daughter, if the reformists do not succeed, you could be tried and hanged."

"I do not have fear of that. I am not a Lollard, or a Lutheran. I have the faith of the king and the queen."

"The king, who has been excommunicated. Do you understand what that means? That he cannot attend Mass and look upon the host. That he cannot have the burial rites, unction. That his soul is damned."

"But he does attend Mass."

"Given by priests who defy Rome. Frances, this is not done."

I got to my feet. "You must understand, Father. This is a new time, and I embrace it. If you could hear what Anne tells me about the corrupt monks and priests—they are wallowing in worldliness. They have vast wealth and lands and mistresses and children. You cannot tell me that this is good."

"Of course not. There will always be men who abuse their offices."

"But there are so many of them." I paced a little, as Anne often did, knowing that the jewel at my throat winked in the firelight. "Why is His Grace the king wrong to make them pay?"

"He is not, if they are truly corrupt. But he is sweeping good men aside with the bad."

I shook my head. "Indeed, he is not. The good men realize that the Church needs reform, and embrace it."

My father went silent. I stopped pacing. The expression on his face was so sad that I rushed to him and fell to my knees. "Father, what is it?"

He brushed a strand of hair from my forehead. "You are so young, my daughter. I do not want to lose you."

"You have not lost me." I caught his hand and pressed a kiss to it. "You will never lose me, Father. And I will bring prosperity to the family. I know this."

He continued to study me sadly. The look broke my heart, but I could not understand it.

I longed to make him smile again, and I would. Anne would marry me to a wealthy and noble man. In my head, I made this man handsome and strong to suit me. She would give my father a title higher than baronet, and more lands, and wealth. My father would smile at me, and my mother would no longer look upon me in rage. She'd be grateful to me, and thank me, and tell me she was proud of me.

It would happen, and I vowed to make it happen.

Ten

❖

PASTIME AND GOOD COMPANY

JULY AND AUGUST 1533

My visit home dragged down my spirits. The court, when I returned, however, was anything but dismal.

Anne was queen. Anne carried the king's son. Her ladies were young, her gentlemen, handsome. She was Queen of May, and we were her adoring subjects.

The day I returned to Greenwich, I found the ladies in Anne's chamber, dancing. Mary Howard and Margaret Douglas and the others sashayed across the floor, as two musicians played a merry tune in the corner. Anne rose when she saw me, kissed my cheeks, then drew my arm through hers and took me to sit next to her.

Her stomach was extended with her pregnancy, and the room was hot, but Anne's face bore a radiant smile. "You look dismal, Frances. Did the country not agree with you?"

I could not tell Anne the whole of it, for some of the things my mother said had been quite terrible, but I indicated that my father and mother were unhappy with me.

Anne scoffed. "Nonsense, my dearest Frances. I told you that you will never lose while you are loyal to me, and I keep my promises."

"What do I do in return?" I asked. "Your Majesty, I have nothing to give you. I do not sing or dance well, I cannot be said to have the best wit in company, and my poetry is abysmal."

"You listen to the jealous tongues of others," she answered. "Your poesy is fine. Do I not ask to hear it? You have a cleverness with words, and you make me laugh." She leaned to me. "Besides, Frances, you are sweet, and you are true. It is rare to find a lady at court without ambition. So many of them need careful watching."

The lines about her eyes pulled when she said this. I wondered whether the ambitions she referred to concerned the king. He was certainly known to stray.

"I am ambitious," I said. Her gaze switched to me with the intensity of a goshawk's, cruel and watching. I finished quickly, "I want to marry well, to a handsome man."

Her expression softened, and I relaxed. "I have no doubt." She patted my cheek. "Now, join the dance. I must sit because I am so heavy with my king's son, but I like to watch others."

I kissed her hand and sprang to my feet. I knew she was not dismal because of her condition. She liked her fertility, and she made certain that everyone in the kingdom knew of it. She would be the savior of the Tudor line, and we all were certain of it.

I joined the dance then, taking pretty Margaret's hand, letting her pull me into the circle.

I am ashamed to say that in the days and weeks following, I forgot all about my mother and her doleful predictions, and even about my father's sadness. Anne's court was a merry place, and I immersed myself in joy.

I covertly looked for Jack Carlisle after my return, but did not see him. That suited me, because I was still embarrassed about my behavior toward him at the coronation festivities. I had kissed him, and I was not even in love with him. What he must think of me, I could not fathom.

I learned through gossip that he'd been sent on king's business to the north, to Lincolnshire. I vaguely remembered him murmuring that he should ask for a post far from court that night I'd foolishly danced with him in the passage at York Place. What the king's business was, and how long he would be away, no one knew.

As the summer wore on, people spoke of him less and less, and I pushed him to the back of my mind.

Without Jack looking over my shoulder, I abandoned myself to the pleasures of the moment. I do not mean I did anything immoral—I had not lied when I told my mother that Anne liked us to behave modestly. However, I joined with the other ladies in singing and making merry and flirting.

I studied, and honed my skills, and became a very accomplished flirt. Margaret Douglas was best of all at it, and she taught me much. I learned how to peep up at a gentleman under my lashes when I listened to him, how to purse my lips to make him think of kissing, how to smile over my shoulder when I walked away.

As a result, I was no longer the ignored nobody daughter of a baronet, but a lady sought after for dancing and conversation.

Best of all, George Boleyn came to court often. The king kept him busy with journeys to France as an envoy, but George still found time to attend his sister. They were quite fond of one another, Anne and George. They often sat side by side, heads together, while the rest of us danced or sang or performed little vignettes for Anne's pleasure.

George was quite rich, having been given large grants of land and income when Cardinal Wolsey had fallen from power. He ignored his wife, Jane, who had joined Anne's ladies, and mostly devoted himself to his sister.

I studied him from afar with longing. My palms still sweated when I saw him. A smile from him could brighten my entire day; the days when he did not notice me were dismal and dark.

I flirted with the other gentlemen, but my heart belonged

to George. I knew I could not marry him, which was a draw-
back, but I greatly enjoyed my daydreams about him.

> His limbs fine and strong, his lips speak sweetness
> When he breathes into my blessed ear.
> When he doth approach, my heart trembles.
> I die for one sound or one tenderness.

I sighed when I wrote it, like a forlorn lover.

One afternoon, after we'd moved to Windsor so the king
could hunt, we had music and dance in Anne's presence
chamber. George actually approached me and chose me as
his partner.

His hands felt warm in mine as he handed me into the
circle. I swayed this way and that, my skirts held gracefully. I'd learned much since I'd awkwardly danced with
Jack in Calais. That had been cold November, now it was
high summer, and warm and delightful.

George smiled. His dark eyes held mystery, like Anne's.
Like Anne, he could smile without moving his lips, just by
turning his eyes a certain way. He did so now, following me
with his gaze as we stepped and touched and backed away.

He placed his hands on my waist as he spun me round,
and I knew that I wanted him to kiss me. I had been pining
over him for months, but I had not, until that moment, had
an opportunity to move beyond admiration.

I wanted him to kiss me as Jack had the night of the
coronation festivities. I remembered that kiss, the press of
Jack's lips, the taste of his tongue in my mouth. I wanted it
to be George I tasted, wanted his touch to caress my cheek.

When the dance was finished, George walked me back
to the ladies who clustered near Anne. He kissed my hand
before he turned and sauntered away.

"You are very bold," Margaret Douglas remarked.
"Have you set your sights on the fair George?"

She spoke in a low voice behind her fan. Jane, George's
wife, stood not far from us, her rabbity face pinched. She
grew annoyed when George gave attention to other women,

but she did not like him herself. I thought this rather selfish and inconsistent of her.

"Is it bold to accept the compliment of a dance?" I asked, smiling the knowing smile I'd learned.

"It is bold to look at a gentleman so, under the nose of his wife."

I reflected that Margaret ought to know, because she did such things all the time.

"I merely smiled at him," I said.

"Yes, my dear, of course you did." Her blue eyes glinted. At eighteen, with her fire-red hair hanging long, she was a lovely young woman, indeed.

Of all the ladies, only Margaret suspected my designs on George Boleyn. The others thought my tastes lay elsewhere, on Jack Carlisle. I enjoyed the puzzled looks they shot me when I did not mourn that Jack had gone to Lincolnshire.

Lady Margaret, more canny and perceptive than most, suspected which way my heart leaned. I tried to give her a bland smile, because she would store the information for her own use if she could.

My desire for George and his kisses made me somewhat foolish, unfortunately. Later that afternoon, when I saw George slip away from Anne's presence chamber, I contrived to do so myself.

I hastened through cold halls of Windsor, the stones holding chill even in high summer. Two years ago, Queen Catherine had stayed here while Henry hunted with Anne by his side. I had heard that when Catherine tried to carry on in her capacity as wife and queen, as though nothing were wrong, Henry grew angry at her. He snubbed her, and at the end of the visit, he banished her. He sent her to the More, a house in Hertfordshire that had belonged to Wolsey, and forced their daughter, Princess Mary, to go live at Richmond and not see her mother.

I ought to feel more pity for Catherine, I knew. But I was smug, and much of Anne's thinking had rubbed off on me. If Catherine had been a better wife, I decided, she would still be here at Windsor, mending Henry's shirts and presiding over the dancing.

Also, if Catherine had still been queen, I would not be here with Anne. I would be in Catherine's dull court or at home enduring my mother's barbed criticism and my father's worry about finding me a husband. I would be trying to please them both and failing.

My life was splendid now, and a kiss from George, I knew, would make it perfect.

I hurried toward the king's chambers, where I had seen George heading, pretending to the passing servants that I was doing nothing more than carrying out an errand for Anne.

I mounted a flight of steps, my breath coming fast, hoping I would find him before long. My hands were cold, and my feet, already tired from dancing, began to ache.

I entered a high-ceilinged chamber that contained nothing but hanging tapestries, tall pieces from another century. Instead of admiring the scenes and thinking of the fingers that had woven the threads with skill, I muttered that a room with no handsome gentleman in it was not worth the trouble.

On a sudden, I heard a great lot of voices and the tramping of feet coming my way. Not servants. Gentlemen of the court.

Servants I could have shrugged away, or ordered to stop their gossip, but meeting a crowd of gentlemen alone in a chamber was not what I wished. Worse, I heard Henry's voice among them.

There was nothing for it. They blocked my way out, so I ducked behind one of the tapestries.

"She refused?" the king was saying at the top of his voice.

I peeked around the tapestry. I was well in the corner, in the shadows, and the light from the high windows did not touch me. About half a dozen gentlemen in embroidered finery and glinting jewels entered the room, surrounding the king. George Boleyn, I saw to my disappointment, was not among them. Servants skulked behind them, ready to serve on a moment's notice. Mark Smeaton, the musician, who was about my age, followed as well. He'd become rather a pet of the king and Anne, though he was not high-born by any means. He enjoyed entertaining them and being spoiled by them.

"I am afraid so, Your Grace."

The speaker was Jack Carlisle. What was he doing here? I wondered. He was supposed to be in the north where he could not plague me.

"By what right does she defy me? I gave her everything, saved her when she was starving as my brother's widow, and now she defies me?" Veins stood out on Henry's bull neck, and his face was mottled. "To reject my authority, to acknowledge another authority over me, is treason."

"Yes, Your Grace," Jack said neutrally.

"Tell me again, what you were told."

The king breathed heavily. Jack's face was white. I sensed that he did not want to speak words Henry would not want to hear, but he had no choice. I felt a bit sorry for him.

"She will not answer to the title Dowager Princess of Wales. The ladies of her household and her steward refuse to use it."

Henry looked at him for a long moment, his eyes filled with fury. "Does she know what I can do? Does she know that I can crush her any time I like?" He raised a great hand and closed his fist. "I have spared her only from pity."

Perhaps, I thought. That, and the entire country might rise up if he threatened Catherine with death. If all the women of England were as enraged and stubborn as my mother, Henry would dare not stray a step from his fortified castle.

"She has dug the pit that she lies in," Henry continued. "She will never see her daughter again. I cannot fathom what those two women would get up to if they closeted themselves. Send word."

"Yes, Your Grace," Jack said, bowing his head.

"Now." Henry forced himself to calm, pasted an eerie smile on his face. "There is dancing and music in the queen's chambers. The ladies, I am sorry to say, have not missed you, Jack. They dance and sing and are merry all the day. It is a fine thing to see."

Several gentlemen chuckled in agreement. Jack did not smile.

"Let us go there," Henry continued. "Beautiful ladies are just the thing to relieve my pique. Find one you like and haul her off, Jack, my boy. You need something to unbend your neck."

The other gentlemen hooted with laughter. A few clapped Jack on the back.

Henry waved his servants to precede him from the room, and the gentlemen moved through the doors back into the dim halls of the castle.

Jack lingered. Whether he did so to avoid continued teasing, or whether he sensed something suspicious in the room, I do not know.

At that moment, I realized another reason I did not like tapestries. They were dusty. Small animals also liked to live in them and leave their droppings behind.

The result was inevitable. I sneezed.

Jack had uncanny hearing. He swung around. I rubbed my nose hard, trying to stifle my sniffles, hoping Jack would go away.

He would not, of course. He walked to the tapestry, his body straight and tall, and yanked back the corner.

We looked at each other for a heartbeat. His gaze was unreadable and a bit cold. Usually Jack only made me cross, but now as he stared down at me, tall and severe, I felt chilled and very alone.

"What are you doing here?"

"What are you?" I countered, trying to quell my uneasiness. "I thought you had gone to Lincolnshire."

He seized me by the elbow and dragged me from hiding. "I am not the person hiding behind a tapestry, listening to the king. I ask again why you are here."

"Perhaps I had an errand."

"Perhaps you are a liar."

"You do not need to know everything," I said disdainfully.

His eyes held anger. "You were either spying on His Grace, or you had a tryst. Which is it?"

"Why should I answer? Either admission would not benefit me."

He released my arm. I rubbed it. My velvet sleeve felt good to my cold fingers. He wore velvet, too, a deep green doublet embroidered with gold and a dark green half cloak trimmed with ermine. Jack always dressed well, always had his hair combed and trimmed. I knew he must be wealthy, being heir to an earldom, but I had never given it much thought.

"You have no deceit in you," he conceded. "I doubt that you would spy on His Grace for your or another's gain." He folded his arms and gave me a stern look. "That means you had a tryst."

"Perhaps I did." I shoved aside a strand of hair that had come loose. "A tryst with a very handsome gentleman indeed."

My tongue tripped on the lie, but I tired of his condescension.

His voice went quiet. "Which gentleman?"

"Never you mind."

He studied me a long time, his eyes steady. I grew nervous. "Never you mind," I repeated.

"This is not a game, Frances."

"Oh, but it is. Flirtation is a great game, and an art. One you have not learned, it is apparent."

He reached out and gripped my chin between his gloved fingers. He did not hurt me, but he held me firmly. "If you were wise, you would unlearn these lessons."

I lost my temper. I'd had enough of him, and my mother, and Mistress Longacre, telling me what a fool I was.

"Plague take you, Jack," I snarled. Mistress Longacre could give a man an evil stare and curse him roundly. I was not so impolite, but I had learned a thing or two from her. "If I am sought after, it is my own affair and nothing to do with you."

His face went as red as the king's. "Do not be a child.

You cannot afford to be one any longer. You think of kisses and games, but the gentlemen think of much more than that. I know this. I hear them."

"Do you?" I was curious, despite my alarm at his mood. "What do they say?"

"Nothing very much, because I stop them talking. But it is dangerous. You are unprotected. And now I find you skulking behind a tapestry, on your way to meet a gentleman. Have you lost your senses?"

"The only gentleman I am in danger from at the moment is you," I retorted. "I am in great danger of being offended by your rudeness and your assumptions regarding my character. I am in danger of becoming undignified and kicking you in the shins."

He did not smile. "If I decided to take your virtue, at this moment and in this place, could you stop me?"

I was angry. I jerked from his grasp. "I would have a good try. In any case, you would not."

"You are too trusting."

Something in his voice frightened me. Jack, for all his high-handed ways, was well mannered and inoffensive. Indeed, few men at court could match his refinement. Even Anne, raised at the French court, said admiring things about him.

But I realized in this darkened room with him looming above me and nothing behind me but a dusty tapestry, that I did not truly know him. I had looked upon him as an annoyance, as I sometimes did my cousins, not as a man.

The exception was the night he had kissed me in the tower room in Calais. I did not count the time he kissed me after the coronation, because I had been tipsy, and he must have been as well, to do such a thing.

He was tall, strong, older than me by at least six or more years, he was one of Henry's trusted friends and a member of the privy chamber. He had been knighted, he would one day be the Earl of Pennington, and he had influence, power, and money. He was privileged among a court of privileged men.

I, on the other hand, had little. Anne's favor counted for much, but perhaps, in this room far from the light and gaiety of the queen's chamber, it counted for nothing.

"If I wanted you," he said, his voice deadly quiet. "I could have you. So could any gentleman whom you were foolish enough to meet alone."

He stood so close, I smelled the velvet of his doublet and outdoor scents that clung to his cloak. "If you cried out," he said, "you might bring help. But who would be blamed? The gentleman of good family, or the young woman fool enough to meet him in an empty room?"

I swallowed. "You are trying to frighten me."

"I am. You ought to be frightened."

"I do not want to be."

He took a step closer, and I backed all the way to the tapestry. "The court is a frightening place," he said. "It is slippery and devious, and you are too innocent to be in it."

"I have been here nearly a year," I pointed out. "And I have been quite all right."

"Things change, and they change rapidly. The Duke of Norfolk is angered because Anne does not reward him as much as he thinks she ought. The Duke of Suffolk openly despises her. In spite of everything, her position is precarious. And you are so close to her."

His manner was so strange, his gaze so intense, that my mouth went dry. "What are you running on about, Jack? I have nowhere near the power of a duke."

"If your family tries to make an ambitious marriage for you, using Anne's influence, you will be in danger. The great families scheme and ally with each other and fight one another far more viciously than any European power. And here you are in the midst of this maelstrom, a pawn buffeted about, while the players watch and wonder what use to make of you."

I began to shake. I did not like that. "You are mad. No one has any interest in me."

"They do," he said. "You are one of the new queen's favorites. She has much power. Can they use you to get close to her, to gain a favor? Or perhaps to rid themselves of her, perhaps to poison her?"

"Poison?" I looked at him in horror.

"They may well try to use you to tear her down. Her position is precarious. The right information in the right ear could give her enemies great advantage."

"Do you mean people would expect me to spy on her for them?" I asked, aghast.

"Indeed."

"Well, I never would." I put my hands on my hips. "I never will, and you can tell them that."

He softened suddenly. Jack was a rather handsome man, and his smile suited him. "I will drop hints that you are viciously loyal. As long as you are telling me the truth."

"I am not a liar. As much as I have disappointed my mother, she did raise me to believe that a lie is a mortal sin."

His brows climbed. "And she allowed you to come to court? She is a brave woman."

"She does not want me here. She hates Anne very much."

His smile vanished. "Do not say such things too loudly. We are all in precarious positions."

"Even you?" I asked.

"Yes." He gave me an unreadable look. "Especially me."

I wondered what he meant. I did not know much about Jack's family, but I thought Henry trusted Jack implicitly. I realized as I watched him that although I viewed Jack as a nuisance and a gentleman who liked to spoil my fun, I should not like to see him arrested. Nor did I much want to see his head gazing mournfully down at me each time I crossed London Bridge.

I touched his sleeve. "Take care, then, Jack."

He started, as though his mind had been on other things. He took my hand and moved it from his arm. "Go back to the queen's chambers and do not wander about on your own again."

He turned to leave. The man exasperated me. I never understood why he scolded me so. No matter what, he always confused me. I decided to punish him a little.

"Are you not going to kiss me good-bye?"

He swung around, his half cloak flaring. "You think too much about kissing, Frances."

"I never mind it when you kiss me."

That was true. There were several gentlemen at court I did not want near me, but I rather liked kissing Jack. I hoped I could practice with him, so that when I at last was able to kiss George, I would not make a mess of it.

Jack stepped to me. He cupped my face in his hands, resting his thumbs on my cheekbones. "I could wish you truly meant that."

I wanted to scoff, *Of course I meant it,* but my tongue had gone heavy and lay dormant at the bottom of my mouth.

He leaned down and kissed me, so fleetingly that I barely registered the touch.

I raised on my tiptoes, trying to follow his mouth as it moved away from me.

He arrested the motion and stepped back. He watched me with dark eyes, while I tried to recover my dignity.

"It was not much of a kiss," I said, pretending to be haughty.

He made a noise of exasperation. I thought he would whirl around and leave me there, but he hooked strong fingers under my elbow and more or less dragged me back to the more inhabited part of the castle.

Eleven

❦

THE BIRTH OF A PRINCESS

WE remained at Windsor through the warm August days. The king hunted and was merry and thought of returning to Calais in the autumn after his son was born.

Court life was happy, although after Jack's warnings to me in the tapestry room, I looked upon those around me with less naïveté than previously. Jack was not a stupid man, and I knew his observations would be apt.

True, people wrote to Anne or used their connections to speak to her, asking her to either intervene for them in a private matter or to bring up a matter for the king's or Cromwell's consideration.

But I began to watch eyes. I began to notice that courtiers did regard me in speculation, like the Duke of Norfolk when he visited the queen's chambers one day and found me sitting next to Anne.

"I hope you are well, Your Grace," he said to her, bowing his head. I sensed an ironic note in his voice, which was not lost on Anne.

"Why would I not be well?" she asked. "The king's son

keeps me good company." She rested her hand on her swollen belly and shot him a look of defiance.

I wanted to warn her to take care. The duke was an oily man; even Jack did not have to explain this to me. Norfolk had encouraged Anne to win the king, not for her glory, but to elevate himself. The Howard family was a powerful one, and they'd kept their position by cannily detecting which faction to join or leave at the right time.

The duke went away then, but I did not like his smile. I wanted to tell him that when Anne was mother of the king's heir, no person would be as powerful as she.

THE baby prince was expected in October. Six weeks before that, in the middle of August, we traveled from Windsor to Greenwich so that Anne could begin her confinement.

Workmen had frantically repaired and renovated the rooms where Anne would live out her seclusion. A great bed stood in the center of the bedchamber, fantastically carved and ponderously heavy.

The bed gave the room a somber but majestic air. A false ceiling had been built above it, and the walls were hung with tapestries and draperies, shutting out air and light and noise.

But every luxury had been provided for Anne, including new linens, which we ladies had hurriedly sewed, golden ewers, fine cloths, a carved wooden font for a quick baptism should it be needed, and an altar where Anne could pray each day.

Anne also had commanded that the sumptuous cloths that had wrapped the Princess Mary at her christening seventeen years ago be fetched from Catherine's household for the new prince. The request sent new waves of anger through the men and women who supported Catherine. These cloths had been brought from Spain, they argued, from Queen Isabella's court. They were not for the new mistress, the upstart daughter of a mere courtier from Kent.

"I shall have them," Anne said to Henry. "Nothing is too good for our prince."

But in this, Anne was thwarted. The cloths were never relinquished. This battle, Catherine won.

I handled what Anne did acquire, fine velvets and embroidered satin, cloth of tissue and cloth of gold. I savored their lovely textures and rubbed them to my cheek when no one was looking. The cloths would drape a little prince, the hope for the king's future.

On the twenty-sixth of August, Anne and her ladies processed to her chambers for the official beginning of her lying in. Servants and Anne's chamberlains preceded us, carrying candles, and then Anne came with her chosen ladies, the midwives, maidservants, and me.

My mother would not approve of me attending a birth, since I was still unmarried, but Anne had clung to my hand and told me I must stay with her.

"But you will have so many other ladies," I pointed out. I felt flattered that she wanted me to witness the birth of the prince, but on the other hand, confinement for six weeks in a soft, quiet room while Anne's pregnancy came to term seemed rather tedious to me.

"I want you. You love me. Not many do." Anne deliberately softened her expression. "Besides, I want a sonnet about the occasion, and what better lady to write it than my own dear Frances?" She'd patted my cheek, and I'd curtsied and said I'd be honored. There was not much else I could say.

The gentlemen of Anne's household and the chamberlains and footmen left us before the chamber doors closed, shutting out the male world. The doors emitted a hollow sound as they banged together. I looked at them, the doors of a jail, confining the queen until she either failed or emerged victorious. Death or triumph awaited us.

CONFINED or no, Anne continued her daily routine as queen. She read letters from petitioners and answered the same, she wrote instructions for her chamberlain and gentlemen of the chamber, she wrote to the king, she wrote to

Cromwell. She asked for favors to be done her petitioners, or she advised said petitioners that she could not help them.

I often delivered papers and letters to Anne's gentlemen, who waited outside the privileged confines of the queen's lying-in chambers. I gladly accepted the task, happy to escape the stuffy, deadened rooms for a few minutes, at least.

Anne, her abdomen swollen beneath her gold-laced garments, was serene. She was still ill in the mornings, and often she'd take to her great bed and lie quietly, her face white. We ladies fretted and prayed when she did this, fearing the child would come too soon or be dead when it did arrive.

But Anne remained resolute. She often asked me to read things out to her, letters, poems, the scriptures she liked best. She would hold my hand and listen to my voice, sometimes drifting to sleep in the midst of it.

One morning, only two weeks into her confinement, she paced about the chamber restlessly, her hand on her back.

"Do take down a letter for me, Frances," she said. "I would like Cromwell to help a priest whose plea I received this morning. He is quite zealous, poor man, and the monks continuously fine him. I will be indeed happy when these monks and bishops are put into their places. Heavens, Frances, I have seen priests feast from solid gold plate every day while the parish goes hungry, both for food and spiritual guidance."

"Yes, Your Grace," I murmured, scribbling down the requisite words. Anne always grew incensed when she learned of a reformist parson being persecuted.

"I want him to—"

She broke off. I glanced up. Anne was staring at me, eyes wide, but she looked straight through me.

I flung down the pen and paper and ran to her. "My lady, are you ill?"

She continued to stare, her dark eyes wide like a startled doe's. And then something splashed to the stones at her feet. She moved away, dazed, and gazed down at a wide wet patch on the floor. I saw blood in the water.

She put her hands to her belly and gave a loud cry.

Fear shot through me. I dashed to the door of the inner chamber and shouted, "Help, help, the queen."

My cries brought the midwives and the matrons at a run. They poured into the room and surrounded Anne, who stood half bent over, panting.

"The prince is coming," I said hysterically.

The most experienced of the midwives put her hands on Anne's distended stomach. Anne threw back her head and cried out, her face covered with a sheen of perspiration.

"He is indeed," the woman proclaimed. Her face creased with worry. "It is a bit early."

I bit my lip. Everyone in the kingdom assumed that Anne and Henry had not consummated their love until January, when they'd wed. I knew better. I remembered the cold tower room in Calais, when Henry had at last drawn Anne into his arms. I remembered our leisurely journey back from France and through the countryside of England when Anne and Henry had been almost constantly together.

I knew that the prince had likely been conceived in the first days of December when Anne and Henry were tasting their first love. The child was not early. In fact, if anything, he was a bit late.

The chambers exploded with activity. The midwives shooed me away and half carried the queen back to her bed. They stripped her clothes from her body and got her settled into the great bed of state, covering her with the linens brought for the purpose.

I hovered, uncertain what to do. When my cousin had dropped out her babies, all three of them, she had squalled for a few hours, then pushed them into the hands of the midwife. My aunt habitually spent her daughter's labors in a swoon, always certain my cousin would die.

I now understood my aunt's fears. Anne moaned in grievous pain. I hung onto the bedpost, fearing I'd have to watch the life drain out of her while she tried to bring the prince into the world.

The midwives took over with smooth confidence. Anne

might be queen, but in this chamber, they reigned. The two midwives discussed, their wimpled heads together, Anne's condition and the time it was likely to take. If Anne heard them, she made no sign.

They made her comfortable among the pillows and pressed their hands to her belly when the pains were greatest. They seemed smiling and at ease. My throat was tight with worry.

"Frances," Anne said. She held out her hand to me. I took it. Her fingers were cold and damp. "I will not die, Frances." She looked at me with heavy-lidded eyes. "I promise this."

"No, Your Grace."

"You will not let me. You will hold onto me and keep me anchored."

"Yes, Your Grace." Tears slid from my eyes.

"Would you like a child, Frances?"

I sniffled. "No."

That brought a smile to her wan face. "Yes, you would. A strong boy to show to his father. And then you would know that your life was complete."

My cousin's brats had never seemed to make her life complete. She was fond of the things, but each one seemed only to make her existence more difficult.

It was different, I supposed, if one were queen.

Anne held my hand all through that hot morning and into afternoon. Another lady had taken word to the gentlemen of the chamber, who had run with it to the king's men. Henry had been busily planning many festivities, including a grand joust, to welcome the baby prince.

I babbled this to Anne when she begged me to talk. We laughed at the gentlemen and imagined them jousting and falling from their horses.

The afternoon waxed, the sun shining strong behind the hangings. Near three o'clock, one midwife had Anne's bare leg hooked over her shoulder. The other midwife hovered with cloths. I held a basin in shaking fingers, sloshing water over my brocade gown.

Anne let out a scream that shook the room. The midwives seemed to find this encouraging. "Not long now, Your Grace."

I saw the child, its head jammed against her opening like a log in a too-narrow stream. I stared, fascinated. "He has red hair," I announced, awed.

Anne began to laugh. The midwife shot an annoyed glance at me.

Anne's laugh become another wail. Her face turned bright red, and she squeezed her eyes shut. She clenched her fists and gave one final, heartrending push.

The baby slid free, out into the warm September afternoon, and landed in the midwife's outstretched arms.

Quickly she cleared its nose and mouth, and the infant drew in its first breath. Its angry cry split the air, a long-drawn-out howl that proclaimed this infant would be a monarch to be feared.

I, the midwives, Anne, and the other ladies in the chamber began to laugh.

"Blessed be," I said, wiping tears from my face. "He is lively, Your Grace. And certainly healthy."

The midwife who had caught the prince went quiet at my words. "Aye, the babe is strong."

She looked worried. I stopped laughing. "What is it?"

Anne half sat up. "What is the matter? I want my child." She stretched out her arms.

The midwife looked at her companion and pulled back the cloth in which she'd caught the child. The other midwife's face fell.

"What is it?" Anne said in panic. "Tell me at once. Frances, make them tell me."

The midwife did not answer. She came around the bed, the infant half unwrapped. The poor, rather messy mite roared, its face red with Henry-like rage.

The midwife placed the baby in Anne's arms. As Anne gathered it to her, I saw what had so distressed the midwife.

The baby was healthy, large, and robust. It had a shock of red hair, pink skin, a wide mouth, and tiny, perfect fingers.

She was also, quite clearly, not a boy.

Anne bent over the princess, her eyes full of tears. "Not your fault," she said, kissing the little one on the forehead. "It is not your fault."

THE king canceled the jousts. Jousts, I gathered, were only appropriate for the birth of a prince.

The other festivities, however, went as planned. In the chapel at Greenwich, the choirs sang Te Deum, the heralds proclaimed that the heir had been born, letters flew far and wide to announce the safe birth, and the king rejoiced that the princess and her mother were healthy.

The princess was certainly vigorous. Her wails could split my ears, and we ladies smiled at one another when we heard them. A loud baby meant a strong baby.

She had fine curls of red hair, a plump body, fingers that could seize with a powerful grip, and a tiny, amazingly expressive face.

She resembled Henry excessively, and this fact kept Anne's hopes high. "She is his child," she'd say with a smile when the babe's demanding yells kept us jumping night and day. "I have borne a strong and healthy babe. I can do so again."

Her confidence shone, but outside her chambers, I heard the whispers of disappointment. Anne had not fulfilled her role as queen. Was God displeased that Henry had put aside his rightful wife? Those who might have switched their allegiance to Anne had she borne a prince, now edged back to the side of Catherine.

The christening fell on that Wednesday, the tenth of September. The princess had been born on an auspicious day, the day before the feast of the nativity of the Virgin Mary, which promised the child a bright future. Anne and Henry chose the name Elizabeth—through a flurry of messages and letters; the two did not see one another—after Anne's mother of the same name, and Henry's mother, Elizabeth of York.

The procession to the church of the Observant Friars

began at Anne's chamber door, although neither Anne nor Henry attended. Anne was still in confinement, and Henry wanted to step back and let Elizabeth gather all the attention.

Many of the great ladies of the land were there, including the Dowager Duchess of Norfolk, the Marchioness of Exeter, and the Dowager Marchioness of Dorset, who became her godmothers. Mary Howard went along, and so did I, although I could not count myself a great lady. No one noticed me, in any case, among the finery and the highest ladies and gentlemen of the land.

The church had been transformed. Red cloth hung from the walls, and railings had been erected around the church to keep the spectators back. A huge silver baptismal font stood in the center of a platform, and a canopy of gold and red hung over it. The church blazed with candles.

Elizabeth was not the hoped-for boy child, but she was still Henry's heir and evidence of his fertility. Anne's supporters, most notably her brother and the archbishop, said audibly that where Anne could produce a healthy girl, she could produce a healthy boy. Surely the next child would be the prince. The whispers of Anne's detractors might continue, but the words of the archbishop and George Boleyn carried much weight.

I helped undress Elizabeth behind a drape, then the Dowager Duchess of Norfolk carried her out. The archbishop raised Elizabeth above the font, speaking the service. Then he wet his fingers and traced the cross on Elizabeth's forehead, baptizing her in the name of the Father, Son, and Holy Spirit.

The archbishop then thrust a candle into Elizabeth's hand, and the dowager duchess helped her to hold it. At that moment, five hundred torches flared to life and trumpets blasted. My heart swelled with the light and music.

The torchlit procession traveled back to Anne's chambers, and she received her child with a smile of joy and pride. Small Elizabeth had impressed the nobles of England, and Anne knew it.

We had a celebration then with feasting and wine and

music, and all of Greenwich was merry. I imagined they were merry in London, as well, because the king had ordered that wine be served free to all. Whether the citizens of London acknowledged the princess or not, I was certain they acknowledged the free wine.

Anne emerged from her cushioned chambers several weeks later, after a purification ceremony called churching, and again took up the mantle of being queen.

Elizabeth had a grand suite of rooms in Greenwich and was looked after by a wet nurse and a bevy of ladies. Anne visited her whenever she could, nearly bursting with pride at the lovely daughter she had borne.

Other than that, the routine of court went on as usual.

Anne's influence extended not only to helping reformist priests, but also to making advantageous marriages for her friends and family. Anne Savage, who had attended the queen at her wedding at York Place, married Baron Berkeley. Mary Howard, my friend, was to marry the Duke of Richmond and Somerset.

The duke was Henry Fitzroy, the king's son by his former mistress, Bessie Blount. Richmond was tall and redhaired with a sunny smile and a boisterous nature. He was so like the king that no one questioned who was his sire. Not being legitimate, Richmond would never inherit the kingdom, but he had much wealth and power, and was an excellent catch.

Anne caught him for Mary Howard. The king liked Mary, who was pretty and sweet and well-mannered. Anne convinced Henry to waive the large dowry that the Duke of Norfolk, Mary's father, would have had to pay for so advantageous a match. This pleased the duke but infuriated his wife, the duchess. She hated any of Anne's schemes and made certain that everyone in England knew it.

And so I had the pleasure of being a bridesmaid at Mary Howard's wedding.

Mary was fourteen. She gripped my hand as we waited in an antechamber for the ceremony to begin. "Frances," she whispered. "I do not know what to do."

" 'Tis simple," I replied. "You stand before the priest, and he speaks for what seems hours, and then His Grace, Richmond, gives you a ring, and you are married."

Her fingers clamped mine. "I do not mean that. I mean in the wedding bed."

"Oh," I answered. I had nothing to say, because other than knowing that the woman and man drew the curtains around the bed and then joined together with breathy sighs, I had no idea myself.

As a country girl, I was acquainted with the method in which sheep and horses and cows mated, and once I'd glimpsed my cousin and her young husband in the meadow. However, what truly happened between a man and woman, I did not know. One of Anne's ladies had giggled to me that one did not even need to completely remove one's clothing. I had remarked that that must be a mercy, because then no one need catch cold. The lady had thought me quite funny.

"I know," Margaret Douglas said. She smiled her dazzling smile, her red hair made still more luxurious by jewels and a white satin hood. "A man is powerful until he wants a woman. Then he is weak. Quite weak."

"How can that be?" I asked, curious.

"Because his wanting fills his mind. He will do anything for it. A woman can use that to her advantage. It is our strength."

I thought of a few of Henry's courtiers who did get hot looks in their eyes and follow pretty women about, but I could not believe this a universal truth.

Jack Carlisle, for instance, would never stoop to pursuing a woman for bed games. He had kissed me several times, but never looked in danger of pursuing me. I did not interpret that as an insult; I simply knew that Jack was incapable of giving in to base lust.

Mary's grandmother bustled in to fetch Mary, and Margaret and I ceased giggling over men and the wedding bed. Mary still looked worried.

She needn't have. As both she and Richmond were only

fourteen, they did not consummate the marriage at once. Mary slept without him that night, with me to keep her company. Three years later, Richmond was dead, without Mary ever going to his bed.

Twelve

⁂

THE TRIUMPH OF MY MOTHER, OR, I AM MARRIED

CHRISTMAS 1533

MARY Howard's marriage to the king's son seemed to set up a flurry of matrimonial intrigues at court. Strange as it may seem, I became caught in them.

My mother had ceased speaking to me, of course, but my aunt kept up a stream of gossipy letters, so I knew of everything that went on at home. In November, she informed me that no less than two gentlemen of the king's household had written to my father asking permission to court me.

"Your father turned them both away, dear Frances," my aunt's letter prattled. "Although I can understand no reason why. Both are rich, and I imagine quite handsome, or they would not be at court."

I could not imagine which gentlemen she meant. Certainly none had ever hinted marriage at me. A few had responded to my flirtations, but no gentleman seemed in danger of pledging himself to me.

I put away the letter and thought no more of it.

In December, Elizabeth and her new grand household moved to Hatfield, not far from Hunsdon. Not long after that, Henry sent his other daughter, Princess Mary, to live there with her.

Mary went with reluctance. When Anne read a letter from her uncle Norfolk that Mary had arrived in Hatfield but refused to acknowledge Elizabeth as princess, she grew wild with rage.

"How dare she?" she snapped. She flung the letter at me. "Read that."

I skimmed the pages. Norfolk wrote in a priggish style, much like himself, his words filled with annoyance. He had bade Mary pay respects to Princess Elizabeth when she arrived. Mary had replied, "I know of no other princess in England but myself." She did, however, say she would condescend to address Elizabeth as sister.

"I will box her ears," Anne cried. "If she vows to insult me, she will be punished."

Anne did send harsh letters to Hatfield instructing the new steward of the household, Sir John Shelton, and his wife to be very strict with Mary. They should confine her to her chamber if she refused to eat at table. If she insisted on being called "princess," she should be slapped.

I thought this a bit harsh on the poor girl, who was very near to me in age, but Anne's anger came of great frustration. If Anne had borne a son, Mary's disobedience could have made little difference. But the question of who was heir was still a touchy one. Mary and her supporters viewed Elizabeth as the illegitimate child and herself as the legitimate one. And they always would.

ANNE tried to put aside her frustrations by lavishing gifts on her daughter for Christmas and presiding over the festivities at Greenwich.

Greenery lined the halls of the Greenwich palace for Yule; purple arras hung from the galleries, and boughs twined the railings. The king lit candles every Sunday for Advent, and we feasted.

The nights we dined in the hall, Anne and Henry sat

close together. He often laid his thick hand on hers and shot her looks of longing. I knew that Anne wanted to be pregnant again, and the manner in which the king looked after her told me that she soon would be.

Rumors, of course, flew at court that the king was already tiring of Anne, that he had given up on her because she'd borne a girl child, that he had taken another mistress. If that were true, I missed the signs. Henry was immensely proud of Elizabeth and was even now negotiating to get her married off in some match that would be advantageous to him. He had been pleased at how easily Anne had delivered Elizabeth and reasoned that the next child would be a boy.

Henry's eye roved, yes; he was that sort of man. But if he had affairs, no one knew with whom, and he certainly stayed often in his wife's bed. At the Christmas celebration, Anne's face glowed with womanly satisfaction. She was still admired, and Henry loved her.

The hall was hot and lit with braziers and a huge burning log in the center of the room. Enormous roasts of pork and beef filled the tables, accompanied by pies both savory and sweet. We drank wine and mead and laughed at the king's fool, who tumbled this way and that and managed to fall into a barrel of ale and cover himself with it. Mark Smeaton played and sang and cast hungry looks at all the women.

I danced in a little pageant we ladies put on for the king and queen. I was one of the angels who'd brought the news of Christ's birth to the shepherds. I much doubted the angel would twirl bawdily and wave embroidered robes to the music of virginals and hurdy-gurdies, but I played along.

I danced among the tables, the ladies and I raining apples and sweetmeats upon the gentlemen and nobles. A hand caught my draperies as I glided past. George Boleyn released me and smiled as I whirled away.

My heart beat hard and fast. His smiles had increased of late, and I thought that perhaps he'd turned his interest to me at last.

Jack, as usual, was all frowns, not smiles. I deliberately danced to him and emptied an armful of apples into his lap. He scowled, but the courtiers and king's privy gentle-men laughed loud and long.

At the end of the room, I danced out, hot and breathless. The courtyard was freezing, but the air felt good on my flushed skin. I walked about, my heart beating hard, and laughed up through the arched courtyard to the leaden black sky. The December night was cold, but inside was warmth and joy, and I was part of that warmth. It wrapped me, and I reveled in it.

A hand caught me and whirled me to a brick pillar of the courtyard wall. I gasped. I had one wild hope that George Boleyn had followed me, but then saw that it was not he. The gentleman who'd seized me was Thomas Seward, an obscure young man who'd recently come to court. He had a spotted face and bad breath, and I did not like him.

I suddenly realized we were very much alone and that my draperies were not as modest as I would have liked. His narrow eyes roved me, making me feel unclean.

Swallowing my alarm, I gave him a freezing glance that I'd learned from Anne. "Excuse me, sir. I must return to my lady."

His sour breath poured over me. "Frances Pierce. You are to marry me."

My heart near stopped. "You are forward and out of place, sir. It is not for me to say whom I marry."

"I know." He smiled. His black hair hung in hanks from under a pushed-back velvet cap. "My father wrote yours. Your father had the audacity to write back that the match was unsuitable. He, a countrified baronet."

I blessed my father's perception and tact. If he had given his permission for me to marry Thomas Seward, I think I would have died.

"If I am daughter of a countrified baronet, what interest can you have in me?" I countered.

"You are close to the queen." He neared me until less than a handspan of space existed between us. "And she has much influence. The people of England hate her, but the court and Cromwell listen. That is much more important."

I tried to step away from him, but he hemmed me in. "Why should you think I'd intercede with the queen for you?"

"Because I will be your husband, and you will obey me."

I raised my chin. "You will not. My father turned away your offer. Why you even speak to me is beyond my comprehension."

He seized a handful of my long hair. "Because when I compromise you, you will be forced to marry me. You would not like to be sent from court in disgrace, would you?"

Fear pounded through me. I remembered Jack's words on the summer night in Windsor: *If I decided to take your virtue, at this moment and in this place, could you stop me?*

I could not have stopped him, I realized. And I could not stop Thomas Seward. If I screamed, I would be ruined. I had come dancing out here in my draperies after I'd thrown apples at gentlemen like a wanton. Anne always struggled to keep her ladies pious and calm—a mighty task—and I suddenly wished I had listened to her.

What would Anne do? Blame me? Banish me? With cold certainty I realized that if Anne were angered, she'd turn her back on me. I'd seen her do it to others, and I'd foolishly believed her justified.

"You will not have me," I tried.

He pressed me into the wall, hands heavy on my shoulders. "I will. Henry Norris also wanted you, but the king opposed the match. But I will have you."

I pushed at him. He slapped my hands away. He fumbled at my breasts, and I grew sick with loathing. He terrified me, but I was more terrified to scream.

My entire life focused to that moment. Everything I had done, everything I had gained, everything I had learned was to be shattered by this foul man and my own folly. A pit of ruin gaped before me and I teetered on its edge. If Thomas Seward raped me, he would destroy me.

A strong hand seized Seward's shoulder and hurled him away from me. I fell into the wall and slid down the stones, scraping skin as my legs folded under me.

I brushed the hair from my eyes and looked up to see Seward hanging from the grasp of Jack Carlisle. Jack's face was red with rage, and Seward regarded him in fear. I do not know what Jack said to him, because my ears rang, and I could not hear.

Jack shook the loathsome Seward like a dog and flung him away. Seward hit the wall. He scrambled to stay upright, then, eyes wide, he regained his feet and scuttled away into the darkness.

I sat folded in on myself, my breathing unsteady. I saw Jack's feet in fine brocade shoes next to me, and his firm calves in green and white hose. The sight was somehow comforting, and I found I could not raise my eyes to look anywhere else.

"What have you done, Frances?" he demanded, his voice harsh. "Why did you lead him out here?"

His sharp words cut through my terror. "I did not lead him," I said. "He followed me."

"What were you thinking, dancing out here alone in the dark?"

"I wanted air."

Because he did not reach to help me up, I pushed my draperies out of the way and struggled to my feet. I wanted to run away into the palace and not stop until I reached the safety of my chamber, but my feet would not move.

"I am sorry, Jack." Tears filled my eyes.

"Thank Jesu I saw him leave the hall. I did not like the way he watched you. Then I saw you smile in that coy way and run out, daring any to follow you."

Daring George to follow me, I thought. *Only George.* But George never had.

"Please do not scold me, I cannot bear it." I sniffled. "You are wise, and I will always listen to you."

"Frances." He touched my cheek, wiping away a tear. "I do not believe you, you know."

"Always," I promised. "You are wise and I am foolish."

He sighed. "I wish I could take your word. You are far too impetuous."

"I know. My mother said it would lead me to trouble."

He was silent a moment, watching me. I knew I should return to the hall, but suddenly, I did not want to face all the people and merrymaking again, especially if they, like Jack, had seen Thomas Seward follow me out here. I had ruined my reputation, I realized, simply by leaving the hall.

Through a haze of tears, I realized that Jack was speaking again.

"I am glad you think me wise, Frances. That will make it easier for you to accept me as your husband."

I was still an entire minute as his words penetrated my senses. I looked up. "Husband?"

"I sent a messenger to your father. I received his reply this morning. He is willing to negotiate with me to be wed to you."

"Wed?" I repeated the word in panic.

"Yes. He is willing to give me a bit of land in place of a large dowry."

My father had always worried about my dowry, not having enough to make an advantageous match for me. I stared at Jack, my mouth dry. "But why should you be wed to me?"

"Because you need to be married. It will keep you from harm."

I gaped at him. The man who would one day take me to wife had always been a comfortably vague figure, someone handsome and wealthy who would simply materialize when we stood before the priest. I had never connected that husband with a real person, and certainly never Jack Carlisle.

"Perhaps," I said, "but why to you?"

"Why not to me?"

A thousand reasons, I thought. I grasped at one. "You do not like me."

"You are incorrect."

I could not meet his gaze any longer, so studied the gold embroidery that crisscrossed his doublet. I touched a thread on his chest and felt his heart beat hard beneath it. "If you marry me," I argued, "if I become your wife, then you will tire of me. You will take a mistress and break my heart."

"You read the future, do you?"

"It is the way of gentlemen. Every woman knows it."

He tilted my face upward. "I believe I will be satisfied enough with my wife."

"But your wife will be me."

He smiled gently. "At least you have agreed to that part of it."

I pulled away. "I have not agreed. I was not even informed."

His smile vanished, and he became cool Jack Carlisle again. "The matter is settled. I had hoped to discuss this with you, but Seward spoiled that. He may choose to tell the tale of this night far and wide, so we had better marry quickly."

My alarm returned. "How quickly?"

"The banns will be read this Sunday. We should be wed after New Year's."

The world fell away from me. I clung to one last hope. "Anne will never let me go. She needs me."

"Anne is pleased with the match. She believes it will be advantageous to you, and she is correct. I will be an earl, and your station will be elevated. The king also likes the idea. He finds you charming, and it will remove me from the field."

"Field?" I asked, puzzled. "What field?"

"The matrimonial field. There are several females of royal blood that I might try to snatch, such as Margaret Douglas. I believe Henry wants me safely out of the way."

My heated blood cooled slightly. "That is a bit insulting."

"It is the way of things. You are not highborn, and I am not important."

I stepped away from him. The cold wind swirled my draperies, and I no longer liked the chill. "That is why we are well matched? We are the stray dogs no one wants?"

"I would not say so. And no, that is not the only reason."

"I do not think I wish to marry you, Jack Carlisle. You are a prig."

His familiar look of impatience settled on his features. "The matter is finished. We wᵢ l wed at New Year's." His voice softened. "I will ensure you do not regret it."

"I believe I already regret it."

I glared at him, groping for more words to throw at him, but I suddenly burst into tears. I was angry at myself for crying in front of him, but I could not stop myself. I cried tears of rage and frustration and sorrow at the end of my hazy dream.

I thought Jack would scold me, but instead he drew me into his arms, pressing me to his broad chest. He tumbled my hair and dropped a kiss to the top of my head.

"Hush," he said in a strangely gentle voice. "You will not regret, Frances. I promise."

THUS it was that I stood in the queen's chamber the day after New Year's and married Jack Carlisle.

The queen had given me a fine New Year's present, as she had all her ladies, a palfrey of my own with the saddle to go with it. I longed to leap onto this lovely horse and finely tooled furniture and ride far away as fast as I could.

I got married instead.

Anne had dressed me in a kirtle of yellow satin with an overrobe of cloth of gold. Intricate embroidery covered my sleeves and the kirtle, and my hair hung in a honey-brown wave down my back. Mary Howard, now the Duchess of Richmond, and Margaret Douglas had brushed my hair into a shimmering wave and pinned a hood to my head. They had enjoyed themselves dressing me, while I'd stood numbly in the midst of them.

Anne herself clasped a jeweled necklace about my throat. She kissed my cheek, her lips warm. "You are lovely, Frances. May you and your husband have as much happiness in your marriage as I know with mine."

Anne had begun to believe herself with child again. Her midwives reserved judgment, but she was ill in the mornings and had missed her courses, and would not be swayed in this opinion. She considered herself destined to bear the king's son.

To emphasize this, she had given Henry as a New Year's gift a gold and bejeweled fountain. Around the base of this fountain three maidens hovered, water streaming from their nipples. I found it an odd gift to give a man, but Mistress Marshall explained that it was a symbol of fertility.

I clung to Anne after she straightened my jewelry. "Will you still love me?"

"My dear, cleaving yourself to a husband is not the end of things. Nothing will change. You will still wait upon me, and he upon the king. You are old enough to share his bed, and you will, that is the only difference."

"It is a great difference," I mumbled.

She laughed, as did the other married ladies, and they began to give me ribald advice.

"If you hold your legs tightly, it does not hurt so much," Mary Carey said.

"Not even with a king?" Margaret Douglas remarked, pretending innocence.

Mary shot her a venomous look. "Guard your tongue, my lady."

"Margaret," Anne chided. I could not decide whether Anne were angry at her for mentioning the fact that Mary had been the king's mistress, or because Margaret meant to hurt Mary. Margaret fell silent but looked pleased with herself.

Mistress Marshall said, "With most men, it is so quick, you scarce know it happened at all."

The married women whooped. I did not know what to make of this.

"Be happy if your husband notices you at all," Jane Rochford, George's wife, said sourly. A few ladies shot her looks of sympathy.

"Sir John Carlisle is a handsome man," Anne said. "You are lucky in that. Thank God for it."

"As handsome as Northumberland?" Margaret Douglas murmured. I stared at her in horror, hoping Anne hadn't heard. Gossip implied that Anne had never fallen out of love with the Earl of Northumberland, whom she'd nearly married before she'd met the king. Northumberland was now married himself, most unhappily so, if I believed what I heard.

If Anne noted Lady Margaret's dig, she said nothing. The other ladies began discussing how I might encourage my husband to finish more quickly, squealing with laughter at their own bawdiness.

Anne straightened my gown, and I grew more nervous. I had no knowledge of men, and Jack was not the most patient of them. The idea that I might disappoint worried me a bit. What if he should find me wanting and callously ignore me, as George Boleyn did to Jane? I had always viewed this as Jane's own fault, because she had a sneering disposition, but what if Jack viewed me the same?

When the ladies led me out to the chamber where the gentleman waited, my insides churned, and my mouth was dry as dust.

None of my family was present. My aunt had written to me, saying that my mother was much better but would not think of coming to Greenwich. My mother approved, however, of Jack Carlisle. She had known his mother, the Countess of Pennington, who had been a very proper lady. She had heard that Jack had reformist tendencies, but he might be made to see his error.

My aunt gushed on, congratulating me on finding the son of an earl, and a handsome one at that. My father had written to tell me that Jack Carlisle was a splendid fellow. They all seemed to love Jack.

I was the one, of course, who had to enter the chamber where he waited and marry him.

He wore green and gold brocade, his sleeves slashed to reveal green and white satin, his colors. His cap was black, his dark beard neatly trimmed against his face.

I stepped next to him, my legs quivering under my heavy skirts. He took my hand. He wore gloves, but the warmth of the cloth could not penetrate my frozen skin.

I remember little of the ceremony. The priests spoke

Latin, which I knew little of, though Jack murmured responses as appropriate. Jack slid a ring with a very large ruby onto my finger, then the priest blessed us, and then we had Mass. At the end of the ceremony, I found myself married.

Anne had insisted on a feast for us. It was nothing near as lavish as any of her own spectacles, but she'd ordered a large banquet table spread with food in the main hall, and musicians, and dancing.

I could eat little, but gulped warmed wine in desperate thirst. Jack sat next to me, seemingly at ease, taking the ribbing from his fellows with good nature.

Anne pressed me to dance, and Jack and I did steps in the center of a circle of married gentlemen and ladies, while the unmarried danced on the outside. Even Anne and the king joined with the married couples.

I could not feel my feet. Jack surreptitiously pushed me this way and that, and people remarked that I seemed to be in bright spirits. Jack kept hold of my hand, I noticed, near the entire night.

All too soon, the dancing ended, the elderly went off to their beds, and the ladies swooped upon me.

Laughing, they took me back to Anne's chamber, where they undressed me. Off came my beautiful cloth of gold skirts and satin sleeves. Off came my embroidered stomacher and bodice and hood. Off came my underskirts and stockings, and finally, my chemise, leaving me with nothing.

They wrapped a robe around my bare skin, then I was propelled, quite against my will, through doors to another chamber, in the center of which stood a bed.

This bed had been decorated with ribbons and greens and flowers that streamed from the bedposts and the tester. Bedding of thick quilts and linens filled it, and a garland twisted across the headboard. A brazier warmed the room, and braces of candles cast a warm glow.

The ladies had given me a nightcap to keep my hair confined, but they made me relinquish the robe.

"In you go," Mary Carey sang, and she pulled the covers back for me.

I climbed beneath, drawing the warm coverlet over my nudity. My arms had gone all over chills. The ladies settled down to keep me company, giggling and laughing over their jokes until I nearly ran mad.

I think it would not have been so bad had Jack come in alone. But he, too, was accompanied by a horde of gentlemen, all of them tipsy. He was dressed in nothing but a long garment that looked somewhat like a nightshirt, except that it was velvet and embroidered. His eyes held a slightly glazed look, as though he had partaken in a bit of wine himself.

He wore no nightcap, and his hair, always curly, twisted in unruly locks. He glanced swiftly at me hunkered under the blanket and turned to his comrades.

"My friends," he said. He held up his hands, and the gentlemen at last quieted to hear what he had to say. "My friends," he repeated, then lowered his hands. "Go away."

After a second of stunned silence, the gentlemen burst into laughter. "He is keen," Henry Norris said. "He is very keen."

The others made more bawdy jokes, then mercifully, another said, "Let us leave them to it."

The gentlemen clapped Jack on the shoulders and at last trickled out of the room. Mary Howard smoothed my hair one last time and hugged me tight, before she followed the other ladies out the door.

I found myself alone in my wedding bed with my husband.

I felt his gaze on me, but I could not bring myself to meet it. There I sat, fine Frances, now Lady Carlisle, my knees drawn to my chest and the covers pulled to my chin.

I expected Jack to chastise me, to get on with the business of being a displeased husband, but he only looked at me.

"The room is cold," he said.

My teeth chattered. "I suppose."

Jack turned and added more fuel to the brazier, which crackled and burned white hot.

He returned to the bed. In one motion, he stripped off his robe and stood bare before me.

In my childhood, I had seen the naked bodies of my father and my younger cousins, but I had paid them no mind. One does not notice the men of one's own family. The nakedness of one's husband is much different. In the moment before he burrowed into the bed with me, I noted that Jack's body was lean and taut and not displeasing.

Because I did not seem disposed to lie down, he moved to sit next to me. "Frances."

"I do not know what to do," I said stiffly. "I am sorry. I do not know what to do."

He brushed a lock of hair from my face. "Look at me."

I did so. His dark eyes held a watchfulness.

"I am not afraid," I told him. "At least, I do not believe so. But I am not schooled."

He could have laughed at me, but he kept his mouth straight. "There is nothing to fear, Frances. 'Tis only your Jack."

"Are you?" I asked. "Mine?"

He traced my cheek. "Always."

He kissed me, and ever so gently, pulled the cover from my grasp.

I do not recall what I expected, but later I lay with my head on his warm shoulder, my body pliant and heavy, and thought myself a blessed woman. He lay without speaking, his breathing soft, one hand resting on my abdomen.

In the last hour everything had changed for me. I was aware of many things: the difference between being a maid and a woman, the wonder that such emotion could ravish my body, and the realization that I was not in love with George Boleyn.

I never had been in love with him. I had been infatuated and silly. I thought of the poetry I had written, and blushed. My head had been turned by a handsome face, coupled with the fact that he was Anne's brother. I loved Anne; therefore, I must love George.

But George, for all his flirtation, his charm, and his skilled discourse, was not the man I wanted.

"Have I conceived?" I asked my husband.

He stroked my hair with a languid hand. "Hmm? I do not know. It is too soon to know."

"I thought that if I felt such joy, then surely I had conceived."

He gave a rumbling laugh, warm under my ear. "That does not always follow."

"It ought to." I thought a moment, enjoying the comfort of his body. "When we have a child, what shall we call it?"

"You are in a hurry," he said, amused.

"Names are important."

He bent one arm behind his head, his skin dark against the linens. "The first son is often named for the father. For a daughter, I am partial to Frances."

I raised my head. He watched me, his eyes dark, lids heavy. "If I have only girl children, will you put me aside?"

"Very likely not."

"Boy children are important. A girl needs a dowry, and she takes your wealth to another family. Believe me, this troubled my father as long as I can remember. The king put aside his wife because she bore no sons. I cannot help but wonder if you will do the same."

He gave me a bemused look. "You mistake my character, Frances. What children come will come. If none at all come, well, then, they will not."

"That is why you married me," I argued. "So that I will have your children."

"There are many reasons for marriage. Children are only one of them."

I bit my lip. "I can sew your shirts, though I am not expert with a needle."

"I did not marry to gain a seamstress, either. Although I will take pleasure in your needlework."

"I *can* brew ale," I went on. "My aunt and my mother's housekeeper taught me. It is palatable. We may not have chance to sample it, however, if we remain at court."

He traced my cheek with warm fingers. "I did not necessarily marry you for your ale or your needlework or your ability to bear sons."

"No?" I liked the way he touched me. "Then why?"

He smiled. "I wished to marry a young woman called Frances."

"Oh," I said. I felt pleased that perhaps, just perhaps, he liked me. "I am quite plain," I pointed out.

"No, you are not." He put his arm around me. "Now, I would like you to kiss me, if it is not too much trouble."

It was not too much trouble. I rather enjoyed kissing Jack. He tasted a bit of wine and cinnamon, and I liked spiced wine.

The kisses led to more joy, for myself and for him, and when I finally fell asleep in his arms, I was strangely contented.

Thirteen

❦

OATHS, PRINCESSES, AND OTHER TROUBLES

SPRING 1534

My life changed only a little after my marriage. I still served Anne, although now I was known as Lady Carlisle. In time, I would become Countess of Pennington.

A few of the other ladies treated me with more defer-ence after my nuptials, but not all, because most in Anne's court were countesses and duchesses and marchionesses and were not impressed with my new title.

They did tease me remorselessly the first few weeks of my marriage, asking me about my handsome Jack, and passing lewd remarks over my head until I wanted to scream. My blushes and confusion only delighted them.

"What is the difference between Frances and a stream of water?" one would ask. "Very little, because Sir John becomes soaked when he enters both."

"What is Frances's favorite time of day?" another teased. "It does not matter, as long as she is in bed with Jack."

My mother would hardly approve.

Anne admonished them, because she prided herself on keeping her ladies modest, but she tried in vain. A gaggle of ladies with the opportunity to talk about men cannot be silenced.

Jack, still a gentleman of the privy chamber, attended his king as usual. We were given a chamber at Greenwich to share, but much of the time, Anne wanted me to stay beside her just as Jack was required to stay with the king.

Anne was quite happy those early days of 1534, because as I said, she had conceived again, and was certain that this time, the child would be a son.

"I feel it to be so," she told me. "I had a healthy daughter, who grows rapidly by the day. My son will be as healthy."

She spoke with confidence, but I noted a glimmer of worry in her eyes. For a year, Anne had been the promise of a new England, of an heir to the throne who would stop the machinations of others to seize the crown when Henry grew weak and old. If she'd borne a son, the child would have symbolized her complete success.

Now, she still had to fight. Catherine's supporters had not gone away, and even Henry speculated that a woman of Catherine's courage could very well make things difficult if she chose. She was the daughter of Isabella of Spain, who herself had stepped over the bodies of half siblings to reach the throne. Isabella had succeeded in taming the ungovernable and violent nobles of Spain, bending them to her will. Catherine, in spirit, took after her mother.

With this in mind, Henry, that spring, busied himself ensuring that Catherine and his daughter Mary were cut out completely from inheriting the English throne.

Thomas Cromwell and his supporters in Parliament drafted a law that said that the children of Henry and Anne Boleyn would be first in succession for the crown. This agreement became known as the Act of Succession, and I know of few other documents that caused as much tragedy and bloodshed.

The Act of Succession was to ensure that Princess Elizabeth, if no sons came along, would be supported as the heir to the throne. Not supporting her, or supporting Mary instead, would be, quite simply, treason.

At the end of March, when the act was complete, Henry forced every man in England to bend his knee and swear to it. Denying it meant denying Henry.

Even my husband Jack bowed his head and took the oath. Jack did not like the fact that Mary had been reduced to nothing; after all, her parents had assumed the marriage legitimate for nearly twenty years, and children of such marriages were not considered illegitimate. That was canon law, he tried to explain to me.

"I took the oath," he told me in our chamber, his face red with anger. "I was not the only man who promised with reluctance. But I thought of you, and our family, and I took it."

I folded my hands across my stomacher, worried. "You had no choice."

"Oh, there was a choice," he said bitterly. "And I made mine. Others refused. Bishop Fisher and Sir Thomas More. They will be arrested, of course."

Sir Thomas had been chancellor of England, but he'd resigned when Henry had first been named supreme head of the English Church two years ago. I had always been angry with Sir Thomas for not supporting my lady Anne. But Jack looked troubled, and that troubled me.

"What will happen to him?" I asked.

"He will be tried, and made to answer. Whether refusing the oath will be enough to kill him, remains to be seen."

We were somber the rest of the night.

Anne had little use for Sir Thomas More, or for any friends of Catherine. "He had the chance to support the king, Frances," she said to me. "He did not take it. Now he will pay for being pigheaded."

I did not argue with her.

That spring, however, I had other things than politics to worry about, because I found myself quick with child.

I had no idea of this until one morning in February. After gulping down a hearty breakfast, a sudden wave of nausea struck me, and I barely made it to a basin before I was violently ill. After this bout, I felt much better and ate with gusto the rest of the day.

The next morning, I repeated the pattern, and the next day, and the next. But other than the brief illness in the morning, I felt quite fit. Anne suffered a bit more than I did, which she attributed to her advanced age of thirty or so. But she'd smile, her eyes glowing. "By autumn, Frances, both you and I will have sons." She promised that our children would be playmates, my son the privileged companion of hers.

As if to seal this bargain, in early March Anne took me with her to visit Elizabeth at Hatfield. Hunsdon and my own home lay not far from there, and Anne generously offered to let me ride the few miles to visit my family, but I declined. As disagreeable as Princess Mary might try to make our stay at Hatfield, I opined that a visit to my mother would be even worse.

I had gathered, from the reports Anne received, that Mary, daughter of the stubborn Henry and the equally stubborn Catherine, would rather spit on Elizabeth than serve her. I discovered, when we arrived, that I was quite right.

The winter skies were clear but cold, and I was glad to enter the warmth of the house, which smelled of sweet burning wood and venison for our supper. Anne went at once to see Elizabeth.

In the princess' chambers, she held out her arms and Lady Bryan, Elizabeth's nurse, gave the child to Anne.

"Is she not splendid?" Anne cried.

A cloth cap covered Elizabeth's red hair, and her flailing limbs were draped in wool to keep out the cold. She had pretty dark eyes, and she yawned, bathing us in milky breath and showing one tiny white tooth.

I still opined that the child looked much like Henry. Certainly Elizabeth had her father's stern brow and red face.

"She is splendid," I said.

Lady Bryan smiled. "I told her all the day long that you were coming, Your Grace. Her highness seemed most pleased."

Anne bounced Elizabeth in her arms and cooed to her. She was in danger of becoming as soppy as my aunt over her granddaughters. My own mother, of course, had never shown an interest in babies.

"What of the Lady Mary?" Anne asked.

Lady Bryan's brow clouded. "She reacted to your visit as could be expected. She is in her chamber and will likely stay there. You will not have to subject yourself to her rudeness if you do not wish."

"Humph," Anne said. "She must acknowledge me if she is to remain in her father's good graces. He will not stand treason from his own daughter." She sighed. "The little fool. Why does she defy him, so?"

I agreed that things would be better for Mary if she bowed her head and accepted the will of the king, as the rest of us did. But then, Mary had been princess of England for many years, heir to the throne in absence of any brothers. All that had been stripped from her little by little, until she had nothing left but to be a forced maid to the child who had usurped her.

I understood Mary, I think, better than Anne ever could. Anne possessed an iron-strong will, and so did Mary. Anne could not bear to face such a will in another woman and did not want to fight for acquiescence.

"Send Mary a message," she said, her voice tight. "Tell her that I would very much like to greet her. She is welcome to visit me, and honor me as queen."

I busied myself playing with little Elizabeth's fingers so that Anne would not observe my skepticism. Lady Bryan dispatched the servant with a message, and we had but to wait.

The reply came soon. "I know no queen but my mother," Mary's message said.

Lady Shelton, who looked after Mary, relayed this to us apologetically. Lady Shelton had been employed by Anne's kindness, and she flushed as she related the princess's exact words. "She said that if Lady Pembroke, the king's mistress, wanted to intercede with the king for her, she would welcome it."

"King's mistress, indeed," Anne growled. "Foul-tempered Spanish brat. You shall box her ears for that."

"She is unhappy," Lady Shelton tried.

"She is willful and defiant, and she enjoys her defiance far too much."

I had never seen Anne so angry. Her face grew red and her breathing ragged, and I worried about her unborn child. "Perhaps you should take some wine," I said.

Anne turned a blazing eye to me. "Do not patronize me, Frances Carlisle. I am queen of England, and no whore. I am *queen*."

Lady Shelton, Lady Bryan, and I stood mutely. Anne paced, winter sunlight falling through the heavy window-panes, throwing spangles across her skirts.

She swung around. "I will tame the pride of this unbridled Spanish blood if I must pursue this course to the end of my life. This I vow." She clenched a fist.

We could only reply, "Yes, Your Grace."

Anne's mood stayed foul throughout the visit, which lasted only two days. She sent another message to Mary, but Mary replied similarly: "I know no queen but my mother. The messenger must say Lady Anne requests me, and not confuse me."

"Maddening child," Anne muttered as we rode from Hatfield to return to London. "I swear to you, Frances, she is my death, and I am hers."

She remained in a foul mood and I could do nothing that day and the next to please her.

IN April, Jack told me to ask leave of Anne to accompany him to Gloucestershire to visit his father, the Earl of Pennington.

April rains would be soft in the country, but in London, the streets became channels of mud. I was lucky that I could float in Anne's barge from Greenwich to the Tower, to York Place to Richmond, as Anne willed, but any time I ventured out in London on my own, walking became a sticky business.

I had never been to Gloucestershire, far away near Wales, but I imagined it from what Jack told me. The green Cotswolds would be dusted yellow with spring flowers, and lambs would stagger about the fields, the earth fresh and open.

In London, the river stank, and the bodies that pressed me when I ventured out to shop in Cheapside or Honey Lane stank as much.

But I was a wife now, and needed to set up my household. Jack accompanied me when he could, and did useful things such as carry parcels and pay for what I ordered.

On an April afternoon, Jack met me in Cheapside for such an expedition. When I saw his tall form striding toward me through the crowd, my heart leapt. How I could have been so infatuated with George Boleyn, I scarcely knew. The morning after my wedding to Jack, I'd burnt the poetry I'd written about George, and now I all but ignored the man, despite his frequent visits to Anne.

I had, unfortunately, bad news to relate to Jack. "She does not want me to go," I said glumly.

Jack frowned at me over an ell of linen. "Why ever not? I return every year to Gloucestershire, and I have been given leave. I have been commissioned to speak to gentlemen there who are trying to be reformists, to show them that they have support."

Anne was always talking about wooing those of Gloucestershire to continue her reforms. The west of England had been home to the Lollards years before, and its people retained their reforming zeal, she said. I was not surprised she'd use Jack to help her.

Jack was a bit uneasy with the archbishop's and Anne's heavy-handedness regarding religion, but he did believe in the ideas of reform. But while Anne was happy to let Jack go, she equally wished for me to stay behind.

"She is anxious, she says, for me." I rested my hand on my stomacher, which my pregnancy was just beginning to press outward. "She fears a long journey might hurt me."

The look in his brown eyes told me he shared her concern. "I plan to travel slowly, and rest whenever you feel the need, and even when you do not."

"I believe she is more anxious for herself. She has been ill once or twice this spring, and worries."

"Yes," Jack agreed. As usual, when we were about in the city, Jack and I did not speak the names of our patrons. We did not worry so much for the spies, who probably knew much more about Anne and Henry than either of us ever would, but, alas, much of the populace agreed with Princess Mary about Anne—she was still the pretender, the upstart who had dethroned the true queen.

"I still must go," he explained. He looked troubled. "I do not like to leave you here. I married you to look after you."

"I do not believe the court gentlemen will be interested in me at present," I said lightly. "I am growing quite fat."

His mouth quirked, and his eyes took on a light of pride as they always did when he beheld my thickening body. "It is not the gentlemen. Her position has weakened, and intrigue is rife. Anything you say can be repeated and recorded and twisted to use against her."

"I suppose I can bend my head over my sewing and say not a word," I retorted. I still chafed at Jack's notion that I was too naïve for Anne's court and had better follow his instructions.

"Remaining silent at the wrong time can also be misconstrued," he said.

"Then I will shut myself in a cellar and have food slipped through a slit in the door."

I did not amuse him. He hoisted the parcel I thrust at him and led me on through the warren of market stalls. "What I wish is for you to leave court altogether," he said. "I prefer you to live in Gloucestershire with my family, or at Hunsdon with yours. At Hunsdon, at least I could visit you often."

I dropped my skirts, regardless of the mud. "Leave court?" I asked, aghast. I agreed with him that Henry's court could be a tricky place, but I never played its games.

I served and obeyed Anne and had no other ambition, except to write my poetry, which, by the bye, Jack still did not approve of.

"Yes," replied my pigheaded husband. "You are better suited to a quiet life in the country."

"No, indeed I am not. Ask my mother. As a country miss, I was most disobedient and willful and got myself into all kinds of scrapes. Being at court has made me. I have my own attendants. Kings and queens and ambassadors ask me to entertain them. I should be a dull stick in the country with nothing to do but ply my needle and play the virginal, which I do not do very well."

"You would set up housekeeping and look after my father," Jack replied. "That will keep you far busier than sewing. And you will be seeing to our child. You would also be the lady of the house. I assure you, you would not be a dull stick, as you call it."

I put my hands on my hips. "I do not hear you say that *you* will leave court."

"No."

"Why not? It is just as dangerous for you."

"I know my way about." He pulled me aside as two stout housewives with soiled wimples nearly ran us down. "Henry rewards me well," he said in a low voice, "and I have made a safe marriage. He does not regard me as a threat."

"Do cease reminding me that you married me simply because I am nobody," I said.

He leaned close to me so that none would hear his words. "There was nothing simple in my decision to marry you."

I ought to have been angered, but the warmth of his breath through my veil made me not quite so enraged. I had come to learn that Jack liked to tease me, although I was not yet adept at deciding when he teased and when he did not.

"Your health," someone said loudly, and I was saved from answering him.

We stood near a tavern open to the street. Despite the

mud around it, quite a few gentlemen stood drinking ale or wine, and women lined up to buy ale to take home.

A man with soiled hose who had to hold himself up with the countertop, hefted a cup and slurred, "To His Grace the pope."

"To the king," another proposed. "There is no pope, had you not heard?"

The drunk man blinked. "You speak heresy."

"The king has declared it and so have all the fine gentlemen in Parliament," the second drinker said. He was slightly better dressed, with a surcoat and a thick silver ring. "Is the king a heretic?"

"The pope says so," said another man. "He has been excommunicated."

"Has he noticed?" the wealthy man asked with a cynical smile.

The drunk man looked baffled. Then he brightened. "His mistress is a heretic. On that, the world agrees."

That brought laughter. "Aye. A whore and a heretic. A highborn man should keep his wife at home and out of men's affairs."

Eyes turned to me, because while I was not dressed in the finery I usually wore to wait on Anne, my gown was made of costly wool, my sleeves embroidered, and my cloak trimmed with fur. My husband, likewise, wore a fur-trimmed cloak, high boots, and a feathered hat.

"You, sir," the burgher said. "You look a proper gentleman. Is the king a heretic?"

I waited, heart pounding, for Jack's answer. He could not very well say "Yes," and let the tale get back to Henry, or say "No," and incense these men to argument or worse.

My husband smiled. When he bothered to, he could charm. "Whatever we think, he is king. I will raise a glass to him, if you will join me."

He produced a silver coin, laid it on the counter before the landlord, and bade him serve to all whatever they were having.

I relaxed. Jack was no fool. An offer to buy a man ale

could change opinions in the wink of an eye. The landlord snatched up the coin and reached for his pitcher.

"Shall ye drink to the queen?" a woman asked Jack. "Queen Catherine?"

She held challenge in her eye. The woman near her also looked at Jack.

"I shall not drink at all," Jack said smoothly. "My wife and I are newly married, and she tires easily these days." He winked.

The men laughed. The women looked at me, and my stomacher, and said nothing.

Jack raised his hand. "Good day to you." He turned, placed his hand on my shoulder, and started to lead me away.

"Your mistress is a whore," a woman muttered darkly as I passed her.

When my mother had implied the same, I'd answered with hot words. But I did not fear my mother as much as I did this woman with large arms and a mean eye. I decided to follow Jack's lead, press my hand to my belly as though I felt ill, and continue to walk.

"You tell her for me," the woman continued. "A whore and a heretic."

"Shut your gob, woman," a man at the counter said. "She's a lady."

"A lady who serves a whore is a whore. Ain't you?"

I looked up at Jack. He wore a grim look but determinedly steered me away.

"Whore," the woman muttered again, then she threw her glass of ale at Jack's back.

Jack turned and glared at her, but he did not stop.

"Strumpet's jade," she taunted.

A man in the tavern struck her. She shrieked and scratched his face.

That was all it took. Suddenly patrons from the tavern and from the nearby food stalls took up mud and cabbages and began flinging them at us, and at the woman and man struggling in the street.

Jack grabbed my arm and dragged me into a side passage.

We stood in the reeking alley, me pressed against his solid body while the ruckus increased, and we were forgotten.

"They hate her," I whispered. "Why do they hate her so much?"

"The world is changing," Jack said into my ear. "Anne is part of the change. Not everyone likes that."

I knew he spoke the truth, but my spirits were heavy, and I could not banish the chill in my heart.

Fourteen

❦

I TAKE A JOURNEY

WHEN we returned to York Place, I was struck with the differences between the world within the court and the world without. Here, Anne was revered and admired, or at least, those who did not like her did not say so in her presence or the king's. Outside the cushioned bubble of the court, however, she was openly hated.

"When she has the king's son," I confided to Jack, "everything will change."

I firmly believed so. So did Anne.

Just after Easter, Jack left for Gloucestershire. We parted in our chamber, because it was raining and he did not want me walking down to the barge with him in the wet.

He said his formal good-bye and gave me a lingering kiss. I had promised myself I would let him go with dignity, but as he turned to leave, I tossed dignity away and flung my arms about his neck.

Jack held me. He wiped tears from my cheeks. "What are these for?"

"I shall miss you. I do love you, Jack."

His dark eyes filled with surprise, then pleasure. "I shall

remind you of that when I return. If you still love me then, I will know that I have passed the test of your devotion."

I pulled away from him. "Do not joke. Do you think that I will change my mind about you once you are out of sight? I am not such a featherhead."

"No, but George Boleyn is due to return from France, and I will not be here."

His mouth was a straight line. I stared.

"Nonsense. I care nothing for the queen's brother, save that he is the queen's brother."

He shot me an unreadable look. Jack was certainly handsome in his traveling cloak with his curling hair close-cropped and his dark eyes watching me. "That was not always true," he said.

I had never told him of my fancy for George Boleyn, but he was not a stupid man and must have guessed it. "A girl's infatuation. I fell out of love with Lord Rochford quite easily, I assure you."

"Hmm." He tucked a stray curl behind my wimple. "If you do decide you prefer his charms, tell me at once, and do not leave me to guess whether I am a cuckold. I will not put you aside for it, I promise you."

I folded my arms. "You make me quite cross, Jack Carlisle. It will serve you right if I no longer love you."

He kissed me again, his lips cool. Then he departed the chamber, his boots ringing on the stones.

I watched out of the window as he took the path to the barge stairs, my heart hollow.

JACK wrote to me when he reached Gloucestershire. He told me of the spring fields and the flowers, and of the grand house where his father lived and where we would also live. It had five galleries and several wings, he said, which was ever so much larger than my father's house, or the house of my uncle, the baron.

I longed to see it, and I longed for Jack. The court carried along as usual, but for me, it had lost its savor. I'd objected when Jack suggested that I leave court for good, but without him, it seemed a rather empty place.

The question this spring was a dynastic marriage for Elizabeth. Royal sons were heirs, but daughters were bargaining chips, used to bolster power or to pull it in from elsewhere. Henry would want any foreign prince who married Elizabeth to come to England and become English, but the foreign princes wanted Elizabeth to come to them. The game was about to begin.

With that in mind, Anne took me with her to Eltham, where Elizabeth's household had moved for the spring. Here, Anne explained, we would show off the princess to ambassadors and stir interest in a marriage.

Eltham lay not far from Greenwich. Here the great Edward the Second had established the order of the Knights of the Garter. A new knight was admitted to this prestigious order only when an older knight died. Then every gentleman of the court vied for a position.

Henry accompanied us. The people of Eltham came out to watch him ride in, waving banners and caps. They loved Henry. He had been born at Eltham, and the people embraced him as their own.

The hissing I heard as Anne and I rode past told me that they had not embraced her. Anne, as usual, was surrounded by guards and outriders, in case anyone made so bold as to try to hurt her. She frowned in annoyance at their behavior but said nothing.

Once we reached the palace of Eltham, Anne and I went at once to Elizabeth.

I had never had much use for babies, but I liked Princess Elizabeth. She was lively, quick to smile, and quick to howl if displeased. Her halo of red curls grew longer each day, and at six months old, she laughed and gurgled and rolled about with vigor.

I helped Lady Bryan dress Elizabeth in a gown of yellow velvet with a green satin kirtle and green sleeves embroidered with purple. A cloth of gold cap went on her head. In solemn procession, Lady Bryan bearing Elizabeth, me holding the train of the child's robe, and a gentleman bearing Henry's banner and one bearing Anne's falcon banner, walked into the great hall where Henry had gathered the ambassadors.

I found this all strange, but I memorized the ceremony to write to Jack and also to my aunt, who loved to hear of such things.

We paraded before the ambassadors. They were gentlemen of middling years, dressed in various surcoats and robes of purple and green and yellow. We walked past the standing ranks of them, Lady Bryan holding Elizabeth so they could see her clearly. Elizabeth stared back at them first with a baby's curiosity, then with a baby's boredom.

The ambassadors looked her over carefully. I could almost hear them drafting letters in their heads to send to their monarchs about her appearance and obvious health.

Lady Bryan and I took Elizabeth, alone, behind a screen, and prepared for act two. With a brazier to warm us, we stripped Elizabeth to her skin.

I took the naked child in my arms and again we paraded. The gentlemen's gazes roved her sharply, looking for any deformity or sign of disease that the regal clothes might have hidden. They also, I knew, looked for signs that might show she'd been exposed to witchcraft or touched by the devil, but Elizabeth's skin was clean.

I carried her proudly, noticing the ambassadors' approval. Elizabeth, of course, liked none of this, and began to fuss. Lady Bryan hurried forward to wrap her in a warm blanket, and then we took her back to her chambers, dismissed.

THE little show seemed to have done what it was intended to do. George Boleyn returned from France in May. He immediately sought his sister and reported to her that the king of France not only wanted another meeting in Calais that fall, but proposed that Elizabeth should marry his third son.

Anne smiled her pleased smile. She rose, skirts swishing, pulled her brother down to her, and kissed him soundly on the lips. "Excellent news. Frances, have wine with us to celebrate."

George chucked Anne under the chin and laughed at her. He looked fine as always, in a black velvet doublet, sleeves slashed with silver, and black trunk hose.

He took the wine from the servant who'd hurried forward, and filled three silver goblets. He handed the goblets to us and raised his. "To Princess Elizabeth," he said.

Anne and I sipped our wine. George drained his goblet, and sat on a bench with a flourish. "Pour me more, Frances," he said.

Courteously, I set down my cup, took the flagon from the footman, and poured a stream of pale wine into George's cup.

His dark eyes twinkled as I bent over him. "The ladies of the court of France are never as comely as ours," he said.

I glanced at him in surprise, because he, like Anne, considered French court to be superior in taste to our rather backward English one.

He returned a gaze that roved my face. As I straightened up, he brushed my cheek with his finger.

I flushed. Hastily, I sought out the footman and thrust the flagon into his hands.

"Frances is married, brother," Anne chided gently. She'd resumed her seat on her cushioned square chair, her feet in satin slippers resting on a carved footstool.

"To Jack Carlisle, yes. Well done, Frances. You are learning how to raise your station. You have an excellent teacher." He raised his goblet in salute to Anne.

Anne gave him an irritated glance. "Never mind your teasing. Frances, I want you to leave me now. Send Lady Berkeley to me."

I blinked. Anne rarely sent me from her side, and only if she wished to be alone with the king or an important official. She had never before ordered me to simply go away.

I dropped into a wooden curtsy. "Have I offended Your Grace?" I asked, my voice faint.

She waved her hand dismissively, but I could see the square neck of her stomacher rise with her quick breath. "Not at all. You look unwell. Remember that you carry a child. Leave me and rest."

"You also carry a child," George pointed out.

She frowned. "The pair of you confound me. Do you question the queen's wishes?"

I grew cold, but George's smile deepened. "Who in England would dream of disobeying Queen Anne? You had better go, Frances. My sister angry is no pretty thing."

Anne glowered at him. I curtsied again and nearly fled the room.

What I'd done to anger her I could not imagine. I thought of the caress George had given me when I poured his wine, and the look. A year ago, I would have made a fool of myself at such encouragement.

Did Anne believe I would cuckold my husband with George? A chilling thought struck me. Had Jack told her of my earlier infatuation, believing it to still be true? Did he ask her to watch me, and had she grown angry to discover that Jack had been right?

These thoughts troubled me, gnawing at me as I lay alone in my bed in the darkness.

Anne spoke no more about it but began to not want me by her side as much as usual. She frequently asked her sister Mary to perform the offices I normally did, without explanation. Mary obeyed without saying much, and I stood aside and burned with jealousy.

Not long after George's return, when the buds in the rose garden were just beginning to open, Anne told me to go to Gloucestershire.

She instructed me of this in her large chamber that overlooked the gardens. The scent of roses wafted to us, the promise of warmth and summer.

I gave her a frozen look when she made this announcement, which annoyed her.

"I thought you would rejoice, Frances. You have been melancholy at your husband's absence, quite remarkably so."

"I have been," I agreed. "And I will be happy to join him. But not because of your displeasure. Why are you sending me away?"

Anne's expression softened. She was lovely in the spring light, her oval face cream white, her dark eyes enhanced by the deep violet veil that framed her face.

" 'Twill be only for a little while," she said. "You will certainly return in time for my lying in."

I nodded numbly. But, as usual, I could not obey without question. "Please tell me what I have done to anger you."

"Nothing, my dear Frances. I am thinking of your condition and your need to be with your husband."

I did not believe her, but it would do me no good to say so. I did not dare mention George.

I curtsied. "I will leave if you wish."

"Do not look so downcast. The time will pass before you know it. In the autumn, you will wait upon me and my little prince."

She laid her hand across her abdomen, her irritation fading before a hopeful smile. Henry had already had a cradle made for the new baby, a splendid silver affair carved with roses and set with jewels. He and Anne had also ordered baby clothes of cloth of gold, sumptuous for the christening.

I sank to my knees before her, lowering my eyes. "I would never do anything to anger you, Your Grace, never. I am devoted to you. I will do what you wish."

As I hoped, my dramatic plea made her laugh. She raised me to my feet and kissed my cheek. "Frances, you are absurd."

"Yes, Your Grace," I said.

ONCE she had made up her mind, Anne liked to act quickly. She sent her sister and her own maids to help me

pack for the journey and to put away things I would not
need until my return. Anne even gave me cloth for several
new gowns in both serviceable wool and stately velvet.

I wrote to Jack warning him that my visit was imminent,
and Anne sent the letter by special messenger.

On the first of June, one year after Anne's coronation, I
again boarded a barge. This one, much smaller and carrying only me and two manservants and two maids, took me
upriver past the Tower, past the City, past York Place, then
slowly around the bend to Richmond and Hampton Court.

As the journey went on, we passed Windsor, its round
towers rising majestically from the green hills of Berkshire. This summer, Anne would hunt and hawk there, but
without me. The boat moved on, the imposing castle fading
slowly from sight. With a mixture of misgivings and curiosity, I turned my face to places I'd never before seen.

The lands of the Thames valley rolled on, the river nar-
rowing and becoming more and more shallow. We passed
manor houses and villages, men working fields, sheep
strolling misty greens. Children liked to wave as we
passed, and I tiredly waved back.

We disembarked at villages along the way and slept in
inns, in private chambers that I could now afford. The land-
lords and hostlers and their wives bustled round to serve
me as though I were a great lady, and incidentally, to earn
tips. Their deferential treatment baffled me and might have
tickled me had I not been worried about Anne's anger.

At Oxford, we left the river behind to ride west and a little north for Cheltenham. I stayed the night at Oxford in a
house near the colleges. My two footmen did the difficult
work of unloading all my things from the barge while the
maids argued with the landlady to bring me the best food
in the house.

I sat in the stifling upstairs room trying to choke down
the rather salty soup and dry mutton, about which I was too
tired to complain. The days of sun glaring off the river had
wearied me, and the thought of riding on a hard saddle the
next day made me still more weary. I longed to see Jack

again, but I wondered if he'd scold me for displeasing
Anne. He'd always thought me a fool.

My journey resumed the next day. Fortunately, while
the sun remained warm, the breeze was cool and pleasant.
The servants walked along beside my horse, arguing with
each other, and I diverted myself by settling their quarrels.

At long last, we reached Cheltenham and paused at yet
another inn. This time, Jack was there to meet me.

He reached for me as I slid from my horse, cramped and
hurting, my feet and fingers swollen. I never thought I'd be
so happy to see his curly head again. I lingered for a moment to put my arms around his neck and touch his unruly
hair. He smiled at me and kissed my cheek, to my relief not
seeming angry at all.

We rested for a time at the inn, Jack sitting close to me
and watching me as I drank warm ale. My sting at being sent
from court was lessening the longer I spent in his presence.

Pennington Hall itself also lessened the sting. We rode the
final five miles to it on the horses Jack had brought, a pretty
mare for me with a new saddle, a gift from Jack's father.

The house sat at the bottom of a hollow, its redbrick
wings stretching across a strand of green like welcoming
arms. Windows glittered under deep dormers, and ivy
clung to the walls like a green curtain. A rose garden lay to
the south of the house, its beds a riot of yellow and red and
pink. Rose vines twined among the trees, softening them
with color.

I would live here, with Jack and his father, for the rest of
my life. My children would live here. It was my home.

The thought resonated through me as we walked to the
open front door. *Home*.

My welcome to this house took me by surprise. At my
father's house I was the impetuous young daughter looked
upon by the servants with an indulgent eye or in exasperation. Likewise, at my aunt's house, I was simply the niece
of a lesser family. In Anne's court, I wore finery and jewels
and received privileges from the queen, but any ceremony
was for her, and I walked in her shadow.

The inhabitants of Pennington Hall greeted me as the lady of the house. Inside, I found a dim and cool hall stretching to the back of the house. A gallery ringed it, wood shining and dark. On the stone floor of this hall stood at least twenty servants, from the steward in gentleman's clothes to the housekeeper in an embroidered kirtle to the footmen in green and white tunics, to the scullery maid in linen. All stood deferentially, all turned curious eyes toward me.

The thought flashed through my head that they must be awaiting a prestigious personage, and then I realized that they awaited me.

Fortunately, two years at court had polished my manners, so I did not gape at them or do anything else foolish. I pasted a smile on my face and acknowledged each servant in turn. The girls and women curtsied while the gentlemen bowed, but they did not drop their eyes deferentially. They looked me over with careful scrutiny, taking in every detail of my dress, my hair, my veil, and even my shoes. They scrutinized my servants, as well, who were rather preening themselves behind me.

Their deference to Jack pleased me. At court, Jack was only one of a number of nobles, and he was a somewhat minor one at that. Here, he came into his element. His father was still earl, but he was the heir, and no king's son could have received looks prouder than what these servants gave Jack.

"Lady Carlisle is tired from her journey," Jack said as soon as the greeting ceremony concluded. "She will want to seek her bed."

I had said no such thing to him, but I could not deny the truth of his words.

There seemed to have been a rivalry about who actually led me to my chamber. The apparent winner, a round and red-faced maid, held her nose in the air and told me she'd take me up. Another maid, whose straw-colored hair leaked from under her cap, shot her a vicious look. My maids and footmen from Greenwich accompanied me to ensure that my accommodations were up to their standards, and our little procession wound its way up the stairs.

The chamber we entered was large and airy. Situated in the front of the house, its windows overlooked the lane and the rose garden. The walls had been whitewashed, and the bed hung with white and gold draperies. In the summer sunshine, the entire room seemed to shimmer.

" 'Tis lovely," I exclaimed.

My footmen inspected it and predicted the chimney would not draw, even though the day was warm, and I scarce needed a fire.

My maids undressed me and bound up my hair, then they put me to bed, although it was midday. I sank gratefully into the quilts and pillows, closing my eyes.

I fell into easy slumber. My distress as leaving court had not lessened, but here, in the sunshine, with Jack nearby and the scent of roses at my window, I found something close to peace.

I awoke hours later. Gold fingers of cloud brushed the dark blue sky, the long summer day nearing its end.

Feeling better, I left the bed and, in my nightgown, padded to the window. It lay open, facing south. I could see both the entire western sky lit with sunset and tall hills flooded with sunlight to the east.

I heard the door open behind me, but I did not turn, knowing it was Jack. He closed the door and crossed to me, his footfalls soft.

I did not move. He slid his arms around me, resting his hands on my increasing abdomen, and brushed a kiss to my cheek.

"It is beautiful here," I said.

"It is," he murmured.

I rested my hands on his. "This chamber is too fine for the likes of me." I sighed with contentment. "Though it pleases me."

"The household has been preparing for weeks for you.

There has not been a mistress of Pennington Hall in ten years. They grew quite excited when I told them that the queen had granted you leave at last."

My contentment lessened. "She sent me away."

He raised his head and looked at me. "Are you certain? I assumed her being generous to us."

"No. She has been annoyed at me for weeks, ever since her brother returned." I paused, then voiced my fears. "You did not tell her that I once fancied myself in love with him, did you? Please, say you did not tell her that."

He turned me to face him, his gaze unreadable. "Of course I did not. I would not presume to discuss such things with her. And I would not betray your confidence."

I deflated. "I am sorry. It was an unworthy thought. But she has behaved differently since his return."

"Perhaps he told her something to trouble her."

"I cannot imagine what. His trip to the French court seems to have been a success. When they are together, they laugh and talk for hours. I have never seen two better friends. They even have discourse on the scriptures. George is very learned. My mother would faint."

He chuckled. "We will not speak of it to her. Depend upon it, Frances, Anne is feeling generous because of her own coming child. She has kind feelings toward young mothers."

"Perhaps." My thoughts remained troubled, but I let him soothe me. "Are you pleased to see me, Jack?"

"Most excellently pleased."

I kissed him. He returned the embrace, then he took me back to the bed. He helped me into it, then he undressed himself and got in beside me. I wrapped my arms around him and thanked God for delivering me safe to my husband.

I met the Earl of Pennington, Jack's father, the morning after my arrival.

My own father was a vague man, but kind, and had

spent years being cowed by my mother. The earl was quite different. He had gray hair and sharp, dark eyes, and regarded me with keen scrutiny.

"So you are Anne's favorite," he said. We stood in the rose garden, me deferentially facing the earl, Jack just behind me.

"I have that honor, my lord," I said.

I hoped I would not do anything dreadful, such as hiccup. I wanted this man to believe me dignified, at least.

The earl took my hands and briefly kissed my cheek. "Welcome, Frances. I am pleased that my son chose you. He has told me much of you."

If Jack were relieved, he made no sign. I said, "I am very provincial, my lord."

The earl smiled. He tended to smile more than his son. "We are quite provincial here. Nothing like court. Which suits me."

"Court is a splendid place," I objected. "There is something new every day."

His smile dipped, then resumed, less warm than before. "It no longer holds my longing. I prefer dull walks in the dull country." He squeezed my hands. "Welcome again, Frances. The servants are instructed to obey you. Take guidance from Jack, and you'll not go wrong."

I curtsied again, politely. I wondered about the flash of sadness I'd seen in his eyes, but I sensed that I should not ask.

The earl offered his arm, then proceeded to lead me about the garden. The subject of court was not raised again.

Fifteen

❦

THE END OF A HOPE

Looking back at that month of June 1534, I believe it the happiest of my life. And then I question the belief, because perhaps it was simply the last June of my innocence. I was young and in love, the child inside me spoke of a happy future, and Pennington Hall was at its most beautiful.

I spent the days walking or riding with Jack or wandering about the Hall, becoming used to the fact that I was mistress of the place. Daylight lingered in the sky until nearly eleven o'clock and reappeared near three, so I remembered that time as one bathed in sunshine.

The child in my belly grew and began to kick with vigor. Being kicked from the inside was a new experience to me. Jack liked to press his hands over my abdomen and smile when he felt his child move.

I learned the routine of Pennington and soon fell into my duties. The housekeeper and cook began to consult me on menus and foodstuffs, wine, and ale, I was given keys to every door and cupboard in the place, and I was waited on hand and foot. Granted, I did have to stifle quarrels between my Greenwich servants and the Pennington servants, but after an exasperated scolding the first week, they settled down and merely smoldered at one another.

I made plenty of mistakes, but the housekeeper kindly steered me into safer waters. I tried to remember what my mother had done throughout the years of my childhood, but I recalled only her ordering the servants about and lamenting that life in England was nothing so easy as in France. I never remembered her making certain the butter was sweet, the bed linens aired, her husband's shirts mended, and the mead correctly brewed, as I did as mistress of Pennington. I brewed ale as well, although I had to throw away the first batch. No one laughed at me, save Jack. The second batch, however, was quite drinkable.

The servants still regarded me as a court lady, in spite of my becoming a housewife. We had a formal supper every evening with myself and Jack and the earl in finery. Footmen dressed in green and white livery served the meal that I had directed, wiped our hands, and poured wine.

After supper, I would decline to play the virginal, as I played clumsily, and we'd ask the earl to play instead. He had a fine touch on the instrument.

When the weather was fair, we walked; when it clouded, we played cards or chess or simply conversed. This was easy conversation, without the contrived witticisms of court ladies and gentlemen. At court, one was always trying to think of a new quip or clever saying in order to keep others from thinking one a dullard. Here, we talked and listened as though we were interested in what each of us had to say. I found it restful.

I still wrote my poetry. One early morning in mid-June, I could not sleep, and so crept to the table in our room, opened my writing box, and began to scribble.

"What are you writing?" Jack asked sleepily from our bed.

"Verses for the new prince," I replied.

"He will not be able to read them."

I looked up at my husband, who watched me from the bed, his dark hair tousled with sleep.

I put my tongue out at him. "I am writing them for Anne."

"I thought you had given up poesy."

"No, indeed. I simply do not tell you because you scold me."

"I see."

He did not sound angry, and he did not laugh.

"Anne likes my verses," I said. Then I felt downcast. "Leastwise, she did."

He was silent a moment, then said, "In truth, Frances, I am happy she sent you from court."

I hooked my slippered foot around the leg of the chair. "Why, so that I can sew your shirts? My seams are never straight."

"No, because you have an unguarded tongue."

I laid down my pen and contrived a haughty look. "I had hoped that when you professed to love me, you would cease twitting me about my shortcomings. Alas, it is not so."

I still did not goad him into emotion. Jack twined his hands behind his head. "The mire thickens, Frances. Anne is not accepted as queen, despite everything Henry has done. Very soon, any word from any subject against Anne will be treason, punishable by death. One slip of the tongue, and arrest can follow."

"I would never say anything against Anne," I insisted.

"You might not mean to. But enemies abound at court, ruthless people ready to shove aside any person they perceive as a threat to them. An enemy can take what you say and twist it into something treasonous. Or imply that you knew of another's treason, and said nothing."

I stared at him. "An enemy? But I stand in no one's way."

"Jealousy abounds," he said. "You are close to the queen, a position others want. Your marriage to me protects you somewhat, but not entirely. I am happy that you are far from there and will be forgotten."

I sprang to my feet. "But I do not want to be forgotten."

My heart thumped. "You cannot understand. I lived my entire life knowing I was nobody, and not a very accomplished nobody at that. I could never once please my mother, no matter how hard I tried, and my father was not much impressed with me, either. Then Anne plucked me up and made me into somebody. She loves and trusts me and made me her confidant." I struck my chest with my hands. "*Me*. Nobody Frances, who none ever thought would amount to anything. Including you."

A few tears spilled down my cheeks. Jack said, "Frances, come here."

I balled my fists in frustration, but I went to him. I disliked how he reminded me that he married me to protect me. But I went to him because he was my husband, and I'd promised to obey him. I also went because I was cold, and I knew the bed with him was warm.

He held the covers for me while I climbed in beside him and settled down next to his body. He put one arm around me, and I laid my head on his comfortable shoulder.

He said, "Do you know why my father lives here at Pennington, not in London or at court?"

"It is beautiful here," I pointed out.

"But rather remote."

I nodded into his shoulder. "Yes, I had wondered."

"A dozen years ago, the Duke of Buckingham was executed."

"Yes." Everyone at court knew the story. Buckingham had married his son to Ursula Pole. Buckingham's family, the Staffords, and the Pole family were direct descendants of the Yorkists, and Buckingham had combined the two in this marriage. The twisted politics of this baffled me, but most people agreed he'd been unwise.

"I believe all would have been well, if Buckingham could have kept quiet," Jack said. "But he speculated more than once that Henry would never have sons. And everyone was reminded that Buckingham's line had a better claim to the throne than Henry, a man descended from a trumped-up Welsh soldier."

My eyes widened. "Did Buckingham say that?"

"Not so precisely, but everyone understood. Buckingham was arrested, tried for treason, and executed. Quickly. My father, long a friend of his family, tried to speak up for him."

"Oh." I bit my lip.

"My father tried to explain that Buckingham simply liked to talk and meant nothing by it. But Henry needed to prove a point. Any talk, however idle, about ending the Tudor line had to be punished—blatantly and publicly.

"Henry was fond of my father and had promised me a place in his privy chamber. Henry said that my father could avoid Buckingham's fate by declaring, in writing, that Buckingham was a traitor. Or my father could leave court. Because my father believed that the charges against Buckingham were manufactured by Cardinal Wolsey to get rid of the man, he could not bring himself to say such things. My mother, too, had fallen ill, and he wanted to be near her. So he chose exile from court. All because he said one sentence to the king: 'I know Buckingham well, and he means no harm.'"

"Oh," I said again.

"My father had no intention other than pointing out that Wolsey was mistaken about Buckingham. And yet, my father found himself banished. He was lucky that Henry considered *him* harmless enough to let him retain his title and his lands. The best of the Buckingham estates were redistributed to the Dukes of Norfolk and Suffolk and other of Henry's favorites."

He fell silent. The morning breeze brushed a tendril of hair at his forehead.

"I am sorry," I whispered.

Jack shifted a little, as though the bed was growing uncomfortable. "He does not regret it. He was able to spend my mother's last years with her, here, where she was happy."

"But you went to court," I said.

"Yes, Henry still offered to bring me into the privy

chamber. Perhaps it was an apology to my father; I do not know. But I learned to tread lightly."

"And marry a nobody so that Henry will not worry that you have dynastic ambition?"

"Yes."

I looked at him. His eyes were dark and filled with something I did not understand. "And if I had been a duke's daughter, like Mary Howard? You would not have touched me, but run after the first safe woman you could find?"

"Had you been a duke's daughter, I would have risked the king's wrath. I would have promised to remove myself to the far corner of the barren north if I had to."

"You are trying to make me feel better."

He smoothed his palm over my hair. "I am trying to convey the truth."

I let him touch me, mollified somewhat. I knew that Jack had affection for me, but I did not believe it was deep love. I did not believe he felt at all what I felt for him.

"Frances," he said, his voice husky.

He needed to say nothing else. I slid my body on top of his and kissed him. His eyes darkened with passion, and we left the bed quite late that morning.

I mulled over Jack's story of his father during the next few days. I thought I understood now why Jack had given me warnings from the moment he'd met me. He knew me for a naïve country girl, and then he'd seen me rise at an alarming rate.

He must have wondered, as others must have wondered, what Anne meant by favoring me. And I, silly thing, had let it go to my head. No wonder Jack had hovered round trying to discover what I was about.

I thought of his warnings again when word came at the end of June that I was to return to court at once. The message was not that Anne had forgiven me, as I'd hoped, but something more dire. Anne had miscarried her child.

* * *

I stood by Anne's chair in her bedchamber at Greenwich, where she rested in the dark, her face pale and drawn.

"Frances." She seized my hands, and I knelt at her side. "Oh, Frances, God has taken this away from me, and I do not know why."

I struggled to understand as well. My mother would tell me that it served her right, that God punished her for being presumptuous, for daring to rise so far above her station, for daring to challenge Queen Catherine.

I more practically wondered whether an accident had befallen Anne, or if she'd had some upset that brought the baby far too soon. Six months gone myself, I touched my stomacher and wondered if the same fate was in store for me.

As though in response, Jack's child kicked me, hard. I winced.

Anne saw me flinch, and her expression became strained. "Go away," she said viciously. "Leave me be."

Mistress Marshall came forward, her eyes anxious. I struggled up from the floor, curtsied, my vision blurred, and fled the room.

ANNE, always strong, soon recovered. When she did, she sent for me again. She hugged me to her and kissed my cheek. "My poor Frances. I do so need you beside me, especially now."

We cried together, and then I wiped away my tears. "You will have another child. This time must have been unlucky. Look at the princess. She is healthy and strong and never ill."

Anne did not brighten, but she looked less morose. "Indeed, Elizabeth is all that makes her father proud."

"You will have a son as healthy as she."

I believed it in my heart. Many women miscarried children, including my aunt and my mother. My aunt had lost one child, my mother three. And yet, they'd borne

healthy children as well, who lived to grow up and be nui-
sances to them.

But I knew Anne was thinking of Catherine, who'd been
with child no less than eight times and had only Mary to
show for it. Henry had lost patience with Catherine. Would
he with Anne? I prayed not.

The lovely silver cradle with the roses and jewels was
taken away and never seen again.

Henry went off on his summer progress, traveling to
Buckinghamshire with his retinue, but not with Anne.
Anne was still somewhat ill, but her enemies construed this
separation to mean that Henry was tiring of her.

Henry, however, kissed her good-bye with plenty of
passion, and I knew that it was only a matter of time before
she was with child again. If it is a woman's lot to lose children, it is a queen's lot to become belly-full again and
again until the nursery is filled with sons.

Anne moved to a house called Guildford, where Henry
planned to join her later. She and I wandered about the
park and entertained ladies and gentlemen during the
month of July, and I missed Jack.

Jack had returned with me to court but now was at
Henry's side, hunting and hawking in Buckinghamshire.
At Pennington, I had been mourning being sent away from
court; now, perversely, I longed for the quiet days walking
with Jack and his father in the Pennington rose garden. I
became annoyed at my own inconsistency.

George Boleyn had been sent to France to postpone the
Calais meeting between Henry and the king, ostensibly because of Anne's illness. I knew, though, that Henry was
having a temper tantrum because the French king had been
breaking promises, and Henry never liked that.

For instance, Francis had gone ahead with the marriage
of his oldest son to Catherine de Medici, a relative of Pope
Clement. Francis had promised to postpone the marriage to
force Clement to not excommunicate Henry, but I suppose

Francis more wanted the pope and the Holy Roman Emperor on his side than he wanted Henry. In the triangle of France, England, and Empire, Henry was now odd man out. He hated being odd man out, and so he did the equivalent of putting out his tongue. He delayed the Calais meeting until he was good and ready for it.

In any case, Henry did return from Buckinghamshire to meet Anne in Guildford, and the usual summer pastimes of hunting and hawking and riding and flirting continued.

By September, relations between myself and Anne seemed as normal, although I sensed an undercurrent of tension that had not existed before. At least, everything was as normal for me as could be with my belly huge and unsightly. I could barely walk on my swollen feet, and Anne kindly allowed me to sit in her presence whenever I wished.

Relations between Henry and Anne returned to normal as well. They appeared everywhere together and slept together at night. We all waited for Anne to announce that she was again with child.

However, it was not Anne who was discovered to be pregnant that September, but her sister, Mary Carey.

One day I tottered into an inner chamber into the midst of a flaming row between Anne and Mary. Mary had sunk into tears, but she folded her arms and glared at her sister defiantly.

"Are you mad?" Anne demanded. She'd clenched her fists, jewels flashing on her hands, her black eyes blazing as bright as her diamonds. "Did you think of your son? Did you think of *me*?"

"The entire world does not stop for you, Anne," Mary blurted.

"It does. It does. I am queen. You are my subject. You obey." She drew herself up, magnificent in her velvets and gold. "Even were I not queen, you have disgraced the family. Father will banish you, you little fool. What were you thinking?"

Mary was not cowed. "I love him."

"Yes, but was that reason to *marry* him? If you wanted a husband, you ought to have left it to me to find you one."

"I married to not disgrace him," she flashed. "Perhaps you cannot understand that."

"No, indeed, I cannot." Anne caught sight of me. "Frances, what think you? My dear sister has gotten herself married to a fool of a man, secretly and without permission. To William Stafford, who is nothing. Even Frances had my permission and blessing to marry, and she was wed to an earl's son, not a nobody. You are the *queen's sister.*"

Mary made an imploring gesture to me, her face mottled with weeping. "I fell in love. Is that so much to condemn a woman?"

I looked from Anne to Mary. "Perhaps," I said in a small voice, "you ought to have mentioned it."

"And have him sent away?" Mary cried. "Everything has been taken from me, including my only son. I wanted this. I love him."

Anne nearly screamed in exasperation. "Love, love, stop bleating about love. You have ruined yourself. Can you believe, Frances, she tells me she has been 'in love' with this man for nearly two years. Under my nose, without a word. She goes from the king's bed to a nothing. His Grace will not take kindly to the insult."

"What choice did I have?" Mary gasped. "The king never meant to marry me. He was finished with me, and he wanted you. Where did I have to go?"

"You were the widow of a perfectly respectable gentleman," Anne retorted. "I have wardship of your son and the keeping of you. I would have thought a privileged position at court serving your queen a fine thing."

"It was not enough," Mary said sullenly.

"Well, it was much more than you have now. You cannot stay here, you and your William. You have married beneath you and disgraced yourself and me. William Stafford has the keeping of you now."

Mary wiped her eyes. She might be the pretty Boleyn,

the compliant Boleyn, but she was still a Boleyn. She looked her sister straight in the eye. "I married him to seize a bit of happiness. I did not want a throne; I wanted someone to love me."

If she meant to knock Anne from her heights, she did not succeed. Anne shot her an annoyed look. "You are a little fool, and I can no longer help you. Go and have joy of your William and your love. You belong to him now."

"I will," Mary said furiously. "I've had enough of court and lies and *you*."

She swung about, her skirts swishing, and pushed past me out the door. She did not even say good-bye.

Anne was in a foul temper for days after that and found fault with everything I did.

TWO more things that happened that September worth noting were, first, Pope Clement, who had blocked Henry's divorce and then excommunicated him, died. Henry was quite pleased and thought he might convince the next pope to reverse the excommunication. He began campaigning to petition the next pontiff.

The second thing of note was my lying in.

Unlike Anne, who had an entire suite well-provisioned for her, I had a small chamber to myself and one maid. The midwife would not be sent for until it was time. Jack had to make do sleeping with the gentlemen again.

I kept myself busy sewing and reading and writing poetry. Ladies came to visit me from time to time, including Anne, although she did not like to stay. For the most part, I was left alone to brood.

Margaret Douglas always brought with her the most delicious gossip, so that I did not feel entirely left out.

"Jane Rochford has gone from court," she said, her lovely eyes smug.

I raised my brows, delighting her with my interest. "Has she? Why?"

"No one is certain, but she had a row with her husband.

She says George has no use for her, which is true, and that he spends all his time with Anne. How unnatural, Jane says, for a man to be so fond of his sister." She looked heavenward. "His sister is the queen, the silly fool, and I do not blame George for having no interest in Jane. She is a dull stick with a sour disposition. George likes ladies to be lively and pretty."

I knew that Jane Rochford disliked her husband and Anne, and had actually expressed sympathy for Princess Mary and Queen Catherine in Anne's hearing.

"Poor Jane," I said.

Margaret snorted. "Her own fault. Anne is quite jealous of you, you know, but promised gifts all the same."

Her words cut, as she'd probably meant them to. Anne had sent me off to my confinement with a prayer and a kiss, but I had seen a small resentment in her eyes.

Margaret embraced me and gave me a kiss that she said came from Mary Howard. After explaining to me that having a baby ruined a woman's slimness forever, she departed, her smiles sunny.

My pains came upon me without warning in the middle of a cool September night. I woke to the feeling that somebody was twisting my insides all around, and I cried out. The maid came, eyes wide, then ran to fetch a midwife.

I waited alone for two hours for her return. Pain came and went. It would rack me and make me want to double over, holding my belly, then it would subside. My body would tease me with feeling better for a while, and then pain squeezed me until I was screaming with it.

The midwife at last came, scolded the maid for leaving me alone, then took over with brisk efficiency. My husband had been told, she said, a smile on her face, and hadn't he gone over white? Sir Henry Norris and the queen's brother had taken Jack Carlisle away to drown him in a barrel of wine.

"Poor, sweet Jack," I said, and then the pains came again, and I could not speak.

The midwife told me after, that I'd done it easily. I did

not believe her. I remember only hours of mindless pain interspersed with brief interludes of calm. The midwife sang little tunes, most of them bawdy and funny, I suppose to keep up my spirits.

I lay on the sheets, naked and sweating, certain I would die. When I begged for a priest for unction, the midwife laughed and said I was a good girl and I'd do fine.

As morning brightened, the vigorous child within me dove into the world to land in the waiting hands of the midwife.

His howls pierced the room. I fell back to the pillows, sobbing in relief. The midwife crooned, "Now, here's a bonny boy to give to a lady."

She bathed him while I lay exhausted and defeated on the bedding, then she wrapped him tightly and laid him in my tired arms.

I gathered him to me, looking in awe at his tiny face and tiny nose and tiny mouth. He glared at me with Jack's eyes, then opened his mouth and bellowed in rage.

This made the midwife and the wet nurse, who'd been hurriedly fetched, laugh. "Aye, he's a lively one. He'll make his papa proud," the midwife said.

"His mama is proud, too," I whispered. My breasts began to tear, just like the water from the teats of the fountain Lady Anne had given Henry at New Year's.

But a highborn lady never suckles her own child. I handed him to the plump, young wet nurse, and watched my son draw his first drink.

Sixteen

❦

MY MOTHER PAYS A CALL

NOVEMBER 1534

My child was christened John Anthony James Carlisle, and Anne lavished gifts upon me and him. She wore a brittle smile as she presented me with costly baby clothes, a cup, and a few small jewels.

"He is beautiful, Frances," she said. "A credit to you and Jack."

Anne visited my child only once, and there was no more talk of John becoming the playmate of her children.

Jack had not much to say about small John to me, but when he entered my chambers and first met his child, he stared like a man transformed. He fussed a bit, as was his way, instructing the servants to take strict care of us and on no count let either of us take ill. Then, my maids told me, he went about court swelled with pride, as though he'd done something very clever.

I reminded him once that I had been the one to suffer the night of agony, but I never spoke of it again, because he became worried and insisted I stay abed for nearly a fortnight.

My son grew and thrived and became the focus of attention. Ladies came to visit his cradle and coo. Gentlemen clapped Jack on the back and congratulated him on his virility. The king gave our son a small grant of land, so that when he grew older, he would be baronet of a minor holding.

After the story Jack had told me about his father and Henry, I was surprised the king would reward us so, but with Henry, one never knew. He could wax generous with one hand and strip someone of everything he had with the other. Or perhaps Henry merely wanted Jack in thrall to him. In any case, Jack graciously accepted.

MOTHERHOOD suited me, and my heart was light, but as fall turned to winter, Anne's mood became black.

This was mostly because of two incidents. The first was that the emperor's ambassador, Chapuys, spread the rumor all over Christendom that Henry had taken a new mistress. Chapuys speculated that Anne would be put aside, just as Catherine had been.

The ambassador professed to be delighted. He enjoyed nasty stories about Anne, the more scurrilous, the better. He took care never to acknowledge her as queen, and still paid homage to Catherine. My mother would have liked him.

That Henry did have a mistress, there was no doubt. He was a man who loved women. He had pursued mistresses under his first wife's nose, and saw no reason not to do it under the nose of the second.

I never learned this lady's name. She could not have been a woman of the court, because, were that the case, all of us would have known who she was. At court, you could not cough once without people across London the next day asking if you were well.

I speculated that the lady might have been a noblewoman Henry met on his progress during the summer, when he'd been without Anne. A smitten or ambitious woman would no doubt take full advantage of finding Henry alone.

In any case, this lady began writing letters to Princess Mary, ensuring her that she now had a friend who would intervene with Henry for her.

Anne knew of Henry's propensity to chase women. She laughed of it sometimes. But this was different. This was wooing Princess Mary behind her back, which implied that Elizabeth was not the legitimate heir. Anne wrote another letter to Lady Shelton instructing her to be more diligent in punishing Mary.

Henry visited Anne one morning after she'd received another report from Hatfield about Mary's rebellious behavior. "I fault you, Your Grace," Anne said angrily, waving the letter at him.

Henry's thick neck reddened. "These matters are for you to sort out."

"You said you wanted to bring Mary under your heel. Well, if your women go to her behind my back, what can I do?"

The flush moved up his face to his forehead. I, pretending to sew in the corner, sensed his embarrassment. Wives were supposed to look the other way at their husband's affairs, not interrogate them about them.

"Women's prattle," he growled. "Gossip and prattle. It means nothing."

"Nothing?" Anne cried. "I have fought at your side for everything you have. I have worked to repay you for what you have done for me. I have tried to do your will, sought to oppose your enemies who would see you weak. And you reward me by breaking my heart?"

Henry lost his temper. His great hands balled, his eyes flashed, and I closed my eyes against the coming storm.

His voice rose to shake the beams. "I break *your* heart? Is that my only task in life, to look after your heart? Do I have nothing better to do than soothe the fears of women?"

I peeked at the pair of them. A vein on Henry's forehead pounded, and his dark eyes narrowed. He was a fearsome sight. Anne did not cower. She stood with her head high, her shoulders thrown back, her eyes holding challenge.

"Remember," he snarled. "I raised you from nothing, and I can send you back where you came from whenever I choose. If I want a lady, you swallow and bear it, as your betters have done.

Anne did not wilt. "She is interfering with our child."

"Let her," Henry roared. "It is *my* will that is obeyed, not hers, not yours."

He snatched up a cup that rested on a nearby stool, threw it hard into the wall, and turned and stormed from the room.

In a mirror image, Anne snatched up another silver goblet and sent it hurtling after the first. I squeaked and ducked.

Anne seemed to remember I was in the room. "Frances," she snapped. "How dare you?"

I said nothing. It was hardly my fault I'd been caught in the room when she began railing at Henry. If I had tried to leave without being dismissed, I would have been equally punished.

Anne seemed to realize the truth of it, just as the truth of Henry's words must have sunk in. "Go away," she said. "Go look after your son."

I laid down the shirt I had been mending, curtsied, and tried to leave the room as quietly and deferentially as I could.

"Insolence," she called after me. "You are an insolent nobody."

I fled. I reached my chamber, shaking and cold, tears flowing.

When I reported the incident to Jack, he looked troubled. "You know what she meant, do you not?"

I nodded. I had thought of it all afternoon. "She means that I am flaunting my son when she has none. I am not, but she thinks so."

"Yes." He glanced at the cradle where our son slept—at last. He had fussed and cried and played and fussed for hours before finally dropping off. This is why even young parents look old.

"I believe it is time to send him to Gloucestershire," Jack said, "to my father."

My heart sank. I was quite attached to small John, and

the thought of sending him away upset me greatly. "I do not want to."

"Nor do I. But he is a constant reminder to the queen of her failure. And to Henry. I would rather he be safe in Gloucestershire, and forgotten."

I bit my lip. Many families of Jack's station fostered out their sons, and mothers gave the raising of their daughters to governesses and nurses without thought. Anne, who greatly loved her daughter, had turned her over to the keeping of the Sheltons and Lady Bryan without fuss. This was what was done.

I had known that one day I would have to let John go. But no one told me of the great wrench I'd feel when required to.

But I worried about Anne's anger. Jealousy made people do odd things, and when those people were as powerful as Anne and Henry, people like Jack and I had reason to fear.

I clasped Jack's hand. "Send him," I said. I gulped, trying to hold back tears.

Jack nodded. He began making arrangements the next day.

BEFORE we could send John off, an event occurred that I'd never dreamed would happen. My mother arrived in London and sent word to Greenwich that she wanted to see me.

I was still angry at my mother and her words about Anne, but I viewed her abrupt arrival in alarm. I feared she had come to tell me some bad news, such as the illness or death of my father or aunt.

I asked Anne for leave to go to London, and grudgingly, she granted it. So on a rainy November day, Jack and I, my son's nurse, and John, who was bundled up until nothing showed of him, took a barge to London. We huddled under a canopy that could not keep off the damp, and climbed out at stairs near the Temple. From here we walked to Fleet Street and a nearby inn where my mother had taken rooms.

This area of London was pleasant enough, filled with

middle-class houses and the lawyers of Lincoln's and Gray's Inns. I wondered why my mother had chosen to stay here, when she could have stayed near the houses of the nobility, but while my mother was a great snob, she was also one for economy.

The house looked quiet enough on the outside, but the inside bustled with activity. Servants hurried about carrying bedding, trays, firewood, and sundry items, harried looks on their faces. The landlord gave us a dark look when I asked for Lady Pierce and jerked his chin in the direction of the hall.

My mother's voice floated from the gallery above. "If you wish an elderly woman to be miserable, then you will *not* bring new linens." A maidservant rapidly descended the stairs, muttering under her breath.

I called up to the gallery in trepidation. "Mother? Are you well?"

My mother looked over the railing. She took in me, my tall husband with his cloak and sword, and the nursemaid and bundle of baby.

"Climb the stairs and see me, Frances," she commanded. "That is, if this wreck of an inn does not crumble around us."

I hurried up to her without anything so dire occurring. My mother looked me over, then condescended to let me kiss her cheek.

Without a word to Jack, she turned and led the way into her private chamber.

The room was comfortable and warm with benches, a table, and a bed hung with heavy curtains. A fire burned high to counter the cold rain beating at the shutters.

My mother turned in the center of the room and fixed her stare on Jack. "I suppose you are the husband?"

Jack had removed his hat and now carried it under his arm. He bowed. "My lady, I have that honor," he answered in her language.

"Never mind your fancy manners. There is not much honor in being married to Frances. She will never bring you riches. However, you look as though you have enough farthings in your pocket to take care of her."

I peeped at Jack, worried that he'd take offense, but the corners of his mouth creased, which I'd come to understand was a sign of amusement. "I will do my best, my lady."

"Is everything well at home?" I ventured.

My mother nodded. The hair on her forehead had gone a bit grayer since I'd seen her last, but other than that, she looked quite the same. "Everything is as it should be. I decided to come to London to see my grandchild."

"Alone?" I asked.

"Yes, alone. I am not feeble-witted."

"Last summer, you were unwell."

"I am feeling better now." She turned to the nurse. "Let me see him."

The nursemaid hastily folded back the corner of the blanket. My mother peered at John's scrunched face and closed eyes for a long time. I noted a softening about her mouth.

"He is much prettier than your cousin's brats," she pronounced. "One day he will be an earl and wear a fine sword like his papa."

I relaxed. My mother had little use for babies, finding them messy and noisy and too much bother. But I knew by her words that she approved of this one, and also of Jack.

She sent for wine, and we seated ourselves on the benches and drank. The nursemaid held baby John who, mercifully, chose to sleep.

My mother enjoyed herself complaining about London wine and the unsuitability of the inn. Then she turned to Jack and began to quiz him about Pennington Hall. She wanted to know where it was and how large, how many acres it farmed, what his father planted, how many servants he had. I was mortified, but Jack answered readily, as though he did not mind.

Once she had thoroughly probed Jack about his father, his place at court, and Pennington, she turned to the gossip of home.

"Your cousin is with child again." Her lip curled. "I know children are necessary to carry on a line, but the line of that varlet she married should be broken."

She took a sip of wine. Jack had bent his head over his cup, so I could not tell what he made of this.

"Your aunt Mary is beside herself with joy," my mother went on. "But she's always been a fool of a woman. Which reminds me, Mistress Longacre has been accused of witchcraft."

I jumped. "Good gracious." I was not entirely surprised, because Mistress Longacre liked to spit at people and promise curses. I was a bit surprised, however, because she'd been cursing people for scores of years, and no one had ever reported her to the witchfinders. "Who accused her?" I asked curiously.

"Your silly cousin, of course. She said that Mistress Longacre gave her the evil eye, and then your cousin went home and found a diamond-shaped crease in her bed linens. She was convinced that Mistress Longacre had hexed her." My mother made a face. "Of course Mistress Longacre looked at your cousin askance. The girl hasn't one whit of sense. I glare at her far more severely."

"Was Mistress Longacre arrested?" I asked, holding my breath.

"Indeed, no. I sent the inquisitor who arrived packing. Mistress Longacre mumbles at everyone, and we take no heed. I told the inquisitor she was a foolish old woman who could not predict that the sun would set in the evening. And your cousin retracted her accusation."

"She decided she was mistaken?"

"No, I gave her a good hiding. Mistress Longacre and her friends enjoy pretending to be witches; I see no reason for an inquisitor to come poking about our business. At least Mistress Longacre is not a heretic."

She fixed her eye on Jack, who returned the stare neutrally.

"Mistress Longacre does like to dose people with her blackberry wine," I said.

"No harm in that. Blackberry wine does some good. If you ignore her chanting and dire predictions that the queen will burn, she is a harmless soul." My mother brightened.

"Or perhaps she means that one of the strumpet's houses will burn to the ground while she is inside it."

My eyes widened, and I glanced fearfully at the closed door. "You should not say such things."

"My dear, everyone knows my views. I could spout them far and wide, but I am wise enough to know I can change nothing. Our king chose to put aside his wife and take a whore and bear bastards, and we all must live with it."

The nursemaid listened from the corner, lips parted. Jack remained stone-faced.

Fortunately, my mother left it at that and began quizzing me about my new life as a wife and mother. The subject of Anne was dropped.

Jack and I slept the night at the inn. Jack said little to me as we snuggled down in our chamber, but then, the nursemaid and baby John snored at the other end of the room. I rather liked being this close to my child, and when he woke in the night, I got up with the maid to soothe him.

My mother departed London the next day, satisfied that I had married somewhat decently and produced a child that would not shame her. She kissed my cheek as she pulled on her gloves and awaited her horse and groom.

"Do remember to be humble, Frances, despite your finery and your title," she said. "Do not get above yourself, it is quite unbecoming."

So saying she turned away, admonished the hostler for not holding the horse correctly, and bade her footman boost her into the saddle. We had been dismissed.

Jack said nothing at all on the boat back down the Thames to Greenwich. John fussed a bit, and the nurse and I took turns holding him. Jack watched the south bank slide by and remained silent.

Not until we'd gained our chamber high under the eaves of Greenwich castle, did I confront him.

"My mother approves of you, at least," I said nervously. "I believe she would, even were you not an earl's son."

Jack stared out of the tiny window, his back to me. He'd

removed his cloak, but his yellow green velvet back told me nothing.

"Oh, Jack, please answer," I begged. "Are you dismayed? Will you put me aside?"

He did not say anything for a long moment, then I heard a snorting sound. He swung around. He was laughing.

While I watched, bewildered, he slid down the wall, his legs folding up, and held his sides.

I strode to him. "Why is it funny?" I demanded.

He wiped his streaming eyes. "Because I love you," he said. He reached for me, pulled me down on the floor with him, and held me close, still laughing.

THE second event to upset Anne that November was the arrival of a French minister. This minister was the admiral of France, Philip Chapot, Sieur de Brion, and he'd come to talk about, as George Boleyn had indicated last May, the marriage of Francis' third son, the Duke of Angoulême, with the princess.

Except he did not say Princess Elizabeth. He said Princess Mary.

Henry had stared at the admiral in outrage. "Is this meant to be an insult?"

The admiral looked perplexed. A marriage between the first daughter of Henry and the third son of Francis was no insult. Except, of course, the admiral did not know that Henry was trying to break Mary's spirit and promote the children of Anne.

Or perhaps he did know, and simply did not care. King Francis liked to play his cards, and he would do just as he pleased.

"Indeed, no," the admiral said. "Is the arrangement not with the Princess Mary?"

"There is no Princess Mary," Henry snapped. "The only princess of England is my daughter Elizabeth."

The admiral took this in his stride, pretending that there was simply a mistake in wording. "The king did not mention

Princess Elizabeth by name. I will speak of it when I return to France."

Henry, who had hoped to celebrate the admiral's visit by drinking to the new betrothal, was furious.

"They took it in the spirit that I am certain the French king meant it," Jack told me, lying in the dark in our bed. "That they consider Mary legitimate and Henry's marriage to Catherine still good."

"But in Calais," I protested, "Francis danced with Anne. He acknowledged her. He gave her gifts on her coronation."

"Times change," Jack said. "Last year, he wished good relations with Henry. This year, he wishes good relations with the emperor."

"*Men,*" I said sourly. "Kings especially. They tire of their alliances faster than they tire of their mistresses. Women are never so inconstant."

Jack squeezed my hand under the bedclothes. "Do not condemn all of us, my dear."

"I have not watched you long enough to make a decision," I said. I made him laugh, but I was not entirely joking.

Henry tired of his own new mistress, and before long, we heard no more about her. He also proved sneering Chapuys wrong that his marriage with Anne was disintegrating. One night, while I ran through Greenwich palace on an errand, I came across Anne and Henry in a dark and empty chamber.

He was holding Anne against a wall. At first I was alarmed, thinking he meant to hurt her, and then I heard her laugh. It was the throaty laugh of a woman who knew her power, who knew that she held the man before her in thrall.

"Nan," Henry said in a low voice. He threaded his fingers through her loosened hair. "You drive me mad. Your pride makes you beautiful. I want you."

She laughed again and drew him into her arms.

I quickly and quietly backed out of the chamber, then positioned myself nearby to ensure that others did not disturb them.

Seventeen

❦

I Am Banished

SPRING 1535

THAT February was cold, with wind crackling in chimneys and blowing round the eaves. I sat in luxury in Greenwich and worried about my boy in Gloucestershire.

Jack's father wrote regularly and told me that John was well, but as he was a man, he did not fill in the details dear to a mother's heart. John's nurse could not write me, of course, because she had not the skill. So I was left to fret and miss him. Jack found his father's letters quite thorough, but then, Jack, too, was a man.

Anne took as much pain over Elizabeth as I did with John. A year and a half old, Elizabeth now toddled about, running into things and sitting down hard as children do. She spoke as well, saying a few phrases in English, and a few in French, because Anne spoke much French to her.

February brought a new vexation for Anne. Despite Anne's seduction of Henry that I'd witnessed in December, in February, he began chasing another mistress through the halls of Greenwich, this time Anne's cousin, Margery Shelton.

Anne was enraged. "I vow, Frances, the women of my family have run mad. First Mary, now Margery. Seducing His Grace is bad enough, but Margery flirts outrageously with Sir Henry Norris and Francis Weston, who is wed himself. If she is not married off soon, she'll come to grief."

"Yes, Your Grace," I said, not so much because it was required, but because I agreed with her. Margery was enjoying herself far too much.

Even as Henry took Margery to his bed, he continued to punish men hostile to his marriage to Anne. Several more acts were passed to reinforce the Act of Succession and to make it treason, subject to death, for any man or woman to speak against Anne or dare call Catherine queen. For this reason, I was glad my mother had gone to bury herself safely in the country.

Later that year, Henry used these acts to condemn Thomas More, once a mentor and confidant, and Bishop Fisher, Queen Catherine's steadfast friend. Unlike Bishop Gardiner, who had eaten humble pie and given up his house and lands to keep his life, Bishop Fisher would do no such thing. Jack told me, in private, that he admired the man, and Thomas More, for standing by their convictions.

This alarmed me, because Jack was a man of principle. I'd come to learn that, despite his avowal that he could tread softly, if Jack believed something right with all his heart, no king or threat would sway him. So far, Jack supported Anne, because he, too, liked the thought of a reformed church. But if Henry were ever to do something to which Jack heartily objected, he would object out loud. Henry already kept an eye on Jack because of his father. I could certainly lose my husband to Henry's rage if Jack were not careful.

These fears were fanned by what happened that summer. Thomas More was tried, and a group of lawyers led by Master Cromwell, Anne's staunch supporter, carefully examined the evidence against him.

Now, from what Jack told me, I understood that Thomas More was the trickiest lawyer of the lot. He nearly came through the trial unscathed, but he would not, in the end, take the oath Henry wanted him to take.

"If these acts of supremacy and appeals and succession are not valid," More said in his final speech, "then whatever oath I gave would not be valid." In other words, Jack explained, he could not break laws that were in themselves unlawful. And therefore, he was innocent.

It to me sounded like men twisting words to suit them, but apparently, everyone took More's speech very seriously. But Henry's will was more powerful than startling speeches, and More was condemned to death.

More was old and ruined and had grown ill during his stay in the Tower, and he said he was ready to die. I imagined he was also disillusioned, that by standing against what he thought was wrong, he had been broken.

Bishop Fisher, while he was a prisoner, was made a cardinal by the pope. This, of course, incensed Henry. So, that summer, before we all left for a progress to the west country, Henry made examples of him and Thomas More, as well as four leaders of Carthusian monks who had held out against Henry about the divorce.

The monks were hung, then castrated and disemboweled while they were still alive. Jack tried to keep that knowledge from me, but of course the ladies heard it and talked it over in gruesome detail.

Among the people of England, Anne was much blamed for the monks' deaths, and then for the beheading of Bishop Fisher and Thomas More. But it was Henry's hand who signed the condemnation, Henry who gave the nod to Cromwell to go ahead with the executions. I believe that Henry simply did not like his will crossed, and Anne had little to do with that. Thomas More and the others resisted and displeased Henry; therefore, they died. Anne only watched.

SUMMER AND AUTUMN 1535

I eagerly anticipated our journey to the west country, because we would go to Gloucestershire, and I could see my son. Anne and Henry had given Jack and me leave to spend a few weeks at Pennington. I thought on the lovely days I'd spent with Jack there last June and looked forward to repeating them.

Along the way, we visited a man called Poyntz, who'd built an entire wing onto his house just for Anne's stay. She slept in elegant chambers, and we dined off of Venetian glass. This Poyntz was a reformist, and Anne and Henry wooed him as much as he wooed them.

We visited many such reformists, Anne and Henry reassuring each that they had not been forgotten. These men and their families greeted Anne with joy, which made a change from the missiles and angry words that usually pelted us.

The progress should have gone to Bristol, but we received word of plague in the city, and so stayed away. Jack and I left the party for Pennington Hall.

We spent two glorious weeks walking in the rose garden, dining with the earl, playing with baby John, who could crawl and laugh. We lay in our bed in the summer night, either making love or simply lying together, savoring the peace of our home. I loved Jack and Pennington and John, and I thanked God for my good fortune.

All too soon, we had to leave Pennington to journey again to London and York Place. I cried when we departed but vowed to dry my tears. Court was always interesting, and I was still with Jack. He talked of arranging another visit after New Year's, and that was only a few months away.

However, before this occurred, disaster came upon me.

ANNE summoned me one day in September to a sunny chamber in York Place, the very one, in fact, in which I'd left her in Henry's arms the night before her coronation.

She stood in a square of sunshine before a window, her dark blue skirts rippling with the light, jewels glittering at her fingers and throat.

When I arrived, she dismissed all the servants and told me to shut the door behind them. Her stance was quiet, but her body quivered, her skirts moving slightly, and her eyes were stark and cold.

"Your Grace?" I asked, uncertain.

Anne held out a piece of paper between her slim fingers. "Frances," she said.

The tone of that one word struck me with dread. Anne was angry, but with an anger so deep it went beyond her usual frustrated rages.

What had I done? Had she been informed of my mother's diatribes against her? I trembled. My mother had refused to be quiet in the inn rooms, and any number of people could have heard her.

What if she'd had my mother arrested? Anne had the power to do so, or at least, to tell Henry to make it so. I would have to plead for my mother's life, and mine, and possibly Jack's as well.

"Come here," she said.

I crossed to her, shaking with every step. Anne turned the paper around and held it before my face. "Explain this," she said in a cool voice.

She held a long sheet of parchment covered with my handwriting. Along the edges of the paper were stylized letters intertwined with leaves and flowers. The letters were F and G. *Frances and George.*

I started, and then my face grew hot. She'd found one of my verses written in the height of my infatuation with George Boleyn. How, I could not fathom. I kept my poems locked away, and I thought I'd burnt those particular poems the morning after I'd married Jack.

"It is very bad poetry, Your Grace," I tried.

Anne's eyes narrowed. "This is not a matter for laughter, Frances. You wrote these verses about my brother. My brother and yourself."

I swallowed, "Long ago. Before I married Jack. Then I realized how foolish I'd been. I thought I'd destroyed them."

"You apparently did not," Anne said crisply.

"I was quite foolish," I babbled, "and young. And I did

not realize that I was in love with Jack Carlisle. What I felt for Lord Rochford was mere infatuation, which I have put behind me."

My words, if anything, enraged her further. She took a step forward and slapped me across the face with the paper.

I reeled back in shock, my hand going to my cheek.

"I believe, my dear, that you are missing the point," she said in a ringing voice. "Did you think you could ally yourself with my brother, that you could raise yourself by winning his heart?"

I shook my head. "No, I never thought—"

"I brought you here from kindness. I took you from nothing, because you showed loyalty to me when so many others did not. I nursed you, a foolish girl, and let you wait upon me when so many more deserving should have. I trusted you, I loved you. And all the time you were using me to gain prestige, to worm your way into my family. The impertinence of it!"

I shook my head so hard that my veil swung. "Your Grace, I never thought that. I only saw a man with a fair face."

She began to pace, as she always did when agitated. "You saw the queen's brother. You did not admire him, you wanted him. You wrote intimate words about him, you dared believe that you might become important through him."

"I swear to you, I never believed I would become anything to him."

"But you wanted it. If these prattling verses tell me anything, it is that you wanted him with all your heart and with your body. And you wrote it all down, for an enemy to find and bring to me. You humiliated me."

Tears streamed down my face. "Your Grace, I never dreamed it would humiliate you. I meant to destroy all of it. I cannot imagine how any person found it." I sniffled. "Was it Margery?"

She ignored the question. "And you stand before me and tell me that you wrote more of this deceitful twaddle. You ungrateful toad. What did you want from me? Did you hope to ensnare George so that he would have me do anything for you?"

"Never—"

My words were useless. She was lost in her tirade.

"The appalling deceit has cut me to the heart. I gave you gifts with my own hands and taught you and raised you. I made you a marriage that you could never have hoped to make with your ineffectual father and your oh-so-pious mother. You would have married a pig farmer if not for me. I made it so you could marry an earl's son and be a noblewoman. I did." She slammed her finger into her chest. "And all this time you have been laughing up your sleeve at me, wondering how much more you can squeeze from me. I have half a mind to have your marriage invalidated. Do you understand me?"

Her words fell like knives. "Please do not take Jack from me. I love him. He is my life."

"I see you switch your love quite easily. First George, then Jack."

"I did not understand. I did not understand until my wedding night, but I love Jack and him alone."

"And not your queen?" she asked, eyes dangerous.

I sank to my knees. "I do love you, Your Grace. You did take me from nothing, and I never understood why. But you have my love and my loyalty, always, I swear to you."

"I thought I did." Her voice lowered a notch. "I thought you were loyal to me, the one person I could trust to not have ambition, to not want to best me, to not want to see me fall."

"I am, I promise you."

"No, Frances. I have no one. Only the king. Even my uncle, who gained so much from me, speaks against me. Your own mother calls me whore and strumpet."

So, she *had* heard that. "She means nothing by it."

"I assure you, she does. She believes that I am not Henry's wife, nor his queen. She does not simply say it; she believes it."

"I do not believe it. I love you as my queen and my friend."

She closed her eyes. "Friend. You presume to call me *friend*." She opened her eyes again, and spoke with finality. "I do not want you to speak anymore, Frances. I want you to go. Away from me, away from court. You will travel to Gloucestershire and stay there. I no longer wish to see you."

"No," I gasped. "Please do not send me away."

I caught an expression of indecision. Anne was suspicious by nature; she had to be. I saw her struggle to decide whether I wept because I was truly heartbroken to be sent from her, or whether I were upset that I'd been exposed as an ambitious deceiver.

"I want you to go," she said. "If you behave yourself and try no trickery, I might consider recalling you to court. For now, I do not want to see you. Go."

I had lost. Tears streaming down my face, I struggled to my feet and somehow fled the room.

The halls, as usual, teemed with people. Courtiers and servants, ladies and gentlemen stared at me as I hurried past, my face twisted with weeping. I ran until I gained my chamber, then I collapsed upon the bed and lay there as one dead.

JACK found me hours later. I lay prostrate in the dark, having shed all the tears I could shed, or so I thought. My veil and wimple had come off, and my hair lay in a thick tangle across my back.

Jack sat down on the bed next to me, but he did not touch me.

"I have prepared a boat to take you upstream tomorrow," he said.

I rolled over. The room had gone dark, light from the candle he had brought with him flickering over his face.

"Are you not coming with me?" I asked.

The glint of candlelight obscured his dark eyes. "I will remain here. Henry has not given me permission to accompany you."

I sat up. "Why not? She cannot mean to punish me so by keeping me from you."

His voice took on a patient note. "It is better this way. People remember what happened to my father. If you and I both retreat, it will seem the entire family is in disgrace. I will stay and be a loyal courtier. You stay quietly in the country, and eventually this will mend."

He was so cool, so unlike my Jack, that I began to panic. "Do not look at me so. It was naught but a piece of silliness, and I very much regret it. I do not understand why the queen is so angry. It meant nothing."

"It was a liberty." His words were chilly. "She decided to take it as an affront to her generosity to you. In time, she might begin to see that you acted only from foolishness, and forgive you."

I caught his hands. "What about you? Will you forgive me? Or do you believe that I am still in love with him?"

His hands did not move in mine. "She showed me the paper, Frances."

The look he gave me near broke my heart. Whatever love he had borne me no longer showed in his eyes. He had seen my secret thoughts about a man, a man not him.

I blurted, "It was a child's infatuation, nothing more. I do not love him. I love you."

He wanted to believe me. I saw that in the grim twitch of his mouth. "I forced you into this marriage, Frances. You did not want it. I went to the queen and asked her to help me. She ordered your father to deny all suits but mine."

I stared, openmouthed. "So that is why . . ."

"She agreed because she liked you and wanted to reward you. As well, she cut out the daughters of enemies who might seek alliance with the Earl of Pennington."

"And it kept you from making a political marriage," I finished.

"Yes."

I wiped my eyes with the back of my hand. "She used me." I sniffled. "So did you."

"It is the way of court," he said.

My chest felt as though a heavy weight pressed on it. I

was a fool, a humiliated fool. Jack had used me. Anne had used me. And I'd only thought of love.

"I wish I'd never come. At home, no one ever made me love them and then turned about and broke my heart."

"Infatuation, you said."

"Not for you. Not for you, Jack. I said that I love you. Do you not believe me?"

He regarded me for a long time. Then his eyes closed, shutting out the bleak light, and he gathered me against him. He held me, stroking my hair, his hand so strong. But I cried again, because I knew he did not believe me.

He knew I'd married without choice. He knew I would have dismissed him had I been able. He, like Anne, thought my tears were for regret of my fall.

When we drew apart again, tears also stood in his eyes, but he did not break down. Jack never did.

I parted from him the next morning on stairs leading down to the Thames. A small barge holding baggage and my servants waited for me under crisp, autumn air.

The night before, I'd shamelessly begged Jack to lie with me one last time, and he had. I regretted my need now, because it made it that much harder to leave him. I admit that part of my request had been hope that he'd lose himself in desire and forgive me.

My tactic had not worked. Such things never did with Jack. But I so much feared that his anger would solidify in my absence, and that he would happily forget all about me. There were plenty of lovely and flirtatious females at court waiting to catch his eye, and all knew that Frances was being sent away.

On the stairs, I clung to him. "I will write you," I said. "Promise you will read the letters before you put them on the fire."

I'd hoped to make him smile, but he remained somber. "I'll not burn your letters."

I did not quite believe him, but I let the point go and hugged him.

His arms tightened around me once, then he brushed a kiss to my lips. "God be with you, Frances," he murmured.

Before I could even return the wish, he handed me down into the barge where my maids and footmen waited, and the boatman pushed off.

I watched his figure on the stairs as long as I could, until the view was obstructed by my tears.

THE journey was the worst of my life. The boat tossed about and made me ill, and when we landed at Oxford, rains began and did not cease all the way to Cheltenham. I could not sleep whenever we stopped for the night and could barely eat.

My two maids, the same who had accompanied me last year, ceased their bickering and became alarmed that I would die before we reached Pennington. Their crying and muttering over rosaries did nothing to soothe me.

When I at last reached Pennington Hall I felt old and ill. But the sight of my son standing on his sturdy legs beside his nurse, his fingers in his mouth, made me realize that exile had its compensations. I went down on my knees and hugged him hard. He looked so like his father that I burst into tears.

I felt my exile keenly, but being at Pennington Hall did soothe me. I came to realize, as the days went by, that Anne had been far less cruel than she could have been. She might have sent me to my father's house to suffer my mother's petty triumph. She could have sent John away to be fostered, even to someplace as far away as France. She could have found some way to publicly disgrace Jack in order to punish me.

She'd at least let me come here to be with my son, to a place where the inhabitants welcomed me.

Jack's father, to my surprise, kindly told me that the debacle was not my fault.

"They are afraid," he said to me soon after my arrival. I'd at last been able to eat and drink without heaving everything up again, and my shaking had finally calmed.

"Who is afraid?" I asked.

"The queen. Her position depends upon her bearing a boy child, and this she has not done. Now, things are still murky. Is she his wife, or isn't she? Is Elizabeth legitimate, or is Mary? People do not like uncertainty."

"But what has that to do with me?"

The earl smiled wisely. "You bring to her mind what she has lost. Or rather, what she has not gained. Henry took her from nothing and made her queen. She took you from nothing and made you a noblewoman. She tried and failed to have a male child. You tried and succeeded. She is self-made and ambitious. She easily believes that you are as well. She judges others' characters from her own actions. With most people, she is right. But with you, she was wrong. You are a kind young woman, with no ambition other than happiness."

I warmed to his words, though he could not soothe me entirely. "You were exiled, too," I said. "I felt sorry for you, before, but I understand, now."

He nodded. "I was very angry at first, and hurt that I was not trusted. I had been quite proud of my place in the privy chamber. But I came to realize that at court, a man's worth and his integrity is valued as nothing compared to his ability to please and flatter. Not to mention the ability to change loyalties with the flicker of an eye. I came to prefer my solitude."

I bit my lip. "Jack is no flatterer. He can be quite forthright."

"I know. I worry about him. I tried to instill in him the need for discretion, but he does have his opinions."

"He generally knows how to keep silent."

The earl and I exchanged a glance, then sank into our own worried speculation.

* * *

I wrote Jack every day. I do not know if he enjoyed my prattling letters of life in the countryside, but I needed to write them. I liked to picture him receiving the papers far away in London and Greenwich and Hampton Court. I hoped, too, that a stream of reminders of his loving wife and son would keep at bay any interest in pretty court ladies.

> Dearest Jack,
>   The weather continues fine, although the women of the village predict that the year was too dry for a good harvest. Your father said no, we had plenty of rain, but they love to be dismal and so take no notice. Your son continues to grow, and we all have much to do chasing him about. He speaks new words every day and will soon be as learned as a bishop.

> Dearest Jack,
>   The harvest turned out well indeed, and food is stocked throughout the village for winter. The women now predict that the grain will spoil before spring because there is too much of it. The earl very patiently says nothing. A spate of violence occurred at Pennington Hall ending in my maid Katie breaking a crockery jar over her husband Tom's head. Tom had allowed a dog to catch one of the best laying hens, and although the hen was rescued, the poor thing no longer lays eggs. I had to be quite cross with them both. Little John has learned to say "eggs," "hen," and "lackwit."

I wrote these anecdotes to make Jack smile and also to make him realize that I took my duties as his wife and mistress of Pennington Hall seriously.

Jack wrote back far too infrequently for my comfort, but gentlemen have difficulty writing long and effusive letters. When he did write, he spoke only of practical matters, such as where he accompanied Henry to hunt or to meet ambassadors, what such and such meeting at Calais accomplished.

I read Jack's missives eagerly but always ended disappointed. I wished his letters would express some sentiment of regret, show some sign that he missed me. But he finished each of the few letters he sent with a word to his father and to John, and then closed with just his signature.

Nothing can make a woman feel more elderly and unwanted than a letter from her husband that ends with no expression of love. I always finished my letters to him with "Missing you and counting the days until I am with you again, dearest husband, your loving wife, Frances."

It cut me that Jack never acknowledged these sentiments nor returned them.

He did write at the end of October that Anne was again with child. This news relieved me greatly. If Anne carried this child to birth, even if it were another girl, it might restore faith in her ability to bear children. She might forgive me, and let me return to court.

I begged Jack in my next letter to give her my felicitations, but left it to Jack's discretion whether to actually do so.

What I did not tell Jack in that letter was that I, too, had a child quickening in my womb.

I could not keep this news from him forever, of course. My maid would soon know, and then everyone would know. But I was not ready to tell him the secret.

I am not certain what stilled my pen. Did I fear Jack would think me unfaithful and the child not his? Or did I fear that he'd ask leave to see me, and our meeting would be awkward and uncomfortable? Whatever the reason, I did not write, at least not yet.

And then, as we cleaned Pennington Hall from top to bottom for Christmas, my hand was forced. One afternoon I fell quite ill. A dull pain gripped my body and would not cease, and one of the manservants had to carry me to my bed.

That evening, I miscarried my child.

Eighteen

❦

THE SPANISH QUEEN
AND EFFECTS OF A JOUST

JANUARY 1536

CHRISTMAS was cold and dark, and the New Year dawned even darker. I recovered my health from my ordeal, but not my spirits.

I could not bear to write Jack of the incident, so my father-in-law did instead. Jack's answer came swiftly. He said that I was to be well looked after and not allowed to strain myself. He also said that he could not come home. Henry would not let him go until the summer.

As I lay in bed during the long, dark hours of the turn of the year, I grieved. I understood what Anne had experienced when her child had died inside her. I felt a failure. I felt cheated. I felt that God had punished me for my misdeeds.

The earl blamed my forced journey to Pennington, when I had been so ill. My mother wrote and blamed the thin air of Gloucestershire, and told me that Mistress Longacre believed I had been placed under a hex. My mother bade me to remember, however, that Mistress Longacre was a daft old woman. She advised that I find my husband at once and try to have another child, and to take comfort in the one I already had. That, she said, is what she had done.

Jack blamed nothing and no one. The tone of his letters changed from formal missives to worried questions, and also great relief that I had not died myself.

"You may think me hard for rejoicing," he wrote. "But I thank God every day that he did not take you from me as well." This letter he ended, "Ever your fond husband, Jack."

I kissed his letters, but my heart grew heavy. It seemed a long time until summer and seeing him again.

On the twelfth of January, the earl came home from business in Cheltenham, quite agitated. He burst into my chamber, where I sat, sewing by firelight, and dropped into a chair.

"What think you, daughter," he said. His eyes were agitated, his graying hair wild from the winds outside. "Queen Catherine has died. Six days ago."

My needle fell from my nerveless fingers. Jack had written that Queen Catherine was very ill, and that the king seemed in a strange mood; in turns relieved, then morose, then merry.

"Oh," I said blankly.

He sat back, sighing, his square face troubled. "I have heard the most appalling stories that I hope are only rumor. They say the king, at hearing the news, got himself up in a costume of yellow and danced in a lively way with the queen's ladies. The queen, too, celebrated with the king. Catherine's supporters are appalled, but they dare say nothing."

"The poor woman," I said. I had never had any patience with Queen Catherine, but to have her death celebrated was heartless. Anne I did not blame so much, but Henry had been married to her, had sired a child with her.

"Aye, it is a sorry pass that such a proud queen should die alone and forgotten."

We both sat thoughtfully for a time. "It seems disrespectful to say it," I began, "but 'twill make things easier for Anne. There is only one queen now."

"I am skeptical," the earl answered. He let his fingers

dangle over the arms of the square chair. His hands were strong, for all he was fifty. "If Anne's enemies wish to weaken her, they can say that putting Anne aside no longer means the return to Catherine and the pope. Henry can begin fresh, still head of the Church, and begin a new court. The gentleman I spoke to in Cheltenham had already heard such gossip."

I flung down my sewing and jumped to my feet, unable to keep still. "When will it end? Henry chose her because he loved her. Why will they not let it be?"

"Because every man at court wants power. They are willing to do anything to get it, including step over the bodies of their enemies. There are those who feel that Anne had her chance and has not measured up. They are ready for the Boleyns to lose and themselves to win."

"I hate it," I said. "I hate it so much."

His look bore sympathy. "I know. Court is exciting, and court is entertaining, but court can also be deadly."

I stopped pacing and clasped my hands. "And Jack is there alone."

"Yes," he said unhappily.

I said, "When I first met Jack, he gave me all sorts of warnings about court intrigue. I thought him too priggish for words. But he was simply trying to tell me to be prudent and wise. Poor Jack. I upbraided him shamelessly."

The earl smiled. "My son sometimes needs upbraiding. He can be a bit of a stick, but what happened to me angered and frightened him. He was a lad at the time, but he was already acting as a page for the Duke of Norfolk. He has seen what intrigue can do firsthand."

"He told me that Norfolk was untrustworthy," I agreed.

"Jack did not want to become a member of the privy chamber," he said. "But he agreed in order to not disgrace me. To turn down the most privileged position at court would have angered Henry to no end."

"I am happy he did," I said, resuming my seat. "If he had not gone to court, and if I had not, I would not have met him."

"True." He smiled. "And I should not have such a fine daughter-in-law."

Tears filled my eyes. "You are impossibly good to me."

"You care for Jack. He chose well."

"I only hope he thinks so," I said glumly.

We received a letter the next day from Jack, which confirmed the news that Catherine had died, and also confirmed that Henry seemed delighted. "Elizabeth had been brought to Greenwich, and he sent for her, then he paraded about with her, dancing and showing her off to the ladies and gentlemen. And he has become mad for jousting. We've had several tilts since then. I took a slight fall and hobbled about like an old man the next day, but Henry would have nothing for it that I rode again right away. Fortunately, I have healed quickly."

Anne also told Jack to give me her blessing and sympathy as well as best wishes for my recovery. Jack ended the letter with news that, while he'd been writing the letter, he received word from Anne that he might send for me.

"And so, Frances," he concluded, "I will travel upriver as far as Oxford, and you shall travel from Gloucestershire, and we will return to London together."

Two months ago, I would have rejoiced that Jack and Anne both wanted me back. Two months ago I would have, on the instant, tied a few gowns into a cloth, slung it over my back, and hurried off in the direction of Oxford.

Now, in dark January, tired and empty, I scarcely wanted to move, let alone make the long journey to London.

However, it is not a wife's choice to do as she pleases. Also, thinking of high-handed Jack all alone in the maelstrom of Anne's enemies decided the matter. The maids and the housekeeper packed my things, and the earl gave me a gift of money to have new gowns made when I reached London. On the sixteenth of January, I set off.

I was lucky in my weather. The skies remained blue and clear, which meant that it was very cold, but the crisp air and bright sunshine cheered me a bit.

Oxford was a pretty sight, with its spires poking up into

the winter air above the river. Jack had directed me to an inn called the George and Dragon, and when I reached it, he was at the door to meet me.

The smell of boiled mutton assailed me as I ducked under the lintel, and then Jack caught my hands.

"Frances, well met." Under the curious stares of the landlord and his wife and far too many servants, he kissed my cheek.

I felt suddenly shy. I knew my nose was red and raw from the cold and my clothes were stained with mud. I was also aware of how tall he was and how strong, and how much I did not want to let go of his hands.

I had to, of course, so that I could climb the stairs to the chambers he had hired for the night. He led me inside, his hand comfortably on the small of my back.

The outer chamber contained a table and chairs, upon which waited a flagon of wine and a loaf of crisp bread. The inner chamber had a bed, large enough for two, I was pleased to see, although the bed took up most of the space.

I removed my cloak and hung it on a peg. I drew my sodden wimple and veil from my head just as Jack entered the bedchamber and closed the door.

"It is cozy," I said, feeling my nervous hiccups welling up inside. "We will have difficulty dressing without banging our arms and legs into the walls. I suppose I might have to sleep in my stomacher if my maid cannot fit in here to unlace it."

"Frances." Jack put his fingers over my mouth. His eyes held not desire, as I expected, but joy.

I went straight into his arms. He kissed me over and over again. "Every day I wondered if I would see you again," he said. "Every day I wondered if you would die and leave me alone."

"You would not be alone," I said, my words muffled against his chest. "You have your father and John."

He did not seem to hear me. "And the last thing I had done was scold you. I was so angry because I'd known you did not want to marry me, and by God, you'd never written silly poetry about *me*."

I looked up at him. "Did you want me to?"

He gave a short laugh. "Nay, but I did not want you to say such things about another. And then my father sent word how very ill you were, and that I should prepare myself for the worst."

"Was I that ill?" I asked, surprised. "I do not remember much."

"You were. My father said you were fevered, and out of your head much of the time. The day I heard you were out of danger, I made my way to the chapel and lay prostrate on the floor. I thought God had tried to punish me for my anger and pride and jealousy." He kissed my lips. "I very nearly lost you for my own folly."

My heart swelled. I had been so sunk in despair that it felt odd to rise above it again. It was rather like awakening from a terrible dream, and not remembering, for a few blissful moments, why you had been so frightened.

"I am here now," I told him.

He showed me then, by word and by deed, how happy he was in this regard.

WE left Oxford the next morning and arrived in London after an easy journey. As we rounded the bend in the river from Berkshire into Middlesex, passing the round towers of Windsor, my heart lightened still further. In spite of the dark predictions of Jack's father, I began to remember my joyous journeys along the Thames with Anne and the ladies. The square bulk of Richmond, the towers of the abbey of Westminster, the green of the Temple, and the walls of the City all increased my excitement.

We disembarked at Greenwich and made our way to our customary chamber high in the castle. I went about touching everything, pleased and happy to be back where I belonged.

Anne did not send for me right away, and scarce seemed

to notice I'd returned. None of the other ladies paid much attention to me, either, except Mary Howard, who embraced me and sat down with me for a long session of girlish gossip. The king's infatuation with Margery Shelton had cooled, she reported, and he seemed to be once again interested in Anne. Everyone was certain that this time, Anne would bring the hoped-for son.

I was pleased that Henry loved Anne again, but still she did not send for me, and I worried.

My acceptance back into the court, when it came, happened in an odd way. Jack had escorted me to some shops in Greenwich one afternoon so that I could purchase pins and ribbons and cloth to make John a new cap. As we made our way back through the palace, we came upon Henry and his noisy entourage just returning from a hunt.

Dressed in hunting clothes, with his cloak carelessly thrown over his shoulder, Henry could have passed for an ordinary country gentleman, that is, had not the other gentlemen been circling him like dogs around their master.

The gentlemen were flushed and laughing with the tired joy of a successful day and in anticipation of wine and the company of ladies. I thought they would pass us without word. They almost did.

At the last minute, Henry stopped, cloak swirling, in front of Jack.

I dropped into a curtsy, but Henry took no notice of me. "Sir Jack," he bellowed. "Well met. We joust tomorrow. If you have finished with women's errands by then, you will join the answerers."

Jack bowed. "Of course."

"I shall try not to hurt you when I topple you again." He roared with laughter. The other gentlemen laughed along.

Jack winced, then gave him a rueful smile. "I will try to bear it, Your Grace."

"Excellent. Come to supper, man. Your lady can attend the queen."

"Yes, Your Grace," Jack said.

And that was that. Or so I hoped.

* * *

THE jousting took place the next day under fine weather. However, it had rained in the night and the tilt yard was slick with mud. I sat in the royal box with Margaret Douglas and Jane Seymour and a few other ladies. We shared some mirth at the poor grooms below, who slipped in the mud and came to grief. I suppose this was cruel, but it felt good to laugh at something silly.

Anne did not attend today, preferring, she said, in her condition, to remain at home with her ladies. She told me to go and watch the men, since my husband would be jousting. She said it with no particular malice, but likewise, with no particular warmth.

At supper the night before, Anne had allowed me to pour her wine and hold her ewer, though she had not spoken to me much. She had been surrounded by ladies whenever I was near, so I had no chance for a private word with her. I could only wonder whether she'd forgiven me. Her cool eyes told me nothing.

Jane Seymour, down the row from me, scanned the field with avid eyes as the jousting began. I looked at her, puzzled. Quiet Jane had never seemed interested in riding or jousts; indeed, she took interest in little but sewing and praying.

I followed her gaze out into the field and saw that it had riveted on the king.

Ah, I thought sagely. *Another infatuated lady.* Perhaps she sought to replace Margery Shelton in Henry's affections. I could have told Jane it would come to naught. Henry liked ladies who were lively and pretty, not pale and meek.

I looked away from her, no longer interested, and focused my attention on the games.

The challengers wore red feathers in their helms, the answerers green. Henry could be made out not only by his fine armor but by the gaily colored sleeve Anne had given him as her favor. A dull blue sleeve, mine, decorated the helmet of my husband.

Margaret Douglas kept up a rapid litany of gossip, filling

226   L A U R I E N G A R D N E R

me in on events I had missed while rusticating in the country. She knew each gentleman below by his banner and style of armor, and had much to say on their looks and manners.

"Henry Norris is splendid, is he not? A fine gentleman with a well-turned leg. You would know all about that, Frances. Your husband is as handsome as God can make a gentleman, for all he has no use for flirtation."

"Aye," I said, trying not to let her goad me. I certainly did not like Margaret talking about flirting and Jack in the same breath. I was keenly aware that she and her flashing eyes had been here all winter with Jack, while I'd been far away.

"Ah, there he goes," she said, nudging me.

My husband had been loaded onto his horse, and now he took his lance from his squire, the pennant snapping in the wind.

I bit my lip. I enjoyed watching Jack joust, but it was a bit unsettling when one's own husband hurtled himself toward another armored rider and lance at breakneck speed.

The two men met with a crash in the middle of the tilt yard. We heard the horses grunt with effort. My husband's lance struck his opponent square in the shield, shattering the pole into a hundred fragments.

I cheered and waved my handkerchief. A fine hit for my husband.

The horses thundered on, then the riders turned them and trotted back to their corners of the field for new lances.

Jack won that match. He rode from the field, acknowledging the cries of the ladies with a wave of his arm.

When he next took the field as an undefeated knight, he faced the king.

Margaret nudged me and said loudly, "Now we shall see who is the stronger, shall we not, Frances? And we will kiss their bruises when it is done."

The other ladies laughed appreciatively. I saw Jane smile and blush. I gave Margaret a sharp look and did not answer.

I turned my attention back to Jack, wondering whether he would allow the king to win. Henry grew angry if he thought a gentleman was holding back for him. He would rather win against great odds and therefore be the strongest beyond dispute. I did not want Jack to incur his anger; then again, I did not want Henry to beat my husband bloody just to prove he could.

Jack saluted him, then clanked down his visor and readied his lance. Henry did the same. I could imagine Henry's delighted chuckle. Jack was a good rider, and Henry liked to beat the best.

Jack started down the muddy field at a slow gallop. So did the king. The horses gained speed. Faster and faster they plunged, huge legs moving, plate-sized hooves churning mud.

At the last minute, both men slammed their lances into position. One more stride, and then each struck the other man's shield. Two lances splintered hard, pieces flying upward into the clear air.

Solid in his saddle, Jack galloped away to the end of the field. Henry rode to the other, equally at ease.

They passed each other again, trotting, to their own ends, Jack saluting his king as he rode by.

Jack settled himself again, reaching for the lance his attendant handed him. I clasped my hands, excited.

The signal fluttered. Jack pressed his heels into his horse and the beast leapt forward. It thundered down the yard, and Henry's horse thundered toward it.

Jack's lance came down. A split second too late, Henry's followed. Jack's lance struck Henry's shield and shattered. Henry's lance glanced off Jack's shield, and then they were riding past.

Jack loped back around the rail and started for his side of the yard. At that moment, Henry's horse shied.

Henry was a good rider. As the horse danced sideways, Henry kept his seat and turned it.

An attendant came running. Before he could reach the king, the excited horse slipped.

Whether Henry was off balance because of the lance he still carried, or whether he'd twisted in the saddle too suddenly, we never knew.

Down went the horse. Down went the king. The lance flew wide and clattered to the muddy earth. The king's foot came out of one stirrup. Henry landed flat on his back in the mud, his other foot still caught.

The horse rolled right over him.

Margaret screamed. I sprang to my feet. The other ladies did the same, except Jane Seymour, who sagged from her seat.

Down on the field, Jack swung off his horse, steadied by his attendant, who'd sprinted forward. He slammed his visor up as he hastened toward the king.

Henry's horse rolled all the way over and struggled to its feet. Shuddering, its eyes rimmed with white, it loped off toward the stables, grooms in pursuit.

On his back, Henry never moved. Jack shouted orders. The king's attendant unbolted Henry's helm and dragged it from his head.

Henry lay utterly still, eyes closed, his face drawn and bloody. No matter how much Jack and the attendants tried, they could not wake him.

HENRY lay in a stupor for two hours while all the court held its breath. When he at last awoke, demanding weakly to know what had happened, the physicians pronounced that he had not been seriously hurt. We breathed out again.

Henry kept to his bed for a time, but his health was robust, and soon he was up again. I feared that he might blame Jack for the mishap, because he'd been tilting against him at the time, but Henry did not. A fair fall on a muddy field, he said, and snapped for his physicians to cease fussing.

Henry recovered quickly but soon faced another crisis. A few days after the tournament, Anne miscarried their son.

"It was a boy child for certain?" I asked faintly when Jack brought me the news.

He nodded. "The midwives say it was male." He hesitated. "They also said the child was—not right."

"Not right? What do you mean not right?"

"A monster, some are saying. Deformed."

I stared at him, openmouthed. The winter sunlight filtered into the room and marked highlights in his dark hair.

"Deformed?" I shuddered. "This cannot be."

"The tale grows worse, I am afraid." Jack folded his arms, his face lined with tiredness. "Henry claims that the child cannot be his."

I gaped. "Is he mad? How could he be so cruel?"

I remembered the days of darkness after I'd lost my child. If Jack had begun asserting that he had not fathered it, I think I would have lost my wits.

"He is protecting himself," Jack said. "Someone as mighty as the king cannot be thought of as producing a deformed child. It must be a demon child, wrought by adultery or witchcraft."

"Dear Jesu, he *is* mad."

"This is a great blow to him. It would have been a son, a prince. He will say anything in his rage."

I clenched my hands. "I want to go to her. I need to go to her."

So saying, I swept out of the room without taking leave. Jack did not try to stop me.

The midwives and Mistress Marshall let me in without fuss, to my surprise. I expected to find Anne in bed, but she was up and sitting at a writing table. She busily scribbled on paper, but her face was white, her dark eyes sunken.

"What is it, Frances?" she asked wearily.

"Let me help you." I fell to my knees on the cold floor beside her. "Please, direct me. Let me help you in some way."

She gave me a tired look. "No one can help me. I have failed."

I seized her hand, which felt thin, like a layer of sticks. "You are strong. You will get better. You can try again."

She gave me a half smile that looked a bit fey. "No, my dear. The world has changed. His Grace no longer loves me."

"Do not say such a thing. He is disappointed. He will come round. He always does."

"Perhaps." She did not believe me.

"Let me help you," I begged again. I suppose I wanted to make up for having a thriving boy child waiting for me in Gloucestershire. I suppose I wanted her to know that I understood her pain and fear. Perhaps I simply wanted to tell her I loved her.

At last Anne softened. She touched my cheek. "Dear Frances. I should have left you in Hertfordshire when I found you. You are too sweet to be true."

"I am glad you did not," I said fervently. "I was nothing until you brought me here."

She managed a smile, but it was strained. "You are kind. Perhaps I will believe you, and take heart."

I felt a little bit better, though not entirely.

BOTH Anne and I had misjudged the king's anger. His fury ate him all the way through. He searched for a focus for his anger and found one: Anne.

When she resumed her duties a few days later, he came to her presence chambers and told her, in front of her collected ladies and gentlemen, that she had failed him. She could not even do, he said, what a nursemaid in a hovel could do.

By then, Anne had recovered her spirits. "Blame your horse," she retorted. "My uncle Norfolk told me of your fall, that you lay near death on that field covered in blood. My despair turned my womb sick. Can you fault me for grieving for you?"

Henry snarled. "It was only a fall from a horse, woman. I take them all the time. When have you begun being driven mad by tittle-tattle?"

"Since I was your wife, sir," she said icily. "Since you began to shut me out of everything."

"A wife's place is to warm my bed and give me children. Which you have proved you cannot do." He swung around and began to storm out. Ladies parted before him like startled butterflies. "I'll have no sons by you, 'tis certain," he sneered, and then he was gone.

Nineteen

❦

THE RISE OF THE SEYMOURS

EARLY SPRING 1536

WINTER continued in a somber mood. Catherine the queen was buried and gone. Anne and Henry both convalesced. Henry had not been sore hurt, as I said, but after his accident, he became difficult to read.

As Anne regained her strength, however, she regained her confidence. "I easily conceive," she told me and her other ladies. "I will again, soon."

But as the days dragged on, she did not. Henry, I understood from whispers, rumors, and Jack's reports to me, did not go to her.

My husband did not come to me, either. It might not be politic, he explained, for me to conceive at the moment, for us to flaunt our fertility when the king and queen had been having such difficulties.

I agreed with him, at least the sensible part of me did. But I craved him with my heart and body and found our enforced distance unbearable.

"I wish I was your mistress," I said one afternoon, when we snatched a few moments together.

He gave me a bemused look. "What are you saying, Frances?"

"I mean that if you'd taken me as your mistress, we would not have to worry what children came or did not come. No worry whether the child was a boy or a girl. We could just be in love, and everyone would think us romantic."

He started laughing. "You have odd ideas, my dear."

"But true," I said wistfully. "If we were lovers, no one would pay any attention to us."

"But you would have no reputation," he pointed out. "And not be mistress of Pennington Hall. And your family would turn you out."

"I know," I said gloomily. "Sometimes a reputation is a very inconvenient thing to have."

Jack continued to laugh, then he kissed me roughly. I clung to him, a little too much, so he detached me and cut our visit short.

I felt a little better, however. I'd seen the longing in his eyes and knew that his decision to not touch me chafed him as well.

As for Anne and Henry, things between them had the appearance of being as usual. They attended Mass on Sunday. They entertained ambassadors together. They showed off Princess Elizabeth. They scowled at the supporters of Princess Mary, who had grown in number since Catherine's death. I heard George Boleyn observe that he hoped Mary went the same way as her mother, and soon.

Anne tried to stifle whispers and cynical remarks that Henry was about to put her aside, by being every inch a queen. There was only one queen in England now, and her name was Anne. Elizabeth was the legitimate heir, and that was that.

But under the surface, things changed.

In March, Henry brought a young man called Edward Seymour into the privy chamber. Henry had spent some time the previous summer at the Seymour family home, Wolf Hall, in Wiltshire. He'd been impressed with the hospitality he'd received and already liked Edward. So, that spring, he offered Edward the chance to serve him, and Edward jumped at it.

Jack whispered all this to me the nights he slept in our bed. He still did not want me with child, so we only lay quietly together and slept or talked.

Tension, he said, in the privy chamber ran high. "George Boleyn senses he is being pushed out," Jack said. "And he is. Seymour and young Nicholas Carewe are worming their way in. The king no longer bristles as much when people speak against Anne. Seymour and Carewe support Mary. And Edward's sister Jane has caught the king's eye."

I had noticed this last. My speculation during the joust that Henry would not return Jane's interest had proved to be wrong. I could not imagine what he saw in the girl. Jane was not very pretty, and she'd mastered obedience far better than I ever would. She hadn't a word to say for herself.

"Another infatuation," I insisted. "He has done this before."

"Yes," Jack said grimly. "But he's put aside a wife for a mistress before, as well. No one can forget that. Even if Jane only becomes his mistress, Henry will listen to Edward Seymour."

I bit my lip. "But he's done so much for Anne. He defied the *pope,* for heaven's sake. He changed the entire country. Why do all that to simply throw her over?"

Jack raised up on his elbow and regarded me with tense eyes. "Henry believes that God is punishing him for what he's done. He also told me he believes Anne must have snared him with witchcraft. Why else would he have behaved as such a madman? He no longer claims it is love of a woman that guided his actions, but the wicked power of the Boleyns."

I thought about this a moment, my heart squeezing. "What about you, Jack?" I asked. "While the Boleyns and the Seymours are dancing for position, what about you?"

Jack lay down again, lacing his hands behind his head, as he liked to do when thinking. "Henry has not come out and asked which side I am on, but I sense he will soon."

"And what will you say?"

I waited for his answer, fear in my heart. I would always stand behind Anne. She'd given me so much, and I owed her my life. I could not abandon her because a few gentlemen in the privy chamber now felt bold enough to speak against her.

But would I have to stand against my husband?

"I do not know what I will say," Jack replied at last. "But I cannot remain neutral for long."

"You cannot be against Anne," I faltered. "Can you?"

To my relief, he shook his head. "I do not believe Anne should be put aside or ignored for a new mistress. But I do not think Henry did right by Princess Mary. She is a child of his blood, and he drove her to rebellion. This rift is of his own making."

"I know all that, Jack." I stared down into his face. "But what will you say? Will you be with George Boleyn or Edward Seymour?"

I studied him intently, not liking the look in his eyes. Not lying with him of nights already had put distance between us, and I did not want a new gulf to push us farther apart.

He said quietly, "I have not decided."

I started to argue. He abruptly told me to go to sleep, and would say no more about it.

I began to keep a jealous eye on Jane Seymour. As usual, she favored a maddeningly demure manner. While she dressed in the finest court style, she contrived to look as modest as possible. If Jack had not told me about her brother, and if I did not see for myself the king's blatant attentions to her, I would never have believed such a quiet woman could attract a man like Henry.

Anne became cool and distant with all of us ladies. She shot many angry glances at Jane Seymour but never said one word. In short, she was neutral and cold, but I could see that her coldness covered great anger.

Jack, too, distanced himself from me. I do not know if he regretted his words to me regarding his choice—or, I should say, his indecision. He did not come to our bed again after our discussion, and my heart was sore.

I was confused and alone and frightened. Until now, Jack had been the one person with whom I never felt I had to guard my words. Suddenly, I thought that perhaps I did need to choose my words with him. What would happen if he decided to support Seymour and his sister against Anne? He knew I would never waver in my love for her and that I would have to oppose him.

These thoughts ate at my heart.

Court gossip was rife, and of course, revolved around Jane and Anne.

In late March, a delicious story circulated that the king had sent Jane a letter and a purse of gold sovereigns. Apparently, Jane had told the messenger, on her knees, to take back the gift and beg the king to remember that she was a virtuous maiden. She was quite flattered and bewildered at the king's attention, but she could not accept it.

"She learned her lessons well," Margaret Douglas whispered to me. "I've heard the tale of how Anne herself refused the king's suit and turned him away. She fled to Kent, and he panted after her like a dog. Of course, Anne's protests that she would remain a virtuous woman made His Grace's flame burn the hotter. Jane is simply following her example."

Anne realized this truth. Although I do not think at that point she believed Jane would win, she had to concede that Jane knew how to play the game.

The next blow to Anne fell when Henry moved Thomas Cromwell out of the chambers Cromwell used at Greenwich. Then what did he do but invite Edward Seymour and his wife, and Edward's sister Jane, to move into these vacated rooms?

Anne was furious that Cromwell, whom she'd always regarded as a friend and supporter, could have capitulated so quickly. The ladies whispered in glee, and I worried.

Margaret Douglas, the font of all gossip, murmured to me, "You do know why Cromwell's chambers, do you not?"

I confessed that I did not. She explained, "There is a

passage from Cromwell's rooms that connects with the king's."

I gaped, to her delight. "What happened to Jane being a virtuous woman?"

"His Grace has intimated that he will refuse to see Jane without a chaperone." She rolled her eyes. "How utterly proper of him."

I wondered how Margaret viewed Jane's rise in the king's affections. Margaret was not a supporter of the reformed religion. In fact, I thought her a friend of the Seymours, but with Margaret Douglas, it was difficult to say which flag she flew.

By Easter, Anne was miserable with jealousy. She had also come to realize that men like Cromwell, who'd always professed to support her, had been simply supporting themselves all along. Jane now had influence, not she.

But Anne was still queen. I attended Mass with her in all her regalia. *No matter where Henry strays,* she seemed to say, *I am still his consort.*

ON Easter Tuesday, things began to happen that I did not understand, much of it involving politics between England, France, and the Holy Roman Empire. But, as it turned out, these things were very important and led to disaster.

I could not ask Jack to explain matters to me, because I rarely saw him alone, so I had to grasp what I could on my own.

Apparently, Charles, the Holy Roman Emperor, had promised Henry that he would delay the new pope's written declaration that he would organize an invasion of England and try to topple Henry from the throne. The king of France, on the other hand, was threatening to help the pope make good his promise.

Cromwell, now the king's secretary and more trusted than ever, saw this as an opening to switch England's alliance from an ever-more-hostile France to the Empire.

I knew that France and the Empire and England changed

alliances with each other all the time, depending on the mood of the monarchs, or who was married to whom, or who was going to be duke of Milan, which was the current fracas between France and the Empire.

Cromwell sought to take advantage of the breach. Anne agreed with him, and their rift seemed to heal slightly. Queen Catherine, who'd been the emperor's aunt, was dead, and it was high time Emperor Charles acknowledged Anne as queen of England.

To that effect, Cromwell staged a bit of drama at Mass on Easter Tuesday.

Anne and Henry attended at Greenwich Chapel as usual. I was not sitting with Anne at the time, but I saw everything. In the middle of the service, Anne descended from the loft to take communion. In a nice orchestrated move, no doubt thoroughly rehearsed by Cromwell, Anne passed the emperor's ambassador. This man, Chapuys, one of Catherine's great friends as I have said, had never consented to recognize Anne as queen, or even to meet her.

Rustling filled the chapel as courtiers turned to see what would happen. Even the bishop at the altar held up the proceedings to watch.

Anne turned to look at Ambassador Chapuys as he stood before his seat, and with a slight nod, acknowledged him. We held our breaths. Chapuys stared back at her in some dismay. Then, with a quiet look, the ambassador bowed.

The collective sigh flowed over the chapel, then excited muttering began. Cromwell smiled, and so did Anne.

I think it was that night that everything began to unravel. I stayed with Anne in her chambers while George Boleyn entertained Ambassador Chapuys, but I heard the tale of how Henry, for reasons of his own, suddenly destroyed the carefully built spun-sugar house that Cromwell and Anne had built around the hoped-for alliance with the Empire.

Although the other courtiers laughed and joked during the evening, Henry remained sullen and quiet.

Suddenly, Henry swept to the ambassador and burst out, "So, you wish me to reverse my decision to exclude my daughter Mary from the succession, and for that you will help me befriend the new bishop of Rome?"

"Indeed," said the ambassador smoothly.

Henry went red in the face. He suddenly began dancing about the chamber, speaking in a piping voice. "Henry! Henry! Come and please us, Henry, and we will give you pies."

The ambassador, as well he might, looked shocked. So did Cromwell. The other courtiers, including my husband, watched with dismay.

"If Henry does not play, Henry will not have pies!" The king whirled around and thrust a thick finger at Ambassador Chapuys. "You dare. You and Charles. If I do your will, you will be kind. If I do not, you threaten me. Go tell your damned Spanish emperor that England belongs to me, as it belonged to my father. What I have done comes from God's will, and mine. Now, go away."

The ambassador stared in astonishment, but he was an ambassador. He did not argue; he merely bowed and took his leave.

"Your Grace." Cromwell tried to intercede, but Henry threw him off.

And so the ambassador was sent back to the emperor empty-handed. Henry turned his wrath on Cromwell for proposing the entire scheme in the first place. Henry had never forgiven Charles for so blatantly supporting Catherine throughout the divorce, never forgot the possibility that Charles could invade to help the old queen. He never wanted to forget.

Cromwell realized that he'd made a grave error and that his position was in peril. To save himself, he struck out and found his easiest victim, my lady Anne.

Henry wanted Jane. Cromwell wanted to appease Henry. Anne was in the way. So Cromwell moved, swiftly and decisively, against her.

At the time, I paid little attention to these events. They

belonged to the world of men, and it made small difference to me whether England was tied to France or the Empire or to no one. As long as wars did not come along to grieve us, I did not pay much mind to politics.

But Jack did. He watched with worried eyes, and after the imperial fiasco, he told me I must ask leave of Anne to return to Gloucestershire.

This did not please me at all. The queen and king would begin a progress to Dover and Calais after the celebrations of May Day, and Anne had bade me to come. I saw this as a chance to return to her good graces, and I informed Jack that I would go with her.

Jack upbraided me, his lips white, for disobedience.

"Disobedience?" I shouted. "How can I disobey you when you never speak to me? How long has it been since you came to me as my husband?"

Most of our quarrels had ended, up to that day, in rueful laughter and kisses. This one did not. Jack stormed away, leaving me bitter and weak.

APRIL 1536

As spring went on, Henry continued to pile more cruelty on Anne. Not only did he make no secret of his new and somewhat maudlin affection for Jane, but he also made plain he no longer cared for the fate of Anne's family.

George Boleyn had been suggested as the next new Knight of the Garter, a member of that prestigious order having died the year before. Henry had two names put before him, Nicholas Carewe and George. Anne, of course, pushed in favor of her brother. However, on St. George's Day, April the twenty-third, Henry snubbed Anne and chose Master Carewe.

Cromwell, the toad, saw, rejoiced, and made his move.

On the last Saturday in April, I followed Anne into her presence chamber along with several other ladies. While tensions at court ebbed and flowed, and the king flirted with Jane and humiliated his wife, life went on. Anne asked me to attend her mostly because she needed an extra pair of hands sewing for the coming progress.

I did not mind because I was pleased to follow Anne about again. I hoped the best for the Calais trip. Perhaps when she and Henry found themselves again at Calais castle, they would remember the tower room and Jack and I leaving them to spend their first night together. The romance of it could hardly be forgotten.

I hoped against hope that Jack would remember, too. We'd shared our first kiss in Calais. Perhaps, I thought sorrowfully, our romance could be rekindled as well.

As we entered the presence chamber, I saw a young man standing at the window. He did not look around, but I knew who he was. Mark Smeaton, the musician who'd become a great favorite of Henry's and Anne's.

Anne looked slightly annoyed to find him there. "Why do you tarry here, Master Smeaton?" She noted his mournful expression and gentled her tone. "Come, tell me why you look so sad."

Smeaton turned. He gazed at her with heavy brown eyes, then put his hand on his heart. " 'Tis of no moment."

The words were harmless, but I thought him impertinent. Even the highest gentlemen bowed to Anne and called her "Your Grace" and did not speak familiarly to her. Smeaton was becoming full of himself.

Anne said sharply, "Guard your tongue, sir. You may not look to have me speak to you as I should a nobleman."

Smeaton did not look abashed. He bowed. "No, madam. A look sufficed me."

He bowed again, and turned and left the room. Anne glared at his impudence, then jerked around and made for her seat. The ladies whispered until Anne ordered them to silence. We began sewing, and I thought no more of the matter.

* * *

THE next day, Sunday, we took up sewing again, after Mass, again in Anne's presence chamber. The morning sunlight warmed the room, carrying the promise of summer heat. Having spent the winter always cold, with my mind dark, I welcomed it. In June Jack and I could return to Gloucestershire together. We would walk in the gardens and lie side by side in our bed, the scent of roses entwining us.

Or at least we would if Jack ever forgave me. I feared that Jack perhaps would send me home in June but stay here with Henry. I had no idea what he'd decided regarding his support of Anne or Jane, because I rarely saw him these days, and we never spoke.

I wiped away two tears of self-pity, and for distraction, focused on the low-voiced conversation Anne had begun with Henry Norris.

"Margery Shelton," Anne was saying. "My cousin."

Sir Henry smiled gently. "Aye, I will acknowledge that she is your cousin."

"She needs to be married," Anne said. She sounded annoyed. "I must ask why you have not done so."

Sir Henry looked slightly abashed. "I had not thought to marry any lady, Your Grace."

"Come, come, sir. You have been a widower five years. Is there no lady whom you would have as your wife?"

Poor Sir Henry. I watched out of the corner of my eye as he flushed then whitened. He could apologize for trifling with Margery, but Anne might decide that the only way Norris could make up for toying with her was marriage. Norris might find himself bound into a marriage he did not want before he could even draw a breath.

He decided to worm his way out of the question by flirting. "I would tarry a time," he said, sending Anne a coy half smile, "before I marry."

I tried not to roll my eyes. This approach did not always work with Anne. She was master of flirtation and expected lesser beings to bow before her.

Today, she decided to be displeased, even horrified, at his presumption.

"Do you mean to prefer me?" she said, lowering her voice.

"Perhaps," he said, still flirting.

Anne lost her temper. "Do not tell me you seek dead man's shoes. If aught came to the king but good, you would look to have me."

I looked up, astonished at her statement. She held Henry Norris with a glare from her dark eyes. Sir Henry spluttered, startled out of his flirtatious banter. "No, madam. If I should have any such thought, I would my head were from my shoulders."

"Such things have happened," Anne snapped. "Beware of what you say. I could undo you if I would."

Sir Henry floundered in a manner distressing to watch. "I never meant an insult to you, madam. I am unworthy of such thoughts."

Anne cooled, but she glanced about the room, noting the sudden silence. "Go to your almoner, and tell him I am a virtuous woman," she said to Sir Henry. "And have yourself shriven."

Sir Henry, looking slightly appalled at the way the conversation had gone, bowed and nearly fled the room.

As with the encounter with Mark Smeaton the day before, I thought the exchange not worth commentary. Anne had accused Sir Henry of wanting her, and perhaps she was right, but I assumed no one would pay attention to such nonsense.

I had forgotten that at court, one tiny spark can burn down an entire castle. By that afternoon, Anne's enemies had fanned the incident into high flames. And Henry, her husband, confronted her.

Anne knew he was coming. She sent her ladies away, and then she clutched my arm and told me to run and fetch the princess Elizabeth, who was visiting for the coming May Day celebrations.

I hurried in my errand, running back to Anne's chamber on the heels of the nursemaid. Elizabeth, pretty with her halo of red curls, squalled at being bounced in the nurse-maid's arms.

We heard Henry shouting as we tumbled into Anne's chamber. "Madam, your conduct has always been lacking as a wife. Sharp words and haughty gestures are not what a gentleman desires. And now I find the reasons you were harsh with me, eh?"

"Never would I give you cause to doubt me," Anne said. She sounded desperate, pleading, very unlike herself. "The love I bear you runs deep, more than a woman for a man or a lady for her king."

He did not seem to hear her. "I have given you everything, at your command. My heart, my realm, my wealth, more than any mere woman ever deserved. And you pay me back with deceit and lies, with a friend who was dearer to me than any brother."

Spittle flecked his lips. Anne's eyes were enormous. "I swear to you, upon my heart, I am innocent. 'Tis gossip, nothing more."

"You twit me over a harmless and chaste flirtation," he growled. "While on the other side of your face, you spurt threats to me and carry on with your lovers. The child you lost cannot have been mine."

Anne swung to the maid and held out her arms for Elizabeth. "*This* is my only child, and she is wholly and faithfully yours."

She gathered Elizabeth to her. Elizabeth was nearly three years old now. She was a pretty child, with her mother's dark eyes, but when she lowered her brows, her father's expression shone from her face. She lowered those brows now and said imperiously, "Down."

Anne hugged her and kissed her cheek.

"Do not hide behind the skirts of your child," Henry began. But already his flush had receded and his scowl had lessened. Elizabeth had worked her magic.

"She is our child," Anne said. "Our hope."

Henry glared at Anne, then at Elizabeth, who glared right back at him.

His growl, when he spoke again, had receded to a rumble. "Madam, your conduct is deplorable. I dislike my courtiers murmuring and whispering in my ears. Mend your ways and behave like a queen."

Anne bowed her head, her dark locks mingling with Elizabeth's red ones. "I strive to return as much honor as you have shown me, for the love I bear Your Grace."

Henry said, "Humph," and did not look convinced, but at least he left her. His angry stare lingered on me as he walked away, and I dropped into a curtsy and pretended not to notice.

Twenty

❦

PRISONERS IN THE TOWER

HENRY canceled the journey to Dover and Calais, to my disappointment. He nearly canceled the May Day festivities and jousts as well, but at the last moment, he changed his mind. A harried staff, learning that the jousting was on again, hastily prepared the tilt yard. The royal box was hung with cloths bearing the king's red and gold standards, and the queen's blue and violet colors. Anne entered, her face betraying none of the strain I'd seen there yesterday.

Jack, in his armor, took his place on the field. This time, the king had included him on his side. Sir Henry Norris was to lead the answerers.

Jack wore my favor in his helm again, I saw to my relief. My gaze followed him as he walked about awaiting his turn, sunlight glinting on his armor.

Suddenly I craved him. I wanted him with me, up in our chamber in the sunlight. I wanted him to undress me and touch me. It was a mindless craving, and I know not what brought it on. At that moment, I simply wanted to be far from here with his hands and lips on my body.

I breathed a sigh of regret. Anne glanced sharply at me, then away.

The jousting began. We ladies behaved as usual. We cheered the winners. We groaned when a knight fell, and offered kerchiefs to mop his blood. We waved for our favorites and threw flowers to them. Anne sat rigid and regal. I stewed in my own lust and wanted my husband.

Sir Henry Norris' horse for some reason decided it did not want to joust. When Sir Henry clapped his legs against its sides, the obstinate beast bucked and spun but would not run. Sir Henry tried to canter him about to release his bad temper, but to no avail.

Perhaps the horse was hurting, perhaps he'd been spooked. One never knows with horses. When a horse decides it is having nothing to do with what you want it to do, all of God's angels cannot change its mind.

The king laughed at his friend's plight and commanded one of his own horses to be brought for Sir Henry. The grooms stripped the furniture and cloths from Sir Henry's charger and transferred them to the new horse. At last, Sir Henry was mounted again. We cheered.

The jousts finished in the afternoon, with the king's side winning, of course. The rest of us made our way to the hall where a great feast had been prepared. The long evening would be warm, and we'd dance and drink and eat for the joy of life and spring.

May Day festivities could become bawdy, and I would maneuver to have Jack at my side when that happened.

But as the feasting began, I could not help but notice that several people remained notably absent: Sir Henry Norris, the king himself, and my husband Jack.

I took to my chamber much later that night, dismissed my maid, and undressed myself. I put off my wimple and veil, then my stomacher, which my maid had unlaced. I slid off my bodice, then my skirt. I laid the clothes carefully over a bench, smoothing each garment as I went.

I'd stripped all the way down to my skin, then pulled on a thick, loose robe. With my feet stuffed into slippers, I padded to the bed and sat upon it.

The night turned cool. Nights would not warm until long summer days saturated the land with heat. I pulled the robe close and stared into the fire, my heart numb, my mind racing. At the festivities, which had indeed turned quite raucous, I'd heard terrible whispers of terrible things. People had looked at me sideways when I tried to speak to them, and would not answer my questions.

As time ticked by, I became more and more troubled.

Near three in the morning, I heard a tread outside the door. My heart in my throat, I leapt from the bed, hurried to the door, and thrust my head into the dark passage. "Jack, is that you?"

"Go back inside," my husband answered. "You'll take cold."

He near pushed me back into the chamber. His doublet and trunk hose were soiled and stained, the cloak he flung on top of my velvet clothes wet and coated with mud. His damp hair dripped on the floor, and he was shaking.

"You are the one who is cold," I said. "Your hands are freezing. Come, sit by the fire."

He did as I instructed, sinking into a square chair and resting his head in his hands. Firelight danced on his dark hair, the curls outlined sharply against his skull.

"Would you like wine?" I asked, anxious.

He drew a breath. "Aye. Please."

I poured some into a cup and brought it to him, a dutiful wife. My hands shook so hard that I sloshed liquid over the rim before he caught the cup and took it away from me.

He drank, and I traced the swallow down his throat. His face was dark with unshaved whiskers.

I set the flagon on a table. "What has happened? Why were you not at the feasting? Where did you go?"

I did not want to sound like a harridan, but my voice shrilled.

"London," he said. He drank another swallow of wine

and closed his eyes. "London with the king and Sir Henry Norris."

"Why? What did you do there? I have heard frightening things, Jack. I've heard that Mark Smeaton was arrested. But I could not discover why."

Jack did not look at me. " 'Tis true. Young Smeaton was arrested. And interrogated by Cromwell. Then he went to the Tower to be put on the rack."

My eyes widened, horror chilling me. "Why? Did he murder someone?"

"Only the queen's good name," Jack said humorlessly. "In the end, he confessed that he had indeed been the queen's lover, and so, God help him, had Sir Henry Norris."

I stared, dumbfounded. *"What?"*

Jack said nothing. I began to babble. "What are you saying? That cannot be true."

"The king believes it true." Jack's tone was somber. "At the joust's end, Henry suddenly gathered up Norris and me and a few others and said we would ride to York Place. All along the road he questioned Norris. Was what Smeaton said true? Was he the queen's lover? Was Norris Anne's lover as well? If he would confess, then the king would pardon him. Norris was astonished. He said the conversation yesterday was misunderstood, though foolish, but the queen is virtuous and Norris, guiltless."

"I was there," I said. "I heard him and the queen speaking. I heard the entire thing. I know there is nothing between them. I can tell the king."

Jack gave me a sharp look. "No. You will stay well out of it. Anne has plenty of witnesses to her character, and so does Norris."

"Did the king pardon him, then?"

"No." He drained the goblet. "Norris was arrested when we reached London. He will be taken to the Tower tomorrow. The manner in which the king behaved, I am surprised he did not arrest the lot of us."

Cold struck the pit of my stomach. "He could not. Why should he?"

Jack looked up at me, eyes dark. "Because he is crazed with anger. Anne has disappointed him deeply. If he can put her aside, then he will be wifeless, free to choose whom he pleases to be queen."

"Jane Seymour," I said softly. "Oh, dear God."

"Very likely. Edward Seymour has done his work. They were waiting, Cromwell and the king, just waiting for an excuse to move. They have found it. Adultery against the king is treason."

I put my hand to my throat. "But it is a lie. I have been with Anne all these years. She has no more committed adultery than I."

He flashed me an ironic glance. "Do not put that forth as a defense, I implore you. Any word, any slip of the tongue, can be taken as an admission of guilt. Cromwell has one of the finest legal minds in the kingdom, and he will put it through every twist and turn he can to have a case." He set the goblet on the floor. "That is why I will restate my wish to send you to Gloucestershire. I want you far from here while all this transpires."

"Abandon her?" I cried. "And abandon you?"

Jack went stern. "Your loyalty does you credit, Frances. But I do not want you here. I do not want you to be called as a witness. Cromwell likes to move swiftly; if he has to take time to send to Gloucestershire and then wait for your return, he might decide not to bother with you."

I hugged myself, the wide sleeves of the robe swallowing my nerveless hands. "You fear what I would say to him."

"I fear that you will be accused of being a go-between. You are very close to the queen, and there are many jealous of that position. They might see this as a way to destroy you. They'd put you forth as a procuress, or some such."

"But that is all nonsense," I protested.

"It does not matter. It will not matter what is true or what is false. Cromwell will act; he will do anything to remain in Henry's good graces. He will ensure that things happen the way the king desires."

I clutched his shoulder. "In that case, you must go to

Gloucestershire yourself. We will retreat there together. You said you might have been arrested tonight. If they can think of me as a go-between, they can accuse you of the same."

He shook his head. "I am not so certain. I have kept my distance from the queen."

I wished he would look at me, but he directed his gaze to the fire. "You said it will not matter. I am frightened for you, Jack. Do not send me away, to live every day fearing and not knowing, and uncertain I will ever see you again."

"If you were in Gloucestershire, I would be sure that you were safe."

I snatched my hand from him. "That is all very well for you. What about me? I should go ill with worry, and I have had enough of being ill, thank you very much."

At last he did look up at me. His eyes held a mixture of annoyance, amusement, resignation, and fear. "You have no propensity for obedience, Frances."

"I know that. I had thought it quite obvious."

He clasped my hand, though he did not caress me or squeeze my fingers. "Very well, we will watch and see what happens. But I want you to promise to speak to no one. Keep silent and contrive to be as overlooked as possible."

"I excel at that," I answered. I remembered my terrible need for him this afternoon, and if anything, his frightening news had increased it. "Jack? Come to bed?"

He looked up at me, eyes haunted. I swallowed the bubble of hurt inside me.

"Frances—" he began.

"Please."

His voice turned harsh. "If I share a bed with you this night, I will not be able to stop myself."

"Good." I lifted his hand and pressed it to my bosom. "Please, Jack. I need you."

He regarded me for a long, silent moment. I could not decide if the look he gave me came from love or anger.

Then he nodded, rose from the chair, and led me to the

high bed. His boot caught the goblet, and it spun away. Drops of wine sprayed the floor like blood.

THE next day, a council summoned Anne and questioned her. It was headed by William Fitzwilliam, the royal treasurer, and her own uncle, the Duke of Norfolk.

I do not know exactly all that was said in the examination, because I was not allowed in, but I knew what she said when she came out. "Norfolk used me very ill," she flashed. "I have done him every favor he has asked, all my life, and raised him high in the king's grace. And now he wags a finger at me and tuts me for my behavior. My own character, he said, has brought me to this."

She looked furious, then she sat, as though her legs could no longer hold her. "And now he abandons me," she finished, her voice limp.

They came for her not long after that. I had striven all morning to do as Jack said, to be as inconspicuous as possible. I quietly ran errands that would take me away from the queen's chambers and tried to sit unobtrusively when I had to be in the company of other ladies.

The Duke of Norfolk entered the presence chamber, his long face cold and neutral. "You are to come with me," he said to Anne.

"Where to now?" Anne's voice cracked.

"The Tower of London."

Silence fell like a dropped anvil. Even Anne's direst enemies looked shocked. It was one thing for a nobody like Mark Smeaton to be arrested, even for Sir Henry Norris to be taken to the Tower. But Anne was a queen.

Anne's long-fingered hand closed over my arm. "Come with me, Frances."

I started, staring up into her white face, lined like death.

"Leave her," Norfolk snapped.

"I need someone to wait upon me. I want Frances."

"You will be provided for."

Anne's voice rose, hysteria edging it. "Am I to have no one I trust? I need her."

Norfolk's dark gaze moved to me. I saw in its depths the sharp intelligence of a man who could find a way to use any tool to further his own purpose.

"Very well, bring her. Come along."

Anne kept her hand around my wrist and dragged me behind her. Her fingers were ice-cold and shaking, and she never once looked at me.

As we scrambled down the slippery steps to the river and the waiting barge, I wondered if anyone would remember to tell my husband that I was on my way to the Tower.

Twenty-One

❖

FALL FROM GRACE

THE barge was somber and plain, nowhere near the brightly painted, flower-bedecked craft that had carried Anne upstream to her coronation. No boats rode alongside us spouting fire or music or rose petals. No banners fluttered, no minstrels sang, and we wore no cloth of gold.

A crowd flocked the streets and around the Tower gates. Word traveled quickly, I reflected as I steadied my lady out of the barge. All of London, it seemed, had turned out to see the humiliation of the queen. The women taunted her and called her witch. They gloated, they screamed insults.

I glanced briefly at the crowd and saw, to my shock, two faces very familiar to me. One belonged to my mother. The other was the black-hooded visage of Mistress Longacre.

My mother stared at me, her eyes wide in horror. I could not stop; the escort kept us walking at a brisk pace, and Anne would not let go of me.

"Tell Jack," I cried to her. "Go to Greenwich and find Jack!"

I do not know whether she heard, or understood, or moved to obey. She watched me go, her mouth open in dismay. Uncharitably, I wondered whether that dismay stemmed from worry for me or worry that my disgrace would be hers.

The lieutenant of the tower was Sir William Kingston, a tall man with a sloping forehead, and he waited for us inside the Court Gate.

Anne fell to her knees, more or less dragging me down with her. She looked up into the circle of faces, her uncle Norfolk, the lord chamberlain, Cromwell, and Kingston. "Jesu, give me mercy," she said to them. "I am an innocent woman."

They studied us at their feet, unmoved. *This is our world,* they were saying. *You have invaded it, unwanted.* They would not help her.

I assisted Anne to stand. "Master Kingston," she gasped to Sir William, "shall I be put into a dungeon?"

Kingston bowed, but his face was like granite. "No, madam. You will go into your own apartments, which you have used on happier occasions."

He meant the chambers rebuilt and decorated for Anne's coronation. The irony was not lost on her. "No, they are too good for me." She fell against me, sobbing, then her sobs changed abruptly to loud and shrill laughing.

The gentlemen exchanged glances, as though they'd expected nothing else from wicked Anne.

I slid my arm around her waist to support her. She leaned heavily on me as I led her deeper into the Tower and to the sumptuous rooms that were now her prison.

KINGSTON tried to have me removed. A few other women, besides his own wife, had been summoned to attend Anne, including Margery Horsman, who had been a lady of the wardrobe and never liked her. But Anne begged him to let me stay.

Mistress Horsman unwittingly helped me remain, because she remembered quite well the day that Anne had quarreled with me and sent me packing to Gloucestershire.

She told Lady Kingston she was certain I would be nursing grudges against Anne.

"She will be as good an attendant as I," Mistress Horsman said somewhat smugly.

Lady Kingston wanted Anne's attendants to be as hostile to her as possible. And so, on the strength of Mistress Horsman's belief, I remained.

However, even those haughty ladies could not be unmoved by Anne's plight. At first she would neither drink nor eat. She paced the chamber, unmoved by our pleas that she sit and rest or take food. She babbled and chattered or laughed in hysteria. Over and over, she pleaded her innocence.

"I cannot understand it at all," she said. She strode back and forth, her hands going to her neck, fumbling with her jewels, gripping her dress. "To be used so, as queen. 'Tis not to be borne, nor understood. How did those two men, innocent of everything, come to be here with me?"

I begged her to cease speaking, to sit with me and take wine, but she waved me off.

"He is a good man, Sir Henry, and virtuous. His flirting is a game, naught but a game. Sir Francis Weston is far more a rake and always will be. 'Twas Weston himself loved Margery, and more than his wife it was said."

Lady Kingston hovered on every word. When Anne was to sleep, and I lay in the room with her, she babbled on about bits of court life, going over and over the incident with Norris, trying to ferret out where someone had misinterpreted it. 'Twas Weston, too, she said, who said that he loved one in Anne's chamber more than his own wife or Margery Shelton—Anne herself.

Not until well into the next day did Anne at last fall silent. She went into a sort of stupor, and then slept. When she awoke, she was shaking and hungry but could eat little.

She let me serve her dinner, which she picked at, although she did seize her cup of wine with relief. She seemed more herself after that, but began to fret.

"What will become of my father and my poor, sweet

brother? My mother will die from this sorrow, because of me. And my sister's child, he is only a boy. Will he still be cared for? I am ashamed that I have brought this all upon them. Would I could see my brother one last time. Dear George, my sorrows will trouble him greatly."

"Your brother, madam," Kingston said from his position by the door, "was arrested and brought to the Tower yesterday."

Anne stopped in midword. She stared at the master for a stunned moment, then she laughed. She could not stop laughing. "At least he is near," she said, and then she picked up her cup of wine and drank to him.

Sir Francis Weston was arrested that day. From what I understood, he denied the accusation that he'd been Anne's lover as well, but ended up a prisoner, anyway.

Those two weeks were the most bizarre of my life. If Jack or my mother tried to get a message to me, I never heard of it. I felt isolated and alone.

Every day we'd hear a report from Sir William or Lady Kingston, and it seemed that every day a new and fantastic charge was brought and another arrested. On Thursday, it was William Brereton, groom of the privy chamber. I supposed his charge, too, was adultery with the queen, which is the accusation they'd leveled even at George Boleyn.

On the eighth, I heard that two more men, Thomas Wyatt whose poetry I'd so long tried to emulate, and a man called Sir Richard Page, had been arrested.

I held my breath as the roll of names marched in, waiting for Kingston to announce that of Jack Carlisle. If these other gentlemen could be accused of the preposterous charge of adultery with the queen, then what was to stop them from accusing Jack? He'd never told me whether he'd remained loyal to Anne or pledged himself to Jane. Had he perhaps, for safety's sake, decided to join Edward Seymour?

Or, perhaps because of Jack's straitlaced nature, no one thought they could make a charge of adultery stick to him. I noted that they'd arrested men already a bit lascivious, like Weston and Sir Thomas Wyatt, who were notorious for pursuing ladies even when married themselves. If they brought in Jack, who was a model of propriety, the case might dissolve like the air it was. Or perhaps they simply hadn't manufactured the evidence yet.

These thoughts tormented me, and I nearly fell into as much hysteria as Anne. Traitors died a terrible death, like the Carthusian monks had last year, castrated and disemboweled and quartered while still alive. I have no idea how long the condemned lived through this ordeal, but the thought of Jack enduring it made me sick with fear.

Anne begged Sir William to let her send for the king or Archbishop Cranmer. He constantly denied her. She was allowed to see only Sir William and his wife and the ladies who looked after her. She continued to hold great hope, however, in support from the archbishop, who she swore loved her.

But as the days passed, no word came from either him or the king.

FROM the windows of Anne's chambers in the Tower, I could see the Tower Green. The grass had gone emerald with coming summer, and small white flowers poked through it. Crows, black and big-bodied, flapped there.

Inside, in the chamber behind me, Anne paced and talked, as she did every day. At times she was merry and made many jests, then she would fall into despair and wish to die.

I gazed out over the green and the rooftops beyond in melancholy. Somewhere out in the world men and women carried out their daily lives, sat down to table together, watched their children together, went to bed together. They would discuss the highly entertaining spectacle of the queen's arrest. Out there in the world today, some, very likely my mother, were saying that Anne was having her comeuppance at last. Others would be shaking their heads over the so obvious political plot to remove her.

I wished and wished I could be one of these people,

reading the news with amazement and discussing it with
Jack. I wished it was no more to me than a piece of scandal
that I mulled over, comfortably outside it.

Then I would weep quietly, because I was wicked in
wanting to desert her.

Lady Kingston was a font of information. Pious and disapproving, she nonetheless knew, through her husband,
what Cromwell and his council were up to. With a touch of
glee, she related it to the rest of us ladies.

"Jane Rochford has told much," she said. "She agreed
that there was much familiarity between the queen and her
brother beyond what so near a relationship can justify."

"Nonsense," I said, then closed my mouth. I had observed much affection between Anne and George, but
nothing that convinced me that it was anything untoward.

"Not nonsense, my girl." Lady Kingston seemed to rel-
ish the details. "I hear that another lady said that the queen
would allure him with her tongue in his mouth, and his
tongue in hers."

I could not keep still this time. "But I have waited upon
the queen for four years. I have never seen such things."

Lady Kingston gave me a pitying look. "Then thank God
that you have not. Likely she sent you from the room before
she performed such abominations. Perhaps the one good
she did was to abstain from corrupting your innocence."

I wanted to scream and protest, but I knew it would do
no good. Even Anne counseled me to silence. "Say nothing, Frances," she begged in a whisper one evening. "I do
not wish you condemned with me. I will answer at my trial
to any question. They will not be able to bring witnesses,
because it is all false. But I do not want you to have to face
the court."

She gave me a stern look, every inch the queen, and I
promised her.

ON the afternoon of the eleventh of May, Margery Horsman, who herself had been summoned by Cromwell to tell

stories against Anne, relayed something that froze my blood.

"What think you, Lady Carlisle?" she said to me. "My lord Cromwell has been brought a sheaf of poetry written by the queen to her brother. In it she describes all manner of longing for him and waxes on about the turn of his leg and the silk of his hair." She shook her head and made disapproving noises. "Who would have thought such licentious things went on under our very noses?"

I stilled. "Poetry?"

"Aye, a long parchment of it. And names in the margins."

"You saw it?"

"Nay, not I. But I heard many speak of it."

I stared at her one long, numb moment, then I turned from her and ran, not minding if I was rude.

I searched the chambers for Lady Kingston, finally finding her in Anne's dining hall. Anne was in one of her merry moods and was teasing her other ladies and Sir William.

Lady Kingston followed me to a corner with bad grace. "What is it?"

"I must see Master Cromwell," I hissed. "Can you arrange such a thing?"

Lady Kingston eyed me sharply. "Why?"

"I have thought of something to tell him."

"Tell *me*," she said. "Tell me what you have, and I will convey a message."

I contrived to look mysterious. "It is for his ears only."

Lady Kingston had much of my mother in her. She drew back her hands to box my ears, but I stepped quickly out of reach. "It is important, my lady. You do not want to keep any evidence from Master Cromwell, do you?"

For a long moment, I thought that she gladly would keep it from him if she could have joy of slapping impertinent Lady Carlisle. But then, perhaps Cromwell would blame Lady Kingston for withholding a damning story.

Lady Kingston satisfied her need for violence by taking me by the ear and marching me out of the room.

Next, I had to convince her husband, who was just as

reluctant as his wife to have me bother Cromwell. But I knew—I believed with all my heart—that I could save Anne's life. I could collapse the nonsense case against her.

Sir William finally understood that I would stubbornly demand to see Cromwell until he and I turned to dust. He had been instructed to deliver to Cromwell anything Anne or her ladies revealed, and he, too, did not want the consequence of withholding a piece of evidence.

At last, without letting me say a word of assurance to Anne, he took me out of the Tower. We went down through the confining gates to the water, out into open air. I took my place on a small boat with Sir William, who directed the bargeman to row us upstream to York Place.

I was out of the Tower, back in the world, free, as I'd longed to be. In my agitation, however, I could rejoice in none of it, not the soft spring air, the green of the far bank, or the cool of the river. I glided through, seeing nothing.

We landed at York Place after what seemed too long a time, and I scrambled up the slippery stairs to the doors, following the swing of Sir William's dull black cloak.

The first person I saw when I entered the palace proper was my husband Jack.

It tells much of my agitation that I did not run to him at once. He stopped in midstride to wherever he was off to and stared at me. "Frances? What the devil?"

I had spent nearly two frightening weeks wondering if he would be safe and if I would ever see him again. And now that I beheld him, now that I could go to him, I could only look at him imploringly and blurt, "I cannot speak to you. I am here to see Cromwell, and I must to him at once."

I swung around, skirts swirling, and hurried after Kingston, who was marching smartly through the passages.

Jack came behind me, his footfalls swift. "What is this all about? Tell me at once."

"I can save her," I said. "I can, if only I see Cromwell."

He put a frantic hand on my shoulder and dragged me to a halt. "No."

"I cannot explain. But he has evidence that is false, and I must tell him. Do let me go, Jack."

He would not. I squirmed to get away from him, but he held me fast.

My heart beat swiftly. If Jack tried to forbid me seeing Cromwell, I would have to fight him. I could be arrested myself for so blatantly disobeying my husband in public. I could be put in the stocks or given some other punishment like wearing an iron mask with a hideous face, to let everyone know I was a scold and a harridan.

Sir William looked behind him. "Lady Carlisle," he said peremptorily.

His loud voice made Jack loosen his hold. I slipped from him and ran after Kingston.

I followed him into an antechamber, and Jack came after me. Kingston told me to wait, then asked a servant to admit him to Cromwell. The servant opened the door at once and ushered him inside.

As soon as the door closed, Jack began arguing. "Frances, you have no business here. Come away with me, now."

"I cannot. You will see."

"Why must you always defy me?"

"I am sorry, Jack. I know I am a terrible wife, but I cannot bother with that right now." I bit my lip. "If I could see the king, 'twould be even better."

He was white to the lips. "None have seen His Grace. He is speaking to no one. He still swears that Anne is a witch, and he cannot risk letting himself near her."

"He will think differently when Cromwell hears me."

I shook all over, half-crazed with the idea that my words could change everything. Jack said nothing. His face was white, the lines around his mouth strained.

"Damn you, Frances," Jack began, but then the servant returned, and he fell silent.

The manservant bowed to me and told me to follow him. He did not extend the invitation to Jack, but Jack came anyway.

For a place of interrogation, the room we entered was comfortable. I had been housed in the luxury of Anne's Tower rooms, but the simple elegance of this chamber—carved wood, tall fireplace, tapestries, and square wooden desk—was refreshing.

Cromwell sat behind his desk, his long nose and slightly fat face offering no comfort at all. I'd never liked his eyes, narrow and dark and penetrating. He was a man of law and a man for himself, those eyes said.

Sitting near him were the gentlemen who had questioned Anne at Greenwich—Lord Audley, the lord chancellor; Sir William Paulet, the controller of the household; and Lord Fitzwilliam, the treasurer. These four men gave me the eye and made me feel as they had Anne at the Tower gate—a foolish woman presuming to intrude in their privileged world.

It was Fitzwilliam who spoke. "You claim to have evidence against Lady Anne?"

I bristled that he used her former title, but I could not afford to quibble.

"The poem," I said. "The poetry that was addressed to George Boleyn—Lord Rochford."

Cromwell leaned forward, his eyes glittering with interest. "Yes? You know about that, do you, Lady Carlisle?"

"Aye." I clenched my hands against my stomacher. "I know Her Grace the queen did not write it. It is false. She never in her life said such things about her brother."

Lines firmed in Cromwell's face. The answer displeased him, but I did not care two straws for that.

"It was found among her personal papers," he said. "It familiarly addresses her brother by his given name. The handwriting resembles hers."

"That is because I have always tried to imitate her writing; it is so fine." I drew a breath. "I wrote that poetry, my lord. I said those things about the queen's brother."

The room went utterly still. The snap of a log in the fire-place was loud as a cannon shot.

Cromwell's fingers moved on the paper before him, a dry sound. "You wrote it for her, you say?"

Pig, I thought. "Indeed, no. I wrote it for myself."

His mouth flattened. I felt like a fish on a line, squirming and dancing to free myself from the hook.

"Adultery is a serious offense, my lady," he said.

"This is not about adultery," I cried. "It is about a silly girl who admired a man above her station and wrote foolish words about him. I meant no harm, and I never dreamed any but myself would see it."

Cromwell looked at me for a long time. "You are an impertinent young woman." He adjusted a paper. "The poetry seems to have been mixed in with the queen's papers; therefore, I assume it hers."

"Because she discovered it, and was very, very cross with me. She punished me, believe me, my lord."

He went quiet. I sensed thoughts spinning behind his eyes, thoughts I did not trust. He was a man not so much concerned with truth as how he could bend truth to serve his needs.

I threw open my hands. "I wrote the words, before my marriage. I thought those things; the queen did not. The letters on the margin are F and G—Frances and George. The foolish dreams of a foolish girl. My lord, you must believe me."

He gazed at me in silence. His colleagues gazed at me, too.

"It seems I must," Cromwell said at last. I nearly cried in relief.

Cromwell's hard gaze flicked to Jack, who stood behind me. "Sir John, what say you of your wife and her confession?"

Jack came forward. He walked slowly, deliberately, to the desk. I could sense his thoughts, as slick and precise as those of Cromwell. "My wife has recently become with child," he said.

Cromwell's brows flickered. I remained stone still. I had done no such thing, or at least, I would not know whether I had for some time. Jack and I had lain together on the night of May Day, and my courses were not due for another week or so.

"My felicitations," Cromwell said with polite disinterest.

"She becomes overwrought at these times and speaks nonsense. But she does say the truth about the poems. I saw them when she wrote them, before our marriage. They were a foolish bit of hubris in one very young."

"Indeed they are."

I held myself still, hiding my alarm at Jack's lies. He'd never seen this sheet until Anne showed it to him last August.

Cromwell studied Jack in calm assessment. His shrewd gaze moved from Jack's velvet hat down his gold slashed sleeves to the diamond on his finger, and all the way to his flat, brocade shoes. Jack Carlisle was every inch the wealthy courtier, handsome, aristocratic, and friend to the king. I, in my velvet stomacher and French hood, was every bit the courtier's wife, although I was never so neat as Jack.

Time ticked by as I watched Cromwell decide what to do with us.

Jack was wealthy, Jack had powerful friends, Jack had always supported Anne. On the other hand, I was a nobody, of no noble lineage, with a mother openly hostile to Anne.

Cromwell's white fingers twitched as he ran his gaze over us again. Then his eyes summed us up and decided, *Too weak to be a threat.*

"Sir John," he said smoothly. "Take your wife, and go."

Jack inclined his head, put his hand under my elbow, and steered me away.

I looked over my shoulder. "Will you free her? She is innocent of this."

"Lady Carlisle." Cromwell's voice froze the air. "She stands accused of treason against the king. That is the highest crime in the land. There will be no forgiveness for that."

I stared at him, cold to the bone. Jack pulled me round and at last got me out the door.

He towed me along passages, through blocks of sun-shine from high windows, and down into the gloom of the lower palace. I barely saw where we went.

In an empty chamber, Jack swung the door closed.

"I had to save her," I sobbed, my face wet. "I had to."

"I know," Jack said. He gathered me to him and let me weep.

Twenty-Two

❦

The Tower Green

I asked to go back to the Tower and Anne. Sir William Kingston assumed I would. Jack tried to prevent me.

"Let me do this," I begged. "She needs me. I am the only one there who loves her."

"*I* need you," Jack growled. "What happens if you are condemned with her? If they cannot make adultery stick, they will try witchcraft. Either way, they will condemn her for treason. They might condemn you for helping her. That means burning, for a woman. Do you think I can stand by and watch that happen to you?"

His face was white, the fear in his eyes deep.

"She has not been tried yet. They have no evidence."

"Frances, they need no evidence. You noted how Cromwell behaved. They will condemn her without proof; they will invent the proof. The question is not whether she will be condemned but who will go with her."

I shook my head. "It cannot be so. These men know the law—"

"And how to use it to their advantage. The men of

Chancery have moved against the aristocrats, and the aristocrats will lose. The king even now plans his wedding to Jane."

I gasped. "How can he?"

"Guard your voice; who knows who is listening?"

"If she is to lose, if the king is to marry Jane, I must go back to her. All the others hate her. We cannot leave her all alone in a pack of enemies."

"I know you love her, but I want you safe—"

I drew myself up. "I vowed to serve her. I will not break my word. I will not leave her when she is so afraid."

I thought he would shout at me, but Jack placed his hands on my shoulders and rested his forehead against mine. "I wish you were not so bloody brave."

"I am not brave. I am terrified." I traced his cheek. "I am worried for you, Jack. I fear every day that you will be arrested as well."

He straightened. "I have already been questioned."

My heart thumped with fear. "What? Why? Tell me what happened—quickly."

"They decided that I had carnal relations with the queen three years ago, in the spring. Thank God they picked that time. I was able to, without doubt, prove I was in Dunstable, at the side of Archbishop Cranmer day and night."

I remembered Jack's detailed letters of the divorce proceedings of Catherine and Henry. "And they let you go?"

"I believe they concluded that I would not be of interest to the public."

I breathed out. "Thank God for that. Have a care, please, Jack."

"I had been very careful, until I saw my wife dashing up the water stairs to announce to Cromwell she'd written poetry to George Boleyn."

I stared at him, stricken. "Are you saying they will question you again? And I am the cause?"

He tried to soften his expression, but I saw in his eyes that he meant exactly that. "I believe they will watch us to

determine whether they can make use of us." He tucked a
lock of hair under my veil. "Go to her. I will be obsequious
to Cromwell and the king and try to keep my neck from the
noose."

Fear pounded in my throat. "Please take care. If I lost
you, I think I would die."

He gave me a bemused look, as though surprised my feelings for him ran so deep. "Kingston is waiting." He kissed
my forehead. "Go to her, Frances. And God bless you."

ANNE nearly fell upon my neck at my return. She'd
feared they had taken me away from her. I hugged her back
and assured her I'd stay at her side, whatever came.

She hugged me and kissed me, then recovered her dignity and ordered me to bring her wine.

Lady Kingston heard, through her husband, that
Cromwell had decided to withdraw the poem as evidence.
She looked disappointed, but she had no idea I had any
connection to it. I suppose Cromwell was keeping that to
himself, for his own reasons.

The trials of four of the accused men, Sir Henry Norris,
Mark Smeaton, Sir Francis Weston, and William Brereton,
began the next day at Westminster Hall.

These gentlemen had real trials, with the commission of
oyer and terminer and a jury. Lady Kingston reported to us
the lurid details she learned from her husband. The four
men were accused of adultery with the queen on divers
and sundry occasions. Norris, Weston, and Brereton each
answered firmly that they were innocent. Young Mark
Smeaton, on the other hand, pled guilty, a bit pathetically.
But only he had been tortured, only he stood before the
judges with his hands bound.

The other three refuted every charge. They answered, as
Jack had answered, that they'd been elsewhere on the spe-
cific days accused.

It scarcely mattered. That afternoon, in the very hall
where they'd served Anne during her coronation feast, all

four were found guilty of adultery and treason. They would be hung, disemboweled, and quartered at Tyburn.

Anne's eyes filled with tears when she heard the verdict. "That they should come to such a pass because of me," she whispered. "I pray the king takes pity on them." Then she fell into a stupor again and did not come out of it for some time.

Thomas Wyatt and Sir Richard Page were not tried, though they remained prisoners in the Tower. I hoped that the king and Cromwell believed their innocence, or at least that they could not come up with enough witnesses against them.

The trials were a sensation up and down England, Lady Kingston said. Everyone believed Anne guilty, said wasn't it just as they thought? They blamed her for every ill done for the last seven years, and thought her exposure and inevitable punishment just. Anne had been called whore and Jezebel for so long—now people gleefully believed it literally true.

Three days after the first trials, on May fifteenth, Anne came to answer her accusers.

She stood trial in the Great Hall in the Tower in front of several thousand avid spectators. She would not face a commission and a jury as the others had, and neither would her brother. Because they were nobles—Anne, Marchioness of Pembroke and daughter of an earl, and George, Viscount Rochford—they would be tried, as was law, before the Lord High Steward and the nobles of the land.

The Lord High Steward appointed for this day was the Duke of Norfolk, Anne and George's uncle.

I stood among the spectators and hated the Duke of Norfolk. He sat under a canopy at one end of the room, shuffling notes and trying to not pay attention to the gathering crowd. He was powerful, he was a peer, he had the ear of the king, and he was Anne's kin. And still, he looked upon Anne with sad eyes as though she had done something terrible to *him*.

The jury consisted of the highest peers in the realm. The Duke of Suffolk, who had always hated Anne; the Earl of Surrey, Norfolk's son, acting as earl marshal. Henry Percy, the Earl of Northumberland, who'd once been secretly betrothed to Anne, had made the long journey from the north. I was pleased to see he looked ashamed of himself.

Cromwell, I'd heard, had tried to get this young man to say he'd been "married" to Anne before Henry had begun courting her, so that they might declare her marriage with Henry invalid. But Northumberland would not say it. And I could see, by the way that he looked at Anne across the chamber, that he still loved her.

Cromwell himself was there, carefully watching the proceedings.

I half hoped the king would come. He would look upon Anne standing straight and tall before her accusers, and remember how he'd loved her. He'd remember how she was mother to his beloved daughter Elizabeth. He might be moved to pity.

But Henry never appeared. Anne's enemies were too smart for that.

Another person who did not appear was my husband. I searched the stands that had been erected for the spectators, but I searched in vain. Jack was not there.

Lady Kingston led Anne in. I had not been allowed to attend her, which was why I watched, my hands cold with sweat, from the stands.

Anne seated herself in the offered chair before those assembled. In private, she had been nearly mad with fear, but in public, in this place, she held her head high. She might be fighting for her life against her false accusers, but she was still queen. Her dark eyes held those of the men before her, and the haughty curl to her lip had returned.

My heart swelled with pride. They might condemn her, but they could not break her.

They accused her thusly: that she had cohabitated with and had carnal knowledge of her brother and other lovers in divers and sundry times and places, and that she and Sir Henry Norris had planned to marry after Henry's death. She was accused of poisoning Catherine the queen to her death and of plotting to poison Princess Mary.

Anne heard the charges calmly. She dismissed each accusation easily with an explanation that belittled their evidence. She showed no hysteria, no fear, only cool scorn. I could see the jury of peers, including Norfolk, growing worried.

Her uncle Norfolk, I supposed, had counted upon her breaking down. As he chewed his lip and rearranged his thoughts, I began to feel sorry for the man. He wanted a guilty verdict, and Anne was taking away all his cards.

At one point, Norfolk brightened. "You admit that you gave gifts to one Sir Francis Weston?"

"Of course," Anne said, looking him in the eye. "As I give to all gentlemen of my husband's chambers at New Year's. And the king gives gifts to my ladies."

The crowd murmured, and the hostile jury shifted.

They could not do it, I gloated. They would not. They had no proof. Cromwell would lose.

Norfolk finished the questioning. Anne waited, as seemingly at ease as she would be presiding over a ball, as the peers deliberated.

They did not take long. Norfolk asked Anne to stand. She did so, as though bestowing upon him great favor.

I held my breath as Norfolk asked for the verdict.

"Guilty," Suffolk pronounced with satisfaction.

A sick feeling began in the pit of my stomach.

"Guilty," said Surrey, Anne's cousin and Mary Howard's brother.

Northumberland took a deep breath, and his voice came out a weak whisper. "Guilty."

The word hit me like a physical blow. If Northumberland, who had loved her, could speak thus, then Jack had been right. These men cared nothing for justice. The king wanted Anne condemned, and condemned she would be.

I could not stop it. Jack could not stop it. Even Cromwell, who had lit this fire in dry rushes, likely could not stop it. Norfolk, the highest duke in the land, was himself swept up in the fire.

Every lord who had knelt to her at her coronation

pronounced the word, every lord lent their voice to destroy her.

Guilty.

Norfolk at least let tears roll down his gaunt cheeks when he said the final "Guilty."

He swallowed noisily and finished, raising his voice a little. "Thou shalt be burned here within the Tower of London, on the Green, else to have thy head smitten off, as the king's pleasure shall be further known . . ."

Anne remained standing calmly. The jury murmured to each other. "Beheading?" I heard one say, "that is not the law. A woman is burned, and that is that."

The Earl of Surrey waved for quiet. The crowd, rippling and rustling and murmuring, turned to Anne, waiting for her final speech.

Anne looked them over, her accusers, her family, and the people of London who hated her. If she saw me among them, the one lady who loved her dearly, she made no sign.

"I am not afraid to die," she began. Her voice was clear and ringing. The crowd hushed, leaning toward her, straining to lap up her words.

"If I am guilty as judged," she said, "then I will die as the king wishes. I regret only that I have been the cause of the deaths of those innocent and loyal within this place." She fixed her gaze on Northumberland, who was pale and shaking, then moved it to her uncle. "I do not say that I have always borne toward the king the humility that I owed him, but may God be my witness if I have done him any other wrong."

If Suffolk and Cromwell and her other enemies hoped that she would break down, weeping, and confess they had been right all along, they did not know my lady Anne. She was stronger than they. She always would be.

"Take her down," said Norfolk.

And she went.

Lady Kingston and her husband led Anne out of the hall. As the crowd shifted, getting ready to watch the next trial, I again looked in vain for my husband. I never found him. I learned from Lady Kingston later that the king himself had summoned Jack to attend him—to play tennis.

THE peers shuffled papers and resettled themselves, making ready for George Boleyn's trial, which would commence immediately.

I lingered long enough to witness the commotion surrounding the young Earl of Northumberland, who had collapsed. I could not help feeling small satisfaction, though I knew he'd not the choice to help her. None of them had. Cromwell, the son of a brewer, fighting to keep Henry satisfied, had bested a queen.

I saw George brought in. He was thin from his two weeks in the Tower, even though he'd been well housed. His eyes flashed black fire, as sparkling and regal as Anne's. George Boleyn was no fool, and those trying him had no evidence, and they knew it.

I hurried from the hall before they could close the great doors and begin the trial, gathered my skirts, and ran through the courts and halls to Anne's chambers.

She was there, pacing, her back straight, her head high. The ladies watched her fearfully.

When I appeared, she strode to a table and called for pen and ink. "I must settle my affairs," she said calmly, seating herself, "and provide what I can for my daughter and my sister and my ward. Frances, attend me."

That night, however, she held me when the others left us, and wept in black grief.

GEORGE Boleyn's trial caused another sensation. I heard from reports afterward that he, like Anne, clearly refuted all charges that he'd lain with his sister in her bed at any time. He was a clever man and kept the jury hopping on legal niceties.

At one point, George was handed a paper with an accusation written on it, because, Norfolk implied, it was too scurrilous to be spoken aloud.

George read it out anyway. The report was that Anne had told his wife, Jane Rochford, in French, that Henry the king "had neither potency nor force" in bed.

The jury was shocked, Cromwell furious, the crowd thrilled.

After that, George was found guilty and sentenced to a traitor's death. In his final speech, he, like Anne, insisted on his innocence but expressed worry for his creditors. He owed much, he said, and feared they'd be ruined if the king confiscated his lands and moneys.

AND so it was over. Cromwell had what he wanted. There was nothing left but for Anne to die.

"What will you do, Frances?" she asked me softly as we prayed together that night at the little altar erected in her rooms. I'd never had much use for prayer, even though I repeated them by rote. Now, for the first time in my life, resting on my knees, my head bowed, asking God for his pity brought me comfort.

"What will you do when I am gone?" she asked me again. "Will you return to Gloucestershire and your son? I am proud you have such a son."

I swallowed tears. "I do not know. I cannot see anything beyond this, Your Grace."

We were quite alone. All the others had gone to bed, save Mistress Horsman who pretended to watch from the door to Anne's bedchamber, but her snore betrayed her.

Anne placed a cool hand on my head. "You must think of much beyond. You must think of your husband and small John. You must think of your life, and your own soul."

I knew she wanted a response. "Yes, Your Grace."

She went quiet a time, then she said, "He loved me once."

"I know," I whispered.

"He loved me as a man loves a woman." She smiled, the old sparkle returning to her eyes. "I held him in my palm, Frances. His passion for me was everything."

"Yes."

"I can be a hard and cold woman, I know. More like a man, sometimes, and gentlemen do not like this. When my uncle Norfolk told me to play upon the king's interest in me I saw no reason not to. Uncle Norfolk is an ambitious man, and I was an ambitious woman. I burned with such fire." She sighed. "Perhaps if I'd simply been a woman . . ."

"His Grace loved you for it," I pointed out. "He loved you for your fire."

"Aye, mayhap." She stared off into the darkness. "But when fire burns too hot, one reaches to snuff it out."

My eyes ached with tears. "He is unjust."

"Nay, say nothing against the king. He is law and un-questioned. Do not forget that."

I nodded. She fell silent again, her head bowed.

I thought Anne calm and praying, but suddenly she drew a ragged breath and dug ice-cold fingers into mine. "Help me, Frances," she said. "Help me. It is so very dark."

ARCHBISHOP Cranmer at last came to see Anne the next day. She greeted him with joy, and then they closeted themselves in Anne's inner chamber, alone, for several hours.

Lady Kingston tried to find out what they were saying, but failed. She looked put out, stabbing at her sewing in the outer chamber, her ear cocked toward the door.

I hoped against hope that Cranmer had found a way to convince Henry to give Anne a reprieve, to let her retire to a house, as Catherine had, instead of putting her to death. But when he emerged from the rooms much later, his face held great sorrow, and I knew that he had not been able to save her.

I followed him to the doors of the chamber and could stand it no more. Before his servants could stop me, I pushed past them and stood face-to-face with the archbishop.

He was a man of middling height, with a square jaw just fleshing out and intelligent dark eyes. He took me in without surprise and without contempt. The lines about his eyes were deep, his mouth flat with pain.

"Why can you not help her?" I whispered. "You of all people could help her."

Two of his servants reached for me, ready to haul me away, but Cranmer stopped them with a gesture. "Child," he said. "You love her."

"Aye. I thought you did, too."

His eyes were bleak. "And I wish I did not, else I would not feel as I do. I cannot help her. She is in God's hands. None of us can. We can only do nothing, or die with her."

"But that is not right," I cried. "It is not fair."

"It is the way of the world," he said, his voice not unkind. "I grieve that it is so. If you love her, child, keep alive what she tried to do. Keep alive the reforms she wished to make, keep alive the Church."

I stared at him. He was looking beyond Anne's death, the death of one person, and seizing on a higher purpose. To me, that meant the same as conceding defeat.

"I care nothing for the Church," I said viciously. He recoiled. I saw Sir William bearing down on me, bent on dragging me away. "I care nothing for your reforms. I only care that you could save her, and you do nothing."

"Lady Carlisle," Sir William said in a thunderous voice.

Cranmer only looked at me sadly. "There is nothing to do."

I wanted to storm at him, to shout like Henry did until everyone bent to his will. But I was not Henry. I was Frances Pierce, after all this time, still nobody.

I balled my fists in frustration, burst into tears, and fled him.

* * *

ANNE's brother George and the other four men died on the seventeenth of May. The king, at least, had granted them one mercy: instead of being dragged across London and quartered at Tyburn, they would be hanged until dead on the Tower Green.

Anne would die on the nineteenth. Henry had chosen beheading, and had sent to Calais for the executioner. His sword, it was said, was quite sharp and his accuracy, superb.

I thanked God that at least Anne would not be burned alive. I believed that even Henry could not let a woman who'd shared his bed and borne his child die in the agony of flames.

On the seventeenth, Anne stayed in her chambers and prayed. Her mood was dark. "My sweet brother has come to this through my fault," she said. "May God forgive me."

She barely noticed me there. While she knelt at her altar, head bowed, lost in grief, I slipped away and ran through passages and through gates until I could look out onto the Tower Green.

Crows hopped about the grass in lazy anticipation. I cursed them under my breath, though I knew they were only foolish creatures with no understanding. The scaffolding rose high above the walls. A crowd had gathered on the green and outside the gates.

The condemned men were led out one by one. George faced the crowd without fear. He looked fine and handsome as ever, though he wore rusty black and his hands were bound behind him.

His dark gaze lingered on me, hiding in the shadow of a gate. He gave me a faint nod, as though in farewell.

Then he turned to the crowd and spoke, "I acknowledge the sins for which I am judged," he said clearly. "I who have loved the Gospels did not enough follow them. For if I had lived according to the Gospel as I loved it and spake of it, I had never come to this."

When he finished his speech, the rope went around his neck. Still he watched the crowd with dark eyes, as proud and cool as his sister.

Francis Weston gave a speech himself, in a faint voice, that he was a sinner and had thought he'd have much more time in his life to make up for it. William Brereton asked those watching to judge whether he were innocent. Sir Henry Norris said nothing. I swallowed, my throat aching.

They, too, bowed their heads to let the hangmen settle their nooses. Francis Weston moved his lips in prayer. Mark Smeaton would not even look up.

The hangman covered their heads with hoods, and then they were just bodies, faceless and featureless.

I turned and fled. I did not want to hear the creak of the ropes, the groan of the crowd, the death rattles of George Boleyn, a man I had once desired, and four other innocent men as they were hauled high.

THE next afternoon, we received news that made me wish the archbishop a special place in hell, right next to the horrible Thomas Cromwell.

Kingston explained to Anne that Archbishop Cranmer had annulled her marriage to Henry and rendered Elizabeth a bastard.

I raged and could not understand. Why, if Anne's marriage was invalid, was she punished for adultery? If Henry wanted the marriage annulled, why not have Cranmer do it before the trial, and so spare her life? I went hot with fury, and hated the king.

Anne was already grieving her brother, and the blow nearly put her mind into disorder. Her mood became strange, even crazed.

"They shall call me Queen Anne the Headless," she said one moment, and burst out laughing.

"Or," she said, calming the next, "Anne the Martyr.

Depend upon it, terrible things will befall this land when I am executed. Rain will not fall on England until I am set free."

I watched her worriedly, wondering if she'd gone mad. It hurt me to see her so, my beautiful Anne, once so prepossessed and witty, making speeches now grim, now bordering on the ridiculous. She laughed and became almost flirtatious, then plunged the next moment into somberness and prayer.

Anne was to die the next day, on Friday. Thursday dragged by, unbearably long. Even Margery Horsman and Lady Kingston, who disliked Anne, were nervous and watched the clock.

I tried to sit vigil with Anne that night, but I fell into heavy slumber, and when I awoke in the wee hours, she had gone to pray with her almoner.

I dressed myself and sat watching the window until dawn broke. Anne entered her main chamber to hear Mass, and I joined them. She asked to see the consecrated host and swore on it that she was innocent.

It made no difference.

Anne had thought she'd die at dawn. As the chambers filled with May sunlight, she became impatient. "Master Kingston," she said. "I thought to be dead by this time and past my pain. Why the delay?"

He bowed. "I do not know, my lady."

He lied. He did know why, and I did, too, but we'd been admonished not to tell the queen. In effort to control the mob, the real time of the execution had been concealed. I'd also heard that only Englishmen would be allowed onto the Tower Green to watch the execution. She would die before her people, and her people only.

"Take comfort, my lady," Kingston went on, flushing. "There will not be any pain."

Anne looked at him, her eyes enormous. She put her hands to her neck. "I heard that the executioner is very good," she said in a merry voice. "I am pleased, for I have but a little neck."

She started to laugh. I watched her, my heart heavy.

* * *

LATER that morning, Kingston and Anne's ladies and I accompanied Anne to her place of execution.

The same crows strutted in the grass. The swordsman from Calais waited on the black-draped scaffold, sunlight glittering on his blade. He would earn twenty-six pounds for his deed this day, and return to Calais and his family tomorrow.

Only a small number of people had gathered, the confusion of the time of execution having been effective. The watchers murmured when they saw Anne approach, and went silent.

I nearly jumped when I spied Jack near the forefront of the gathering. He wore dark green and a black cloak, and the breeze ruffled his dark curls. His face was drawn and somber.

He held my gaze for a long time. I saw in his eyes pain and remorse, regret and anger that he could do nothing to stop this, and behind it, quiet love. He knew why I had returned to Anne, and he loved me for it.

Of my mother, I saw no sign. I wondered whether Jack had sent her home, or whether she'd chosen to stay away. I was glad she was not there; I could not have borne her satisfaction.

Anne walked beside me. She wore a simple gown covered with a fur-trimmed robe, and I had braided her hair to bare her flawless neck. She glanced behind her from time to time, but her eyes were blank and resigned.

Kingston guided her up the steps of the scaffold, holding her carefully so she would not trip. The ladies and I crowded behind her.

She drew herself up before the small assemblage that huddled on the green, her enemies and her friends, who had come to watch her die.

She seemed to draw comfort from them. She was queen, she was studied at holding attention and making anyone who watched her, hers.

"Good Christian people," she began. The crowd quieted, murmurs dying away. I saw her uncle Norfolk, his face quiet, and her own father, eyes red with grief.

"I am come hither to accuse no man," Anne said in her clear, queen's tones, "nor to speak of that whereof I am accused and condemned to die. But I pray God save the king and send him long to reign over you, for a gentler nor a more merciful prince was there never, and to me he was ever a good, a gentle, and sovereign lord."

I gritted my teeth, hating Henry, and hating that after all he had done, she still admonished us to love him.

Anne finished, asking all to pray for her. She stepped back, flashed her glorious black gaze around the crowd, and knelt.

As I lowered the blindfold to cover her eyes, she whispered, "Write verses for me, Frances. Write them so all will know what happened here. Write them for Anne your queen."

"Yes." I could barely form the words. "I will."

I tied the blindfold with shaking hands, then knelt beside the other ladies, tears dropping to my hands.

I prayed God to take her soul. I prayed that God might see fit to let the king send a reprieve. I prayed that I might die the moment she was struck down so I would not have to live with the memory of this day.

My lady bent her head. Her face was white but calm and serene. I heard her whispered prayer, "To Jesu I commend my soul. Lord Jesus, receive my soul."

The Calais executioner stepped behind her. Some small noise made Anne raise her head and turn as though to look.

And in that moment, she died.

Epilogue

The ladies and I wrapped Anne's body in a sheet and carried her across the green to the chapel of St. Peter.

I worked in a curious numbness to undress her and clean her and lay her out. I sensed that later I would break down, but now my body went through motions without my heart understanding what I did.

The ladies remained beside her, praying. I rose painfully to my feet and stood looking down at the woman to whom I'd given my life.

"And wild for to hold," I whispered, "though I seem tame."

I heard nothing save the quiet weeping of the ladies. I kissed my fingers and reached them toward her body.

"Good-bye," I said.

I walked away from the chapel, across the green, where even now the crowd was dispersing. The executioner had collected his fee and gone.

I wandered through the Cole Harbor Gate back into the Tower. I walked slowly, ignored by servants who hurried about their duties as usual. Rooms still had to be kept, linens washed, food prepared, gardens weeded. Against grand events, the minutia of life ground on.

I thought my feet would take me back to Anne's rooms so that I could begin clearing away her things, but I found myself walking, as if pulled, to the queen's garden.

I found my husband there, sitting on a low stone bench. His hat rested on his knee, and the wind ruffled his dark hair. My son had the same tightly curled hair, only a shade lighter, like mine.

I walked to him and sank down beside him, not looking at him.

We sat silently, side by side, lost in our own thoughts. Around us the gardens were budding, the hedges, grass, and trees filmed with yellow, blue, and purple blossoms.

We sat for a long time, and no one heeded us.

Jack said, "Northumberland has taken very ill."

"He ought to," I answered with a hint of fire.

"He could not have saved her."

"No."

The breeze fluttered a bright red blossom on a bush before us. A sparrow landed at the base of the bush and poked its beak into the earth.

"I do not understand what they wanted," I said. "I do not understand why she had to die."

"So they could live," Jack said softly. "In the end, it was her or them."

"I still do not understand why it should be so."

He closed his warm hand on mine. "Because it is a game. If you join the game, you play for the highest stakes. You agree to risk all. That is what Anne did."

I stared straight ahead of me. "She did not have a chance."

"She did, at first. But the game shifted, and she could not. You and I were nearly caught in it ourselves."

I bowed my head and thought for a while, wondering when my numbness would wear off and I would feel again. I knew that what I would feel would devastate me.

"You warned me," I said after a time, "that I did not have the wherewithal to survive here. You were right."

His hand tightened. "No. I was wrong. You have amazing strength, Frances."

I did not feel strong. I felt weak and beaten.

"She asked for you," he said. "Jane Seymour."

I lifted my head. "Asked for me?"

"She and Henry will wed in a few days. She asked Henry to ask me to have you join her ladies. She likes you. When the king played tennis with me, he asked."

I stared at him aghast, through a film of tears.

He gave me an understanding look. "I told him that you were unwell, that you needed to retire to Pennington. I told him I did not know how long it would be before you recovered."

"Thank you," I breathed. I could not imagine a worse purgatory than having to wait upon the woman who had sent Anne to her grave.

"I asked leave to accompany you," he went on.

I closed my eyes, a modicum of peace stealing over me. The vision of Pennington Hall rose before me, its wings stretching out like welcoming arms, the riot of roses climbing the trees, the long days of sunshine, the evenings before the fire listening to the earl and Jack speak in quiet voices. My son would be there, running about the house and grounds, his unruly curls so like his father's.

"Home?" I asked him. "We may go home?"

"Yes," my husband said, and then he rose, and took me there.

Turn the page for a look at

Plain Jane

A NOVEL OF JANE SEYMOUR

by Laurien Gardner

Coming in July from Jove Books

The Phoenix in the Forest

JANE felt warm. Too warm. She pushed back at the heavy covers confining her slim body. Her fingers clutched feverishly at furs and fine spun wool, seeking to free herself from the embrace of the enveloping softness that was making her burn.

Firm hands—the fingers cool against her skin—pushed the covers back.

Confined, bound, desperate, Jane tried to turn. The same hands, respectful and soothing, pushed her back. Another hand held her own—a large hand, enveloping but soft.

She closed her fingers hard upon it, and the hand clutched hers, feeling cold and moist against her parched skin. There was a sound, low and crackling, pervading all. Hail? No. Fire. It was the crackle of the fire.

The heat. Jane was burning. There was a fire. She would perish. Her mind conjured up images of a great conflagration, of fire eating walls and roofs and crawling, devouring, unforgiving, toward her in her bed.

"The heat," she whispered. "Burning."

"Jane," a voice said. A familiar voice.

The hand enveloping hers squeezed her fingers, and there was a great intake of breath, a ponderous sigh. Jane knew the sound of that sigh, she knew the voice, but she could not quite remember.

She fought to open her eyes. It felt as though twin weights rested on her eyelids, and all her efforts could only gain her a narrow sliver of light and vision. As if the world had become straightened, narrowed.

Turning her head slowly, she saw a large woman by her. Or rather, she saw the ample bosom of a woman rising and falling with deep breaths. It was covered in a rich red brocade surcoat. From that bosom cooing sounds emerged, the sort of noise a certain type of woman makes under her breath to calm babies, puppies, and invalids.

Jane didn't know who the woman was or why she was near. She turned her head away and saw at the foot of the bed two men in dark attire, their heads inclined. A faint whisper of Latin issued from them, soft-sweet in the heavy, closed-in atmosphere of the room.

It wafted in the air, crisp, familiar, and formal like incense at high mass. Rolling her head further upon the pillow, Jane saw a roaring fire upon a deep, wide fireplace. Too hot, she thought. Far too hot. She smelled her own sweat tinged with the sharp tang of fever. She tried to speak, but no sound came from her parched lips.

The woman attending her raised her gently on one arm, supporting Jane against her bosom, the brocade rough against Jane's cheek.

Yet someone understood. A metal cup touched her lips. Sweet claret flowed upon her tongue and dripped down her throat. Jane swallowed. Again and again she swallowed with a sense of relief. She was released and fell back, gratefully, upon mounded pillows.

She managed to open her eyes a little farther and allow her curious gaze to fix upon the tapestries on the wall and the rich furnishings of the room. The bed was hung with heavy, intricately worked curtains that half-obscured the two praying priests.

Where was she and why were they praying? She could not remember anything at all, and her eyes dwelt wonderingly upon the great carved walnut bedstead above her head, far richer and costlier than any furniture she had ever had.

Why was she in such surroundings, and why was she so hot?

She felt as though a fire consumed her from the inside, as though the room were an oven within which they meant to roast her. The heat made her languid and slow and seemed to make her breathing difficult.

Her wondering gaze took in carvings up near the ceiling, gilded wood and inlays. A unicorn, a rose, and the moto *Bound to serve and obey.*

Her gaze rested on it, fascinated, slow. It all felt so far away and strange, like the background of an obscure painting.

The hand holding hers squeezed, and she turned to look at it. It was a huge, powerful hand covered in a layer of fat. A massive signet ring shone upon the middle finger.

Jane recognized the ring, and blinked at it in confusion. It was King Henry's ring.

The king. It is the king. She tried to rise. She must get up and prostrate herself before her sovereign.

But the woman in red held her down, and the king patted her hand with his free hand. "Jane, Jane," he said.

He spoke tenderly to her. The king was her friend.

Jane looked anxiously at the king's large face, his eyes fixed on her with peculiar kindness and concern. He squeezed her hand again. "Jane," he said. "You must live. And give me many sons."

Sons? The king was . . . her husband?

But it couldn't be. She'd known since she was nine that she would never be married. She wasn't beautiful enough for anyone to wish to marry her.

This was a dream. A strange dream. She must waken.

The sights, the sounds, the smell of her own sweat, the feel of oppressive heat all receded. There were images in her mind and they overpowered all, shining clearer, brighter than anything outside. Her eyes fell closed.

"The queen, the queen," a woman's voice cried. "Someone help me."

But Jane did not hear. In her mind, she was a slight girl of nine running down a cool hallway at Wulfhall, her family manor.

I

The crisp, cool sunlight of autumn fell richly upon the stone walls of Wulfhall in Wiltshire.

Filtered through the red and gold leaves of Savernake forest, it lent a gilding patina, making the stolid stone building look like a rough common pebble that had been polished to look like a jewel.

The manor, traditional dwelling of the family that acted as guardians of the Royal Forest, bustled with the routine activity of a rural household. Grooms coming and going, maids tending to cleanliness and food preparation, entered and exited through various doors. At the kitchen door, a dozen hares were hung by their feet, waiting skinning and cleaning.

In the kitchen garden, a maid sang an old ballad while picking through the herb patch.

Three blond children, two boys and a girl, stood in front of the great detached barn at the side of the house. They were children of the Seymour family, the current owners of Wulfhall.

Edward was twelve, Tom ten, and Jane nine. The boys had taken it into their heads to get their horses out for a run and, with the help of a young stable boy little older than they, were saddling them.

Jane stood a few steps away, looking on.

"If we had the king's permission," Tom said, "as he gives Father twice a year, we could have a great hunt." Ruddy, bright-eyed, and stocky, he was fastening his saddle on sloppily, while smiling at the prospects of an imaginary sport. "We could hunt a deer. I bet I could bring down a buck with my bow."

His brother, Edward, older and quieter, was also more careful and exact. He gave Tom a long, doubtful look. "We'll ride through the glades," he said.

"Jane, aren't you coming?" Tom asked as if only then realizing that his sister hadn't gotten her own horse and was making no move to saddle up.

The little girl shifted from foot to foot and edged away. Her threadbare, pale green dress left her thin calves and slippered feet uncovered. "I don't know if—" she said. "I don't know if I rightly may." A slip of a child with a cloud of spun-sugar hair and skin so pale that it appeared green in certain lights, she trained huge, eager eyes on her brothers, clearly longing for the sport and the race through the autumnal fields.

They always had a grand time while Tom shouted instructions as though they were all esquires on a royal hunt.

And she could almost feel the cool wind on her face, the horse beneath her, the excitement of racing out with the boys. The oldest daughter of the family, born after four sons of which Edward was the oldest surviving and Tom the youngest, she had grown up being treated as one of the boys.

Three years before, she would not have hesitated to saddle her own horse and go riding with her brothers, with no question to anyone. But the last three years had brought a change, as the nurse hired to look after Jane and her sisters had taken it into her head that Jane was growing wild and must be curbed.

She was a kindly, poor kinswoman, distantly related enough to have only a tenuous claim on the Seymours, but well brought up enough to know the rules. She paid great attention to propriety and behavior in those she pleased herself to call the young ladies.

Not that Jane minded, usually. The nurse, Anne, taught her embroidery and sewing, and Jane enjoyed the fine, demanding work and was good at it, learning designs quickly and executing them to perfection. But Anne was all too reluctant to let Jane go running with Edward and Tom.

And yet . . . And yet, Jane could almost feel the horse gathering speed beneath her, she could almost smell the spicy air of autumn amid the golden splendor of ripe crops and yellowing leaves.

"You should go ask your nurse, Jane," Edward said. "Mayhap she'll allow you to come with us."

"Why, only yesterday father said good riding and hunting were necessary accomplishments of any gentlewoman," Tom said. "I'll wager he wants you to acquire them right enough, Jane, if he expects you to marry well."

His boisterous words and encouraging smile defeated Jane's hesitation. She turned on her heel, headed into the house by the door nearest the stables, and ran down the long gallery that led to the family quarters.

The gallery was deep and narrow. On one side were portraits of her ancestors, going back to the thirteenth century, when the limning was done in paints that had faded and the figures represented were distorted, the heads out of proportion, so that ancient Seymours and Esturmis looked not quite human but like those titans and dwarves that ancient stories spoke of.

The Esturmi family had held this manor and the honor of keepers of the Royal Forest till a Seymour had married the last Esturmi and, with her hand, taken manor and honor.

Jane had heard all these stories from her older brothers, who'd heard them from her father, and every time she went through the gallery, no matter how fast she ran or how little she was thinking of house and ancestors, she got a sense of how long her people had been here and that the blood that ran in her veins was ancient and respectable.

That day she smiled a little at the long row of serious-faced men and the occasional stern-faced woman, though her mind was wholly on her nurse, both anxious to reach her and dreading her response to Jane's request.

Nurse would be in Jane's room, or in Elizabeth's room, at this time of the morning. She might very well wonder where Jane was. She might very well have already looked for the girl to set her at some mending task, or some other needlework. Or to sit her before her virginals, practicing the music at which Jane was wretched indeed.

The thought of how Nurse's lips would purse and how displeased she would look at Jane's lateness made Jane stop running and start walking, haltingly, down the hallway.

The house being made of stone, it was colder inside than out. Even the full heat of summer never penetrated the long gallery. And the windows that opened on the other side of the hall faced the wall of the great barn, too close by to allow direct sun in the house. Though glazed with panes divided by lead into small rectangles, the windows let in a hint of cold breeze through their imperfect jointures. Jane longed more than ever to be out, in the sunlight of fall.

She didn't want to face Nurse, who might be displeased so early with Jane over her absence this morning. But neither did she want to go back and admit to Tom that she lacked the courage to ask. After all, though the nurse had authority over the girls, she was only a servant, and Tom would remind Jane of this in withering tones.

By the time Jane reached the end of the gallery, she was walking slowly and halting often. Just then, from her right, her father's voice came, with a hint of stern reproach, "Jane, now."

Jane stopped and froze. She looked around wildly, thinking her father must be somewhere behind her and reproaching her. Perhaps the nurse had already gone to him?

But look as she might, she didn't see Sir John anywhere.

"Jane is so plain," her father's voice said, calmly, clearly, in the tone of someone who continues an interrupted conversation. "I doubt we can get her a marriage. Or at least a creditable one. Not on any dowry we can command."

Jane blinked. Her father was referring to her as too plain to marry? Why? And to whom would they marry her at nine, who would mind her looks? Looking around again, she realized the voice came from the barely open door of her mother's small sitting room, where Jane usually went for her instruction in music.

Shocked by being called plain and by a hint of unconcealed disdain in her father's voice, Jane gaped and thought *He's talking to Mother. Mother will no doubt defend me. Mother always says it's the beauty of the soul that counts.*

"Jane is indeed, plain," Jane's mother said, her voice containing no hint of offense or heated defense of her progeny. "And yet," she sighed, "you know plainer than she have got married before."

Jane's father made a sound in the back of his throat, a sound she knew full well from when John Seymour discussed the value of his ewes' wool or the price of lambs with their shepherds and thought the shepherds were far wrong.

"Aye, plainer have married," he said, "but not without a dowry. Not without some enticement to bring the young man to the altar. Come, come, Margery. Think of your daughter's face. Those protruding eyes, those thin lips, the receding chin—no, Wife, we should thank the Good Lord that Elizabeth and Dorothy are not as plain as Jane is. They will get good marriages, good husbands. But that leaves us still with Jane."

Jane's mother sighed. "Well then," she said. "It is a good thing that Jane is the oldest of the girls, and of a good, steady temper, too."

She paused for a moment and Jane could picture her threading her needle in the interval, because Jane had never seen her mother hold any conversation without her hands being busy at some domestic task of sewing or embroidery.

"She'll help me till the others marry and then we'll find the money for an offering to a convent and give her to the church. Some small convents don't demand too much. And she can go in and spend the rest of her life decently, without remaining forever an old maid and a burden on her brothers as they go on to greater things."

"Well, and that's good enough," John said and sighed.

"But how she should be born so plain when your beauty was reputed all over the countryside . . ."

His hint of reproach was ignored by his wife, who instead said, in a firm voice, as if she were holding back comments about John's female ancestors, "Cousin Francis wants to take Tom with him to court. He says he could use a boy of such cleverness on his foreign missions."

"Francis Bryan?" John Seymour asked, in a tone of great astonishment. "What a great opportunity for Tom, for Francis is a friend of the king himself."

"Yes, but . . . perhaps a little bawdy withal. And Tom is young."

John made a sound of dismissal at his wife's mention of their kinsman's less-than-reputable character. "Every male at court who is close to the king is reputed bawdy. It means nothing. A little too much drink, a bit of wenching now and then. It signifies nothing at all. Though to be sure, Tom is perhaps still full young . . ." His voice trailed off, as if he were thinking.

Jane became aware of herself where she stood in the hall. Her feet were cold in their thin slippers and a breeze from some open door somewhere played the hem of her dress around her ankles. A thin dress and nothing much for the daughter of the manor to run around in, but her parents had never taken great pains over ensuring that Jane looked her best, and now Jane thought she understood why.

Her hands clutched at her skirt in distress and her small teeth clamped on her lower lip. They thought her plain. Too plain to marry, to plain to display. Plain.

Her logical mind fastened on the list of faults her father had enumerated. She knew her own face well enough. In her room, she had a polished silver round she used as a mirror, and though Nurse had always discouraged her from contemplating herself in it, and Jane's mother talked of the demon of vanity hiding within mirrors, Jane had spent long enough in front of it, while arranging her hair in the morning.

Thin and silk-soft, her hair shed all binds, all clips, all

attempts at controlling it, and the family had too many daughters and too little money to afford her a skilled maid who could fashion her hair into something less than frightful. So the task fell to Jane herself, and while seeing to it, she had stared at her own features long enough.

Her chin did recede, and her lips were indeed thin, and her eyes did poke out a little, giving her an impression of perpetual surprise. She'd seen the way nearby landowners and her parents' friends would smile at her sisters and then let their gazes slide over Jane as if she didn't exist.

She'd heard—more in jest than in actual planning— several matches talked of for Elizabeth and even for little Dorothy, who was just learning to walk. But no landowner, no neighbor, no friend had ever joked about matching their likely lad to Jane.

Because she was plain. And yet her brothers with much the same features were not regarded as being less worthy. Everyone talked of how bright they were and how far they would go in the world.

Jane let go of her skirt and lifted a hand to her hair in a desultory gesture. Her parents talked of sending Tom to court. And they'd always talked about how bright Edward was. Jane was bright, too—or at least, she had a steady and capable mind. Why should that not count? Why would it be different for a girl?

And what fault was it of hers if God had made her plain? Surely all of the work of His hands was pleasing, no matter what form it took?

Jane shifted a little on the floor and frowned at the door of her mother's room, from which the sound of her parents' voices still issued. She was no longer attending to their conversation. She was no longer interested. She'd heard their opinion of her and their plans for her, and she was surprised and angry.

She did not want to be a nun. She wanted a family. She wanted a husband who'd look at her with the same love and desire she saw in her father's eyes when John Seymour looked at Margery.

"Jane?" Edward's voice came from behind her, hesitant.

She turned to see her brother walking down the hallway toward her.

"Jane, have you asked? Can you ride with us?" he asked. "Only . . . Tom is anxious to leave. He says the ride will be at its best before the heat of noonday."

Jane realized she had been standing there long enough that she'd had time to ask her nurse for permission two or three times over. She felt the cold trails of tears down her face.

Oh, do not let her have to tell Edward what she had just heard. Not steady, unimaginative Edward, who would tell her that her parents were right and that she should be sensible about it all.

She covered her face so Edward wouldn't see her distress. She wanted neither sympathy nor mockery, and most of all, she did not want his sense and reason in this matter. There was nothing reasonable about this. It was a blight come upon her for no cause.

"Jane, what is wrong?" he said.

She could not stand to explain. Her face covered, she shook her head and ran away from him, down the hallway to her room.

Nurse was not there, the bed was carefully made as Jane had left it. Jane locked her door and flung herself facedown upon her woolen blanket.

The tears came then, fast and unstoppable.

It wasn't just that she was plain, but that her parents thought so and that they thought her plainness and lack of grace would prevent her ever being anything in life, save perhaps a nun because the Lord didn't care how ill-favored his brides were.

"Jane?" Edward's hand knocked lightly on the door. "Jane, if you don't come, Tom and I will go. I can't hold him back much longer."

Jane wanted to reply, but she could not because her voice would drip with the unsteadiness of tears and shake, brittle with self-pity. She could not talk without giving away her distress. And Edward was a good person; if he heard her distress he would demand a complete explanation. Or worse, he would tell her parents.

She remained still, quiet. For a while, she was aware of his presence there, outside the door, and could imagine him, his hand raised to knock again but hesitating. Presently, she heard him walk away, headed for his ride through the morning-still glades.

And Jane would be left behind now as she would be left behind in life. Always the one left at Wulfhall until she became enough of an embarrassment that her parents would dispose of her to the cloister.

She cried for she didn't know how long. It seemed to her that at some time someone tried the door—another of her brothers, or perhaps Elizabeth or even her nurse. Whoever it was asked no questions and made no sound beyond trying to open the door and leaving.

After a long time, Jane got up and looked at herself in the mirror. It was highly polished and gave her back her reflection with just a slight tinge of ghostly distortion. Her face was as her father had described it, save that her eyes were now rather swollen from crying and her hair, having come lose, made a pale hallo around her unlovely face. None of which improved her appearance.

How strange it was that, if a woman's face were her best weapon in the battle of life, she should have come to it armed with such paltry and insufficient weapons.

And yet, the intent, too-pale blue eyes that looked back at her from the mirror showed a more acute expression than she was used to seeing in people she met.

Jane had always been a good girl, quietly following her brothers, pacifying their quarrels, pleased enough to join in what they contrived for their own amusement. She had taken her mother's and nurse's impositions and done her best at her needlework and her music, though she didn't enjoy the latter very much.

Now, her pale eyes showed something like a fire of rebellion. Her small fists tightened on either side of her body.

Her father had called her plain. And said that this made her fit for nothing but maybe the convent.

Well, let Jane be plain. The Good Lord in His mercy had given her good and plentiful understanding, and that ought to be enough to make up for her plain face. She looked in the mirror, determined, intent.

Aye, she'd wager her good mind against any woman's prettiness, her understanding against any woman's wiles.

Looking at the pale blue eyes in the mirror, she vowed to herself that she would do better than any of her ambitious brothers or pretty sisters.